A Dickens of a Crime Mystery Series
By Heather Redmond

A Tale of Two Murders

Grave Expectations

GRAVE EXPECTATIONS

HEATHER REDMOND

KENSINGTON BOOKS

www.kensingtonbooks.com

KENSINGTON BOOKS are published by

Kensington Publishing Corp.
119 West 40th Street
New York, NY 10018

All Kensington titles, imprints and distributed lines are available at special quantity discounts for bulk purchases for sales promotion, premiums, fund-raising, educational or institutional use. Special book excerpts or customized printings can also be created to fit specific needs. For details, write or phone the office of the Kensington Special Sales Manager: Kensington Publishing Corp., 119 West 40th Street, New York, NY, 10018. Attn. Special Sales Department. Phone: 1-800-221-2647.

Kensington and the K logo Reg. U.S. Pat. & TM Off.

Library of Congress Control Number: 2019932239

ISBN-13: 978-1-4967-1716-0
ISBN-10: 1-4967-1716-3
First Kensington Hardcover Edition: August 2019

ISBN-13: 978-1-4967-1719-1 (ebook)
ISBN-10: 1-4967-1719-8 (ebook)

10 9 8 7 6 5 4 3 2 1

Printed in the United States of America

For Rachel and Joseph

Cast of Characters

Charles Dickens* A journalist

Kate Hogarth* Charles's fiancée

Fred Dickens* Charles's younger brother and roommate

Mr. George Hogarth* Charles's newspaper editor and Kate's father

Mrs. Georgina Hogarth* Kate's mother

Mary Hogarth* Kate's younger sister

William Aga A journalist at the *Evening Chronicle*

Daniel Jones A blacksmith

Mrs. Addie Jones Daniel Jones's wife

Edmund Jones A blacksmith

Hannah Jones Edmund Jones's spinster sister

Prince Moss A lower-class youth

Pietro Ferazzi A landlord

Miss Haverstock A tenant

Mrs. Julie Aga An underemployed actress

Evelina Jaggers	Miss Haverstock's foster daughter
Osvald Larsen	An escaped convict
Ned Blood	An escaped convict
Breese Gadfly	A songwriter
Lady Holland*	A famed hostess
Reuben Solomon	A dealer in old clothes
Lucy Fair	The leader of the Blackfriars Bridge mudlarks
Little Ollie	A mudlark

*Real historical figures

That was a memorable day to me, for it made great changes in me. But it is the same with any life. Imagine one selected day struck out of it, and think how different its course would have been. Pause you who read this, and think for a moment of the long chain of iron or gold, of thorns or flowers, that would never have bound you, but for the formation of the first link on one memorable day.

Charles Dickens, *Great Expectations* (1860)

Tribes of the wandering foot and weary breast,
How shall ye flee away and be at rest!

George Gordon Bryon, sixth Baron Byron
"Oh! Weep for Those" (1815)

How can you expect us to show kindness, when we receive none?

Richard Cumberland, *The Jew* (1794)

Chapter 1

Chelsea, London, June 20, 1835

The ancient magazine had been pushed under Charles Dickens's Selwood Terrace door sometime on Friday night, after the household had retired.

"Here." His brother Fred thrust the crackling papers into his hands. "I found this on the floor." Fred, a gangly almost fifteen-year-old, was dressed to go out in a cut-down frock coat, a shawl, and gloves.

"Was there a note?" Charles, still in his dressing gown, regarded the yellowed pages and scarred cover of *Migrator Magazine* with bewilderment.

"No." Fred shrugged. "I'm going to the bakery for fresh buns. Do you want anything?"

"Please. When you return, I expect you to work on your Latin lessons while I finish an article," Charles said.

Fred squeezed his cheeks toward his nose with his fingers, forming his amiable face into a pout. "It's going to be a perfect summer day. I'd rather walk into the countryside."

"Not until you've done your lessons." Charles went to the

water jug and found just enough water left for tea. He poured it into the kettle and handed the empty can to his brother.

"Very well," Fred said with a hint of desperation. "But my stomach is growling."

Charles gave his brother a cheery wave of goodbye and stirred the fire in the hearth, attempting to bring it back to life. While the day would be a pleasant one, with no hint of rain, for now a decided chill permeated the air.

He heard the click behind him as Fred went out the door. After tossing a fresh lump of coal onto the grate, he went back to the magazine, settling into a mostly unstained armchair he'd picked up from a Holywell Street secondhand furniture dealer. Since he'd kept his lodgings in Holborn, he had a limited furniture budget.

Still, it was worth the inconvenience to be closer to Kate Hogarth, his new fiancée, during the summer months. He wanted to see her without the time expenditure of a five-mile walk. The early part of their courtship over the past winter had burned through a great deal of shoe leather.

The publication date on the top sheet read "1785." Who would hold on to it all these years, only to shove it underneath his door? He was a parliamentary reporter, a sketch writer, and an occasional theater reviewer, not a collector of stirring tales of past times.

When he flipped through the pages, he found a scrap of faded hair ribbon, a brown that might once have been lavender, tucked into the binding. The title of the marked article was "Death of a Jewish Child."

Charles winced at that. The death of any helpless creature excited his natural sympathy. Was this the part of the magazine that the unknown sender had wanted him to read? He leaned toward the fire and perused the page.

Four children followed their leader, nine-year-old
Pete, down the ladder behind his house in Lime-

house. The tide swept out, leaving a beach full of fine pickings for an intent and cunning eye.

"Sharpish," Pete ordered, a disdainful eye on the two girls, Han and Goldy.

"I know," snapped Goldy. She had already bent her head, focused on the beachscape under her nose. The only Hebrew in Pete's gang, she was prized for her unerring ability to pick out unbroken pipe bowls.

Han went toward a large rock and cast herself over it, belly down, then inspected among the stones for salable items the river had cast up.

Eddie, Han's younger brother, kicked over a rock. On the other side lay a china doll, face pressed against the sediment. He picked it up, then made a rude remark when he saw half the face was caved in. Throwing it in Osvald's direction, he jeered, "'Ere's a mother for ye."

The boy's hand shook as he plucked the ruined doll from the seaweed bed, where it had fallen. His mother had died from a blow to the face by her brutal, drunken husband, but Eddie had no sympathy for Osvald's loss.

"Lookee 'ere," Pete called. "Come quick, lads."

"A barrel," Goldy cried. "Is it full?"

Pete ignored her, breathing heavily as he fought to control the spirit-scented barrel. "Get behind it," he ordered Eddie. "Take the other side, Os!"

The three boys managed to push the barrel out of the water onto a patch of pebbles that was only damp.

"God's teeth!" Pete swore when he saw the bottom of the barrel was missing.

"No grog for us," sulked Eddie.

"Where's me pipe?" Pete asked, turning in Goldy's direction.

She held out a tiny bowl with a long, wide crack on one side. "All I have so far."

With a wave of his hand, Pete smashed it from her grip. As the pipe fell, the momentum of his movement swung Goldy's hand into her face, causing her to slap herself on the nose. She sobbed loudly.

"Shut up," the gang leader snarled after a moment's shocked pause.

Goldy sniffled and pressed her fingers to her injured nose. They came away with a smear of blood. With a shriek of irritation, she flew at Pete and pummeled the stocky boy with undersized fists.

He clouted her on the side of the head. "Stop crying!" he ordered.

But she wouldn't stop and spun around, dizzy from the clout.

"Into the barrel," Osvald said. "That will shut her up, the greasy slattern."

"Into the barrel," Eddie repeated, kicking the girl's feet out from under her. When she fell to her knees, he stood over her, hands on his hips. "She's only a dirty Jew."

Osvald grabbed the back of her ragged dress. The fragile cloth ripped as he picked her up. She screamed as he dropped her into the barrel headfirst.

Pete leaned a hand against the barrel. For a moment, all was silent, except for the slap of oars on the water as a rowboat went past, sending waves flowing over the rocks.

Then the waves upset his footing, and he collapsed against the barrel, making it totter. It fell on its side. Goldy cried out.

"Can't she ever shut up?" Eddie complained, kicking at the barrel.

It moved. A larger wave came in.

"Tide's early today," Pete observed.

Another wave. The barrel bobbed in the rising water.

Goldy beat against the barrel. Her dirty bare feet spilled over the edge.

Eddie kicked at the barrel over and over again until another wave came and pulled the barrel a good four feet closer to the dirty Thames.

A larger boat came by, with a complement of rowers working tirelessly. They sent a flurry of water toward the dampening beach, but the wave caught the barrel.

Han screamed as her playmate disappeared into the muddy brown waves. "She'll drown. She's in headfirst!"

Eddie clutched his sister's shoulders and shook her. "Quiet now. We never saw her today, do you hear?"

The children ran away, damp and shivering. Smoke from the forge at a nearby shipyard stole over the beach, making it hard to see the river. They climbed up the ladder behind Pete's house, one by one, none of them looking back, leaving Goldy to her watery fate.

Charles blinked hard as he came to the end of the story. Such a tragic tale within the damp-marked pages of this old periodical. A tale to make one rue humanity, in its depiction of cruel children and their immoral ways. He wondered if one of his neighbors, Miss Haverstock or Mr. Gadfly, had taken him seriously when he chattered about writing a historical novel and had slipped it to him for inspiration.

The door to his chambers opened as Charles turned the page.

Fred handed him a neatly wrapped bundle of buns. "Is the kettle hot?"

"Yes, it should be by now."

Fred peered at him. "Are you well?"

Charles closed the magazine, which sent a waft of mold spiraling into his nostrils. He sneezed. "Perfectly. I was quite transported by the article I just read."

Fred dug into his pocket for a handkerchief as Charles sneezed again.

"Thank you. Just the magazine irritating my nostrils." He set it on a pile of papers, far away from the heat of the fire or the damp of the windows.

Fred went to the mantelpiece and reached for the stoppered china jug that held their tea leaves. "Did you deduce who left it?"

"No, but it's a sociable building. Dotty old Miss Haverstock from upstairs could have found it in her belongings, or Mr. Gadfly could have picked it up when he was perusing at the stalls, looking for inspiration for his songwriting. Then there are our unpredictable friends, William and Julie Aga."

Fred shook their teapot until the leaves were disbursed to his satisfaction, then covered the teakettle handle with a rag and gently poured the steaming liquid into the pot. "I was surprised when they moved in. It's quite a walk for William into the city."

Charles stood and stretched. "They seem happy enough. Besides, William and I can walk to work together." William was a crime-focused reporter at the *Morning Chronicle*.

"Do you think so? You can hear William's cheery whistles from half a mile away, but Julie looks drawn to me."

"She had some sort of illness in the spring. High-strung people have these problems."

"Maybe she left the magazine to tease you."

Charles rejected the idea. "No, there was nothing funny about it."

"Shall I let the fire die down?" Fred asked.

"You might as well. It should warm up now. Why don't you do your lessons this morning, and after that, we need to tackle our windows. They are so frightfully dirty that it is hard to see in here."

"What about my walk?"

"This afternoon," Charles promised. "You won't get any-where in life without applying yourself. I have to write a sketch before I can please myself."

The Dickens pair worked diligently at the elderly, rickety deal table they'd pushed in front of the fire to catch the last of the heat. A knock came at the door just as the bells of St. Luke's tolled 10:00 a.m.

"I'll get it. You keep translating," Charles said, rising. He pulled off his fingerless gloves and dropped them on the table.

He opened the door a crack. "Hogarths!" he boomed when he saw the young ladies.

His fiancée, Kate, smiled at him, her heavy-lidded eyes bright-ening. She wore a crisp cotton dress, its thin stripes of red creat-ing cheer. Her bonnet had been trimmed with matching ribbons. He still couldn't believe she was his, though she'd accepted his proposal of marriage in the early days of spring, three months after her father had introduced them.

Her sister Mary, dressed in a summery floral print, held up a basket and pulled back the cover. The luscious sight of straw-berry scones and butter greeted him.

"Such a pleasure, my dears." Charles opened the door wider. "Fred is in the parlor, and we were about to eat."

He shut the door after they entered, careful to keep their wide skirts from being caught. Fred rekindled the fire and boiled more water. The girls laid out four plates on the table, with the dish of scones and the crock of butter in the central place of honor. Charles found a butter knife in his box on the mantelpiece and handed it to Kate.

"Do you have enough chairs?" Mary asked.

"There are four, yes," Charles said, pointing behind her. "I imagined many pleasant mornings like this when I moved to be close to my dear Hogarths."

Mary asked Fred about his translations, and they discussed the Latin poetry he had set aside in favor of their repast. Charles found the catalogue detailing the kitchen equipment that was deemed necessary for every new home and shared it with Kate.

"Do we really need all these specialized brushes?" she asked with a hint of anxiety.

"The more the better," Charles said. "You know how the soot goes everywhere, but you can't let it win. We are planning to tackle our windows this afternoon. They are a dreadful mess."

"It is rather dim in here," Kate said.

"I'll run home and get our special cleaning solution," Mary offered. "And Father has a translation of Caesar's *Gallic Wars* that Fred might like."

Fred snorted.

Charles spoke over his brother. "The cleaner would be very useful."

"Go quickly, Mary, but assure Mother that Fred is here to chaperone us," Kate said.

"Yes, go quickly," Fred added, "because I'm going out as soon as this poem is ready."

Mary snorted at the younger boy's order. "I'll be back as soon as I can, for Kate's sake."

She flounced off. Charles and Kate shared an amused glance at the antics of their strong-willed siblings.

"Have you learned Latin, Kate?" Fred asked.

"A little." Thus enticed, Kate bent over Fred's side of the table.

Charles picked up *The Times* and flipped to page three to read the parliamentary news. He read the lengthy article about Mr. Buxton's speech.

"*The Times* has put in quite a lot about Buxton's antislavery speech," he remarked. "I have to write my own analysis for the *Chronicle*, but my thoughts are taken up by cruelties even closer to home."

"What do you mean?" Kate asked.

Charles reached for the ancient copy of *Migrator Magazine* and showed it to her, explaining how it had come into his possession. "Keep your handkerchief close by, because it has mildewed." He opened it to the correct page and set it next to Fred's translation.

Kate reviewed the page as Charles picked up the last of the dishes and set them in a bowl on top of a chest that they used as a makeshift sink. Then he retrieved his notes on the Buxton speech and picked up his quill, considering his own take on the subject. *The Times'* comments on lashings excited his sympathies, so he went through his notes, seeing if he had anything their reporter had missed.

After a few minutes of intent reading, Kate closed the magazine. And sneezed.

Fred giggled. "You were warned, dear Kate."

She wiped her nose daintily as Charles set down his quill. "You were reading about children from some fifty years past, Mr. Dickens. Surely the horrors of modern slavery are more real than murderous children from long ago."

"Do you think children are better behaved now?" he countered.

Kate smiled at him. "I hope we shall find out next year. With any luck, we can be married at Christmas."

He patted her hand. "With luck."

"We have been engaged these past two months already," she reminded him.

"I am hoping for Christmas, if we can find and furnish a suitable home."

"Ahem." Kate cleared her throat.

"Yes, my darling?" Charles asked.

"You know what would distract me from the wedding?"

"What?"

She fluttered her eyelashes at him. "A mystery, of course."

Chapter 2

Charles pointed to the ancient magazine on the table. "There is a murder right in front of you."

"Spare me the distant past," Kate said. "And find me something fresh. If a disgruntled planter had shot Mr. Buxton, but no one knew he had done it, now that would turn my thoughts away from our future home for a time."

"I should hardly think it Christian of me to hope a Member of Parliament be killed just to please you," Charles said dryly.

Kate wiped a crumb from the table. It landed on the floor. "Of course not, but London is a big city. I'm sure you'll find something to amuse me."

"I don't even know who left me the magazine." Charles bent down and picked up the crumb, then dropped it into the fire.

"You have yet to leave our rooms today, Charles," Fred pointed out. "All you have to do is call on the neighbors to solve that mystery."

The door rattled then, and Mary came in. The sisters set to work polishing the interior of the parlor windows, clearing away the soot that was forever accumulating on the glass.

Charles went back to his table and his unfinished article. The window rattled as Mary and Kate opened it to clean the outside. Having buried himself deep in the Buxton matter, Charles didn't register the activity around him until he heard a shout, then a shriek.

Mary was leaning too far out of the window. Seeing what was about to happen, Fred jumped to his feet and reached for Mary just as she fell out the window.

"Mary!" Kate screamed.

Charles rose quickly, upsetting his chair. Another shriek sounded; then he heard a call from the lane.

"I've got her, lad. You can let go."

Charles rushed to the window to stand next to Kate. They leaned out. Just next to the hedge at the bottom of the four-foot drop, Mary lay splayed across the arms of the young blacksmith, Daniel Jones, who lived down the street.

Kate clutched Charles's sleeve as the man gently set down her sister.

"Best brush off your skirts, pet. I always have sawdust on me clothes," the affable local blacksmith said.

"Mr. Jones!" Charles called to Mary's rescuer. "You're a lifesaver. Thank you!"

Kate clasped her hands together and added her thanks.

Mary smiled up at them. "No harm done."

"Indeed. She's just a slip of a girl," Mr. Jones agreed.

"She slipped right out the window," Fred said, shaking his head.

"I leaned out too far," Mary admitted. "I'm lucky you came along."

"I live right down the lane." Mr. Jones still wore his heavy leather apron, and a jug rested at his feet.

Charles pointed down. "Did you drop that to catch Miss Mary? Is it broken? I'll pay for it."

Mr. Jones picked up the jug. "No, it's fine, Mr. Dickens. As are you, I hope, miss."

Mary sketched a little curtsy. "Very fine, sir. Thanks to you. What is your favorite jam? My sister and I will bring you some to thank you."

The blacksmith grinned shyly. "Oh, you needn't do that, but my good wife can never get enough strawberry, as Mr. Dickens here knows."

"We polished off an entire jar of it when you invited me to tea last week," Charles agreed.

"Watch out for that window," Mr. Jones advised. "That bush there has thorns. One of our cats was caught in it once, and Miss Haverstock had to call on me to rescue it."

Mary pulled a face. "We'll be more careful, sir."

Mr. Jones lifted his cap and pushed sweaty locks of hair off his forehead. "Speaking of Miss Haverstock, have you seen her these past days? My wife usually does for her on Fridays, but she didn't open her door when my wife knocked yesterday."

"We'll check on her," Charles promised. "I haven't been out yet today."

"Very well. Off to fetch beer," Mr. Jones said, settling his cap over his eyes. "Want to join me, Mr. Dickens?"

"I wish I could," Charles said, "but I have to work. I'll see you at St. Luke's tomorrow." The Jones family worshipped at the same local church as the Hogarths did, and Mr. Hogarth, not just Kate and Mary's father, but also Charles's editor at the *Evening Chronicle*, had introduced Charles to the Jones family back in April, after he and Kate had announced their engagement.

When the window cleaning was done, the men having taken charge of it, Charles told Fred he could go for his walk, and he went back to his gestating article, while the Hogarths cleaned the dishes and set everything back in their basket. Mary swept the floor.

Kate had brought some embroidery with her and settled down at the table, while Mary attempted to reattach some buttons that Fred had lost off of a coat. When the church bells struck eleven, she jumped up as if a hot poker had just touched her.

"I forgot. Mother said I had to watch the twins while she paid calls." She tossed down the coat.

"Did you fix the buttons?" Kate asked, unperturbed.

"All but one. You can finish it, can't you, dear?" Mary asked.

"Of course," Kate called as Mary ran for her shawl.

Mary glanced back. "You have to leave, too, since Fred isn't here. Bring his coat with us."

Charles looked up from his papers. He didn't want to be parted from Kate yet. "Why don't we pay a call? Miss Haverstock can chaperone us. I need to check on her, anyway."

Mary flung her shawl ends over her shoulders. "Fine. I'll leave the door open and go, but you must promise to be out the door in under a minute, or I will incur Mother's wrath."

Charles set down his quill. "Never that." He stood and picked up the basket and placed it over Mary's arm.

She sketched a wave and opened the door to its full extremity, pointedly leaving it open as she swished into the tiny front hall.

Kate set down her embroidery and picked up the coat with a frown. "I do hate to be interrupted when I'm in the middle of finishing a flower."

"You never miss a stitch," Charles said, leaning over her. "I love the blue. It matches your eyes."

Kate set down the coat and patted his hand. "You do say the sweetest things."

"I will give up sleep," he said aloud.

"You will not, Mr. Dickens," she said with a giggle. "That will not serve you."

"Why not?"

"Your mind must remain keen."

He tickled her cheek with one daring finger. "But I am such a fool for love. The more I do, the more I earn, and the faster I can afford to marry you."

"Come, fool," she said, standing. "We had better go upstairs. I don't want to have to lie to Mother about never being alone with you in your rooms. You know it isn't proper."

He put his hands on her shoulders. "May I steal a kiss first?"

She tilted her cheek, leaving him a surface for his lips.

"Only there?" he said gently. "Is that all Mr. Dickens deserves?"

"Charles," she whispered, her eyes meeting his.

He grinned and rubbed his nose against hers, then kissed the tip. "That will keep me. Your honor is as important to me as it is to you."

"Thank you." Her cheeks pinkened, and she stared at the floor.

He offered his arm with a gentlemanly flourish. "Let us go upstairs."

"When did you last visit her?" Kate asked, a little unsteady on her feet as she softly took his arm, the pressure of her fingers almost unfelt against his coat. "I admit I am concerned, considering what Mr. Jones said. It was selfish of me not to demand we check upstairs right away."

"You are never selfish, darling. Miss Haverstock uses that stick, you know, because of her bad hip. Maybe she couldn't rise from bed yesterday."

He and Kate stepped into the narrow hall between the sets of rooms. Opposite the front door to the building was a wooden staircase spanning the width of the hall, with extremely squeaky steps. Mrs. Haverstock was a small woman and didn't make much noise going upstairs or moving in her rooms, which were over Charles's. The noise she made was more like that of a mouse skittering than that of a full-grown person going about the business of their day.

As they climbed the steps, Kate having let go of his arm in order to lift her skirts slightly, he realized he hadn't heard the mouselike sounds in days. When had he last seen his upstairs neighbor?

Kate glanced at him, a pinched expression around her eyes. "What is that smell, Charles?"

"Meat that's gone off?" he asked, curling his lips with distaste. He'd smelled something like this before, half a year ago, when he'd been taken to the scene of a bloody suicide.

They reached the top of the stairs. The smell intensified. Kate coughed and pulled a handkerchief from her sleeve and held it to her nose. "Maybe she is ill?"

Charles knew better, now that they were at the unremarkable front door of Miss Haverstock's rooms. "It's death, Kate. It can be nothing else."

Chapter 3

"Should we go for a constable?" Kate asked as they hovered outside the closed door to Miss Haverstock's rooms. The dim windowless landing created a soundless cave. Nothing could be heard from the street; nothing moved inside the building. Yet something very bad had happened here.

Charles shook his head, his reporter's brain needing more information. His words moved through the possibilities, even as he knew the uncomfortable truth. "Not yet. It's been warm in the afternoons. Maybe Rattles, the building's mouser, has died. Or Miss Haverstock went on a journey and left the remains of a joint of beef on the table."

The cool knob turned easily under his hand, but that was not remarkable. Miss Haverstock didn't lock her door. Nothing seemed out of place on the sparse landing, but then, the small space between apartments was empty, and the floor was neat, swept clean.

He pushed open the door and they walked in. The rotting odor rushed out, so strong that he could taste it in the back of his throat. He blinked, attempting to focus his eyes into the bright parlor after climbing up the rather dark staircase.

"Oh," Kate said, gagging a little. Her eyes had adjusted first. Charles saw the evidence of that as her face went pale and she turned her head into his shoulder.

Then he saw what was in the room. Directly opposite them, Miss Haverstock, unnaturally still, perched on a stool against the far wall next to one of the windows. In between them was a red and blue Turkey carpet and a faded brown-velvet sofa, worn on the arms. In front of the sofa, on the rectangle of carpet, rested a sewing basket. Charles saw a pincushion on top of a cloth in the basket. He remembered Miss Haverstock had been embroidering a seat cushion for her foster daughter. She'd worked on it while they shared a dish of strawberries, and she had worried about the fruit staining her fine efforts.

He cataloged all of it in a moment, then forced his eyes back to the strange figure. Miss Haverstock wore a dress he'd never seen her in. The high sash marked it as at least a quarter century out of style, and probably more. It had half sleeves, ruffled over the elbows, and a ruched bodice. The silk had probably once been white or cream but had yellowed. It had fine embroidered work on the skirt and must have been her best dress, the sort she would have married in if she hadn't been a spinster.

He swallowed hard. The room was shut up close. A quick glance showed him that while the curtains were tied back, the windows were not open. But that hadn't kept the bugs from descending upon his friend. He could see movement on her face, around her slack mouth and half-opened eyes. Maggots. A large spider crawled up one hand, which was splayed, open fingered, across her lap. The other arm hung down.

"Where's the blood?" Kate asked, lifting her head from his shoulder for a moment before squeezing her eyes closed again. "There has to be blood, with that coppery smell. Check her dress. Oh, do you think it was the poor old thing's dress for a wedding that never happened?"

"Perhaps. Go stand in the doorway," Charles urged, pushing her gently toward the open door.

As Kate complied, he walked around the edge of the carpet, noting, as he had not before, Miss Haverstock's small tea table, pushed off to the left of the sofa. A service was set out, cups, saucers, and a teapot. An unopened wine bottle squatted next to the cream jug. He craned his neck to look across the few feet between it and him and saw a dead fly floating in the remains of a cup of Miss Haverstock's finest souchong tea.

He forced his gaze back to the body. His gaze roamed the gently wrinkled cheeks of his dead friend. Her chin rested on her throat, and her cap was slightly askew over her coarse gray curls. Her skin bore no resemblance to the color it had had in life. All her blood would have pooled lower once her heart stopped beating.

"How did she die?" Kate called.

Charles shook his head, holding his sleeve over his nose and mouth. It held a hint of grass and soot, which tempered the smell. He could see no reason for Miss Haverstock's death.

He took a step closer to her, staring at her profile, trying to ignore the work of the maggots. Forcing his hand not to tremble, he touched her shoulder. Something crunched in the wall.

She began to tilt away from him. Charles grabbed Miss Haverstock's arm, but she collapsed to the floor, still in her seated posture. That was when he saw the corkscrew embedded in her neck, blood congealed around it and soaking the back of her beautiful dress. Flies and other insects were stuck in it. Even in death, her yellowed skirts stayed demurely in place, protecting her modesty, if not her flesh, from the insects that devoured her.

He glanced away reflexively and saw a hole in the plaster where her neck had met it. Whoever had killed her must have driven the other end of the corkscrew into the wall. He gagged as he looked down at the body, now crumpled on the floor. The side of her neck was mottled. Fingerprints, maybe? Had she been strangled before being propped up in this strange manner?

He heard gagging sounds and raced to Kate, then pushed her out the doorway and into the hall. The ghastly odors diminished somewhat. Downstairs, the steps squeaked as someone came up them. Charles thrust Kate behind him, suddenly afraid the killer had returned.

Instead, he saw his friend and colleague William Aga, who had moved into the apartment across the hall from Miss Haverstock for the summer, along with his wife, the actress formerly known as Julie Saville. William carried a carpetbag, the weight sagging his wide shoulders, and Charles remembered he'd been out of town, covering the aftermath of a steamboat accident.

William's usual smile was worn around the edges, and his top hat bore all the signs of hours riding on top of a stagecoach. His normally well-groomed tawny locks were wind tossed and storm swept, and all of him appeared ready for a good long rest.

"Go for a constable," Charles said sharply, grabbing Kate's arm and thrusting her in his friend's direction. "Take Kate with you. She can't stay here."

"What's going—" William said.

Charles saw the instant his friend smelled death on the air. He must have been too exhausted to notice it before. William dropped his carpetbag in front of his door without finishing his question and put his arm around Kate, then ushered her downstairs.

Where was Julie? Charles could not remember knowing where she had gone, but she couldn't have been home these past couple of days, or she'd have noticed the deadly odor.

Charles took several deep breaths through his mouth alone, steeling himself for a second glance, then turned back into the parlor. He took another careful look around but found it difficult to concentrate, between the insects and the smell. Everything was as he remembered in the room, from the crock of oatmeal on the shelf to a heel of bread covered on a plate next to the crock. Hoping to find a list of addresses so he could notify her foster daughter, he paid special attention to papers but found nothing to even tell him what her name had been.

Miss Haverstock had a second room, a bedroom, but he'd never been inside it.

Finally, he went to her mortal remains and took another look at her neck. He had no experience of such things, but he really did think he saw fingerprints in those bruises. He hoped the abomination with the corkscrew had been done after she died.

When he took her hand, he couldn't bend her fingers or wrists. She was solid, unmovable. Only the insects roamed.

He debated taking a blanket from her bed and covering her decently, if only to attempt to protect her from the spiders, but then he heard a police rattle in the street.

William and Kate had found a constable, and he was sending his signal to any others who might be in the area of Chelsea Division. A couple of minutes later, Charles heard footsteps squeaking on the stairs, and William reappeared, followed by the lone constable.

"Miss Hogarth stayed outside in order to direct the bobbies," William said, panting a little.

The constable, about Charles's age, with teeth stained by tobacco, whipped a dirty handkerchief from between buttons down the front of his tunic and held the cloth to his nose. "Blind me, that's dreadful," he exclaimed. "She's been dead for days."

William went to the body, expression fixed, and knelt down. He removed his hat as he stared at the body. "What do you think, Charles?"

"Maggots, rigor mortis," Charles said. "I know that means it didn't just happen."

"A couple of days have passed," William agreed. "Poor dear. I've been out of town these past four days. When did you last see her?"

"I think I heard her more recently than that," Charles said. "On Wednesday or Thursday? Going up the stairs. But where is Mrs. Aga?"

"Lord and Lady Lugoson returned from France on Wednesday. She went to Lugoson House to help her aunt and cousin settle back in."

"She left when you did?"

"That afternoon," William agreed, coming to his feet as the constable slowly approached him. "I left that morning."

"I saw Miss Haverstock at St. Luke's on Sunday." Charles frowned. "But that's nearly a week ago now."

He heard a liquid cough. The constable spun around and ran out of the room. William sighed as they both heard the sounds of vomiting in the passage.

"Who's going to clean that up?" William groused.

"I guess we are tougher than a constable," Charles said.

"They have a hard time keeping recruits." William put his hat back on. "What a moment for me to return home. You say you heard her on the steps the night after we left?"

"I heard a lot of movement overhead on Wednesday night. Fred complained about it. He couldn't fall asleep." He heard another gag, then spitting. The constable reappeared in the doorway, wiping his mouth. His skin had gone pale, and his eyes were underlined with purple half-moons.

"She probably died about then," William said.

The constable swallowed hard. "You think you heard a fight on Wednesday night?"

"Yes," Charles concurred. "What is your name?"

"Constable Nathaniel Blight," he said. "Can I have your name, please?"

Charles gave the constable his information, then put the heels of his palms against his eyes and pressed hard. "Why didn't I go up to check on her?"

"Why indeed?" William asked.

"I stayed late at the office, deciphering my shorthand about the Irish Church debates in Parliament," Charles recalled. "By the time Fred was complaining, I was half asleep myself. Then, on Thursday, I was busy with a comic bit about the beer bill.

Really, I worked the same kind of hours. I suppose I had forgotten all about the noise."

"Of course, it didn't reoccur," Constable Blight suggested. He sniffed, then gagged again, putting his handkerchief to his mouth.

"No," Charles said bleakly. "She must have been dead by then."

Charles spent the afternoon with Kate at her family's home in York Place, reluctant to return home.

Eventually, Charles went home to Selwood Terrace, despite knowing what was on the floor above him. The body wouldn't be moved until the coroner's inquest, when the jurors would see the murder site and the corpse and would determine the cause of death.

He hovered outside, reluctant to go in. He had seen that the curtains were open in the rooms across the hall from him on the first floor as he came up to the front of the building. Breese Gadfly, a songwriter, was home.

Breese, like the constable Charles had met earlier in the day, was just about his age, but an entirely different sort of man. Breese's parents had had a thousand pounds a year, from a legacy. They'd both died in the past couple of years, and he claimed the legacy had moved to another branch of the family, but Breese had been well educated, remained well dressed, and must have some substantial means of taking care of himself.

Their rooms were nothing special, not even quite as nice as what Charles had at Furnival's Inn, but Breese dressed like the gentleman Charles wanted to be. He wore a new Wellington-style beaver hat, carried a brass-handled cane, and often sported a natty tartan waistcoat under a burgundy velvet frock coat. His facial hair was styled in the manner of King Leopold of Belgium, who had once been married to the heir to the British throne, and Breese had the same kind of leonine quality to his face as that royal personage.

Charles longed to try Breese's tailor, knowing he couldn't afford it just yet. But that didn't mean he didn't enjoy spending time with Breese, attempting to soak up his gentlemanly ways.

He went into the building and knocked on the songwriter's door. Breese opened it in less than a minute, still shrugging on his coat.

"Ah, it's Dickens," he cried, stepping back. "Do you know what that smell is?"

"The mortal remains of Miss Haverstock," Charles said solemnly.

Breese's eyes, already dark, went hard. "What?"

"She was murdered, probably Wednesday night. I discovered the body late this morning. If you think it is bad down here, you don't want to go anywhere near the second floor."

"You cannot be serious!" Breese exclaimed.

Charles held up his hands. "It's a dreadful business."

"When will the inquest be?"

"Monday, I hope. The police have the case."

Breese shook his head. His dark locks fluffed up from his temples, then settled again. "Poor creature. Nothing to do but endure, then. Hot rum and water? I was just heating the kettle."

"Excellent," Charles said, rubbing his hands together. "I will need something to help me sleep."

"What about Fred?"

"I sent my brother to my parents until the upstairs can be cleaned."

"And the Agas?"

"Mrs. Aga was with her aunt and cousin these past few days. William came home today, but I believe he will also stay with the family until the inquest."

Breese nodded. "And you? Am I to be all alone in this house of death?"

"No, I'm going to stay, if I can stand it," Charles said.

"I wonder if we'll have a ghost now. Miss Haverstock strikes me as good ghost material. She was vague enough to be a specter."

"You could say she was dressed as a ghost already," Charles revealed.

Breese poured rum into glass cups, then drizzled hot water from his steaming teakettle over them, before returning his kettle to the hob. He gestured Charles into a comfortable green upholstered armchair in front of the fire, then took the opposite chair. A nice desk rested in front of the window to the left of the chairs. Breese had said he preferred light to heat. Charles had noticed that he burned only the best wax candles, and his air was often sweetly scented as a result. In fact, Charles could not yet detect the smells of death in the air here. Perhaps Breese's nose was keener.

"What was she wearing?" Breese asked, setting his glass to his lips.

"An ancient once-white silk dress and a lacy cap," Charles explained, swirling his glass.

"I only ever saw her in tans or browns," Breese said. "Even when that lovely foster daughter of hers appeared."

"How long have you lived here? I never met the foster daughter."

"Three months longer than you. I moved in on the first of March. I saw Miss Jaggers about once a month, and Miss Haverstock would come down to the front door in tawny silk, maybe secondhand. Not new, certainly, but in a style of the past ten years at least." He chuckled.

"This dress had not been in style for many years." Charles swallowed half his drink, enjoying the near burn to the back of his throat. "But then, she had been staged to some degree. Who knows if her murderer put her in that dress?"

"What?" Breese exclaimed. "*Oy vey*, what a *tummel*."

"She was attached to the wall by the neck. With a corkscrew. There must be some significance in that."

Breese's hand stilled where it had been brushing his velvet lapel. "I am a fanciful character, I admit it, but do you not think she must have been involved in some criminal gang? A band of highwaymen perhaps. She was young in the late century."

Charles laughed. "Where do you get that idea?"

"Just before you moved in—late May, it was—we had a string of thefts in the area. I suppose the landlord's agent didn't tell you."

"The Hogarths didn't tell me," Charles said with a frown. "The Lugosons next door were out of town, so I suppose they missed the drama."

"It was confined to this side of the street, I believe," Breese said. "I heard of five or six house break-ins. The blacksmith's shop down the street was robbed, as well. And then there's this business of a convict breaking out of Coldbath Fields."

"When was this?" Charles demanded.

"That's the thing. It was Tuesday night, or so I heard. And the next thing you know, a woman is dead."

"How do thefts of a month ago, an escaped convict who'd obviously committed only a minor crime, or he'd have been in a different prison, and a murdered old lady tie together?" Charles asked.

Breese polished off the contents of his glass. "I don't know. I could write quite a ballad about this collection of schmucks, I tell you."

"I could write a sketch," Charles said, taking his own last sip. "There has been no crime since I moved in? Could the previous resident of my rooms have been the thief?"

Breese poured another tot of rum into his glass and topped it off with hot water, then refilled Charles's glass. "I hadn't thought of that. That's a reporter for you, always considering the angles."

"True, but songwriting seems to pay better." Charles stared at the fine cobalt Wedgwood jasperware candlesticks on the mantel and the professional-quality oil portrait of Breese's parents that hung above the fireplace. Those were probably inherited, but the full, delicately painted iron coal hod in the corner was a display of present wealth as much as the candles.

"Well, as to the previous inhabitant of your rooms, it was a young couple. Irish. They left for Boston about two weeks before you moved in, so not them."

"Any suspicious characters around?"

"I was never robbed, but the people who lived in the Agas' rooms were. That's why they moved."

The Agas had moved in the same day as Charles, all of them seeking a more country atmosphere for the summer, and with ties to friends nearby. Charles had thought they might stay on here, but he would give up his rooms in September and put Fred back in school.

"What was stolen?"

"They had some nice candlesticks."

"As nice as yours?"

"No, I don't think so. They took the blankets, and some of their clothing, a pot."

"Anything portable," Charles suggested.

"Yes. There wasn't any jewelry. But Miss Haverstock lost a pearl ring and her Sunday dress."

"She was robbed, but not you?"

"Odd, I agree," Breese said. "Maybe I was home when they came to our building."

"Miss Haverstock rarely left, except on Sundays," Charles said.

"She did her own marketing," Breese countered. "I'm sure that's when it happened, whereas I stay home all day, banging away on my piano."

"I'm curious to know more about this escaped convict," Charles said, dismissing the thefts. "The hardened types don't go to Coldbath Fields. The maximum sentence there is just two years."

"So why not just wait out their time?" Breese asked. "Silly to escape from there."

"Must have been very desperate." Charles pushed his hair off of his forehead.

"Desperate souls can murder. It would take only a couple of hours, perhaps less, to walk from the prison to here."

"Whatever caused her death, it must have been some ancient pain. I can't forget that old dress."

"*Oy vey*," Breese said. "Nothing normal about this. Yes, I think the convict must have done it. Broken out to kill the old dear. Do you have a mind to solve the mystery, using your journalist instincts?"

"I solved two murders last winter, but Miss Haverstock's death was nothing like those," Charles said modestly. "It's obviously murder this time, and the police can solve the case. I'm busy courting my future bride, in addition to my work. I've no time to sort out something that will most certainly have an obvious explanation, with the proper amount of investigation."

"Don't protest too much," Breese said with a smirk. "I know how little you bother to sleep."

"Do you know how to find the foster daughter? Someone should tell her that Miss Haverstock died."

Breese shook his head. "No idea."

The next day, Charles stepped out of St. Luke's Church with Kate at his side, enjoying the sight of the blue sky, marred in no way by fluffy clouds that looked like unspun wool.

"We should take a walk," Kate suggested. "It's too nice of a day to stay indoors."

"I thought of checking on Fred." Charles had no intention of spending time in his rooms, not with Miss Haverstock's decaying corpse overhead. It was like living in a slaughterhouse. If he had to spend any time there, he'd have to burn expensive candles like Breese did, to mask the odor.

"I'm looking forward to seeing your entire family. It's been months since I met your mother."

"Yes. You should have a lovely time with them," Charles said vaguely. "I can't believe your visit is tomorrow." He knew Kate had to spend time with the Dickens clan, if for no other reason than she had to understand why some of his money would always go to the care of his mother and siblings, even with his father still living.

Behind them, a heavy door banged against the Bath-stone exterior, and someone came quickly through the porch and down the stone steps.

"Mr. Dickens," cried a strangled East London–accented voice. "Could I trouble you?"

Charles turned around, then smiled when he saw who had greeted him. Addie Jones, the blacksmith's wife from down the lane, wore a black dress as if she were in mourning. A kind woman, she had seen him carrying a broken lantern the week before and had taken it to her family's forge to have it fixed, then had refused to take payment for the repair.

"Were you related to Miss Haverstock?" he asked, gesturing toward her dress.

Mrs. Jones put her handkerchief to her eyes. "No, but, oh, Mr. Dickens! My husband has been arrested in connection with the murder."

Chapter 4

"What?" gasped Kate, staring openmouthed at the blacksmith's wife. "Kind Mr. Jones, arrested?"

Charles, shocked, stood still. He stepped aside when a large parishioner barreled down the church steps and knocked into his shoulder. "Never," he insisted. "Why, your Daniel is a good man."

"He saved Mary from falling," Kate said.

"He didn't charge me at all for mending my lantern," Charles added, "and all the boys in the neighborhood adore him."

"He is an angel," Mrs. Jones sniffed. "Can you help? You're the smartest man I know, Mr. Dickens, with the most learning."

Kate put her hand on his sleeve before he could reply. "Why was he arrested?" she asked.

"Because my husband found cut manacles in the smithy this morning, sir. The police say he conspired to kill Miss Haverstock with the convict, but I can't believe as he'd have any part in helping such a man escape, even if it were his own father."

Edmund Jones, Daniel's widowed father, also a blacksmith, worked at the forge, too, though his joint inflammations kept him from a full day of work. His spinster sister, Hannah, helped Addie with the households.

"Is his father a convict?" Charles asked.

"No, sir, no." Mrs. Jones shook her head vigorously, a little spittle flying from the corner of her mouth. She wiped the moisture away, shamefaced. "Oh, I'm just that upset, I tell you. They are good men, both of them, never caused any trouble."

"I heard a rumor about someone escaping from Coldbath Fields," Charles said.

She nodded again. "That's wot the constable said who arrested him, Mr. Dickens. They traced the escaped man to this neighborhood."

Charles put a hand to his neckerchief. The summer sun made it stick to his skin. "How did they find the manacles?"

"An informant, some secret schemer."

"Maybe the same person who cut off the manacles then put them in the shop and sent word to the police," Kate suggested.

Mrs. Jones put her handkerchief to her eyes. "It was locked up, just that tight. Only one key. That was Mr. Jones's mistake, saying no one but him or his father could enter his smithy after working hours. It's where he keeps all his tools."

"Were you robbed in May? I understand plenty of places were around here," Charles asked, recalling what Breese had told him.

"Not the workshop, but the house," Mrs. Jones said. "They took our Hannah's good bead necklace and my teakettle, a quilt my mother made."

"A strange selection?" Charles asked.

"Nice things," Mrs. Jones explained. "I don't have any jewelry myself, except my wedding ring, and it was washing day, so there weren't clean clothes up on the hooks. I know plenty who lost clothes."

"They can be sold," Charles suggested.

"Yes, you're right," Mrs. Jones agreed. "All that was a good month ago, long before the manacles were found."

"Any sign of a break-in?" Kate asked. "Like a broken window?"

"Nothing," Mrs. Jones insisted. "Nothing of the sort. It's that strange, but I know Mr. Jones didn't have anything to do with them manacles. He'd have told me. No secrets in our house."

"I'm very sorry," Charles told her. "I have to attend the inquest tomorrow since I found Miss Haverstock. I'm not sure what else I can do."

"You'll think of something," Mrs. Jones said. She smiled for the first time, exposing the hole where her eyetooth once had been. "I have faith in you, like I do in our sweet Lord Jesus."

"I'll find out what I can." He nodded at her, then strolled away, Kate on his arm.

"Goodness," Kate said. "That's a lot of faith. But I have faith in you, too, after you figured out how Christiana Lugoson and Marie Rueff died a few months ago."

"When am I to find the time?" Charles groaned. "But I like Mr. Jones. I must help the man." Even if the matter of the manacles made it seem that he wasn't entirely innocent. There must be an explanation.

"I'll help you." Kate chewed her lip as they walked toward a stand of trees on the side of the church. "Do you think my parents would let me attend the inquest?"

"Certainly not. I would not allow it," Charles said. "You weren't called, and I don't think inquests require an audience."

She pouted. "But you'll tell me everything."

His fiancée loved a mystery, so he acquiesced. "Certainly, except for the gruesome bits."

She shivered. "I already saw the body. That was quite enough. What should we do now?"

He leaned toward her ear. "I know you have to help with Sunday dinner. I'll see what I can learn at the police station."

"Very well, Mr. Dickens. I'm sorry I cannot join you."

He smiled at her. "Every moment away from you is painful, darling. Every moment."

He squeezed her hand as Mary joined them under the canopy of leafy trees, then waited for them to leave.

When they were out of sight, he went back to the church steps, where Mrs. Jones stood with her husband's aunt, Miss Hannah Jones; the little girl who lived with them; and a curate.

The frightened wife saw him and trotted up to him. "Did you have an idea, Mr. Dickens?"

"Have you tried to see your husband?" Charles asked.

She shook her head.

"Let's go to the Chelsea station and see what we can learn."

She lifted her skirts and ran back to Miss Jones, all propriety forgotten, then met Charles on the pavement. They walked rapidly toward the police station.

"I thought that given it is Sunday, he might not have been taken to prison yet," Charles told her. "I'd like to know what your husband has to say."

She nodded, her face intent. "I am grateful, Mr. Dickens. I really am."

They reached the police station, only to find a commotion outside. A line of uniformed officers had formed between a cart on the street and the front door of the stone building, and the officers were watching a small group of manacled prisoners make their way to the cart.

"Mr. Jones!" Mrs. Jones cried, running forward again. She tripped on her skirts.

Charles caught her arm. Her outcry caught the attention not just of the officers but also of the manacled prisoners. The three of them, two badly dressed villains and Mr. Jones, who looked out of place with a white shirt and a clean face, stared at her.

Charles pushed his way in between two of the constables and found himself within speaking distance of the blacksmith. Mr. Jones's eyes were red, and his face had contorted with grief and fear. But Charles drew from his reporter's experience and, instead of offering sympathy, went straight to the heart of the matter. There was no time for more. "Tell me about the manacles, Mr. Jones. Did you saw them off an escaped convict?"

Mr. Jones shook his head. "I'd never seen them before, Mr. Dickens. It was a shock to me. I slept beside my wife all night."

"I know you weren't aware that Miss Haverstock was dead," Charles called. "You asked me about her yourself."

Mr. Jones nodded as a constable pushed him. Stumbling forward, he bounced into another of the prisoners. "I didn't kill anyone," he cried as the constable pushed him again. "I didn't help anyone break out of chains."

Mrs. Jones fell to her knees on the dusty pavement as constables helped her husband into the cart. "Where are you taking my good husband?" she screeched.

The constables ignored her.

"Are either of the other men the prison escapee?" Charles asked a constable, his hand on Mrs. Jones's shoulder.

The man spat dark phlegm into the road. "Body snatchers. Caught digging up a grave in an old churchyard."

Charles shuddered. "Thank you." He helped the crying woman to her feet. They watched as the cart rattled away. No one answered when he asked where Mr. Jones was being taken.

Charles looked hard at Mrs. Jones. "Did he sleep next to you all night?"

"As much as I can say," she told him. "I was up myself for a while with little Beddie. But he was there when I left and there when I returned."

An hour later, Charles left the Jones property and went down the lane to Selwood Terrace. Miss Jones had put Mrs. Jones to bed. He had walked across their yard, satisfying himself that the forge was far enough away from the cottage that someone could have sawn off manacles without disturbing sleepers in the other building. The police had simply arrested the first convenient person, without having any good reason to do so.

The weather contrasted with his mood. Late June felt positively joyful, with wildflowers growing on every little bit of soil. Little remained of the gloomy experience of walking these streets last winter.

It seemed like the wrong season to have another murder. Didn't murder belong to cold, wet, dark streets? Yet Miss Haverstock was nonetheless very dead indeed.

The thought was inescapable as he entered his building. The scent of death hit him like a wall of bricks against his nose. His eyes watered, and his stomach lurched. Putting his hand over his mouth, he quickly opened his door and ducked in, then shut it behind him. He took a breath through his nose and rejected the foul air instantly. It was coming through the ceiling.

He took off his hat and clutched at his hair. Should he return to Furnival's Inn? He'd pack his carpetbag with a few things for tomorrow and head to the Hogarths, as planned. They had let him sleep on the dining-room floor, in front of the fire, once before.

After collecting his post, he was back outside, feeling bad for Breese, if he had stayed in his rooms. He argued with himself for a moment, then dropped his bag by the brick wall and went back in to bang on his neighbor's door. Breathing shallowly, he waited for a minute, but no one came to the door, and when he put his ear to it, he heard no motions inside. Breese had probably stayed away, as well.

Charles went back outside and breathed deeply. At least the smell wasn't following him outdoors. Whistling to distract himself, he hoisted his carpetbag and walked over to the Hogarths.

Their house stood alone between their vegetable garden and fruit trees on one side and a walled Jewish cemetery on the other. The gate was usually locked, so he'd never been inside the burial ground, but he and Kate had often walked through the orchard. Across Fulham Road were the market gardens. The area had excellent growing conditions for fruit trees, and Charles was sorry to see the new buildings constantly going up in the area. Soon this would no longer be the countryside.

He remembered promising Kate a picnic when strawberry season came along. After leaving his carpetbag behind the gate barring the Hogarths' front walk from the street, he walked past and checked their garden. The strawberries were ripe. He could smell the sweetness of the fruit. He chose the two best berries, then tucked them into his handkerchief and returned to the gate.

When he knocked at the front door, it was opened almost instantly by Mary. The fifteen-year-old put her hands on her hips and glared at him. "Where have you been? We've been waiting!"

He opened his handkerchief and displayed the berries.

"Ooh." Her fingers hovered over them; then she chose the slightly smaller one and took a bite. "June is the best month of the year, isn't it?"

He grinned at her. "Most months feel like my favorite. Each has its allure."

"Not April," Mary said. "Too much rain." She stepped back so he could enter.

"But the flowers return in April," he protested.

"I suppose April isn't entirely terrible. Are you leaving for a debate tonight?" she asked, spotting his bag.

Charles often traveled to political meetings. "No. I can't stay in my rooms tonight. If your mother won't take me in, I'll head into London."

"Why not?"

He put his fingers to his nose and made a face.

"Kate told me about finding that poor old woman. I can't believe I was merrily cleaning your windows while she was upstairs." She wrapped her arms around herself and shivered theatrically.

"And falling. Did you hear that your rescuer was arrested? Dreadful mess." He dropped his bag inside the door and set his hat on top of it.

"I'd never believe Mr. Jones could do anything sinful. He's such a lovely man. We see him at church at least once a week," Mary told him.

The next youngest sister, Georgina, flounced into the passage. "We have potato soup, asparagus, and a rhubarb sauce for the joint," she announced. "A lovely spread."

"Sounds delicious," Charles agreed. A door opened. He could hear the sound of a violoncello in the dining room.

"There ye are," Mrs. Hogarth said, appearing in the passage. She still wore an apron over her tartan dress, and her dark hair was fluffed up on one side, as if a child's hands had been at it. "Mr. Hogarth was just wondering what had happened to ye. Come, before the soup gets cold."

He followed the girls past the doors to the front parlor, which was rarely used, and Mr. Hogarth's small study, into the dining room. The most used room of the house, it boasted a long dining table with many armchairs surrounding it; a piano; various other instruments, in and out of cases; and an old stuffed chair in one corner. A green baize door led to the kitchen on the orchard side, as well as to the steps to the first floor, where all the family bedrooms were.

The Hogarths had nine living children, all of them at home to fill the bedrooms, from Kate, now twenty, since her birthday the month before, down to twins Helen and Edward, just starting to walk with competence. They were the only two young ones, as Georgina, the next oldest, was already eight.

Charles saw George, James, and William wrestling on the floor next to the piano, while the eldest brother, Robert, attempted to follow along with his father on the keyboard, making a companionable noise.

Mrs. Hogarth scolded everyone in her broad Scottish accent, and the wrestlers stood sheepishly, brushing dirt off their trousers. Much moving about of chairs ensued, as seven older children, their parents, and Charles seated themselves. Soup bowls had already been placed on the table, and after a short prayer from Mr. Hogarth, everyone picked up their spoons.

"Are ye off to a meeting?" Mrs. Hogarth inquired just as Charles lifted his spoon to his lips.

"I cannot stay in my rooms tonight," he explained. "Pray do not ask me the details."

Kate gave a little shudder at his side. He knew she could imagine the state of things. "Can he sleep here tonight, Father? He really can't remain in his rooms."

Mr. Hogarth set down his spoon and scratched his gray side-whiskers. "Verra well. As long as he remains downstairs."

"Of course," Charles said respectfully. "I've never even been upstairs."

Mr. Hogarth nodded and picked up his spoon again. "Have the police made any progress?"

"Not that I'm aware of. It is Sunday."

Mrs. Hogarth shook her head. "Appalling. Kate told me about the dreadful situation with Mr. Jones, Charles. Ye will make it clear to the police that he is a good Christian, won't ye, Mr. Hogarth?"

"I'll send a letter," her husband agreed.

The subject, which none of them wanted to refer to except in the most oblique manner, was dropped. After they finished eating, Charles excused himself to go to Mr. Hogarth's study, hoping Kate would join him for a moment of privacy.

Pulling out a small battered volume of verse, he quoted aloud, "'Laid in my quiet bed, in study as I were, I saw within my troubled head a heap of thoughts appear.'"

"Did you just make that up?" Kate asked, standing in the doorway behind him.

"No." He gestured her in, then, quick as a wink, shut the door behind her. "One of the Tudors. Beheaded, I think."

"A very troubled head, then," Kate said with a giggle.

"Yes. We had better not be in here very long, or your parents will boot me from the house, and I will have to walk into London."

"Or maybe they will demand you marry me that much sooner," she said, clasping his free hand between both of hers.

Her heavy-lidded eyes looked so sleepy, sending his thoughts toward bed and warmth and tumbling bodies. Without thinking, he lowered his mouth to hers.

Chapter 5

No sooner had Charles's lips connected to Kate's soft mouth than she jumped back, releasing him, her fingers going to her throat. Both breathing hard, they stared at each other.

"You make me burn, dear Kate," he said.

"Yes," she agreed softly. "We can't wait too much longer."

A sharp rap came on the door, and Mr. Hogarth spoke. "Kate? Are ye in there? Yer mother wants ye."

The next morning, Charles crossed the Hogarths' orchard into the formal garden that filled one side of the Lugoson property. He collected William Aga, who was about to go out the mansion's door himself. Charles had had a note from his fellow reporter the night before, explaining where he'd be sleeping. Charles caught sight of Panch, the Lugosons' skinny elderly butler, in the hall, a clothing brush in hand.

"He couldn't make you look respectable if he tried," Charles joked as William joined him.

The truth was that William had been welcomed in high circles. Charles envied him his easy way among the upper classes. Some days he didn't even feel equal to the Hogarths.

"Lord Lugoson has a new bull terrier puppy, who shed all over me this morning," William said, shaking out the skirt of his frock coat. "Unfortunately, he's taken mightily to Julie and is crawling into our bed at night."

Charles blushed at William's frank admittance that he and his wife shared a bed. He knew Julie Aga too well, as there had been time a few months ago when she had created problems for him with his courtship. Thankfully, his gaze had been solely on Kate all along, and Julie had developed feelings for William.

"Did you receive the assignment to cover the inquest?" Charles asked.

"Yes. Thank you for reminding me to ask." William nodded as they crossed busy Fulham Road. The inquest into Miss Haverstock's death was being held at an old-style pub that still had seats and a public meeting place upstairs, unlike the new gin palaces that had been springing up everywhere, all doors and counters and barrels leaning up against the walls, with the goal being a person in and out in a minute, full of gin and without a respite from the cares of a working life.

"I have to testify," Charles said. "I found her, after all. This is my first inquest. I still think we should have been called to the inquest for Horatio Durant's suicide, but Matthew Post, his solicitor, kept us out of it."

"Why?"

"I'm sure it was because young Lord Lugoson was with us and he didn't want that to come out."

"Good point," William said agreeably.

The scents of sawdust and spilled beer drifted, not unpleasantly, past Charles's nose as they entered the pub. Ancient stools, worn into a dip in the middle by decades of workmen, were clustered around rough board tables. A rickety set of steps along the right wall led up to the first floor. With no gas lighting here, a fire in the enormous fireplace along the left wall gave a murky sort of light to the space.

William pointed up. Charles followed him to the steps and held the bannister as he climbed, not convinced his foot wouldn't break through one of the sagging treads.

They survived the climb. A dozen men pulled from the streets surrounding Selwood Terrace were in the room, taking the oaths that would make them jurors. The aged boards under their feet squeaked as they shuffled from side to side. A couple of uniformed constables stood with the men.

William nudged Charles. "That's the coroner over there. Listen."

"Once again, the police are interfering," muttered the coroner, a man in his late thirties. The lines of his forehead had been carved by intelligent thought, but the creases around his down-turned mouth indicated a perpetual horrified wonder. "They've arrested a suspect before I can interview him in the inquest."

"Have you appealed to the Home Office, Sir Silas?" his facto-tum, a younger man, asked. A man who was constantly search-ing for approval, he had wide-open eyes, and his clothes were baggy on his tall frame, except for the too-tight buttoned-up waistcoat, which still had toast crumbs attached to the nubby fabric.

"It's too late now." The coroner's irritated gaze moved past Charles to the jurors. He picked up his top hat and pulled it over his neatly waved coal-black hair. "I think we're ready."

"No, sir, we're still waiting for a witness," the assistant said nervously. "At least enough jurors arrived."

Just then, Kate appeared at the top of the stairs, followed by her father. Charles's hands instinctively clenched when he saw her, dressed in her most sober gray dress, looking like a governess rather than her usual ebullient self. They must have called for her this morning, since she'd said nothing before. She was too nervous to smile when she saw him, but her lips twitched as she walked in his direction.

Footsteps clattered along the wooden floor. Charles saw

Addie Jones and her father-in-law, Edmund Jones, who had been lurking in the corner, almost invisible. Mrs. Jones, dressed in black, rushed toward him, her hands outstretched; then she all but fell into Kate's arms, crying. Mr. Jones remained passively in the shadows. Kate was overbalanced and had to lean on the whitewashed wall behind her. Daniel Jones must be the arrested person that the coroner had groused about.

Charles glanced at Edmund Jones. Gray haired and half bent over from a lifetime of work, he had tucked his gnarled hands, with their huge knuckles, against his lapels. Though shrunken, he still gave the appearance of strength.

"That's the last," the assistant said, smacking his lips.

The coroner gestured for the twelve men, all voters on the parliamentary rolls, to sit on the stools provided for them along the wall. "Constable," he ordered, his large frame looming over the seated men.

The taller constable cleared his throat and said loudly, but in a mechanical way, "Oyez! Oyez! Oyez! You good men of this county, summoned to appear here on this day, to inquire of our sovereign lord the king, when, how, and by what means Miss Haverstock came to her death, answer to your names as you shall be called, every man at the first call, upon the pain and peril that shall fall thereon."

Sir Silas tucked his thick, flat fingers under the collar of his freshly pressed waistcoat, displaying a gold watch chain and seals. "I am Sir Silas Laurie, the coroner. Here is what we are going to do today, gentlemen. First, you need to choose your foreman. He will be sworn in first, and then the rest of you will be in turn. After that, we will continue." He made a circle with his index finger, and the twelve men came off their stools and made a loose circle, to discuss who among them was the most distinguished.

Charles's gaze circled the men, cataloging each one. He hadn't been in the parish long enough to recognize them, but he attempted to put them into their rightful place by details of their clothing. He suspected the tallest of them would be chosen. A man of forty or so years, he looked the most prosperous, with a tailcoat of fine black summer-weight wool, and had the bushiest side-whiskers. Twenty minutes passed while the jurors decided and were each sworn in, the foreman with a lengthier oath to recite than the others. Charles was gratified that his candidate for foreman was indeed the man chosen.

After that, Sir Silas drew himself up again and spoke his charge. "Gentlemen, you are sworn to inquire, on behalf of the king, how and by what means Miss Haverstock came to her death. Your first duty is to take a view of the body of the deceased, wherein you will be careful to observe if there be any marks of violence thereon, from which, and on the examination of the witnesses intended to be produced before you, you will endeavor to discover the cause of her death, so as to be able to return to me a true verdict upon this occasion."

He cleared his throat and spoke in less formal terms. "We are going down to the street, and we shall have a fine walk to the late Miss Haverstock's home so that you can view the body. It's not how it was found, unfortunately, but you need to see what was done to this poor woman. It won't be pleasant. She's probably been dead for five days."

The coroner glared as one of the jurors moaned. "After that we'll come back here, and you can quench your thirst before we question the deceased's family and the witnesses. You are lucky. This is the only inquest today, so we won't have to keep you all day long."

One of the constables walked the foreman out. The juror who had protested earlier hung his head as he walked out the door. The others followed, and the second constable brought up the rear, followed by the coroner and his assistant.

Charles, along with the other witnesses, stayed behind, while William followed the group to record the proceedings. The newspapers mostly reported on the juicy parts of witness testimony, quoting them verbatim. William's shorthand skills would be sorely tested once everyone returned to the pub.

Once the jurors were gone, Charles could focus on the others who were present.

Mr. Hogarth opened his tobacco pouch. "They should have chosen a closer pub, but I suppose the coroner has used this one before."

"It will be quite a while before they return," Charles agreed. "Enough time to get good and sozzled, if we were so inclined."

"Can we sit?" Kate asked.

"I should think so." Charles went and collected a trio of stools for them. As they sat, he looked at the others in the room.

The sole woman present, other than Kate and Addie Jones, was quite young, perhaps seventeen or eighteen, and very beautiful. Her golden hair and high color were embellished by the peach silk skirt overlay on her short-sleeved summer dress. She looked expensive in every respect, and her expression was disinterested and serene, even haughty. Kate's gaze had gone directly to the girl, too, and her hands plucked at her serviceable gray summer-weight dress skirt as if it irritated her.

Mr. Hogarth, on the other hand, viewed the girl's companion. The youth next to her looked even younger, but it might simply be a matter of sophistication, for he did not wear the attire of a wealthy person. His coat and trousers were brown wool; his waistcoat was black. His shoes had graying discoloration on the toes and heels, as if the leather was too worn to take polish any longer.

Besides them, the room contained two men, a cadaverous man of some sixty years and a younger assistant, very slim and tired looking, with the kind of frame that never held any fat but only stringy muscle. Charles attempted to define the foreignness of the first man. His clothes seemed cut a bit too tight, perhaps, and the long mustache was not typical for London.

The foreign-looking man approached Charles. He was too elderly for his shoe polish–black hair and trailing black mustache. "You are Dickens?" he demanded, his voice slightly accented, with a glance at his assistant rather than at Charles.

"I am, sir," Charles said after the assistant nodded. "And you are?"

"Ferazzi," the man barked. "I own the Selwood Terrace property."

"Ah," said Charles, offering his hand. "A pleasure to meet you. I had enjoyed my rooms until the late death."

Ferazzi rubbed his nose. "They'll remove the body today. Believe the cart was going to be sent for directly after the jury visited."

"I am glad to hear it. We've had a spot of warm weather," Charles said.

Ferazzi's upper lip curled. "Indeed."

"Who are the young people?" Charles asked, nodding his chin toward the appealing pair as Mrs. Jones cried on Kate's bosom.

"Don't know 'em." Mr. Ferazzi's expression remained harsh.

"I've seen the girl," the helpful assistant said. "When rent collecting."

"A former resident?" Charles asked.

"Miss Haverstock's foster daughter. Name of Jaggers, I believe."

"Ah, I had heard of such a person," Charles exclaimed. "Well, they could not have been of any relationship by blood. Miss Haverstock was so small and dark."

"And Miss Jaggers is a tall, shining creature. Rather like one of them Greek goddesses," the assistant said with a leering grin.

Mr. Ferazzi sneered and stalked off.

"Needs to eat more," his assistant opined as Mr. Ferazzi went down the steps. "If your belly ain't ever full, you ain't going to have a proper decency about you."

"He is not a large man," Charles agreed.

"Sunken cheeks," the assistant said. "That's 'ow you tells it, the signs of want."

"Surely that is also a sign of age in a person," Charles suggested.

"'E's old enough, to be sure," the assistant agreed. "But I've never seen 'im eat anythink, not even a round of toast."

"Who are you?" Charles said. "I don't remember seeing you."

"That's because I 'aven't collected rent from you yet." The man grinned, exposing three holes where teeth ought to have been. "Nickerson's me name. Reggie Nickerson."

"A pleasure to meet you, Mr. Nickerson."

"You'll feel that way until my 'and's out and your purse's empty," Mr. Nickerson said agreeably. "Then you'll 'ate the sight of me. But I mean to do a proper job of it and collect my wage and take it 'ome to the missus so we can keep a roof over our own 'eads, you see."

"Very well put," Charles said. "You'll have no trouble from me."

"I 'ope not, Mr. Dickens, as my employer keeps me ever so busy. Sunup to sundown these past few weeks, cleaning out the rooms on a boarding'ouse 'e's just purchased."

"No trouble," Charles repeated. "I'm a respectable man." He edged away, moving to Miss Jaggers's side.

The beautiful girl glanced at him as he approached. Taller than average, she met his eyes. "Yes?"

"I wanted to express my condolences to you and your companion. I knew your foster mother for a few weeks and enjoyed her company." Charles smiled politely.

"Thank you." Her lashes fluttered. "This is Prince Moss."

Charles inclined his head to the young man. "I did try to find your address so I could tell you the tragic news, but I'm afraid I failed. I hope the police have treated you with sensitivity."

One side of her mouth curled up as Kate rushed to Charles's side. Charles introduced Kate to the bereaved girl.

Kate frowned. "I am so sorry for your loss, Miss Jaggers, and that we never met under happier circumstances."

Miss Jaggers's lips twitched, but she didn't respond, merely glanced at her companion.

Put off by her rudeness to Kate, Charles inclined his head and returned his fiancée to her father.

After ninety minutes, the jurors returned. Their number had been added to by a couple of new men, one of whom was a doctor that Charles recognized. More people who needed to testify.

Charles and Kate had passed the time in between by discussing what furnishings they needed to buy for their marital home, giggling and blushing over what they needed, while Mr. Hogarth pretended to ignore them and read the newspaper. Miss Jaggers had spoken only to her companion after her brief conversation with them. Charles had thought it best to leave her alone, given that she'd just lost her foster mother.

Charles and Kate gave up their stools to the jurors and watched Sir Silas go to the deal table he was using as a desk. He stood over it as his factotum sat down and picked up his quill. Sir Silas dictated to him for a few minutes, and the man scratched away. Then the coroner poked his fingers under his lapels again and stalked toward the jury.

"I shall proceed to hear and take down the evidence respecting the fact, to which I must crave your particular attention. We wish to understand what caused the death, and who. If anyone can give evidence, on behalf of our sovereign lord the king, when, how, and by what means Miss Haverstock came to her death, then let them come forth and they shall be heard." Sir Silas turned and gestured grandly to his assistant.

The man set down his quill. "I call Mr. Charles Dickens. Please state your name, place of abode, and occupation for the records."

After Charles gave the information, the man said, "Please rise and repeat the oath after me."

Charles went forward to face Sir Silas. He nodded, heart thumping, and repeated the oath after the man said it. "The evidence I shall give to this inquest, on behalf of our sovereign lord the king, touching the death of Miss Haverstock, shall be the truth, the whole truth, and nothing but the truth. So help me God."

Chapter 6

✀

Sir Silas spoke rapidly. "Mr. Dickens, can you please take us through the course of events that led you to discover Miss Haverstock's body on Saturday, June twentieth, at Selwood Terrace?"

"Yes, sir," Charles said, feeling his palms sweat as he pressed them against his trousers. He told his story in bare-bones fashion, answering the questions the coroner asked about the position of Miss Haverstock's body before he had touched her.

At the end of the recitation, Sir Silas said, "Before the witness signs his examination, let it be read over to him."

His assistant read back Charles's testimony while he stood there, feeling like a naughty child in front of a schoolmaster.

The coroner nodded to him. "Is this the whole of the evidence you can give?"

Charles thought back. He'd talked about the footsteps on the stairs on Wednesday night, and he'd described what he and Kate had seen in detail. "Yes."

"You the jury, do you have any questions before this witness signs?" Sir Silas asked.

Heads bent as the jurors muttered among themselves. Eventually, the foreman lifted a finger.

"Mr. Dickens, it troubles me that we do not know anything about this lady's circumstances. Do you, for instance, know her first name?"

"I never heard it, sir." Charles laced his fingers together behind his back. "She only ever referred to herself as Miss Haverstock. I believe there are others in the room who might have more information. I knew her for less than a month."

The foreman nodded. "That is all."

Sir Silas sent Charles to the table to sign his examination, then wrote some notes upon it himself before handing it back to his assistant.

Charles felt very sorry to leave Kate, but at least her father was there to support her. He walked past William, who winked at him, and then he went down to the main room of the pub to have a glass of ale and a plate of bread, cheese, and pickle while he waited for Kate to be done.

About twenty minutes later she came downstairs, followed by her father.

"How was it?" Charles asked, rising.

"I could add nothing to your examination," she said. "The foreman asked me if you'd lied about anything. Of course, I said no."

"I'm going to take my daughter home," Mr. Hogarth said. "I have some editing to do."

"I need to pack," Kate said. "Remember, my mother and I are going to spend the night in Bloomsbury with your family."

Mr. Hogarth frowned. "Why don't you cancel your plans? You've had a bad shock today."

Kate set her chin. "No, I'm fine, and Mother hired Hannah Jones to come in for two days and help with the household while we are gone."

"But her nephew is in jail for the murder," Mr. Hogarth protested. "Surely she will need to stay at home."

"No. Mother sent for word before we left for the inquest. She's not canceling. I'm sure they need the money we're paying, with only her brother, old Mr. Jones, to run the forge. Poor Addie Jones is childless, you know. She takes care of a female orphan who is kin to her."

Mr. Hogarth stuck his pipe between his teeth, muttering.

Charles glanced between them both. "I'll escort you home and recover my bag from your house. Hopefully, the body has been cleared and the smell is gone at Selwood Terrace."

"The body may not be gone quite yet. The coroner has to sign the burial order after the witness examinations are completed," Mr. Hogarth said.

"Fred and I can always stay at Furnival's Inn for a night or two, until the air clears."

He followed the Hogarths into their house and took his bag from the dining room. Mrs. Hogarth was all aflutter, giving instructions to her maid. Eventually, Charles escaped the loud, frantic household, carrying his carpetbag. The sun shone down merrily, the weather belying that a woman had been killed and an inquest into the injustice was presently taking place nearby. When he walked past the Jewish burying ground next door to the Hogarths, he found the gate open. He'd never seen it unlocked before.

He poked his head in and saw his neighbor Breese Gadfly sitting in between two new graves. He stepped in softly.

Once he was beyond the gate, he felt the peace of the place. Twenty-year-old leafy trees and a variety of green bushes had been planted next to the walls, creating a hushed atmosphere. On the other side of the walls, through the trees, he could see the St. Luke's bell tower and some of the row houses in the neighborhood.

He walked up to his neighbor, feeling like he should stay on his toes to be as quiet as possible. Breese sat on a patch of moss next to a stone that read "Moses Davis" under a few lines of Hebrew writing.

"Friend of yours?" he asked, noting that the grave dated back only to January. The white stone marker had a complex shape at the top, with wavelike edges and an oval apex.

"No. I just enjoy the peace here. Despite the bodies six feet below, it doesn't smell nearly as bad as our building."

Charles nodded ruefully. "They should have done the inquest on Saturday, but maybe they couldn't round up enough men with such incredibly short notice."

"Neither of us is meant to be an undertaker, that is for sure. I've scarcely taken a bite of food in days."

Charles noticed the songwriter did look pale from the conversation alone. He made sympathetic noises as Breese frowned down at his sheet of paper. "I need a rhyme for *tear*. And not *dear*. It's much too obvious."

"*Near?*" Charles suggested. "*Leer? Seer? Rear?*"

"*Seer*," Breese said, his fingers tapping on his quill. "I like that."

"What have you got?" Charles lifted his coat and sat on the bit of grass around the edges of the grave.

Breese scratched away for a moment; then he sang four lines. "Your beauty and youth are precious to me. I would never see you shed a tear. But sometimes when I glance back at you, I see with the eyes of an ancient seer."

"Interesting," Charles remarked. "Something bad is going to happen to the poor dear."

Breese rubbed his eyebrow with the tip of his quill. "It's meant to be a comic song."

"Ah," said Charles. "For something specific?"

"For a play. The lovesick swain is singing."

"He could predict her early death if she doesn't fall in love with him."

"I suppose as long as the play is comic, then the song doesn't precisely need to be."

Charles leapt to his feet. "The actor can make it so, with exaggerated faces and such." He sang the verse, affecting the exaggerated manner of an eighteenth-century macaroni. When he finished, he executed a flourish-heavy bow.

Breese laughed and clapped. "Bravo, Dickens."

Charles smiled modestly. "I once studied hard to be the new Charles Matthews."

"*Oy vey.* You wanted to be an actor."

"Yes. I even had an audition, but I was so ill that day that my face swelled up and I had to cancel."

"You never rescheduled?"

"No." Charles cleared his throat. "My reputation as an accurate reporter began to grow, and I had plenty of work. The money was good, and in the end, I craved respectability too much to be a professional thespian."

"I understand that, but you do have an ear for verse and song. Why don't you try writing with me? I could use a good rhyming partner."

"I'll join you another time," Charles said. "I have to take my fiancée to Bloomsbury tonight, and then I think I will stay in Holborn for a couple of days."

"Very wise," Breese agreed. "I am sure your rooms are infinitely worse than my own."

Charles stared down at his forlorn neighbor. "Do you want to stay with me in London? You can sleep on my sofa."

His neighbor's eyebrows rose.

Charles hoped he didn't think that his difference of religion would preclude a friendship between them.

"Very decent of you, Dickens, but I think I will stay here. I have a meeting with the playwright tonight in Chelsea."

"Fair enough," Charles said, then hummed Breese's tune again. "Do you have a second verse?"

"Not yet. I—"

Charles heard heavy footsteps. He turned and found a man with a dark scowl on his face approaching. He wore a black velvet cap, and his white beard was very full, like a cloud of whipped cream. His hair hung down from his cap in curly white locks.

"This is no place for singing," the man hissed.

Breese jumped to his feet. "I apologize, Rabbi. My friend was trying to help me."

The rabbi said something in a foreign tongue, and Breese bowed his head in shame. Charles opened his mouth to apologize, but the words did not leave his mouth before the rabbi had stalked away from them, his long coat fluttering around his ankles.

"The dead need their peace," Breese said softly.

"I am sorry," Charles whispered. "I didn't mean to disturb your secret place. I had never seen the gate open before and was intrigued. If you're staying here, can you keep an eye out? I want to open my windows. I don't have much worth stealing, but if you hear anyone prowling around, it's not likely to be me."

Breese held out his hand, and Charles shook it. "I can do that. I'll make up a list of some topics we can write about."

Charles pulled a face. "It's all about girls, isn't it?"

Breese lifted his hand with a world-weary flourish. "But what kind of girl? A milkmaid? A laundress? A shopgirl? A flower seller? A courtesan?"

Charles's lip curled in a sneer. "Not a laundress. I can never find a decent one."

Breese chuckled silently. "Then a laundress it must be, my dear Dickens. For your passions are stirred, and therein lies a song."

"What would bother you? A parlormaid? A duchess?"

Breese's gaze displayed confusion. "All or none. I am indifferent."

Charles sketched a wave, then turned on his heels and marched out of the burying ground. Muttering rhymes to himself, he almost collided with another man as he stepped onto the street.

"Charles! Deep in composition? A new sketch?"

Charles blinked. "Greetings, William. My apologies. I didn't see you there."

William peered over his shoulder. "Never seen the gate open before."

Charles took his arm. "No, but the rabbi didn't like that I was in there. Is the inquest done, or does the jury need to come back tomorrow?"

William lifted the bag he held. "Done. I'm back to the city to write up my notes. Going to spend the night at Furnival's Inn." He had kept his rooms there, as well, so that he had a place to sleep when he worked late.

"It will be a long article?" Charles tilted his hat to keep the sun out. He was starting to feel uncomfortable pressure behind his eyes.

"As you can imagine, Sir Silas was very irritated that Daniel Jones was locked away as the main suspect. I can see how the police and the coroners are going to come to blows, since they have some of the same responsibilities."

"Where does that leave our situation? Was the burial order signed?"

"Yes. I hope our rooms will be habitable again in a day or two. The verdict came in as sudden, violent death by the hand of another, where the offender is not known."

Charles blinked sunspots out of his eyes and walked half a block, searching for a break from the sun. "They didn't charge Daniel Jones?"

William followed him, then stopped in the indifferent shade of a smaller tree. "You missed the bit where the governor of Coldbath Fields testified that a prisoner had indeed escaped."

Charles gasped. "I wish I hadn't."

"Ned Blood," William said. "What a name, eh? The governor couldn't identify the manacles found in the Joneses' blacksmith shop, because the police have them, but no other prison is missing anyone."

"They think this Blood character killed Miss Haverstock, abetted by the blacksmith?"

"Apparently so. When the lovely Miss Jaggers testified, she described a retiring, elderly, homebound lady with no enemies." He shrugged. "An escaped convict looking for portable property is as likely as anything under those circumstances."

"I would agree with Miss Jaggers's assessment of the lady," Charles said, "but no one else has had a break-in since we arrived. That's the part that makes no sense."

"Do you care? Should we?"

"Of course. What if the convict returns to our building?" Charles asked. "Or the thieves? But mostly, Mrs. Jones asked for my help with her husband. There's no help for him if Ned Blood isn't found."

"How do you go about finding a missing murderer?" William lifted his free hand. "You know London better than anyone, but Blood could have gone anywhere since Wednesday night. It's been more than four days."

"People don't usually move very far from what they are used to. I'm sure his associates will have some idea of where he is holed up. Murderers don't get sent to Coldbath Fields. This might very well have been his first kill, and he's probably hiding out, terrified."

William shifted his bag from one hand to the other. "I don't know what he was in for."

"Something with no more than a two-year sentence. For now, there really isn't anything I can do. I have to go to Bloomsbury tonight, and tomorrow I have a sketch due." Charles waved his hand over his face. "I suppose I should visit with Mrs. Jones and see how she coped with the inquest."

"She'll have been dosed and put to bed," William said. "No, enjoy your family time. You want Miss Hogarth to make a good impression on your parents."

"Quite the opposite, I assure you." He pulled William on to

the next tree, searching for better shade. A carriage passed by them on the street, the driver wiping his streaming face with a large handkerchief. "While I admit my mother has some good connections among her extended family, my father's impecunious lifestyle has caused no end of trouble. I hope to never be in debt."

"A good plan, if you do not have wealthy relations," William agreed.

"Not all of us can fall in love with the niece of a baroness," Charles said.

"Ah, but I could not help myself." William smiled fondly. "My Julie is light herself."

"She's a lively one." Charles had never quite trusted his friend's wife, though she generally had a way of angling herself into the right over time. But he couldn't deny the couple's affection for each other, and their heated glances made him quite uncomfortable at times.

"I do wish my Julie and your Kate could be friends," William said. "For they will be thrown together."

"I am sorry for it," Charles said honestly. He preferred not to remember Julie's flirtatious behavior toward him back when they had first met. "But Julie, for however short a period of time, was my live-in maid. I would hope, now that she's a respectable married lady instead of an actress, that the frost would cool."

"Maybe after you are wed," William said.

"Either way, you and I will remain the best of friends," Charles assured him. "It is up, up, up for both of us in our careers. I have my sketches, and you have your monographs."

"Very good." William grinned at him. "We will purchase our mansions soon enough. Why don't you take your papers to Lugoson House? Panch will let you in and make you comfortable in the library for a few hours."

*   *   *

Charles glanced up blindly from his papers when he heard the St. Luke's bells toll four times. Lifting his hands over his head to stretch, he enjoyed the fact that his body didn't hurt, thanks to the Lugosons' luxurious chairs. He'd have to race over to the Hogarths in order to get them in the hackney in time to make it to Bloomsbury for dinner.

He tossed his papers into his carpetbag, then walked swiftly through a maze of passages that deposited him in the drawing room where he had first met the Lugosons and their distinguished guests back on that tragic night in January. Stepping through French doors that led directly onto a terrace, he then descended a stone staircase into a formal garden that edged the Hogarth property.

Charles took deep breaths of the purple-blue lavender that brushed against his knees. A red squirrel dashed across his path, racing toward a stand of trees at the far end of the property. The scent of roses filled the air in the next part of the garden. He then admired white lilies, orange and yellow nasturtiums, and pink and white hollyhocks in turn. Enthusiastic bees buzzed in their favorite plantings. The tall purple foxgloves in one of the final rectangles gave him an uncomfortable feeling, since he knew they could be used to make poison.

He reached the Hogarth orchard. The petals had dropped from the trees, leaving tiny fruitlets behind. He'd much rather stay here, among the trees, than head into urban Bloomsbury, but his family must be faced, and all female elements of the Hogarth and Dickens clans introduced in turn.

Some of the relations had already met. His mother and sisters had been at his birthday party in February along with Kate and her father. Fanny and Letitia would always make good impressions, and his mother had a great deal of flighty charm. Fred, at fourteen, had endeared himself to every member of the Hogarth family but Mary, who was just enough his elder to find the lad less than impressive.

But none of them had met his father, and John Dickens, while at least his wife's equal in charm, was not a parent a young man on the make could be proud to possess. Back when Charles had met Kate Hogarth, his father had recently been released from a lock-up house in Cursitor Street, where his debtors, both landlord and wine merchants, had secured him while Charles raised funds to keep his father from going to prison. Again. Not only had Charles had to borrow money to give to his father's creditors, but he'd also had to support the entire family, and yet his father had been at his old tricks within weeks of being released, asking for loans again. He had a pension from his first career as a navy pay officer, but it was never enough, and his reporting career hadn't been the success Charles's had.

Still, his parents had reunited after his father's sojourn with a laundress out of town in the winter months, and now they had rooms in Bloomsbury.

When he reached the Hogarths' kitchen door, Mary opened it and regarded him with her hands on her hips. "Ready to go a-visiting?"

He tweaked one of her dark brown curls. "That I am, Mary dear. Are your sister and mother ready?"

"There ye are!" Mrs. Hogarth exclaimed, peering around Mary. About five years younger than his mother, she had no gray hair in her dark locks yet, though she'd let her figure expand into soft, comfortable folds and rolls. "I wondered what was keeping ye. The hackney is waiting out front."

He gave Mary a lip-smacking buss on the cheek before following Mrs. Hogarth to the small entry hall, where a bench squatted on the floor, under pegs for coats.

Kate, radiant in a refashioned white dress that she'd inherited from Christiana Lugoson the previous winter, twirled for him. "What do you think?"

"I'd never have known where it came from," Charles said,

admiring the fine silk skirt. Christiana had been a slip of a girl, a couple of years younger than his Kate.

"I fashioned the new bodice from the skirt of one dress and used the rest of the fabric to finish remaking this skirt." She crossed one arm over her breasts to finger the lace on the other short sleeve.

"Very summery," he praised, "and I always like blue ribbons on you. They do so much for your pretty eyes."

She curtsied, belling out her skirt so that the blue ribbons nearly touched his ankles. "La, sir, the things you say."

Mrs. Hogarth opened the front door. "That's enough from the pair of ye. We had best go, or your mother will think we don't want to eat her fine dinner."

Charles's stomach growled. "Never." He picked up the portmanteau Mrs. Hogarth and Kate were sharing with his free hand and marched out the front door. As they walked down the path, George and William poked their heads out of their father's study, waving and shouting goodbye. Kate waved back and blew kisses until Charles helped her into the hackney cab, never an easy process, then did the same with her mother.

They rattled through the streets, moving into Kensington and driving alongside the gardens there. Charles told them about all the blooms in the Lugoson garden, and Mrs. Hogarth said they'd been invited to walk there whenever they liked. Kate asked if he'd seen any new books in the Lugoson library, but Charles had to admit he hadn't looked at the shelves, as he had so much work to do.

"You must take time to look about you," Kate admonished. "You work too hard and I want to know more about poor Miss Haverstock's inquest. Have you heard anything?" Kate asked.

Charles relayed William Aga's comments as they passed Hyde Park, enjoying the sight of people in their finest taking advantage of the long summer day.

"It doesn't seem like anything useful happened. Is that truly just because poor Daniel Jones had been arrested already?"

"I'd like to think poor Mr. Jones would have been exonerated, had he been interrogated at the inquest. I think what needs discovering is any possible relationship between Mr. Jones and this Ned Blood character."

"What a thrilling name," Kate said, wriggling her shoulders. Her poofy sleeves wiggled in turn, as if separately animated. "Ned Blood. Sounds like a pirate."

"Sounds like a murderer," Charles mused. "I like descriptive names. I shall have to do a better job with names in my sketches."

Chapter 7

⁓

The clop-clop-clopping of the horse's hooves finally stopped as the hackney moved from the center to the side of the road in front of the Dickens's lodgings in Bloomsbury. Church bells tolled five times around them as they dismounted.

The family's rooms were over a tailor's shop, and while they weren't any larger than the lodgings of a few months before, at least John Dickens's pension was paying the rent, instead of Charles's and his older sister Fanny's salaries.

"Have you ever used them?" Mrs. Hogarth asked, peering in the bowed window.

"No, but I believe my mother had some coats of Father's made over for the younger boys."

"She doesn't do her own sewing?" Kate asked.

"I believe the light is poor upstairs," Charles said. "Fanny has her singing career, you know, so that just leaves Mother and Letitia to manage the household, and both of my sisters are courting."

"How nice," Mrs. Hogarth exclaimed. "More weddings in the family?"

"Not this year," Charles said. "But maybe next. It's a matter of income, of course."

"Still, it's nice for a woman to know her girls are being settled."

Charles smiled and hoisted their two bags in his hands. One for him and Fred, and the other for the Hogarths. He took them up the stairs behind the exterior door. The air in the stairwell smelled strongly of fried fish and potatoes.

"Are we having fish for dinner?" Kate asked.

"I don't know. The tailor's family lives upstairs, too."

A bang sounded as a door hit a wall. A small face appeared at the top of the stairs.

"Boz!" Charles called. "Come to greet us?"

His brother waved.

As they walked toward him, Kate exclaimed, "Oh, he's a tiny you. Look at all that hair."

"No one would miss mistaking us for brothers," Charles agreed. He dropped the bags on the landing and gave his brother a hearty handshake. "How is school treating you, Mr. Dickens?"

"Well enough," Boz muttered. "But I don't like it much."

"Come in, come in," Mrs. Dickens said, appearing in the doorway. Her hair was frizzed around her charming face, and while the apron she must have just removed had protected the main part of her dress, her sleeves looked like they'd been splattered by grease.

"Mother, you'll remember Mrs. George Hogarth and Miss Hogarth?" Charles said.

"Of course. Welcome," Mrs. Dickens said. "So lovely to see you both. I cannot believe it has been many months since we last saw you."

"It has been too long," Mrs. Hogarth said kindly. "But we'll have the rest of our lives to know each other."

"So very true," Mrs. Dickens said with a tinkling laugh. "This way, please!"

They followed her swishing skirt into the tiny entryway, barren of furnishings other than an empty crate, then went into the parlor. Fanny's piano had been settled under the one window looking out over the street.

Charles's father leapt to his feet from his position on a battered secondhand sofa and bowed to his guests. "Well met, Hogarths!" He shook hands with both ladies, exclaiming over their beauty.

Charles saw Kate cataloging his father, no doubt looking for hints of Charles's future appearance. He saw his father at fifty years of age, graying hair much sparser than it had been, yet still full of the waves he'd passed to many of his children. He'd also passed along his lean build to his sons. His rather sunken cheeks and a sharp beak of a nose, but a strong chin, had not universally appeared in his descendants, however, at least not yet. A ready smile had creased lines around his mouth.

John Dickens rubbed his hands together. "So glad you came this particular evening, as I was craving fried fish. Nothing better, would you agree, Mrs. Hogarth?"

"Oh, I do love it," she assured him. "A good beer batter is heaven."

Mr. Dickens chuckled. "I understand your husband is quite a famous musician. So pleasant to be able to boast of that in our own family."

"We had the pleasure of hearing Miss Dickens sing while my husband played at your son's birthday party," Mrs. Hogarth said.

"Excellent," Mr. Dickens pronounced. "Soon we shall have to reunite them, but tonight I believe Letitia will be the player while Fanny sings, if you will allow the indulgence. Or perhaps Miss Hogarth would like to perform for us?"

"Goodness, no," Kate said. "My best skill is embroidery, not music. It would be a shame to force you to listen to me when we can hear Miss Dickens."

"It is always a treat," Mr. Dickens agreed. "A veritable cornucopia of delights. Charles, why don't you take the Hogarths' baggage into the best bedroom?"

"Oh, we couldn't," Mrs. Hogarth protested.

"Indeed, you must," Mr. Dickens insisted. "It has such a superior mattress that you will think the angels also provided it. Mrs. Dickens has sewn a beautiful coverlet. Miss Hogarth may find it worthy of mention."

"Let us dine," Mrs. Dickens said, touching her husband's arm. "The food is ready. Charles?"

Pleased with the impression his father was offering, and glad his parents were making an effort with the Hogarths, Charles took the Hogarth's bag into his parents' bedroom and deposited it on the bed. Fred jumped up from the rocking chair to the left of the battered dressing table, which their mother had dressed up with a length of lace under her perfume bottle.

"There you are, Charles. Am I going home with you?" his brother asked.

"To Furnival's Inn," Charles said. "Unfortunately, Miss Haverstock was not removed until after midday, and I doubt the air has improved much."

"June is not the right time to die," Fred pronounced.

"I quite agree." He clapped Fred on the shoulder. "What larks we'll have at the old place for a day or two."

"I wish we could go coin hunting," Fred suggested with a sly glance.

"I don't think we dare. Remember how we were scared off by the courting couple last month? I think we'd best wait until the weather changes."

"How about mudlarking, then?"

"Are you so desperate for coin? I won't allow it," Charles declared. "Our little patch by Blackfriars Bridge is full of friends these days, thanks to my charity, but generally, mudlarks are a desperate, dirty bunch. No, if you want to earn some money, I'll pay you to run errands for Mother or me."

Fred gave a frustrated huff. "I could leave school and get employment of my own."

"Absolutely not. School is where you belong, for a while longer at least." Charles ruffled Fred's hair, so like his own. His brother tended to romanticize things, but Charles well knew what it was like to be out in the world, undereducated and too young to take care of himself properly. He wouldn't bestow the same fate upon his brothers, even if they thought they were ready for it.

Letitia stomped into the room, her feet making an elephantine noise for such a small woman. "Dinner, boys. The soup will go cold."

"Boys?" Charles sneered.

Letitia stuck her tongue out at him and flounced away, dark ringlets bouncing.

"She's not much of a lady," Fred said.

"Her force of personality is alarming," Charles agreed. "She's going to become a termagant if she doesn't tame that wild spirit of hers."

Fred let out a whoop and raced out the door, leaving his brother to reflect that Letitia wasn't the only one with high spirits in this family. With a father like theirs, was it likely that his siblings had futures as sober, responsible citizens?

By the time Charles reappeared, his father was seating everyone, giving Mrs. Hogarth the pride of place at the far end of the table and settling Kate next to himself. John Dickens, Esq., as he styled himself, was the perfect gentleman of an older age while he fussed over Kate, who, unlike his own daughter Letitia, was demure, ladylike, and pleasing to his father.

Charles took the seat opposite Kate at the table, resigning himself to being the one to entertain Mrs. Hogarth, since Boz was her other dining companion.

"The inquest was today," Fred said after his father had said a prayer and everyone had hoisted their spoons over their soup bowls. "Was it grisly?"

"No such talk at the dinner table," his mother snapped. "We have guests."

"Even if we didn't have guests, Mrs. Dickens," his father said. "No dissections and postmortems ever at the table."

Letitia giggled. "Were you busy with it all day, Charles?"

"No." He leaned forward, so she could hear him across the table, careful not to drop anything into his beef broth. "In fact, I had a pleasant sojourn in the Jewish burying ground next to the Hogarth home."

"You live next to a graveyard?" Alfred asked, eyes shining. "How thrilling!" Two years younger than Fred, he was the oldest Dickens boy still at home.

"We don't really notice it," Mrs. Hogarth said. "There is a high wall and trees all around. I've never seen it open."

"Unusual," Charles agreed. "Anyway, I had a look at the gravestones. Very odd to the eye, with all the foreign writing, though the lower parts are in English. My neighbor was in there, trying to write a song. That's what he does, and I might try working with him."

"How delightful," Kate said. "I'd love to hear a song you've written."

He smiled fondly at her. "So would I. I did help him with a verse. It helps to have a large vocabulary, so that you have a wide selection of rhymes available."

His father jumped to his feet and declaimed, his hand over his heart, "There was a monkey climbed up a tree. When he fell down, then down fell he. There was a crow sat on a stone. When he was gone, then there was none." His voice rose as Boz giggled loudly. Their father widened his eyes, and his stance became more theatrical. "There was an old wife did eat an apple. When she had eat two, she had eat a couple."

"That's enough, dear," Mrs. Dickens said. "We don't want our guests to think we haven't any manners."

"No different than my husband jumping up from the table to write down a thought on some music he has running through his head," Mrs. Hogarth said complacently. "These geniuses."

Mr. Dickens beamed at the implied compliment and raised his wineglass to her.

Charles, not wanting the poetry to descend into something bawdier, cast about for some other subject. He remembered that strange magazine article.

"Speaking of, err, literature," Charles said. "The morning we found the unfortunate Miss Haverstock, someone had thrust a magazine under my door."

"Something interesting, dear?" Mrs. Dickens asked.

"To begin with, it was fifty years old," Charles explained. "Who put it there? The Agas were gone, and Mr. Gadfly didn't leave it."

"And Miss Haverstock was deceased," Kate added pertly.

"Quite." Charles raised his glass to her, in imitation of his father. "A chilling article resided inside, about a group of bloodthirsty children who basically killed a young Jewish girl who roamed with their gang but wasn't well liked."

"What happened?" Alfred asked as everyone gasped.

"They put her into a barrel, and she ended up drifting out of their hands, down the Thames."

Charles's father looked thoughtful. "Sounds almost like a reverse parable."

"Why?"

"You know the rumors, Charles? About Jews killing children and baking them into matzo?"

"What's that?" Boz asked, his small nose wrinkling.

"A meal they use to make their food," his father said. "There are some delightful ballads on the subject."

Mrs. Dickens narrowed her eyes.

"But I won't regale you with any," her husband said hastily. "I simply mean to say that the usual tale has Christians being killed by Jews, not the reverse."

"I cannot appreciate the intolerance of those days," Charles said. "Why did someone stuff it under my door? That's the real mystery. I cannot understand the point of the article with no context."

"And stuff it under your door while a dead body decayed on the floor above," Letitia said with a kind of ghoulish relish. "It must be a clue."

"Speaking of context," Kate inserted. "I've been thinking about what we saw in Miss Haverstock's parlor, and I think the wedding dress she wore is a key to the murder."

"Why was she wearing it?" Mr. Dickens asked.

"Exactly." Kate beamed. "Was she secretly married? Or jilted?"

"I admit it is an interesting point," Charles said, "and certainly the dress might have been intended for a wedding, but we now know there was a convict in the neighborhood."

"Yes, but—" Kate said.

Charles interrupted. "The convict must be the killer, even though Daniel Jones had nothing to do with the situation and only his forge was used to remove the manacles that were found."

"I think you should move back to London," his mother said, throwing a damper on the conversation. "That Selwood Terrace doesn't sound like a decent place for you or Fred. Murder? Escaped convicts? Manacles?"

"It's as safe as anywhere else," Charles muttered. "But Fred and I are going to spend a couple of nights in town, while the Hogarths enjoy your hospitality."

"I should think so," his mother agreed. "And perhaps you won't return to Chelsea."

"I enjoy being so close to the Hogarths," Charles said.

"Maybe our present rooms are too close to the market. I don't know, but I need to be there to help solve this murder. Mrs. Jones has especially asked for my help."

"She is very distressed," Kate agreed.

"As long as ye don't put yerself into any danger," Mrs. Hogarth said. "We have a wedding to plan."

"Weddings," Kate mused, revisiting her point. "Why would an old lady be killed in an ancient wedding dress?"

"Was it out of style, dear?" Mrs. Dickens asked.

"Oh, yes. Nothing like the present fashion," Kate assured her. "But so lovely."

"Very odd," Mrs. Dickens agreed. "Had it been well cared for?"

"I didn't take a close look," Kate admitted.

"Under the circumstances," Charles's father interjected. He patted Kate's hand. "My dear, you must forget all about it. We'll have Fanny perform some sprightly tune and talk Charles and his brothers into doing comic recitations."

"Oh, you must honor us with one yourself, Mr. Dickens," his wife added.

He inclined his head. "Of course, my dear, of course."

The next morning, Charles and Fred arrived back in Bloomsbury for breakfast, after a short night's sleep in their chambers at Furnival's Inn.

"Good morning, good morning, sirs," his father cried. "Come to check on your lady love?"

"Indeed, Father," Charles said, shaking hands. "And eat, before the long day ahead of me. What are your plans?"

"Oh, a spot of something or other," his father said vaguely. "Might go to the theater tonight, review a play."

His father had all the ability in the world but claimed a chronic illness kept him in too much discomfort to work often. For all Charles knew, it was even true. He'd seen the expression of pain that crossed his father's face when he sat for too long.

They had just finished eating, and Fanny was just saying

something about clearing the table, when something fell against the outer wall of the chamber, loudly and harshly enough to make the teacups rattle in their saucers.

"What on earth?" Charles's father muttered, standing up. "Someone must be moving furniture, but I won't have our meal disturbed."

"We're as good as finished, Mr. Dickens," his mother said. "Dear Charles must leave for the newspaper. We cannot keep him any longer."

Another bang came, louder than the first. His father straightened his neckerchief before storming out of the room.

"Stay here, Kate," Charles said, following his father out. His mother joined the procession, as did Fred.

Charles slid from behind his father as they reached the passage. Across the hall, the door to the tailor's apartment was open. A cloud of dingy, worn underclothing came through the doorway and landed on the boards in a heap.

Mrs. Dickens gasped and retreated to her doorway, eyes averted.

Charles heard raised voices shouting about missing rent payments. More fabric came flying through the door, a bolt of black worsted and a heap of printed cotton that had seen better days. A man with a twisted nose brought out a couple of stools and set them against the wall, sneering at the Dickenses, before he disappeared again.

Then a woman stepped into the passage, a baby in one arm and the hand of a tiny girl in the other. She had the full figure of a woman who'd recently given birth, and her bodice had milk stains on it. Her eyes were reddened, and she had a pack of belongings strapped to her back.

"Mrs. Gordon?" Charles's father queried. "What has happened?"

The woman stared blankly at the pitiful pile of cloth and clothing on the hallway boards.

"Mrs. Gordon?" Mr. Dickens prompted.

"The rent," she said in a tiny voice. "We gave credit to too many gentlemen and didn't have money for the rent last week or this."

"What do you owe?" Charles asked.

"Two pound," she whispered. "We was already behind, sir."

Charles's father shook his head and went to his wife, still in the doorway. They walked into their apartment and left the door open. Mrs. Gordon stared past them, unseeing.

Charles remembered the debtors' prison when he was twelve, his family in the Marshalsea Prison for the sake of a forty-pound, ten-shilling baker's bill. He fished into his pocket and pulled out four shillings.

Pressing them into the woman's hand, he said, "It's all I have. Maybe it will be enough to stave them off."

Mrs. Gordon prompted her little girl to take the coins in her grubby fist. "Thankee, sir, but the landlord, he wants every penny."

Behind her, a man appeared. Charles took a step back as he recognized the figure in the doorway. Small statured, with bottle-black hair and a long, thin mustache. Mr. Ferazzi, his own landlord. He felt a soft touch on his arm and found Kate there.

"Dickens," the man grunted.

"Mr. Ferazzi," Charles said. "Can you accept partial payment for tonight? I will attempt to raise funds for this worthy family tomorrow. They have customers they can collect from."

"They can do that from another boardinghouse," Mr. Ferazzi growled. "I won't have spongers on my property."

"I can ask my father for coin," Charles said with an air of desperation. But his father did not appear in the doorway.

"No doubt we'll be removing your family someday soon," Mr. Ferazzi said. "The lower classes are so improvident."

"My father is a gentleman, sir." Charles's indignant retort brought nothing but a sneer to the landlord's sunken face.

Mr. Ferazzi leaned forward from his waist, his neck craning, vulture-like. "Then what is he doing here?"

He brushed past Mrs. Gordon and went down the stairs.

Kate squeezed Charles's arm. When he glanced at her, he saw her expression was as stricken as his.

A chair came at them, a bulk tossed through the doorway. Charles jumped back, pulling Kate behind him.

"Goodness," she said.

"Go inside," he urged her. "It isn't safe."

She did as he asked, returning to the safety of his parents' rooms.

Mrs. Gordon looked at him.

"Did you manage to hold on to the shop?" Charles asked.

She nodded. "The rent is paid on that for the week."

"Can you sleep there?"

"It's against the rules. Mr. Ferazzi says if he catches us there during the dark hours, we'll lose it, too." She squeezed her baby.

Charles wondered if Mr. Ferazzi was the sort of man to lurk around Bloomsbury in the deep night. His Mr. Nickerson might be, though. Perhaps the men in this gang were even the Chelsea neighborhood thieves.

"Tell your husband you and the children are going to Furnival's Inn for the day. You can open the shop tomorrow, after your husband raises the funds he needs today."

Mrs. Gordon pressed her lips together before speaking. "But Mr. Ferazzi won't take us back."

"I'll reason with him," Charles said. "He understands business, and he's lost more than one tenant recently. He won't want to run his enterprises at a loss."

She sighed. "Two pound."

Another chair sailed out, followed by the tailor. "They said they'd leave the beds until tomorrow," he said. The little girl ran to her father. "They have another job to get to."

"We're going to stay with the young Dickenses today," Mrs. Gordon said with dignity. "Unless you object, Mr. Gordon."

"I must mind the shop," her husband said, eyes wide. "I have three orders I can finish and deliver, to collect the payments. I'll work all night if I need to, though I hope I can gather the coin today." Mr. Gordon drew himself up. Slight and starved as he looked, there was a tattered dignity to the man.

Behind Fred, Kate appeared, holding her purse. She opened the strings and handed Mrs. Gordon what money she had. "For breakfast. Buy some milk for the children."

Mrs. Gordon bobbed awkwardly.

"We should go," Charles said, wondering if his parents would appear again, but they did not. He pushed the slow burn of anger down, deep into his belly. When had they ever shown any mercy? But he must be polite, for Kate's sake. "Thank you, dearest one."

Kate smiled at him. "We shall see you tomorrow."

Charles held out his hand to Mr. Gordon, who took it solemnly. "Come to Furnival's Inn if anything happens," he urged.

"I won't leave my shop alive," Mr. Gordon said, his head stiffening on his neck. "If I lose the cloth or my tools, we are as good as doomed."

"Good luck," Charles said. "I have spent more time than I care to admit raising funds to keep people out of sponging houses."

Chapter 8

As expected, Mr. Hogarth sent a boy to collect Charles not ten minutes after he arrived at his desk after seeing the Gordons and Fred to Furnival's Inn. He set down his penknife and half-cut quill and went to the editor's office.

"How is the visit progressing?" Mr. Hogarth asked from his chair. His curved nose was reddened at the long tip, as if he'd been rubbing it. "Are the Dickens and Hogarth ladies in good humor?"

"I think so, yes," Charles said, leaning against the doorway. "There has been some drama in the building, but inside my parents' rooms, all is serene."

"Excellent," Mr. Hogarth said, pulling out his tin of tobacco. "Harmony is important. One never knows who will end up residing with whom over the years."

"Very true," Charles agreed, though he'd rather have every one of his siblings move in than give either of his parents a bed for the night. He didn't trust them not to trade on his name and spend money he didn't have. "I will have them home to Brompton tomorrow, entirely unscathed."

The editor chuckled. "Very good."

Charles cleared his throat, remembering how his last act of charity had come close to wrecking his chances with the Hogarths. "You should probably know that I brought home three members of the family next door. A Scottish family, the Gordons, the wife and two small children."

Mr. Hogarth narrowed his eyes and scratched at his bushy gray side-whiskers. "A widow?"

"No, sir," Charles assured him. "Her husband is hard at work, hoping to collect the funds he needs in order to have his rooms restored to him."

"What are the chances he will accomplish this?"

"Good, I think." Charles sighed. "They are perhaps not the best at business. I am hard at work on the final stages of my pawnbroker sketch. The Gordons are exactly the sort of people who will end up in front of a pawnbroker if they do not do a better job managing their tailor shop."

"At least they didn't lose that."

"Not so far. I did learn one thing, though. Mr. Ferazzi, who is my landlord, is also my parents' landlord and, of course, the Gordons'."

"Must be a wealthy man. I've never heard of him, though."

"Me either." Charles shrugged. "I don't think I'd want to rent rooms from him again. I know it's a hard business, but his thugs were throwing chairs out the door as if they wanted to destroy what little the family had left."

"Add the tale to your list of sketches," Mr. Hogarth advised. "But not until you depart Selwood Terrace."

When Charles returned to his desk, he finished trimming his quill, then pored over his pawnbroker sketch. The technique he'd employed was that of describing a specific shop on Drury Lane. He half closed his eyes, remembering what had been for sale in the shop, because he thought the description in his first draft lacked something. "Strings of coral with snaps?" He altered the line so that it read, "Great broad gilt snaps." Then he considered his description of the rings and brooches, adding fanciful detail.

He remembered the wives hovering about the front of the shop while men turned in their tools for a bit of coin until they found their next job. The women often carried large baskets of cheap vegetables, while their children ran loose in the streets, many without shoes, none with socks. On a fine summer day, it mattered not, but winter would come again, and then what?

He hoped the Gordons had better luck than the families he'd seen while visiting the pawnbroker.

An hour later, he finished his sketch, satisfied with it at last, and walked it to Thomas Pillar, the under-editor.

"Have at it, Thomas," he invited.

"Thank you." Thomas removed his spectacles and glanced up from his desk, his smile kindly, as usual. His hair had fluffed out around his head. He must have been running his fingers through it while editing a difficult piece. "This is the one for the edition on the thirtieth?"

"That's the one."

"You come up with the most interesting ideas. Have you thought about turning them into a book?"

Charles snorted. "Who would want to read a book by me?"

"I've always thought of you as a young man with a great deal of self-confidence," Thomas said mildly. "I wish I'd applied myself so thoroughly when I was young. If you want to have a book someday, you shall have it, Charles."

"Someday," he echoed, feeling a strange urge to chortle. What a thing to imagine for a young man who'd once spent his days gluing labels to inkpots.

He walked along the editor's passage after finishing his conversation with Thomas. Mr. Hogarth gestured him into his office.

"Sir?"

The editor handed him three folded letters. "These came in. Some parliamentary affairs for you to check into, meetings to attend."

"Excellent. I've just finished my sketch."

Mr. Hogarth nodded. "Can you send William in my direction? I need to give him his assignments, as well."

"Very good, sir."

Charles marched directly to his desk and found that his friend had appeared at his own desk. William was feverishly scratching away at his papers. "Anything new on the inquest?"

"Not yet. The search for the missing convict continues." William set his quill over his inkpot and glanced up. Are those for me?" William gestured to the letters.

Charles turned his chair to face William's desk and sat. "I have three new assignments. You need to go to Mr. Hogarth for yours."

"It never stops, does it?" William muttered. "I'd rather focus on the Haverstock murder."

"I'll help you with it," Charles promised, stacking his letters into a neat pile on his lap. "If you're going to stay in town, we can talk here at the office each day. Then I can carry out the investigation in Chelsea for you. I owe Mrs. Jones that much. I don't think her husband is involved in anything nefarious."

William nodded. "We'll be back in Chelsea, too, but I want the air cleared first. Julie has been through enough this year without that."

"Does she have auditions here in town?" When he'd met Julie, she'd been a sixteen-year-old actress with the love of the lads in the pit. But a series of misadventures had cost her the spot with that theater, through no fault of her own, and she hadn't worked in the past five months. In that time, she had been busy with marriage and newly found relatives.

The newlyweds had moved into a Furnival's Inn front-facing apartment with three rooms and a beautiful bay window, a great improvement over William's two damp bachelor rooms, where ice had formed inside the windows every night in the winter.

"No," William said, not explaining further. "But I promised to take Julie mudlarking on the foreshore tonight. Want to join us?"

"Yes. We should check on our charges. Besides, I need the diversion."

"How is the funding for the Charity for Dressing the Mudlark Children of Blackfriars Bridge?" William asked. "We have not been going door-to-door, collecting."

"No, but there are only four of them that we are in contact with, and as they do not want to leave the bridge, there is only so much money we can spend." They had taken turns walking a hot meal down twice a week to the mostly orphaned children they had befriended the winter before, along with some loaves of bread. Over the winter they had supplied a blanket for each child, as well as a new suit of clothes, then had replaced them with summer clothing. The children also had shoes, though they viewed them with suspicion.

"We could do more," William said. "Julie and Fred can help."

"I don't think either of them should wander the bridge area unaccompanied. I myself felt like I was in danger, until you vouched for me."

"They are tame now, our four," William said. "And it will pay to build our informant network."

"I have wondered why more children don't come to us. I know the mudlarks guard their patches, but surely by now they know there is enough food for more."

"We'll be blunt with Lucy Fair tonight and ask the question. With us backing her, you'd think she'd want to grow her gang."

"I'd rather she tired of the life," Charles said. "Now that she's being fed regularly, you can see she's starting to develop into a woman. She might be thirteen already, and she's going to be in danger from men if she stays in her present profession."

"What would you do with her?"

"Put her into service? Apprentice her to a milliner?" Charles shrugged. "I don't know."

"That's exactly the problem," William said. "She's better off in the life she has, hard as it is. There isn't much to choose from for any woman, much less a girl like her. She's too young to marry."

A boy waved at Charles. He rose and set his letters on his desk. "Looks like I'm being summoned. Knock on my door tonight, when you are ready."

When the Agas came for Charles at ten-thirty that night, he grabbed a twine-wrapped parcel containing a shawl and two blankets he had waiting. He had suggested to Lucy Fair, the mudlarks' leader, that they keep extras in their hidey-holes so that they could clothe others in need. She hadn't been amenable, but if she wanted to sell the blankets instead or use them for her little family, his work had still been done.

Blackfriars Bridge wasn't far. William had a lantern, since only half of the moon could be seen in the sky, but the night was clear, and a canopy of stars shone overhead. Soon their boots were sliding over rock-crusted ground. They could see the mudlarks where the water lapped against the sand, hunting for treasures, or at least anything that might bring a few pence, that the water had cast up.

William lit his lantern. One side effect of feeding the children was their increased strength, and none of them wanted to be attacked because they weren't recognized. He held the light between himself and Julie.

One of the figures lifted her head. Charles recognized the silhouette of a long-legged girl in a tatter-hemmed dress. Lucy Fair. She had her usual trio with her: Poor John, Brother Second, and Little Ollie, the youngest, at about seven years old, or at least the size of a child that age. Additionally, another small figure separated itself as Lucy put her hands on her hips, spreading her stance wide like a sailor. Eddies of water lapped at her bare ankles. As usual, the children didn't want to ruin their boots. He understood that, which was why they had brought the children wooden clogs in April, purchased with the last of the money they had raised that month, but the children found them too clunky to hunt the foreshore in. They were also afraid of damaging artifacts with the clogs, saying that sometimes they found items with their feet.

"Any luck tonight, Lucy?" Charles asked, stepping forward.

"Mr. Dickens," she said crisply, lifting her bucket.

The charity had paid for the buckets, as well, the best purchase they'd made to date.

The Agas walked forward. "Your bucket has a hole already," Julie said, clucking over the gouge on the side. "What happened?"

"An old dagger went straight through. Still not sure 'ow it 'appened," Lucy said. "Bucket's still good enough."

"This li'l dodger needs 'is own," Brother Second pronounced, wrapping his muddy arm around the smallest shape.

William held up his lantern and revealed a small grubby face. "Awfully young, this little one."

"'E's six," Brother Second explained. "Me cousin, aw right?"

"Ah," Charles said. He glanced from boy to boy. Brother Second had obtained, at most, ten years, and everyone's hair was hidden under caps, even Lucy's. But he thought he could see some similarity between the cousins in their stocky build and widely spaced eyes. "Good thing we brought extra blankets. Mrs. Aga can measure you, and we'll get you clothes." As the child was dressed in an old frock coat, tied around him with thick rope, and wore little else, they couldn't clothe him soon enough. "What's your name, my boy?"

The child glanced at Brother Second. When he nodded, the boy piped, "Arfur."

"What made you join the gang?" William asked. "Still living at home?"

The boy sniffed. His hand went into his cousin's. Brother

Second lifted his gaze to the reporter. "'Is ma died two weeks ago. Pa's done nuffink but drink since."

"Are there any other children?" Charles asked.

Brother Second nodded. "Two li'l ones."

William rubbed his chin. "Are you keeping them, too?"

"My ma took 'em," Brother Second said. "But we gots to bring 'em money."

These two small children had had to take on even more mouths to feed. Charles already knew that all of the other children were fatherless.

As Julie fussed over Cousin Arthur, turning him this way and that, Lucy gestured to William. The reporter followed her under the bridge, swinging his lantern. The children had sheltered there during the winter, but then construction had begun on the bridge yet again, and they'd been sleeping high on the shore. They used the bridge only as temporary storage now, because any protection they placed there was soon dislodged by the workmen.

Charles gestured to the remaining three boys, and they went back to the tide's edge. He crouched with them, letting water lap against his waxed boots, and tried to allow patterns to form in the sand, hoping to find anything of value among the rocks.

Poor John went to his knees next to Charles. Bigger than Brother Second, he was the oldest boy in the gang, and the one most interested in the outside world. Charles told him about Miss Haverstock's death, and the boy, fascinated by the missing prisoner, asked a dozen questions. When they had exhausted that topic, Charles shared the story of the murdered Jewish girl, Goldy.

"Oh, tell me something new," Poor John said scathingly. "I've 'eard that one afore."

Charles dropped a round rock he'd been hoping was a lead ball and turned to the lad. "You have?"

"Sure. It's a river story, ain't it?" He tilted his head. "They was mudlarks like us, a long time ago."

"Tell me your version," Charles requested, curious. He assumed it would have the same kind of wild, paranormal elements as the ghost story Poor John had shared last week. However, the story was very much the same as the one he'd read in the magazine. The only real difference was that the other children were named only by nationality. The four little monsters were the Norwegian, the Italian, and the East End twins.

Charles heard footsteps approaching just as Poor John finished. Lucy and William were coming from the bridge, dragging something behind them. Charles stood up.

"Can you believe it?" William asked. He dropped what he'd been dragging in front of Charles. Metal clanked as the unwieldy item landed on the rocks.

Charles kicked at the discovery with his boot. Twisted and broken circlets of metal fell apart, displaying the chain in between. His eyes went wide. "Manacles?"

"Not even rusty," William said with satisfaction, letting the lantern's light spill over them. The cuffs appeared to have been bashed into submission, rather than carefully removed. Dark splotches, which might have been blood, were dried on the metal.

"A second set of fresh manacles?" Charles said in a near monotone, shocked. "These need to go to the police."

"It's a long way from here to Chelsea," William pointed out.

"But not so far from Coldbath Fields." Charles crouched down, pointing to what his keen eyes had seen on one of the cuffs.

William squatted next to him, then ran his finger along the letters cut into the cast metal. "*C* and *F*. You think this has something to do with our murder?"

"That's exactly what I think," Charles said. "That missing Ned Blood could have come into this part of London."

"What about the manacles in the Joneses' smithy?"

"An excellent question." Charles rubbed his chin. "Assuming we are right that Mr. Jones is an honest man, those manacles did appear Sunday morning."

"How did the police know to search for them?" William queried.

Charles gave a mirthless chuckle. "Another excellent question. And if Ned Blood stayed in these parts, who killed Miss Haverstock?"

"What should we do with them?"

"We need to learn more," Charles pronounced. "I'll take these to Constable Blight. Maybe I can free Daniel Jones on this evidence alone."

"It would be a pretty night's work," William agreed. "But it won't happen. They've got a man in custody and won't let him go easily."

Julie came down the beach to them. "You don't think this Ned Blood is still nearby, do you?"

"No," William said. "We don't even know where they went into the Thames."

"Wot will you pay us for them?" Lucy Fair asked, ever practical. She'd long since realized that William and Charles wouldn't ask for any of their treasure without offering coins.

William handed her everything he had in his pocket. Julie kissed Cousin Arthur on the least grimy part of his forehead and offered a boiled sweet to each of the mudlarks, while Charles handed Lucy the bundle, which he'd left on a rock.

"A good night's work," he suggested. "You can shelter under the bridge for the rest of the night."

"Smells like piss," Lucy said scathingly. "We'll be on the beach."

Charles ventured into the three-story, pockmarked stone police station the next day, hauling the manacles in his carpetbag. He felt very grateful to be carrying the metal rather than wearing it.

"Yes?" the sergeant on duty asked, not looking up as Charles approached his desk.

Charles blinked, trying to adjust his eyesight. The windows didn't seem to have been cleaned since winter, and visibility was poor. Not knowing what else to do, he lifted his carpetbag onto the desk.

"What?" The sergeant peered into the bag. His mustache twitched, as did his right hand, but he didn't reach in.

"It's not a live snake. It's manacles," Charles told him. "I'd like to speak to Constable Blight, unless you'd rather I take these directly to Sir Silas Laurie, the coroner, so he can use them for his investigation into Miss Haverstock's murder in Selwood Terrace?"

The sergeant cleared his throat. "The constable is walking his beat, young man. Who are you?"

He drew himself up. "Charles Dickens, of the *Chronicle*. A man was arrested, a blacksmith, because manacles were found in his shop, but here's another set."

"What is your point, Mr. Dickens?"

"Coldbath Fields is missing a prisoner." Charles shoved his own hand into his carpetbag and pulled out the cuffs. "Look here. These are from the same prison."

The sergeant scratched under his reinforced collar. "What do you want the constable to do about it?"

"This creates doubt that the blacksmith had anything to do with freeing Ned Blood, the missing prisoner," Charles snapped. "I want Mr. Jones, the blacksmith, to be released from prison."

Behind him, the door opened. Several voices were shouting. He turned around and saw two men, hackney drivers, by the looks of them, hauling a uniformed constable between them. The constable, a sallow man in his late twenties, was bleeding profusely from the forehead. Behind the trio came Constable Blight, whose grimace marred the otherwise pleasant expression Charles remembered from before.

The inspector on duty came rushing out of his office. "What is all this commotion?"

The sergeant pulled out a length of cloth from somewhere behind his desk and stepped around Charles. He handed the cloth to the bleeding constable, who pressed it against his head.

"Little bleeders were playing with rocks," one of the hackney drivers said, shaking out the arm that had been assisting the constable. "Hit this poor man on the head."

"I need to return to me horse," said the other driver, sidling backward out the door.

Charles stared hard at the man's face before he vanished into the small crowd on the street, suspecting he was a criminal of some kind. Narrow, undersized jaw, pitted skin, very blue eyes, and a missing lower front tooth.

The inspector went behind the remaining driver and the bleeding constable and pushed them both into his office. The slamming door rattled the station wall.

Constable Blight then noticed Charles. He tilted his head, the motion arrested by his reinforced collar. "Mr. Dickens, what brings you here?"

"You'd best return to your beat," the sergeant hissed.

"Give us a minute, so I can tell him about the manacles," Charles said. "It's police business."

"What's this about?" Blight frowned.

Charles gestured the constable over to his carpetbag. He pulled out the manacles and, ignoring the sergeant's noise of disgust, spread them out across the desk. "A mudlark found these washed up near Blackfriars Bridge last night." He pointed at the initials on the cuffs.

The constable yawned, not bothering to cover his mouth. "So that's where the other set went."

Charles felt a headache building behind his eyes. "You knew a second set was missing?"

Constable Blight sighed. "There are two escaped convicts.

They must not have stayed together. I wonder where these went into the river."

Charles's eyes went wide. His heart rate sped up. "Do you know the other name? I didn't hear that it came up in the inquest."

"No. Ned Blood was seen in Chelsea, you understand. The other man has disappeared completely. You'd have to inquire at the prison for the name."

"I will." Charles dropped the manacles back into his bag. He hadn't known Ned Blood had been seen so close to Selwood Terrace. None of this would help Mr. Jones. He'd wasted William's money and his time in pursuit of nothing useful. At least not yet.

Chapter 9

✤

Charles arrived at his parents' rooms for dinner, eager to see Kate. Just seeing her would repair his low mood after the debacle with the manacles. When he reached their floor, the Gordons' door opened and Mrs. Gordon peeked out.

"How good to see you here," Charles exclaimed, stepping to the opposite side of the small passage. "Mr. Ferazzi allowed you back?"

Her skirts were laden with dust. He held back a sneeze with his finger under his nose as she spoke. "His man, that Mr. Nickerson, said we'd have another chance, since my husband paid our account yesterday."

"I'm glad to hear it," he replied, feeling a little of the burden of them fall off his shoulders. They would be unlikely to show up at his door in a new crisis, unlike his own parents.

Mrs. Gordon gently picked up his hand, then dropped five shillings into it. "Your repayment, plus the cost of the food we ate."

"No," he said, instant guilt pricking at him. He handed the shillings back to her. "Please, keep the money for your children."

"I couldn't." She bit her lip.

"You could, as a gift. Hide it away for an emergency."

He touched his hat and went to his parents' door as she called, "Thank you, Mr. Dickens."

As far as he was concerned, the money had been gone, anyway. He sneezed mightily, then wiggled the tip of his nose with his fingers.

His parents' door was unlocked, so he went in, unnoticed. Chaos reigned in the parlor, as the younger boys hopped around, fighting with wooden swords. No wonder they hadn't heard him in the passage.

"Bedlamites!" he called. "Isn't this the dinner hour?"

"Mother burned the bannocks," Boz said. "She started over."

Charles's eyebrows went up. Mrs. Hogarth must have attempted to teach his mother how to make the Scottish oatcakes. "I arranged for a carriage to be here in half an hour. How delayed are we?"

Kate dashed into the room, a smear of flour dusting the apron she wore over a short-sleeved dress of pale pink with a daisy detail in the fabric. Her lips parted in a wide smile. "Charles! I thought I heard your voice."

"Sweet Kate," he replied, kissing her cheek. "You remember we are going to the opera tonight?"

"Of course. What about Mother?"

"The carriage will drop us off at the English Opera House, then will take your mother home."

Her eyebrows scrunched together. "Unaccompanied?"

"No, the Agas will meet us in Wellington Street and ride with her."

"What a perfect idea," Kate said.

"To make the plan work, we have to be done eating in"—he checked his pocket watch—"approximately twenty-five minutes."

"Bannocks need about fifteen minutes' cooking," Kate said. "I don't think we will sit to dine for another ten minutes."

"Then we will have to eat fast."

Kate dismissed that with a wave. "The driver will wait."

A bloodcurdling scream came from deep within Alfred's small frame, and he ran at his younger brother with his sword. Boz countered the attack by ramming his brother with a bony shoulder. They both went down on the hearthrug in a whirl of legs and elbows. Charles stuck his foot into the melee and separated the pair by pressing against their soft parts.

Fanny came in and snatched away the swords. "Quiet now. Father is working."

Charles snorted. "Working? At the dinner hour?"

Fanny frowned at her brother. "We don't wish to disturb him."

"No," Charles agreed. "If it is true. Do you know, I think young Alfred should be trained as a singer? He has at least your lung capacity already."

"It's too expensive," Fanny demurred. "I love music, but I'll never forget how hard it was for Father to pay the fees."

"He has never known how to budget."

Kate cleared her throat, reminding him that a relative outsider was in the room and did not need to hear the old Dickens troubles. "Fanny, would you play? I'd love to hear something. Do you know any of the music from *The Spirit of the Bell*? That's the opera Charles is escorting me to this evening."

"That opera is better known for its flare than its music," Fanny said carefully. "So I have not inquired into learning any of the songs."

"Oh." Kate glanced uncertainly at Charles.

"I know 'The Grateful Heart' from *Hermann*," Fanny offered. "That was an opera from last year."

Charles nodded at her. "I'd love to hear you perform." While Charles deeply regretted the interruption of his own schooling, he never resented Fanny's. It also appeared that she'd met the man she would marry through her music career, though he didn't really care for his future brother by marriage, considering him overly religious. Letitia was being courted by his friend Henry

Austin. He had, in fact, hoped Henry would move into Furnival's Inn with him, but he'd decided to stay with his mother for now.

As Fanny sang, Charles brought Kate up to date on the manacles and his failed hopes for freeing Mr. Jones with his find. Finally, Mrs. Dickens appeared and invited them into the dining room. Charles winced when he saw the time, but had his Hogarths shepherded out of the building only ten minutes late.

His hackney driver, a regular from the stand below his chambers at Furnival's Inn, gave him a dirty look but greeted the ladies politely. The Agas were at the curb waiting when the carriage stopped in Wellington Street.

"I hope ye have another carriage waiting after the opera," Mrs. Hogarth fretted.

"Of course," Charles promised as he slid to the edge of the seat and toward the door. "I won't make Kate walk all the way to Brompton."

Kate laughed. "I'd never agree to it, Mother."

"If anything goes wrong, ye must return to Mrs. Dickens," Mrs. Hogarth insisted.

"A perfect solution," Charles declared. "But I'll have her home."

"Will ye stay with us?" Mrs. Hogarth inquired.

"No. The plan is for Fred to order another hackney at the stand and meet us after the opera. Then all three of us will return to Brompton, and we gentlemen will brave Selwood Terrace tonight."

Mrs. Hogarth grimaced. "Oh, Charles, are ye sure?"

"I'm not afraid of ghosts, only odors," he assured her, then opened the door and swung himself out. He went to his friends and whispered in William's ear, then handed him a couple of extra coins for the driver's wait time.

Kate kissed her mother's cheek. "I'm leaving the valise with you, dear."

"I'll remember," Mrs. Hogarth assured her. Her anxious face

stayed in the window of the hackney while her daughter climbed down.

William gave Kate a wink and helped his wife inside, then climbed in himself. Then Charles heard Mrs. Hogarth laugh at some remark William made. A thump sounded as the door closed. The driver clicked his teeth and lifted the reins. The horses moved back into traffic.

Kate let out a long sigh.

"Tired, darling? Was my family awful?" Charles took her arm and pulled her into the line waiting under the tall arches of the newly rebuilt theater.

"No, they were delightful. Your sisters are angels, and your brothers are scamps, of course, being younger. I can't wait for Fanny and Letitia to receive their proposals. What fun to have us all be new brides together."

"The news is coming shortly?"

"I think so, though a girl cannot ever quite know what is in her gentleman's heart." She giggled. "I had no idea you were going to propose when you did."

"Neither did I," Charles admitted. It had happened on a walk as they inspected the early blooms in the apple orchard. He might have planned a more special moment, but in that instant, he'd known he'd never be perfectly happy without this calm, clever girl beside him. "I hope Mr. Austin and Mr. Burnett plan better than I did."

She smiled warmly at him. "I liked my proposal exactly as it was, full of feeling and hope for the future, rather than you nervous and unsure."

He touched her cheek. "You are a perfect darling, always."

As they entered the theater, Charles saw a frown line form between her eyes. "What's wrong?"

"I worry about you roaming the streets at night. And the foreshore." She shivered. "What if the criminal who'd been wearing those shackles had still been about?"

"That's the beauty of the river. The manacles didn't stay where they went in. Although," he said thoughtfully, "they were hardly a scrap of metal. You'd think they'd have sunk to the bottom."

"As intended," she agreed.

They were ushered upstairs to the second-story box overlooking the stage. The opera had not been particularly well reviewed, and Charles suspected the theater would not fill before the performance. Plenty of humanity's antics were on display below, ready to entertain him. However, Kate was not about to let him sit in silent repose, considering his fellow operagoers, potentially setting the stage for another sketch.

Charles helped Kate with her light wrap, and then they sat next to each other, so close that his leg brushed her skirts.

He closed his eyes, savoring the warmth of her legs under her summer layers. His thoughts went, as they so often did, to how soon they could marry. If only his family weren't such a heavy burden. He prayed his father could keep his finances in line long enough to keep him from delaying his marriage to Kate.

"Do you want to talk about the manacles more?" Kate asked. "Is there any way to use them to persuade the police to release Mr. Jones?"

"No, not since they've revealed there are two escapees. Their case against Mr. Jones doesn't change at all."

"Unfortunate," Kate whispered. "The escapees must have gone in opposite directions."

"I wonder why," Charles said as the lights in the theater dimmed.

He listened to Kate breathe until the overture began, and imagined that sound lulling him to sleep on cold winter's nights. Would Mrs. Jones ever have the comfort of her husband's breathing next to her again? He resolved to do his best to help her.

*   *   *

Fred met them after the opera, and they returned to Brompton. The air in the Selwood Terrace rooms no longer smelled like death, and no one had broken into their scantily furnished rooms.

Still, Charles slept uneasily, as did Fred. The next morning, they both admitted to nightmares, and Fred hadn't even seen Miss Haverstock's body.

At breakfast, Charles related his dream of being harassed by images of bugs crawling on Miss Haverstock. He had to toughen himself. A man should be able to see a dead body without nightmares plaguing him.

Along those lines, he was seized with the desire to visit a prison.

"William," Charles said into the air from his *Chronicle* office chair late the next afternoon.

"Yes?" William pushed his chair over to Charles and reseated himself next to Charles.

"How would you go about a trip to Coldbath Fields Prison? Would someone see us if we just turned up there?"

"Normally, you would write a letter, request an interview with a prison governor."

Charles doodled on his scrap of paper. "But we're reporters, and we only just learned that there was a second escapee. Plus, what if Mr. Jones is being kept there? Maybe we can see him. Maybe he's thought of something that might help."

William flashed a good-natured grin. "You're not a crime reporter, Charles. And I'm sure Mr. Jones is at Newgate."

Charles's doodle turned into a broken manacle cuff. "You are. You should write about it, and I'll go along. Who knows what I'll learn? I can use it in a sketch."

"Then you should make arrangements to visit Newgate," William advised. "No one is going to care about criminals who've done only enough to serve a couple of years on a treadmill, when those at Newgate are facing the rope."

Charles added a second set of irons to his drawing. "I have to start somewhere, and I need to sort out this escaped-criminal matter. What is the connection between them and Miss Haverstock?"

"Poor Daniel Jones," William mused. "He is a sweet man, and his wife is a darling. I thought his father was a tougher sort. I'd not have been surprised if he'd known a criminal or two in his day."

Charles thumped the desk. Now, there was a good point. "Do you think one of the Joneses really did help Ned Blood? That maybe it was Jones senior?"

William chuckled. "Now you're thinking, Charles. You've been so overset with domestic fancies that I'd thought you'd lost your edge."

"We need to speak to the coroner." Charles half rose, but William pushed him into his seat.

"Not so fast, lad. All you would do is manage to have Jones senior arrested and Daniel Jones not freed. Then the ladies will have no one to run the forge. You'll ruin the family."

"But it makes sense," Charles insisted. "Just because old Mr. Jones is somewhat crippled doesn't mean he couldn't have cut off a set of manacles. We know he's strong enough, even if the constables didn't. He works part of the day."

"They will hold both men over for court." William sighed. "It's just supposition right now, and the fact that we know something about the personalities involved. Even if we uncovered a link between Ned Blood and Jones senior, it wouldn't save Daniel now."

"I hear you," Charles said. "But still, we should learn what we can. Let's walk over to the prison and see if someone will tell us about the escapees."

William nodded. "Very well. I'm about done for the day. Let me clean up my desk and we can go."

＊　＊　＊

Two hours later, with the sun still high in the sky, Charles and William arrived at the exterior wall of Coldbath Fields Prison in Clerkenwell. They showed their *Morning Chronicle* credentials to a guard at the front gate. While he stared at them, they stomped dust off their shoes and slapped at their clothing, releasing dry brown puffs. The guard let them enter through the tall prison exterior and into a covered passage that ran past the vagrants' block to a residence in front of the main buildings, all of brick, which contained separate blocks for felons and misdemeanants.

Charles tried not to remember those months when his parents and younger siblings lived in the Marshalsea Prison, though it had been nothing so onerous as this. These days, prisons intrigued him as much as they repelled, though he never forgot those days almost half a lifetime ago now.

A servant with a dirty neckerchief and gin-soaked breath admitted them into the governor's office in the residence to wait for an interview.

"What do you know about this prison?" Charles asked William.

"Houses about a thousand prisoners of both sexes, children, too. Run by local magistrates. It's technically a house of correction, short-term sentences." William fiddled with a small ring he wore on his right pinkie finger. "But you know as well as I do that hardened criminals can be caught and locked away for a lesser crime than those they habitually commit. Still, there must be a few here who could be rehabilitated from a life of evil deeds."

"The public doesn't really care about any of it," Charles suggested.

"They want to know such people are being punished by hard labor. They would prefer the prisoners be kept in silence, in the hopes that they will not be able to train up the next generation of criminals, or to collude in future plans once they are released."

Charles chuckled darkly and peered out of a window. "Which is why transportation is so appealing. Get the men and women of black deeds out of the country." He could see vegetable fields off to the right. He hoped some of the inmates were employed in the open air, though he understood most of them spent their days picking oakum or walking the treadmill.

The heavy office door opened. A map tacked to the opposite wall fluttered on its pins as the door banged into the wall. A man wiping the shiny top of his bald-pated head with a hand-kerchief walked in, followed by another man, hunched and gray.

"I am the governor here," said the first man. "Jonathon Shipley. Who might you be?"

William and Charles introduced themselves.

"Your purpose for visiting?" Governor Shipley asked. "An article for the *Chronicle*?"

"I am the man who took the second set of found manacles to the police in Chelsea," Charles told him as the governor seated himself behind his large desk. "The constable informed me that there were two escapees."

"What do you know about the escaped prisoners?" William asked. Since he was an established crime reporter, Charles let him take the lead.

The governor made a noise in the back of his throat. The other man darted to a cabinet and opened it. Charles saw bottles. The hunched man reached for one and poured some sort of purplish cordial into a fluted glass and put it on the governor's desk.

Governor Shipley poured the cordial down his throat and gargled it loudly, then rattled some of the papers about on his desk until he came up with the relevant document. Charles was surprised the man couldn't come up with the information from memory, but then he had smelled gin coming off the man right when he entered the room, and it was almost six in the evening. The cordial was sweeter, something to help with coughs, probably. The hunched man refilled the glass, but the governor ignored it this time.

After clearing his throat, the governor said, "The escapees were Ned Blood and Osvald Larsen."

Charles squinted. Hadn't he come across the name Osvald recently?

"What do you know about the men?" William repeated.

The governor sifted through his papers, moving phlegm around the back of his throat, and came up with a couple of sheets. "Unpleasant. The continual dampness of these old buildings, you know. Hits me in the lungs."

"I thought this prison was rebuilt only forty or so years ago," William said.

"Brick. Retains the damp." Governor Shipley pointed to a damp patch on the painted wall. "If you poke it, you make a divot. They'll take me out of here on a stretcher, I promise you.

"Now, as to these prisoners. They were both incarcerated on the same day. That's probably how they met, in a general holding cell while assignments were being made."

"They had no known association previously?"

Governor Shipley repeated his phlegmy noise. "Not that I'm aware of, but anything is possible. They could have lived in the same neighborhood even, though Larsen, I believe, is an immigrant."

William pulled out his pencil and notebook. "Do you have descriptions?"

"Larsen is fifty-eight. Blood is much younger, by fifteen years, perhaps. Larsen is a graybeard. Blood is balder than I am," the governor said, touching his forehead.

"Do they have professions, other than criminal?" William asked.

"Larsen was a blacksmith at an earlier stage of life. Still has the musculature." The governor shuddered. "I've seen the man. Blood was a laborer. I don't remember him, but my notes say he was not robust looking."

A blacksmith? Charles didn't like that coincidence, given Mr. Jones's profession. But he kept this piece of unhelpful information in his thoughts and made a different remark. "Larsen would have known how to remove manacles, as long as he had the equipment available."

"But it's Blood who was seen in Chelsea," William pointed out. "Therefore, he's the one who would have needed help from a blacksmith."

"What sort of article are you writing? Backgrounds on the men? I don't have much more for their physical description. Larsen had a beard, but it could be gone now. Blood is said to be unkempt, but that's no surprise."

"Larsen would have an accent, correct?" Charles asked.

The governor flipped through his paperwork, then picked up his cordial again and drank half of his flute. "Norwegian, this says. Came here as a child."

"Anything else useful in your paperwork? Known associates?" William asked.

"No marriages listed, no children. Parents are likely dead."

"Former addresses? Employers?"

The governor flipped through his papers again. A thick sheet of paper fell out.

Charles grabbed for it, recognizing it as a portrait. "Is this Larsen?" He held up the rough artwork, that of an old, bearded man with deep pockets of flesh holding small eyes. The subject had round cheeks and a sharp chin.

The governor poked at the back. "Says it's Larsen." He pulled out a second sheet and handed it to William.

Charles stared at the deeply dissolute face of Ned Blood. The man had a thickly lined forehead, no hair at all, except for the unshaven face, and large piercing eyes. Full lips extended past the facial hair, and as expected, his flesh was molded tightly to his skull. "Where did these sketches come from?" Charles asked.

"One of the guards fancies himself an artist. He does these

while the men pick oakum. The prisoners don't seem to mind," the governor answered.

Charles found that hard to believe. Criminals didn't want to be identified. "May we take these?"

"Yes."

"They are very useful," William said. Charles plucked Blood from William's hand and tucked both sketches into his largest pocket.

"I'm glad to be of assistance, gentlemen. Please don't crucify us. We're investigating the prison break, and of course, you can understand our need to keep all the details quiet. I can assure the public that the situation is under control."

Charles suspected that the governor had no idea how Blood and Larsen had broken free, but he would refrain from criticizing the man to his face. When the governor rose, the journalists did, as well, and the hunched man led them from the office.

"What are you planning to do with the sketches?" William asked as they were escorted from the house and back into the tunnel to the front gate. "We need to get them back to the office so that they can be reproduced."

"It's late. I'm going to take them to the Jones family and see if they recognize either of these miscreants," Charles said firmly. "Now that we know Larsen is a blacksmith, this information might shake off some cobwebs at the smithy. Come. Let's find a hackney and go to our chambers."

Chapter 10

～❧～

Charles left William at Selwood Terrace and went to the Jones property down the lane.

In the yard squatted the heart of their operation, the smithy. A square brick chimney poked out of the roof, revealing the position of the forge. Charles had visited the first time shortly after he took his summer rooms, and had seen the prosperous nature of the operation. Quality brickwork, two anvils, a heavy vise and treadle grindstone. The workbenches had been in good repair and covered in tools. He'd seen horses in the stable, ready to be reshod. The property contained two houses behind the smithy. Edmund Jones lived in one, with his sister Hannah tending it, and in the other lived Daniel Jones, with his small family.

Charles walked past a hired boy chopping wood in front of a lean-to and peered into the smithy. Edmund Jones was bent over the larger of the anvils, shaping a piece of iron over the horn. He looked too busy to be interrupted, and his apprentice had his back to Charles, doing something with a pair of tin shears at a bench.

Night drew near, and the day had cooled, but the intense heat still broke sweat on Charles's face just from him hovering at the door. He turned away and went to the larger house.

When he knocked, he heard fast-running footsteps. Beddie Host opened the door and stared at him, her mouth hanging open.

"Is your aunt home?" Charles asked. He knew the girl had come to live with the Joneses after her parents died a couple of years before.

She nodded and gestured him in, then pointed him into a parlor without speaking. The girl ran off. The windows in the house were closed against the wood smoke and still held in the summer heat, though it was pleasant compared to the intensity the forge generated. He smelled dinner, which must have been roast chicken from the coop next to the barn.

The furnishings were tidy and minimal: a couple of tables, six or seven chairs, and a piano pushed against the wall. Only one painting added character to the abstemious space, but the light wasn't good enough for Charles to discern what the crudely painted landscape was meant to represent.

"Mr. Dickens," exclaimed Addie Jones, coming into the parlor. Her hands were reddened from her day's labors, but she had removed her apron. Wet streaks formed an oval around where the apron had rested on her skirt. "Do you have news?"

He nodded. "I have a couple of sketches to show you."

"Of what?" She gestured him to one of the austere flat-backed chairs and sat next to him.

"It turns out there were two escaped convicts last week. I attempted to find a way to spin that tale into something that might persuade the police to set your husband free, but that didn't do any good. Still, I wanted to see if you recognized either man. Will you take a look?"

She swallowed, squared her shoulders, and nodded. Beddie ran into the room and leaned against her aunt. Did she ever walk, or only race?

He retrieved the sketches and held them out to Mrs. Jones. She squinted at first one, then the other.

"Who's that?" Beddie asked.

"Some very bad men, dear. Do they look familiar to you?" he asked.

Mrs. Jones and her niece both looked blank.

"It was a long shot," Charles admitted.

"I don't think my husband ever left his bed that night," Mrs. Jones insisted. "He had nothing to do with the manacles. He did what he ought to have, as a law-abiding citizen."

"I understand," Charles said gently, "but what if you'd seen one of these men in the neighborhood? One of them was seen around here."

"I have not seen them," Mrs. Jones said, tucking a stray hank of her lank brown hair behind her ear.

He nodded. "Please let me know if some new thought comes to you."

"I will, and, Beddie, you do the same," Mrs. Jones said, putting her arm around the girl. Beddie stared at him while putting a finger in her mouth.

"Can I show them to your father-in-law and his men?" Charles asked.

"I'll take you out there," Mrs. Jones said, standing up. Holding Beddie's hand, she walked out the front door and to the wide-open doors at the smithy. All three of the men were inside now. The hired boy stacked wood, and the other two were still at their posts.

"Father," Mrs. Jones called. "Can we interrupt?"

"Not now. I can't let this cool," Edmund Jones said, pounding away at the anvil.

Charles walked over to the hired boy and held out the sketches. "Do either of these men look familiar to you?"

The boy gawped at him. Charles shook the papers a little. "Can you see them?"

The boy glanced down. "'Oo are they supposed to be?"

"Just some men. Seen them hanging around here?"

The boy shook his head.

"Thank you." Charles moved on to the apprentice.

He had set down his shears and was smoothing out the rough spot on a horseshoe with some sort of square hammer. "Wot's this about?"

"Some men. Trying to find out if they've been seen around the smithy." Charles put his sketches under the younger man's nose.

The man glanced up and down, up and down. "Sorry, but no. Haven't seen them."

"Very well." Charles walked back through the shimmering heat until he stood in front of Edmund Jones, who wasn't nearly as friendly as his son. "It will just take a second, sir."

Irritation creased the man's weathered face, but after a measured pause, he glanced at the sketches. "No. Never seen them."

"Are you certain? Should I come back another time?"

"No, never seen them," the man repeated.

"Let's let them return to their labors," Mrs. Jones called from the doorway.

With a sigh, Charles followed her and Beddie back into the yard. No one in the smithy had ceased working for a moment. Edmund Jones ran a tight shop.

"That's that, then," he said, defeated.

"Why don't you take them to the vicar?" Mrs. Jones asked. "He should know if we have vagrants around here."

"That's a good suggestion," Charles said. "I'm sure my newspaper can send reproductions of these images to all the local police stations, and to the Bow Street Runners, so that they are on the lookout. We might not be able to do anything with the sketches, but someone will find them useful." He patted the child's head and took his leave.

When he reached Selwood Terrace, he felt too restless to go

in, so he decided to visit the Hogarths. Kate would want to consult with him regarding the murder.

Though the hour was late, summer kept everyone but the youngest children from their beds. In fact, Kate and her father were sitting on a bench in the front garden, while Mary tended to the hollyhocks that grew profusely along their front fence. Though twilight had come on, Charles could still see the vibrant pinks and reds of the flowers, and Mary had a ghostly presence in her white summer dress as she cut tall stalks for bouquets.

As he walked up to the gate, Kate stood and waved, looking sweet in a floral-sprigged pale blue dress with a cunning bodice that made her already slim waist appear tiny. Mary trotted over to open the gate for him. He doffed his hat and bowed with a flourish. "Thank you, Miss Mary Hogarth, and good evening."

She curtsied to him, her skirt belling out. "And a good evening to you, sir. I hope you have a treat for us in your pocket."

He reached in and pretended to pull out a stick. "One long shard of flavored ice, just for you."

She took the pretend stick and licked at it delicately. "Ooh, lemon. My favorite."

Kate straightened her skirts and glanced at him expectantly. "Do you have one for me?"

"Even better." Charles bent to her cheek and gave her a loud, smacking kiss.

She giggled. "Why are you here so late?"

He took the images from his pocket. "William and I had these from the prison governor. These are the missing prisoners."

Mary and Kate stared at them for a long moment. Kate clicked her teeth. "It is too bad they are worthless."

"Why?" Mary asked. "The artist displays some skill."

As Mr. Hogarth came toward them, his pipe smoke perfuming the air, Kate said, "The whiskers are blocking most of the identifying characteristics of the faces."

Mr. Hogarth leaned over Kate's shoulder, then nodded his assent to her words.

Kate colored slightly and spoke again. "We need to learn who the victim really was."

Charles shook his head. "It doesn't matter. A stranger killed her."

"Maybe," Kate said. "It's possible. She's quite a mysterious character, though. We met Mr. Small in the lane when we took a walk earlier this weekend. You remember the St. Luke's curate?"

Charles grimaced. The curate tried to wrangle for a dinner invitation at the Hogarths' table whenever possible. He clearly had feelings for Kate. "And?"

"Miss Haverstock did not often attend any of the local places of worship. He likes a bit of gossip, does Mr. Small, and he said that no one around here knew her well, not the Methodists or the Hebrews, not anyone."

"Okay, so she's rather a mystery. But *we* knew her, Kate."

"Not really. What about the wedding dress?" Kate asked breathlessly.

"The wedding dress?" Mary asked.

"Yes, she was wearing an old-fashioned wedding dress when she met her death. People usually just wear their best dress to wed. In this case, it would have long since worn out after, what, fifty years or so. A proper wedding dress assumes wealth."

"And a wedding dress presupposes a wedding," Mr. Hogarth said. "But the victim called herself Miss Haverstock."

"It is odd," Charles agreed. "Women aim for the title of Mrs., never Miss."

"A wedding dress presupposes a wedding was planned," Mary said, her pert nose uplifted. "Not that it took place. Maybe she wore it to confront a spurned lover."

"No," Charles said. "Ned Blood is supposed to be the one

who killed her, and he can't have been Miss Haverstock's spurned lover. The governor said he was in his early forties."

"How old was Miss Haverstock?" Mary asked.

"They said fifty-six at the inquest," Kate said.

Charles snapped his fingers. "The other escapee, Larsen, was fifty-eight."

Kate's eyes widened. "Could they have the men confused?"

Charles stared at the images in his hands. "How? Blood was seen in the neighborhood. One set of manacles was found at the Joneses' forge. The other washed up by Blackfriars Bridge. And Larsen hasn't been seen around here."

Kate took the sketches from Charles and put her finger on Larsen's image. "All he'd have to do is shave off that beard to radically change his appearance."

Charles put his hands in his hair in frustration and knocked off his hat in the process. Mary crouched down to pick it up for him. "Ned Blood is known in the neighborhood. He lived around here. Larsen, if not known around here, would never have been recognized, anyway. There's no reason to believe he wasn't ever in Chelsea."

"The men might even still be together," Kate suggested, flourishing the sketches

"What about the manacles?" Mr. Hogarth asked, pulling out his tobacco pouch.

"I don't know," Charles said, dropping his hat back over his curls. "Except it means that both men are freely walking the streets."

"What a tangle," Kate moaned. "At least we have only one victim this time, unlike last winter."

"With two convicts on the loose, that might not be true for long. Now that at least one of them has become a killer." The twilight sky seemed to have just gone a dark blue. Charles stared up at the starry skyscape, wishing the heavens had some wisdom to offer him.

*   *   *

Charles woke the next morning, hot and sticky, feeling as though his brain had kept churning all night long instead of letting him rest. Kate had kept saying they needed to know who Miss Haverstock was, but what had kept going through his brain during the night was the question of who Larsen and Blood were. He needed to learn the convicts' histories, not Miss Haverstock's. Did Larsen know Chelsea? Had he lived in these parts?

He used up the rest of the water in the basin, since Fred had risen early, saying something about taking a walk, and put on fresh clothes before stumbling into the parlor.

Kate had given him a slice of pound cake before he'd left. He found a fork and took a bite of the buttery confection as he sat in front of his writing desk. When he opened it to pull out paper, he saw the old magazine that had been slipped under his door the week before.

Suddenly, the name Osvald Larsen clicked back into his brain. He paged through the magazine. Yes. His pulse quickened as he ran his fork down the fifty-year-old article. Osvald was the boy with the drunken father who'd killed his mother. Eddie made fun of him with a broken doll. Certainly a boy with that history would turn to a life of crime.

But if Osvald Larsen was the boy in the story, who was Miss Haverstock? And why would someone have put the magazine under his door? Had his neighbor done it before she died? No, that couldn't be right. She'd been dead long before the magazine appeared. Blood? Larsen himself? Someone else?

He heard the St. Luke's bells ringing and realized he had to get to the *Chronicle* for a staff meeting. After swallowing the last bit of cake, he ran for the door, the magazine under his arm and his satchel containing the convict sketches in his other hand.

A few hours later, he had a new roster of assignments relating to parliamentary matters and another sketch idea approved.

As the reporters dispersed, he stood to one side, ready to catch Mr. Black, the other editor, and ask about the old magazine. Mr. Black's habitual and wildly expensive collecting habit might mean he would know something about *Migrator Magazine*.

"Sir," Charles said when the rest of the men had departed. He lifted the old magazine up to eye level. "Might I ask you a question about this?"

Mr. Black took the magazine in his ink-stained fingers and flipped through it. "Before your time." He handed it back.

"Yes, but I think it's a clue in the murder of my neighbor last week. Someone put it under my door on Saturday morning, and I've realized that one of the children mentioned in one of the articles, Osvald, might be the missing companion of escaped convict Ned Blood, who is assumed to be the murderer. His companion is named Osvald Larsen, and that can't be a common name in London. He's the right age, too."

"Hell and damnation," the editor exclaimed. He took up *Migrator Magazine* again and paged through it. "Here is a thought. I suggest speaking to Lord Holland, who backed the magazine and is a longtime supporter of Jewish emancipation."

"He paid for this magazine?"

"It put a positive light on the Jewish people," Mr. Black explained. "Lord Holland was just one investor, but I believe you are acquainted with the man, and it's likely the other investors would be dead now. I don't recognize any of the names on the masthead as being active in publishing any longer."

"Thank you, sir," Charles said. "I shall do as you say."

"Might want to hand that to William," Mr. Black suggested. "As he is the one reporting on the case."

"I will when I know something," Charles said. After all, the clue had come to him.

He returned to his desk and wrote a note to Kate, asking that she make herself available to pay a call on Lord Holland, then wrote a note to Lady Holland in order to make the call possible, as she managed her husband's life. Although the lady was older than her husband, she was presently in better health. The couple had been friendly with William Aga for years and had opened their salons to Charles over the previous winter as his reputation grew.

The next morning, at the appropriate hour, he collected Kate in the entryway of the Hogarth house. For their walk, she wore a straw bonnet and a lacy shawl.

"You look a picture," Charles said approvingly. Kate loved her ribbons, and the straw bonnet had been trimmed with a bright blue, which made his fiancée's eyes light up brilliantly. Her cheeks were pink with health. "I don't recognize that dress."

In fact, the light blue fabric she wore almost matched his summer trousers. They looked as though they had dressed to match. Mary peeked into the hall and waved before disappearing again.

"Lady Lugoson brought us bolts of French fabric when she returned from the Continent," Kate explained. "I think she likes buying things for Mary and me since she doesn't have a daughter living."

"What about Julie Aga?" Charles asked. "She has a niece."

"Julie has an exceptional wardrobe now," Kate said. "I suppose you don't see her very often."

"No, which is surprising, since we officially live in the same building," Charles said. "But it is all for the best."

"It is," Kate said. "My father still dislikes her. But I know her dresses are much flashier than mine."

Charles regarded the bodice of Kate's new dress. It exposed much more of her shoulders than he was used to seeing. If Julie's dresses were cut much lower, they'd be positively indecent. He coughed and turned away, embarrassed.

"Shall I take your arm, Mr. Dickens?" Kate asked, picking up a summer parasol to keep out the sun.

He held his arm out to her and they left the house and went up the street, seeking the crossroad that would take them to Holland House. Usually, when he was invited there, he would spend time memorizing the architecture or admiring the famous interiors. Today his thoughts couldn't focus on any of that. They kept flashing to Miss Haverstock's humble rooms above his. Lady Holland's many jewels and current fashion turned into that yellowed wedding dress, those crone-like, ringless hands.

He felt positively ill by the time a footman opened the door to them at Holland House. His card case nearly dropped when he took it out of his pocket.

"My apologies," he murmured, taking out a card. "I wrote to Lady Holland, but she did not have time to offer a reply."

"I will see if she is available, Mr. Dickens," the footman said and scurried away.

Kate glanced around curiously. The scale of opulence was enough to make anyone feel small. "I thought Lady Lugoson lived well. I suppose all barons are not created equally."

"Especially when one baron is a fifteen-year-old boy," Charles said. "Who knows what toll Lady Lugoson's husband's death had on the family fortunes? The present Lord Lugoson was only thirteen when he took the title."

"Come this way, if you please," said a pretty housemaid who had appeared from a passage off the main hall.

They followed her through a couple of the grand drawing rooms that Charles had been in before. He hoped to allow Kate a peek at the famed Gilt Room, but, alas, the maid took them in the opposite direction and seated them in a cozy room with ancient wood-paneled walls and a thick brick-red carpet on the floor. The fire had been lit, and they sat in upholstered chairs next to an inlaid tea table.

"Lady Holland will be in shortly," the maid said, then left them alone.

"This is the perfect nook for wealthy old people," Kate observed. "Easy to keep warm, well lit. I hope we have such a sweet sitting room someday."

Charles glanced around, noting the many colored-pencil drawings of birds set in frames on the tables and the mantelpieces. "It does have charm, but I'm not convinced the paneling has any real appeal in the modern age."

"Wallpaper would be nice," Kate agreed. "Oh, I do so look forward to having our first real home."

"I do, as well." He smiled.

The door opened, and another maid came in with tea and seedcake. Not a minute later, Lady Holland herself entered. She had an oval face, topped by steel-gray hair, and it was easy to ignore her double chin in favor of the abundance of exotic pearls around her neck. The fabric of her dress bore testament to her reputation for having introduced dahlias to England, as the dark fabric had the lavender blooms painted all over it.

Charles and Kate stood quickly just before she put her first slipper on the carpet, and made their bow and curtsy to the baroness.

"How delightful to see you again, Mr. Dickens," she said.

"And even more delightful to see you, my lady," he responded.

"Is this your future bride? It must be." She smiled at Kate.

"May I present Miss Catherine Hogarth, my intended?" Charles asked.

Kate curtsied again.

"Such a pleasure, Miss Hogarth. You must have a mind as lively as your face is lovely to win such a catch as Mr. Dickens."

Kate's face colored with a pretty blush. "Thank you, my lady."

Lady Holland seated herself with some creaking of stays. The maid, who had remained, poured tea for the trio. When she had left the room, the lady set her saucer in her lap. "I'm afraid my husband is indisposed today, Mr. Dickens, but your letter seemed urgent."

"I'm sorry, my lady. I merely wanted to confer with your husband over this magazine." He pulled it from his pocket and handed it to Lady Holland.

She glanced at the decaying document. "My husband was little more than a child in seventeen eighty-five. What specifically did you want to know?"

"Mr. Black at the *Chronicle* thought your husband may have backed this periodical, since he has supported Jewish causes since his youth. If I may?"

She nodded, and he opened the magazine to the article in question. "This is my particular interest. Someone put it under my door last week, with a ribbon marking this article."

Lady Holland read the first page, her lips moving. "I do recognize the name of the author, but Mr. Smith is long dead, I'm afraid. Given the age of this periodical, all the children involved would likely be dead, as well."

"I believe Osvald is still alive, my lady. The child in this article is of the right age to be fifty-eight now. He is likely to be one of the criminals who escaped Coldbath Fields recently, and could even be the murderer of my neighbor Miss Haverstock. I'm hoping to learn more about him, and what might have led him or his companion in the escape, Ned Blood, to kill her. Someone knew enough to place this magazine under my door. I am trying to learn why."

She worried her lower lip. "I wonder, Mr. Dickens, how your neighbor came to die. I have followed the papers. Miss Haverstock lived above you. Why did she die and not you or, indeed, your downstairs neighbor?"

"That is a most terrifying question," Charles agreed.

"Why was an escaped criminal in the neighborhood?" Lady Holland mused. "Miss Haverstock's death cannot have been random."

"Blood lived nearby at one time," Charles said. "That's the other escapee. He must have known about the smithy, since a pair of manacles were found there."

"Smithy?" Lady Holland said. "Are you certain that this Blood or Larsen had no connection to it?"

"No one there recognized the sketches I have of the felons," Charles said. "But Larsen was a blacksmith."

"They aren't very useful sketches," Kate added gently.

Lady Holland nodded. "I don't think it's of much use to trace the backgrounds of disrespectable people. If I were you, I'd look into Miss Haverstock herself and the smithy people. They are the people whose movements will be traceable, and not those of the criminal class."

"So my fiancée said," Charles offered, with a smile at Kate. "Perhaps this crime really does need the female touch to solve it. I should acquire a sketch of Miss Haverstock and show that around."

"Just so," Lady Holland said. She set her saucer back on the tea tray and rose.

Kate and Charles rose, too.

"You'll have to excuse me," the baroness said. "I had only a few minutes for you today. We have a meeting of the Napoleonic Society this morning."

"Thank you for seeing us," Charles said. He knew the Hollands adored everything Napoleon. "I did have one other request. I've never troubled you with my charity before, but I represent the Charity for Dressing the Mudlark Children of Blackfriars Bridge, and we are presently low on funds."

"Very well, Mr. Dickens. I shall subscribe to your charity."

"How kind you are," he murmured.

The maid came back in the room.

"Annie," Lady Holland instructed, "have the butler give Mr. Dickens forty shillings for his charity."

"Thank you, my lady," Charles said, bowing. He and Kate followed the maid out, then waited in the hall until the butler fetched the shillings, which were tied in a screw of paper. He then opened the door for them and ushered them out.

"I owe you an apology, Kate," Charles said when they reached the road. "You were right that we need to understand Miss Haverstock better."

"She is at the heart of the matter," Kate said gently. "Perhaps we know quite a lot about her already. What do you remember her telling you?"

"You were there for most of our visits," Charles said. "London born, near the river somewhere. She met the regent once. I remember her talking with disfavor about his great size. She seemed to remember the past much more than the present."

"True," Kate agreed, taking his arm as they crossed the street after a carriage went by. "What else?"

"Nothing much." Charles frowned. He tried to disassociate himself from the feeling of Kate's glove on his arm and to remember time spent with the old lady. "At some point over the years, she chose to care for Evelina Jaggers."

"Yes," Kate exclaimed. "She's seventeen. How did this old woman in Chelsea rented rooms end up caring for that gorgeous creature? Why didn't they live together?"

"Yes," Charles agreed. "I need to interview her. No one but us has any interest in saving Daniel Jones, and nothing we've managed to learn so far has helped him."

"I do think everyone but us is on the wrong trail with Ned Blood," Kate mused. "We know Miss Haverstock and Osvald Larsen were about the same age. Don't you think they had some kind of relationship? That would explain the dress."

"It was a lot harder to break an engagement in those days," Charles said. "Given what the prison governor said, we don't even know when Larsen came to Great Britain."

"Maybe Miss Jaggers will know something. There was that young man with her at the inquest. Who was he?"

"Her beau, I expect." Charles pulled Kate away from a man who had approached her. The man had a board advertising a bakery strapped over his torso. "I've had the misfortune of a couple of meetings with Mr. Ferazzi and his representative, Mr. Nickerson. I'll try to learn from them where Miss Haverstock lived before."

"That's a good idea," Kate agreed, squeezing his arm. "Oh, Charles, I know it's all a muddle right now, but you'll sort it out. I don't trust that Mr. Nickerson. Do you think someone in that organization is behind the robberies in the neighborhood?"

Chapter 11

His neighbor Breese Gadfly must have seen Charles come in with dinner, for no sooner had Charles spread out his feast for Fred's exaltation that evening than a knock came at the door.

"Dickens!" Breese said, his nostrils flaring as the tantalizing smell of the pies met his nose. "I thought we might work on our song tonight. I know someone who is forming up a comic piece that's already been purchased for tour in the provinces, and he needs songs right away."

"I have other work to complete," Charles told him.

"You should do it, Charles," Fred insisted from his seat on the hearthrug, where he was wiping soot from their crockery. "You need extra money for all the furniture Kate wants."

Charles glanced at his meat pies. "Seems like good beef, Gadfly. Are you hungry?"

"Certainly. We can go to my piano after we eat."

After they finished, the trio went to Breese's rooms on the other side of the building. Fred stretched out on the sofa with an Ainsworth novel when Breese dragged a chair next to his piano stool. Breese and Charles sat in front of a blank page.

"What should we write about?" Breese asked.

"If we're writing for a specific piece, surely you have a topic already," Charles suggested.

"Oh, young love, you know the sort of thing." Breese played a chord on the keyboard.

"Keep playing that," Charles suggested. "I'll think of something." The feeling of Kate's hand on his arm, for instance.

Breese played the chord again, then embellished it, before starting over.

"In the sunlight, oh, my sweetheart," Charles improvised. "Now switch the key after that."

"I'll start over." Breese stopped and began again.

"In the sunlight, oh, my sweetheart," Charles sang. "When your glove lays soft on my arm."

"Very nice," Breese said. "Then, how about 'I can think of your kisses when we know it's strawberry time'?"

They worked on the song for another hour, draining more from Breese's ale jug whenever they felt parched, until Charles felt quite dizzy and full of laughter. Then something disrupted his giddiness.

He frowned. "I think I heard a knock on the door."

Breese dropped the fallboard over the keys. He stood, then stumbled a little as he went to the door.

"Is Charles here?" asked an anxious voice at the door.

Charles stood, frowning. Fred snored on the sofa, the volume spread open over his face.

When Charles went to the door, he saw Julie Aga in an old, ill-fitting organdy dress that had probably once belonged to her late half sister, mud clinging to the hem. She had dirt on her cheek, too, and a wild expression in her eyes. Her bonnet had gone missing, and tendrils of her wild red hair were in her eyes. This girl reminded him more of the old actress Julie than the polished, pretty young matron she was now.

"William?" he asked, concern sending tendrils of sobriety through the ale haze. He pulled her inside.

"No, Charles." She flipped stray hairs off her face. "It's our mudlark friend Little Ollie. He gashed his hand almost to the bone. It's a long, ugly cut. We were down at the river, and I wondered why he had it tucked in his waistcoat."

Charles's thoughts moved slowly. "What do you need?"

She screwed up her features. "It's infected. We need money for a doctor."

"Did William stay with him?"

"Yes. They are in a hackney, outside. Do you have any money left from the charity fund? Or should I go to my aunt?"

"No," Charles said, feeling quite sober now. "Prov-providentially, I did collect some money recently."

Charles dashed across the hall, which seemed to tilt slightly, and poured out the contents of his charity collecting box, then found a shawl Mary Hogarth had left on his peg a few days earlier. He wrapped it around Julie, who didn't seem to notice her damp skirts. They went outside to where the hackney waited.

After handing her up and swinging in himself, he could finally assess the situation in the faint light of the lantern inside the hackney.

"How is he?" Charles asked William. He could smell the copper scent of blood and already knew it was bad.

"Not good," William whispered. "I don't want to wake him."

Julie pulled the shawl off her shoulders and tucked it around the small boy, who whimpered a little. Only about seven, he wasn't quite too old for tears in the face of hardship. "Should I go back in and fetch some laudanum?" she asked.

"No. Let's get to the doctor quickly. I can't stop the bleeding," William said. "You know of doctors near, yes?"

"Dr. Manette is on the old turnpike road, and he lives and works in the same house," Charles said. He opened the window and told the driver where to take them, then sat next to William and applied pressure to Ollie's wound while Julie cried softly and folded her arms over her chest for comfort.

When they reached the house, the men sent Julie ahead to attempt to rouse the inhabitants. Charles jumped down; then William handed the boy to him. Little Ollie's chest was sticky with blood where his wound had bled through the various bits of cloth—their handkerchiefs and neckcloths and the shawl—they had attempted to wind around his hand.

"Why did you come to Chelsea?" Charles asked, glancing down at the pale face. "He might have died from blood loss."

"I panicked." William wiped his bloody hand across his face. His cheeks were bleached of color, too, as if in sympathy with Little Ollie. "I didn't know what to do. Julie was hysterical at first. I suppose I thought to leave her with her aunt, but then I remembered you and knew you'd manage us."

Charles frowned. A year ago, when they'd first started working together, he'd looked up to William, the elder and the far more experienced one of the two of them. Had he superseded his teacher already?

"The door is open," Charles said as they walked to the house. Ollie started crying, letting out soft, helpless sobs of fear and exhaustion. In the hallway, behind the young housemaid he remembered from visiting here in the winter, when he was researching Christiana Lugoson's mysterious death, Charles saw Dr. Manette coming, still buttoning his tailcoat over his shirt-covered round belly, wearing no waistcoat.

"Mr. Dickens?" the doctor inquired pleasantly, despite the hour. He must be used to such visits.

"You have a good memory for names, sir. I bring you a paying patient. This is Ollie, and he's hurt his hand badly."

"Let's have a look." The doctor came up to them and put a hand on the boy's head. "I'll take care of you, son. You needn't worry."

The boy's eyes rolled up, and he swooned.

The doctor put his fingers to the boy's throat. "Just fainted, poor mite. What is he? A beggar?"

"Mudlark, sir," Charles explained.

"Let's take him into my examination room," the doctor said. "This way. Sarey, please light the fire and all the lamps." The girl scurried ahead of him. Then they all followed.

"It wasn't metal, at least," William said. "Another of the mudlarks was carrying a heavy piece of wood. It fell right on Ollie's hand. He was digging on the foreshore."

"Crushed?" Dr. Manette asked.

"Pierced," William said.

A well-scrubbed table took center place in the examination room. The walls sparkled with whitewash, and mirrors gleamed on each of the four walls, reflecting the lamps. Between the mirrors were glass-fronted cabinets filled with all manner of curiosities, but Charles could think of nothing but Ollie.

Charles laid the boy down on the table. It could have held four of him. The pitiable mite's copious freckles stood out on his pale face, and his stick-straight sandy brown hair was crusted with sand around his scalp.

The doctor pushed his spectacles against his eyes and wiped his hands with a clean white towel, then began to unravel the makeshift bandages. Dark blood oozed from the wound, followed by a gush of new, fresh red blood.

Julie moaned, and her head lolled on her neck. Charles reached for her as she sagged, and caught her just before she collapsed to the floor.

"Take care of my wife," William begged. "I'm covered in blood."

Trying to keep from gagging himself at the heavy scent of blood, of wrongness, Charles picked Julie up and carried her out of the room, unable to forget that the last time he had done this, the girl had died.

But this time, he didn't hold the injured party, but one very confusing actress married to his best friend. He walked down the passage to the receiving room he remembered. The doctor must have been sitting there, for a fire still glowed and the room remained warm. He placed Julie on the sofa and poured her a glass of the ruby port that sparkled in a decanter.

Then he sat her up slowly and put the rich liquor to her lips. She drank a sip, made a sluggish face of distaste, drank again. A couple of sips after that, she pushed the glass away and sat up, her head still parallel to her lap.

"Is Ollie going to die?" she asked.

"Not if infection can be prevented," Charles said. "But obviously, he is badly wounded."

"His hand is open to the bone," Julie said. "I saw more than I wanted to when we tried to bandage it with William's neckerchief."

"You did the best you could."

"William never goes out with money. He says it is unwise after dark. And I never used to have any. Maybe it would have been better if we'd gone for help in London."

"The only difference is if this cost him too much blood," Charles said. "I don't think that is the problem here. Yes, there was blood, but not a mortal amount."

"How I hate the sight of blood," Julie whispered.

"Most people do."

"Don't you ever despair, Charles? You're always so . . . cheerful, so competent."

"I have very dark thoughts at times," he admitted, pouring a glass of port for himself. "But I mean to get ahead in life. That means making friends, as I started out with none, and no one likes a gloomy fellow."

"Is there a part of you in your sketches? Some of them are very dismal, like your 'Watkins Tottle.'"

"I try to reflect our world as I see it." Charles drained his glass.

She shuddered. "I'd rather imagine something better."

"Aren't you happy, Julie? William is the best of fellows. You have family now, nice furniture and clothes . . . ." Charles trailed off. What else could a seventeen-year-old girl want?

Her lips turned down. "I don't have a spot in the theater. I don't have a child."

"You don't need to work, and you haven't been married long enough to have a child," Charles pointed out.

"I want to do something. I met your Kate in the lane the other day, and she could speak of nothing else but your latest mystery. Remember last winter, when I helped you? I enjoyed that. Now I feel merely ornamental."

"You've been a great comfort to your aunt," Charles soothed.

William came in long after Charles had lost track of time. Charles saw his friend's pale face and immediately poured him a drink.

"What has happened?" Julie asked. She rose and touched her husband's arm.

"Dr. Manette had to amputate his hand." William swallowed hard, as if he was about to lose the drink he'd consumed. "I couldn't leave. I had to help hold Ollie down."

"Poor darling," Julie whispered.

"We put enough laudanum into him for sleep now, and he'll stay here," William added slowly. "The doctor has a room for patients."

Charles's stomach clenched. He bowed his head and whispered a prayer.

"It's going to cost rather a lot," William said.

"I'll get the money from my aunt." Julie took the glass from William and set it next to the decanter. "I know we aren't responsible, not really, but we like these children."

"Yes," William agreed, staring down at his shoes. "His life as he knows it is over."

"We need to get our little friends out of the mudlarking trade," Julie said. "Talk them into leaving the foreshore."

"That will just send them to the workhouse," Charles protested. "We need an actual plan."

Julie bent her head. William went to the fireplace and leaned against it, staring into the dying flames.

Charles wondered why William didn't comfort his wife. Was there trouble in the marriage already?

By the time Charles pushed himself up in bed the next morning, the sun had already risen quite high in the sky. When Fred had poked at him, trying to get him ready for church with the family, he'd growled and sent the boy away.

Now he felt sticky, and his head ached from either too much port or too little water. He wasn't even sure why he was awake.

After padding to the jug and basin, he dunked his head in what water was left between them, an inch or two of tepidness, then made his ablutions. When he went to pull up the blankets on the bed, he heard a thud overhead.

He glanced up at the ceiling. Someone was in Miss Haverstock's rooms. Outrage, heightened because of the nightmare with Ollie last night, sizzled through his veins. He reached for his clothes and threw them on without his usual fastidiousness.

Still tying his neckerchief, he climbed up the stairs. He knew the Agas weren't in their rooms, because they'd gone to Lugoson House in order to beg money for Ollie first thing that day.

When he reached the top of the stairs, he saw a chair come flying through the door. His memory flashed back to the Gordons.

"Ferazzi," he muttered. Then he called the name again. "Mr. Ferazzi!"

He heard the stomping of boots, and the old foreigner appeared in the doorway. "If it isn't Mr. Dickens," the man snarled, putting a hand to his glossy black, pasted-down hair.

"Why are you disturbing the building?" Charles demanded. "There is no one here to impress upon the notion of paying one's rent. The lady is dead."

The old man sneered. "Miss Jaggers, Miss Haverstock's foster daughter, has taken what she wants. I have the right to clear out the rest."

"Why destroy these items?" Charles asked, pointing at the chair that had been tossed. One leg lay apart from the rest of the chair, sheared clean off by the impact against the wall. "Shall I direct your attention to the mark that chair made on the wall?" Charles then pointed out the black scratch next to the Agas' door. "That's your responsibility, sir. You've just spent your own coin."

Reggie Nickerson, Ferazzi's assistant, appeared at the door. "Due to be painted, due to be painted, Mr. Dickens. At the end of the season."

Charles doubted that. "I don't care to be disturbed in this manner," he said stiffly. "If this is how your tenants and their possessions are going to be treated, I shall ensure that I do not reside in your buildings again, and neither will my friends or my family."

Mr. Ferazzi's eyes narrowed. "Don't trouble yourself about me, sir. I was prosperous before I ever heard the name Dickens."

Charles turned, and the next thing he knew, he saw the old man's boot kick out a box of tea things. He recognized the teapot Miss Haverstock had kept filled when he visited her.

"Enough!" he cried. What if some crucial detail pertaining to her demise was being destroyed? "I'll buy what's left. How much?"

Mr. Ferazzi's pale lips curved. "I'll let Mr. Nickerson make that bargain." He pushed the little man aside and went down the stairs, the skirt of his frock coat swinging, his legs underneath poking out as thin as a spider's.

Charles grimaced. "What will you charge me?"

Mr. Nickerson rubbed his scruffy chin. "Some nice things here."

"All of which your employer was willing to pulverize into rubble," Charles said. "I'll give you thirty shillings for the lot."

"You knows better than that, Mr. Dickens," Mr. Nickerson

said, leaning against the doorjamb. His eyes glinted. "Five pounds, and not a shilling less."

Charles knew a thief when he saw one. He only wondered if Mr. Nickerson had done more locally than display mere greed. Kate seemed to think so.

"This is already a much-improved morning," Charles said on Monday, sitting at the place of honor at the end of his improvised dining table as Kate placed hard-boiled eggs and toast in front of him.

Mary poured tea for him and Fred; then the girls sat down to watch the Dickenses eat.

"Very nice," Charles praised as he poked at a yolk. "Just how I like my eggs, darling."

Kate smiled. "I'm glad. Another of your favorites checked off my list. But what are all these crates doing here? And that trunk?"

"I bought what remained of Miss Haverstock's possessions yesterday. Cost me the rest of my cash, but it was worth it to have Mr. Ferazzi's men stop desecrating her things."

"They came yesterday?"

"Yes, and treated everything like they had the Gordons' things."

"Landlords can't be sentimental," Mary said. "I expect it's a very hard business."

"So you won't marry a man of property?" Fred asked in a rather hopeful tone, speaking for the first time.

"No, I'll marry a lawyer, like father used to be. Maybe a judge," Mary said. "A man of learning."

Fred stared listlessly at the books stacked on the mantelpiece. Charles glanced at Kate. They both held back grins. Fred still had feelings for Mary, and she returned them in no way whatsoever.

"What will you do with it all?" Kate asked, indicating the trunk.

"Look for clues, of course. Books, albums, although Evelina Jaggers probably took all that and Miss Haverstock's personal ornaments. I really need to pay a call on her." Charles rubbed his eyes.

"I expect so," Kate agreed.

"You should go through all the textiles. Take the clothes and rework them if you can, or sell them to a secondhand dealer or a rag merchant."

Kate nodded. "We can put the money toward our furniture budget. Come, Mary. Let's go through these crates before Mr. Dickens has to leave for London. We can't stay when he is gone. It isn't proper."

"I can help you carry things to your house if you like," Fred said.

"Don't you have translations to do?" Charles asked.

"Sometime today," Fred said carelessly. "They'll keep, Charles. If we don't handle these crates now, our rooms are going to smell like an old woman."

Kate frowned at him. "Open a window if you are so concerned about the smell."

Fred rolled his eyes. "Doesn't it bother you that these things were in the same room as a dead body for days and days?"

"Death is a part of life, Fred. If you aren't used to that now, you soon will be," Kate said.

Charles swallowed his last bite of egg and pushed back from the table. "Here is the clothing. I'm sure Miss Jaggers took all the best of everything, but there is still some good cloth."

Kate went to her knees in front of the trunk that Charles had unlocked for her. She poked around at the dresses. Mary knelt next to her.

"There's quite a bit here that looks to be only about fifteen years old," Mary said.

"She must have refurbished her wardrobe then," Kate agreed. "This is very pretty." She pulled out a cream dress polka-dotted with gold. Gold trim decorated the neckline and the hem of the skirt.

"It isn't so different from today's styles," Mary said.

Charles could hear the smile in her voice.

"This one is more matronly," Kate said as she unwrapped a bit of paper and displayed a navy dress with a white diamond pattern. "All it really needs are new sleeves."

"Did you get a good price, Charles?" Mary asked, tucking stray locks of brown hair back into her braid.

"Very, if there are actually dresses you can wear." He leaned over to examine the cream and gold dress. "I wonder why Miss Jaggers didn't take this one."

"She wouldn't want anything old," Kate said. "Not that sort of girl. You remember how well dressed she was at the inquest, and not at all friendly." She picked up another wrapped bundle. Something fell out and pinged against the floorboards. She handed the bundle to Mary and picked up the object.

"What is it?" Charles asked.

Kate had what looked like a spinning top in her palm. She held it up to him.

He examined it. "Silver. Pointed tip and a spinning rod, but made of expensive metal and very ornate."

"I've seen one of these," Kate told him. "It's a Hebrew toy. I think it's called a dreidel in their language."

"A Hebrew toy?" Charles repeated. "How strange."

Mary had unwrapped the bundle, and she pulled out a silver chain. "Look. The clasp is broken. Do you think she wore that spinning top like a charm?"

Kate threaded the chain through the top of the dreidel. "It does have an loop for exactly that. Was Miss Haverstock Jewish?"

"I never saw any sign of it, but we didn't know her for long." Charles considered. "This area makes sense as a Jewish quarter, with the burying ground nearby. Breese Gadfly is Jewish."

Mary shook out the rest of the bundle, which turned out to be an old evening cloak. Another small item dropped. Charles caught it on the rebound.

"It's a ring," he reported, staring at the simple gold band in his palm.

Kate leaned over him. "A wedding ring?"

They stared at each other.

"Why would she have left such objects in a cloak?" Mary asked. She poked through the fabric. "Look. The pocket has a hole."

Kate went back to the trunk and pawed through the rest of the belongings, but they'd already seen the best of it. "Old stays, old shoes. A tarnished dressing-table set. It could be taken to be resilvered."

"Is there a family Bible?" Charles asked.

"Not in this trunk," Kate reported. "We need to find her parish, if she had one."

"I agree." Charles sighed when he heard the church bells. "I should leave for London. Have a look through the crates, will you, and we'll discuss the matter tonight."

Charles called for Kate on the way home. They walked past the Jewish burial ground gate, which was locked, like usual.

"I had never really thought about this place before," Kate confessed, staring up at the high walls. "Finding that dreidel really made me wonder. I don't think I'd ever had a conversation with a Jewish person before."

"That's because you've never known want. If you'd had to deal in secondhand clothes, you'd have met them."

"She had her tea things, a deck of playing cards, a chipped vase." Kate paused. "Of course, anything finer than her everyday things, if such items existed, would have left the rooms with Miss Jaggers."

"I suppose we have an incomplete record," Charles admitted.

"Fred will be at home, right?" Kate asked.

"Of course, dear, and we'll have Julie downstairs. I want to check on her."

"Did William say much about Little Ollie today?"

Charles's stomach ached anew at the memory of the night before. His exhaustion had kept the remembered horror at bay.

"He was going to check on him on the way home, so we should have news soon."

When they reached Selwood Terrace, Charles sent Kate upstairs to find Julie, then unlocked his own door. "Botheration," he muttered when he saw that Fred was, in fact, not at home. He hated to be made a liar.

As soon as he had the fire laid and the kettle full of water, Kate and Julie clattered down the steps.

"I spent the afternoon with Ollie," Julie announced, walking in ahead of Kate. The young matron wore a dark, serviceable dress with no frills.

"Is he healing?" Charles asked.

"He is still taking a fair amount of laudanum," she said. "The doctor said he's been frantic otherwise and could wound himself."

Charles appreciated Dr. Manette's wisdom. "What about the other children? Do they know?"

"William had to attend a meeting this evening, so he'll be in London late. He said he'd go fetch them after and take them to Dr. Manette's house."

"That will be quite an adventure," Kate said. "They've likely never been in a hackney or been outside of London."

"I expect you are right," Julie agreed. "Maybe that will help them imagine life away from the Thames. I had so many experiences when I was younger. It helped me be less afraid of change."

Charles heard a knock on the door. "Must be Mr. Gadfly from next door."

"I'll put the tea in the pot," Kate said as he went to the door.

Instead of Breese Gadfly, Reggie Nickerson, Mr. Ferazzi's man, stood in the doorway. He took off his cap and frowned at Charles. "Need a word with you, Dickens," he rasped in a grim tone.

Chapter 12

Charles attempted to step into the tiny front hall outside of his parlor to keep whatever unpleasant business the man had out of earshot of the ladies, but somehow, he found himself pushed back into the room, with Mr. Nickerson looming in his entryway and the door closed behind him.

He heard Kate squeak and the rustling of skirts as Mr. Nickerson came forward. Charles put out his hands to stop Kate and Julie from coming too close.

"Now see 'ere," Mr. Nickerson said belligerently. Taller than Charles, he could look down his hooked nose at him. "It won't do, Mr. Dickens. It just won't do."

"What is this about?" Charles demanded, unwilling to give the man any authority.

"You, sir," said the rent collector, poking Charles in the chest, "are behind on rent and will be evicted in a week."

"Balderdash," Charles exclaimed as the girls gasped. "I paid on Friday. My rent isn't due now."

"You've only been paying half your rent, and Mr. Ferazzi, well, sir, 'e won't stand for it any longer."

Charles's stomach seemed to catch in his throat. He forced himself to speak through complete outrage. "That is entirely untrue. I'll show you." He glanced around the cluttered room, panicking when he realized that in this mess, he had no idea where his paperwork was. Had he left it at Furnival's Inn? No, it had to be in his writing desk, and that was here. He took one arm of each girl and pulled them into his bedroom.

"Charles," Kate started.

He shook his head. "It's a misunderstanding, Kate. You know me better than that." He took his writing desk from the nightstand, where it had unaccountably ended up. Flipping through the papers, he could find no sign of rental agreements.

He dumped his papers across the bed and spread them out. Nothing. Trying to be methodical, even as his heart raced, he turned over each sheet as he read it and gathered the rejected papers in a pile. Not that one, or that one, either. Julie picked up the pile and glanced through it, too.

The door opened behind him. It was Nickerson, his gaze scornful. He held up a paper as Julie stared over his shoulder. "This wot yer lookin' for, Mr. Dickens?"

Charles stood from his crouch over the bed and ripped the page out of Mr. Nickerson's hand. It was his rental agreement, all right, but with an amount double what he had agreed to pay. "Where did this come from? The amount is wrong. Look, you can see where it is scribbled over." Where was his copy? Had it been stolen out of his box? He needed to search the rest of his rooms, and the ones in Holborn, as well. Normally, he was fastidious about matters of business. This didn't make sense.

He needed another opinion. Where was William? Or he could go to Breese and see what he paid in rent. "Julie, is this what you pay?"

"I don't know." She lifted her hands. "William handles the rent."

Mr. Nickerson chuckled nastily. "You may think what you

will, but you have no proof of the truth being otherwise. I'll need the rest of your rent now, or we'll plan for the removers."

"Did you break in here? Steal my paperwork?" Charles demanded.

The rent collector bristled. Kate and Julie jumped back.

"Temper, temper," Mr. Nickerson said, waving his finger. "It's 'ard to be a young man trying to impress 'is lady. I unnerstand, Mr. Dickens. But you'll pay everything you owe come Friday, or be tossed out on yer ear, like anyone else." He laughed and walked out, then shut the door gently behind him.

Charles whirled around, his face contorted with anger and embarrassment. "He is lying," he thundered. "He stole my paperwork and wrote over the original. I'd never pay only half of my rent."

Julie put her hand on his arm, while Kate hung back, her hand over her mouth.

"Mr. Nickerson is a bad man," Julie murmured. "Rent collectors always are. I believe you, Charles. I don't know what William paid, but we'd better make sure our rental agreement wasn't stolen, as well."

"I'll bet he's the neighborhood thief," Charles raged. "He'd better not try to steal anything else from me."

"Why didn't you just give him the money?" Kate asked. "Then you would have been done with it until you sorted it out."

Charles took a deep breath, trying to calm down. "I already gave the rest of my ready cash to Mr. Nickerson. For Miss Haverstock's things. I don't have any more until I'm paid on Friday." He put his hands through his hair. "Mr. Nickerson knew it, too. That was part of the negotiation. I told him I didn't have any more money, and he gave me his price."

Kate drew herself up. "We'll sell Miss Haverstock's things to the dealers. And get your money back. The dresses are better than you thought, Charles. You'll get more than you paid."

"I'm not giving Reggie Nickerson one more shilling," Charles insisted. "I paid my rent, and I won't be his victim. I'm not going to be treated like the Gordons."

"I don't understand why you don't have any more money, Charles," Kate said. "How can we be married at Christmas if you are constantly running out of money?"

Charles gritted his teeth. Why was she saying such unsupportive things in front of Julie Aga? "I gave money to the Gordons, remember? And then paid for Miss Haverstock's things. Those were unusual circumstances. I have payments coming for some of my sketches soon. You know I haven't been saving. I've been buying new furniture and kitchen things as I have the money. That was our plan, Kate."

She shook her head, her jaw taut. "I'm not going to live the pawnshop life, Charles. I deserve better. I will leave so you can try to find your rental agreement." She grabbed her shawl off the sofa and went to the door. "Julie?"

"Do you want me to take the dresses?" Julie asked.

"They already belong to Kate," Charles growled. "I gave them to her."

"Oh, well, I'll leave them for now, then," Julie said.

Kate gave Charles an agonized glance, then went out the door.

"If she won't support you through hardship, what kind of a wife will she be?" Julie asked, staring at the door after it closed. "I'd never treat William that way."

"She's a different sort of girl than you." Charles let out a breath and ran his hands through his hair. His heart was still pounding. "You can't expect a gently bred girl who has never known want not to be shocked in a situation like this. She hasn't dealt with the criminal class before."

"She shouldn't have left," Julie said stoutly. "I didn't."

"I know, Julie." Charles lifted his hands. "We've had our differences, but you've a true heart."

She nodded and screwed up her cheek. "Why don't you come upstairs? I'll make you dinner. It will be hours before William is home, and I don't want you to be alone."

"Thank you, but it will need to be quick. I'm going to tear these rooms apart and look for my rental agreement. If it's not here, I'm going back to London to look for it tonight. What choice do I have? Mr. Nickerson and Mr. Ferazzi are attempting to get their revenge on me for helping the Gordons, and this just makes me more certain that Nickerson himself is an accomplished thief."

"Do you think the agreement was stolen?"

"Yes. My windows were open, and no one was here. Anyone could have come in." He shook his head. "I just wanted the smell from poor Miss Haverstock's corpse gone, and now this."

Charles drank too much in the Agas' rooms and didn't relish the idea of stumbling his way into London, unable to defend himself from cutpurses. Instead, he went downstairs and had a chat with Breese, along with two rum and waters. His rent hadn't been raised. Eventually, William returned to Selwood Terrace.

Charles ventured into the small hall. "How is Ollie? Where are the other mudlarks?"

William squinted at him. "You're mumbling, Charles."

Charles pushed curls out of his eyes, except they weren't there. It was only his vision not focusing. "Did Ferazzi raise your rent?"

"No." William narrowed his eyes in confusion. "Ollie is healing but is very sad. He wouldn't speak to the other children."

Charles swayed. He grabbed the doorjamb of Breese's door for support.

The songwriter peered over Charles's shoulder and smiled at William. "Come in," he invited. "We were just drinking, err, talking."

"No, thank you. I assume my wife is upstairs."

Charles belched. "She fed me cold pie and a bottle of wine."

William nodded. "What is wrong, Charles?"

"Reggie Nickerson came to my door, in front of Julie and Kate. Said I was paying only half my rent. Threatened to boot me in a week. Hum-hum-humiliating," he finished, feeling a hot flush in his cheeks.

William stared at him. "You can prove he's lying, can't you?"

"He can't find his rental agreement," Breese explained. "I found mine, and it's a bit more than what Charles thought his rent was, but I have better light in my chambers."

William rubbed his index fingers down the sides of his nose. "I'll find mine tomorrow. But it's not like you, Charles, to be untidy."

"St-stolen," Charles pronounced. "When my windows were open."

"Ah. Anything is possible around here." William nodded. "Perhaps we should all beg Lady Lugoson for rooms for the rest of the summer."

Charles didn't think Kate would like that. Lady Lugoson was very beautiful, and a widow. "I will not be forced out of here," he said very slowly.

"Get some sleep," William advised. "No more drinking tonight."

Charles stumbled into the hall, then turned and bowed grandly to Breese. "Good evening, Mr. Gadfly."

The other man pulled at the seams of his trousers and curtsied. "Good evening, Mr. Dickens."

Charles giggled at the hilarity. William grimaced at the songwriter and put his arm around Charles's shoulders.

"Tomorrow is another day, son. You'll prove the truth to Kate. Don't worry."

When Charles pulled out his key, it fell on the floor. William picked it up and inserted it into the lock, but the door opened from the pressure alone.

William frowned and fussed with the door. "The bolt isn't engaging. It would have been easy for someone to walk in."

"Not very safe, with a murderer l-loose," Charles said. "But I can't get Nickerson to have it fixed, not now."

William pulled off his cap. "Maybe that's the point." He poked Charles in the shoulder. "Go to bed. Start fresh tomorrow. Dawn is only about four hours away."

Charles woke some hours later, spluttering under a stream of water on his face. He blinked and waved his arms, then struggled to a sitting position. "What?"

"You're going to be late," Fred said, putting down a glass. "And you stink."

Charles rubbed his eyes, which were gritty with sleep. "Water," he moaned.

Fred handed a glass to him. He poured the contents down his parched throat. Then he pushed back the covers. It was too much. He let his head drop into his hands.

"Hair of the dog?" his brother suggested.

"No, too much to do today. I have parliamentary meetings. I need to find the rental agreement if I can, and I need to speak to Miss Jaggers about her foster mother." A face-splitting yawn took over. His eyes closed.

When he opened his eyes again, Fred was two feet away from him, waving his hand in front of his nose. "Clean up first. You smell like the bowels of St. Giles."

"Hardly," Charles scoffed. His brother had no idea how bad that could get.

Twenty minutes later, he stepped out of the building. It was the first of July, and he didn't relish leaving the clean air for stinking summer London and work. By midafternoon, he'd kept down a glass of ale and a bun that an office boy had brought him.

William had not appeared. Charles thought, vaguely, that he'd had to attend a meeting out of town.

"Here's that address you asked for, Mr. Dickens," said the

boy, having reappeared again. He thrust a note into Charles's hand.

Charles stared at Miss Jaggers's address. Should he send an advance note or just arrive there? He checked his pocket watch. If he left now, he'd be just within polite hours for calling.

He thanked the boy and reached for his hat and cane, then attempted and failed at a jaunty whistle as he went back into the street. The light, noise, and smell of the Strand assailed all his senses. Fruit sellers walked down the street, hoping to catch men on their way home or people intent on the theaters. Carriage horses stank worse than usual, depositing the remains of their meals onto the road. Sunlight beat down on everything.

Charles pulled the brim of his top hat low over his eyes. He couldn't stand the thought of being enclosed in a hackney, even though it would be dim inside, so he pushed through the crowd, intent on Belgravia.

The sunspots vanished from his eyes as he saw the first trees of St. James's Park, a welcome oasis on his two-mile walk. Thankfully, Miss Jaggers lived in a genteel setting in a quite new brick mews house tucked behind Eaton Square.

A flushed maid opened the door after he knocked. "Yes, sir?"

He produced his card and handed it to her. "I am calling on Miss Jaggers. A matter of business."

"A reporter?" she asked, proving her literacy as she slowly read the card.

"We have met, or rather, she has seen me," Charles explained. "This is regarding her late foster mother."

"Very sad business," the maid said, shaking her head. "Come in, sir, and go into the parlor. I'll see if she is at home." She pronounced the words in a low, gruff voice.

Charles went to the left, as directed, and found a small room, as suited the house. The walls were covered with framed sketches of infants and young children. Sparse furnishings were inclined to comfort. Two rocking chairs were pointed away from the fireplace, and a basket of knitting showed the room was regularly used, rather than saved for callers.

Only a couple of minutes later, Miss Jaggers appeared. She paused, framed in the doorway. Tall and shining, as Reggie Nickerson had described her, and once again, Charles was struck by the youthful loveliness of the girl. He'd been told she was seventeen, though she looked a bit older. Perhaps the calculating eyes aged her face.

"Mr. Dickens," Miss Jaggers said calmly. "I remember you from the inquest. I did not remember you were a reporter."

"I am, but I am not here in that capacity, but as a friend of your late foster mother, and one who would be your friend, as well."

Perfect golden ringlets fluttered as she inclined her head. "You lived in her building, is that right?"

"I did. We have, or had, quite a nice society there, between Miss Haverstock and me, the Agas and Mr. Gadfly, and the Jones family down the lane."

"I remember seeing Mr. Gadfly," she said. "I do not like that sort of person."

Charles frowned. "What is not to like about such a congenial soul?"

"He is unnatural." Miss Jaggers moved ethereally, as if her feet didn't touch the floor, an effect managed by a slightly too long skirt that covered her slippers. When she sat in the rocking chair without a work basket, Charles knew that was her habitual seat. He took a place on the plain blue settee that faced the fireplace.

"What do you mean? That he is of the Hebrew race?"

Her eyes caught the light in such a manner that the bright blue seemed to flash. Those perfectly molded lips curled. "I meant, sir, that he does not like the fairer sex."

"I disagree," Charles argued. "He writes songs of courtship as a profession."

Her long lashes closed gently over her eyes for a moment. "As you say."

Confused, Charles went into a direct questioning more suited to his profession than a genteel call on a lady. "Tell me, why didn't you live with Miss Haverstock?"

"This house was gifted to the nanny of a nobleman for her lifetime," she explained. "Shortly after it was built in the last decade."

That was no answer. "Is she a connection of yours?"

"No, but she has taken in the right sort of young person over the years," Miss Jaggers said. "My parents died in India two years ago, no, three, now. Miss Haverstock arranged for me to live in this house after I left school."

"Were you in India?"

"Early in my childhood," she said. "I came here for school when I was eight, attended by an ayah who worked for the nobleman. It all makes sense somehow." She smiled, exposing a fetching pair of dimples.

"I must admit I find Miss Haverstock to have a confusing personal history." Charles produced the dreidel charm and held it out in his palm. "I realize that Miss Haverstock did not raise you."

"No, but I have known her for nearly a decade. I have known few people more intimately."

Charles nodded. "I purchased the rest of your foster mother's possessions, because I could not bear to see how the landlord's men were treating them. This fell out of a cloak." He showed her the wedding band.

Miss Jaggers squinted and moved nearer to the ring, then pulled back again. Charles suspected she was farsighted and had trouble focusing on his hand. She straightened. "A wedding band?"

"Yes. Was she not a miss, after all?"

Miss Jaggers looked down her perfect pert nose at him. "I

have the family Bible. I know her history. But what business is it of yours?"

"A man is in Newgate because of her death," Charles explained. "I believe he is a good man, not a murderer. His aunt worked for Miss Haverstock. There are two convicts on the loose, and surely one or both of them are the murderer."

Her posture remained ramrod straight. "You are hoping to find some evidence to exonerate this man?"

"Yes. I am hoping to find evidence that one of the escaped convicts knew Miss Haverstock and is therefore the killer. My fiancée is sure that the fact that she was found in an old wedding dress is somehow the key to your foster mother's death."

Miss Jaggers pulled a handkerchief from her apron pocket and wiped her eyes delicately, though there were no tears. "She became strange as she aged. I don't know why she hid her marriage, but I will retrieve the Bible for you. Maybe the names there will aid you."

Charles let out a sigh of relief. "You will help me?"

"I fear she will not rest until her murderer is hanged for his crimes." Miss Jaggers tucked her handkerchief away.

Charles watched her straight, slim back as she left the room, grateful that she wanted to assist him. He still had a headache and did not feel his usual persuasive self.

He had his head against the back of the settee when he heard the rustling of skirts again. After opening his eyes, he saw Miss Jaggers carried a large but not particularly old-looking tome, the family Bible.

She handed it to him, and he set it in his lap. The cover was embellished with the name Haverstock in gold leaf.

"So the name was real, at least," he murmured.

"Oh yes, but she was Mrs. Haverstock," Miss Jaggers told him, sitting again. "I don't know why she didn't claim her proper title."

"Are you connected to the Haverstocks?"

"Yes. My mother's mother was a Haverstock. I was entrusted to my foster mother's care when I came to England, though, of course, she wasn't expected to house me."

Charles opened the book and found the family register, which listed births and marriages. "Do you know what year she married?"

"Seventeen ninety-six, I believe."

That matched the dress. Charles ran his perpetually ink-stained index finger down the list of names until he found the year 1796 and the name Elijah Haverstock, who was born in 1772. His wife's name was Backy Adams. "*Backy* Adams," he said aloud.

"I expect it was a misprint. I can't imagine anyone really being named that," Miss Jaggers said. "I never looked at the Bible until she died. She was always Mrs. Haverstock to me." Miss Jaggers was not a curious creature.

"Was the marriage contested or annulled?"

Miss Jaggers worried at her lip. "I don't think so."

"What parish did they attend? Do you know?"

"St. Anne's Limehouse."

"Limehouse," he muttered. There they were again, in Limehouse, where the Jewish girl Goldy had died. Somehow that old story in *Migrator Magazine* must connect to Miss Haverstock's death. "I see. She was married to this man long before you were born, and he was your relative, not her."

"Exactly, Mr. Dickens. Will this information help you in your quest to free your friend?"

"Perhaps. I sense the story goes back to Limehouse somehow. Did she ever mention Osvald Larsen to you?"

The beautiful girl tilted her head. "No. Who is that?"

"The other escaped convict. There were two, you see. And the name Osvald was in the magazine story. I think the police are searching for Ned Blood in error."

Her slanted eyes widened. "But he's an escaped criminal!"

"Of course they should catch him, but I doubt he has anything to do with your foster mother's death. It's a theory, of course." He closed the Bible.

She rose. "I look forward to hearing that the proper villain has paid for his crime."

He rose, as well, knowing the interview was over. "One last question. Who was that young man who accompanied you to the inquest? I'm trying to understand everyone who might be involved."

Her beautiful face scarcely moved when she said, "Prince Moss is my friend. Miss Haverstock introduced us."

"Are you engaged?"

She was too self-possessed for blushes. "Maybe someday."

He nodded. "Thank you for seeing me."

He left and headed for the river. Limehouse was some six or seven miles east, and it would be easiest to reach the church on the water.

By the time he saw the golden ball on top of the enormous church tower of St. Anne's Limehouse, the dinner hour had long since ended. He decided to proceed, though, and walked through the narrow passage between Limehouse government buildings to the imposing church facade, hoping someone would be about. As he moved up the shallow steps to the front door of the stone church, he heard the melodious voices of a choir. They must be performing Evensong, the Church of England's prayer ritual.

He let himself into the foyer of the church and then walked through the nave. The pews weren't full, but he stood in the back. The music of the organ washed over him. He had no idea what part of the service he'd arrived during, but the music was beautiful. It would suffice for his dinner. A half hour or so passed before the final long note of the organ washed over him. He woke, as if from a dream. Though it might have been hunger that had him feeling so faded.

He watched as everyone filed into the foyer, and listened as parishioners greeted church officials. While considering the elderly priest, he saw an enormous woman attract the attention of a well-fed gentleman. She launched into a jolly tale of her last meal. Somewhere between describing the cream and the pastry, she said something about the man's duties as verger.

When they were finished with their conversation and the woman was departing, he went up to the verger and showed his newspaper identification.

"What can I do for you, Mr. Dickens?" the verger asked, his gaze following the woman, no doubt wishing he could follow her to her next gustatory delight.

Charles cleared his throat. "I want to examine the church books for seventeen ninety-six and verify a wedding."

The man patted his stomach sadly but spoke politely enough. "What is this regarding? Some relative of yours?"

"No, a murder victim." Charles waited a moment for that to enter the man's cogitations. "Do the names Backy Adams, Elijah Haverstock, or Osvald Larsen mean anything to you?"

The man frowned and took a quick look at his pocket watch. "No. Are they parishioners?"

"Larsen is the only one still living, but the other two must have been parishioners in the previous century."

The man chuckled. "I see. Normally, I would put you off, but it just so happens that the records for seventeen eighty to eighteen hundred are in the sacristy. Our rector likes to repair old books."

Charles smiled. "Then it won't be any trouble for me to take a quick look?"

"I suppose not." With another dissatisfied glance at his watch, he led Charles back through the inner doors, then past the altar and into the small room where the rector prepared for services.

It smelled like a holy place. Vestments hung, neatly pressed, on a rack, and Charles saw religious vessels on top of a case. A row of old books leaned on a shelf, held up by a reproduction marble head of one of the Roman Caesars. The bust's sightless eyes watched over one side of the room, while a cross with a very realistic depiction of Christ's suffering held pride of place on the opposite wall.

The verger ran his beefy finger along the shelf, selected one of the trio of oversize volumes, then set it carefully on a prayer-book stand and opened it. "Here you go, Mr. Dickens. What are you hoping to discover?"

"A connection," he explained. "This is a woman I knew who was murdered in her home in Chelsea, supposedly by an escaped convict."

"Indeed?"

"Indeed. I hope to prove that this Larsen fellow knew Mrs. Haverstock or her husband."

The verger patted his stomach again. "Then you want baptisms, Mr. Dickens. You want to see that Mr. Larsen and the Haverstocks are from this parish."

"I know Mr. Larsen is not. He is an immigrant." Charles stood in front of the book and allowed the verger to turn the pages. "There," he said when he spotted the name Haverstock.

"Elijah Haverstock to Backy Adams."

"It matches the Haverstock family Bible," Charles said. "I thought the woman's first name might be wrong."

The verger licked his lips. "Not much information to go on. Just a date. Seventeen ninety-six. The actual wedding date was May sixth."

Charles stared at the crabbed handwriting until it swam into focus. "The groom's parents were John and Mary. Well, I don't think it matters. The young woman currently in possession of the Bible is a connection to Elijah, I believe."

"No listing for the parents of the bride."

"Frustrating. I need . . ." Charles did math in his head. "The seventeen seventies to see birth records."

"Let me take a look." The verger took a ring of keys from his belt and unlocked a narrow door next to the vestment rack, then picked up a lit candle and angled his way through the door.

Charles heard sneezing. Then a couple of minutes later, the man reappeared with a book that appeared to be freshly bound.

"Adams and Haverstock," the man said, leaning the book against another prayer-book stand.

As the verger pored over the pages, Charles flipped back a page in the book that held the wedding information, looking for other Haverstocks and also for Jaggers. He'd never heard the latter name before, though Haverstock was familiar enough, as a hill at least, possibly in St. Pancras. "That's unexpected," he muttered, finding a name two pages back.

"What is it?" the verger asked, his stomach growling again.

"I found a baptism for Backy Adams. Easter Sunday, that same year."

The verger looked up. "Then we won't be finding a record for her in this book. I found Elijah Haverstock, though."

"I wonder where she came from."

"Roman Catholic? Methodist?" the verger suggested.

"I rather think she was a Hebrew," Charles said. "I found a Jewish artifact in her possessions, along with a wedding ring."

"Not impossible, or even implausible," the verger said. "Perhaps Mr. Haverstock brought her to the faith."

Charles nodded. "A Jewish girl. I wonder if she knew Goldy, whom Osvald Larsen likely helped to kill some fifty years ago."

Chapter 13

The next morning Charles had just finished tying his necker-chief when he heard a knock on his door. "Fred, can you get that?" he called from the bedroom.

He heard the door open, then voices greeting his brother. Mary and Kate had come. He hoped Kate had reflected upon their financial conversation and remembered that she could trust him.

In the parlor, his gaze took in his fiancée, in white, with pink ribbons, and Mary, also in white, but with no adornments.

"We brought you fresh bannocks, Charles," Kate said briskly. She carried a small basket, but Mary had a larger one.

"What is that?" he asked, pointing to Mary. He couldn't bear to discover what was underlying Kate's briskness. "Hiding a litter of kittens?"

"No, it's clothing," Mary said. "We went through Miss Haver-stock's things with Mother last night and thought you could sell what we could not make into anything better."

Charles narrowed his eyes. A thrifty woman could make use out of any scrap of cloth. He suspected Kate was trying to help him save face with his financial situation. As if to point out his penniless state, his stomach rumbled.

"Sit and eat," Kate invited. "We can go to Middlesex Street before you go to your office. Mary and I can visit Father."

"Someone like you shouldn't even know the Petticoat Lane area," Charles said. "I don't want you in that place."

Kate tossed her head. "I know how expensive clothing is, and I know how many people have to resort to secondhand clothing, Charles. Perfectly respectable people frequent the stalls."

He sighed. Point noted.

"Hooray!" Fred cheered. "Breakfast? Anything is better than porridge."

Charles ignored Kate's glance of concern and dug into what the girls had brought. He didn't even taste the food as he considered how he would find coins for a hackney to take the girls into London.

While Fred reached for another bannock, Charles excused himself and ran upstairs. William answered the door.

"Can I borrow a few shillings until Friday?" he asked. "I have to take the Hogarths into London with me, and I didn't budget for a hackney."

"Make them walk," William suggested. "You're supposed to be saving for your marriage, not spending for their amusement."

"It's complicated," Charles explained, resentful. William didn't have to scrimp and save for Julie, not even during their engagement, because Julie had come with a dowry and a rich aunt.

William shook his head and reached into the vase just inside the front door, where he kept extra household funds. He pulled out a couple of half crowns and passed them over.

"Sorry," Charles said. "I'll pay you back on Friday. It's been an unusual week."

"Are you leaving now? I'll ride with you and pay the bill. Then you can save that money for the next emergency."

Charles nodded. "I'd be very grateful."

William leaned back in, yelled something to Julie, then came to the doorway with his satchel slung over his shoulder before following Charles down the stairs and into his rooms.

"My dear ladies," William said jovially. "I promised Charles I'd go into town with him today. I hope you don't mind."

"I'll go on ahead," Charles said as the Hogarths smiled at handsome William. "Find us that hackney." Irritated, he went outside and kicked at rocks while he walked toward the nearest hackney stand.

When they reached London, they headed for the Strand first, to drop William off, then went into East London, where the secondhand clothing stalls clustered. They'd get their best prices in the center of the trade.

Everyone in the area was in motion, carrying rough woven bags of clothing, poking at the finer garments strung up over the stalls, sitting at low benches and bickering over payments, their arms waving in the air. A fruit seller walked by, screeching her wares and prices, and a cart with milk and coffee moved slowly down the center of the street, narrowly missing a barefooted boy who ran across.

Charles helped the girls out of the hackney and assisted with the basket of clothing. Acutely uncomfortable, he suggested they check out the wares of the fruit seller first.

"Let's have this done with," Kate urged, taking his arm.

He realized her face had paled. His Kate was nervous. He reached for Mary, who held the basket, and pulled her under the canopy of old shirts and into the comparatively less dusty, less noisy, less filled underworld of the first clothing stall.

As Charles's eyes adjusted to the light, he saw a curious old man seated on a bench, sewing repairs to a frock coat. The tailor had a long, full beard, with white mixed in over red. He wore a tall top hat and had a long black coat buttoned over his clothing, despite the July warmth.

Against the wall of the residential building that served as one side of the stall, two women, one old and one young, worked on a fancy gown. Charles fancied that it had been reconstructed from two older gowns, as the bodice was a different colored fabric from the skirt.

Charles went up to the tailor. "Are you buying today? We have some fine dresses of an old style to sell."

"What is your name?" the man asked, setting down his needle.

"Charles Dickens. I purchased the clothing when a friend died." He winced, suddenly realizing for the first time that the money for Miss Haverstock's things had gone to the odious Mr. Ferazzi, who had no right to it. That money surely belonged to Miss Jaggers.

The man sighed heavily and rose. "Reuben Solomon's shop is an honest one. I will look at what you have to sell and will offer a good price if there is any value in your dresses." He gestured Mary forward.

She stumbled on a bolt of cheap black cloth as she approached him. Kate steadied her, and they clung to each other as the old-clothes man took the basket.

"No cause for worry, little ones. We Jews do not eat little girls, no matter what the stories say." He grinned suddenly, exposing yellowing teeth.

"Why don't you move into the fresh air?" Charles said to Kate. "Maybe you'll find some new ribbons in the stall."

She blinked at him, but Mary pulled her away.

Mr. Solomon nodded. "The bargaining, it isn't for the ladies."

Charles closed his eyes. "Just offer me a fair price, sir. I need to get to work."

"You resent selling these clothes?"

"I meant them to be a gift."

The old man chuckled. "A strange sort of gift. You dress like a young dandy, but you expect your women to wear the castoffs of a dead friend?"

Charles stiffened. "No. I thought they could use the fabric."

The old-clothes man pulled everything out of the basket and set it on an empty deal table. His long fingers twitched through the fabric, separating gowns. "Two twenty-year-old gowns of muslin, with an old-fashioned print," he muttered. "But for a larger woman. Suitable to be cut down. Plenty of fabric in good repair. Two sets of very old-fashioned stays. Not much value there. A short cloak, very much stained."

Charles glanced over his shoulder as the man considered the last dress.

"It's been dyed over as a mourning dress. I can always sell a black dress, I'm afraid," Mr. Solomon said. He lifted the dress to the light. "Not a bad dye job, and it's only about five years old. This is the most valuable piece."

Charles nodded. "What will you give me for them?"

The man named a price that seemed reasonable. Charles raised the bid by half a crown, just to see what would happen, but the man laughed.

"I won't take the stays off your hands if you bargain with me, Mr. Dickens. But you may have any ribbons your young lady chooses as a parting gift."

Charles stuck out his hand, and the man shook it. The man said something in a foreign tongue to the older of the two women. The woman set down the hem of the gown and unlocked the door to the building, then disappeared inside.

"She'll get the money," Mr. Solomon said.

"You are Hebrew?" Charles said.

The man nodded.

"I wonder if you are familiar with the first name Backy? A woman's name?"

"A diminutive of Rebecca, it would be," Mr. Solomon pronounced.

"Could the name Rebecca Adams be a Hebrew name?"

"Certainly. Adam is a Biblical name."

Charles nodded. After the evidence found in her clothing and the church registry, he could well believe that Miss Haverstock had started life as a Hebrew. "I see."

"Where did you see this name?"

"It was the original name of the woman who owned these clothes," Charles explained. "She called herself Miss Haverstock when I knew her, but it turns out she was married to a Mr. Haverstock and was a converted Anglican."

"A rather unusual lady, I expect," Mr. Solomon said.

"Perhaps. She was murdered," Charles confided. "I can't help but feel the reason is buried somewhere in her past."

"I never like to hear one of my people met a bad end," Mr. Solomon said. "I did not know this woman, but I will say a prayer for her."

Charles hesitated, but the old man didn't know Miss Haverstock. "Have you ever heard an old story about Goldy, a Jewish girl who drowned in the Thames after being pushed into the river in a barrel by some Christian children?"

The old clothes man stroked his beard for a moment. "No."

"I read it in a magazine, and then some mudlarks I know were familiar with the story, as well."

"I expect it is a real tale, then, rather than something from the parables of my own people."

Charles nodded. The woman reappeared from the building and handed Mr. Solomon the money. He set it, coin by coin, into Charles's hand, then handed him his basket.

After thanking the man, Charles pushed his way back through the hanging clothes. Mr. Solomon watched as he counted the four ribbons in Kate's hand, and then he nodded his approval. Charles took the ribbons from Kate and tucked them into the now empty basket.

"Let's take you both to your father," Charles said. "It is past time I arrive at my desk."

"Did you get a fair price, Charles?" Mary asked as they started down the street.

"I really wouldn't know," Charles said. "I'm not in the business of selling possessions."

"I'm sure Mr. Dickens did very well, Mary," Kate said in a reproving matter. "And how kind of him to purchase the ribbons."

Kate's approval of his financial dealings set his mind at rest. She had forgiven him for the drama with Mr. Nickerson.

That evening, he turned onto Selwood Terrace with a bottle of good wine and a wrapped meat pie, ready to make a feast of it and forget all his troubles. His tenuous peace, damaged first by his outing to Petticoat Lane and then by a hysterical office visit from a political candidate who felt like he'd been insulted in the *Chronicle*, was injured still further by the sounds of shrieking farther up the lane.

Unfortunately, he recognized that voice. As he reached the front door of his building, he saw Breese coming out.

"What is going on?" Breese asked. "Sounds like someone else is being murdered."

"I'm afraid something has happened at the smithy," Charles said. He handed Breese his food and wine. "Take this in, will you? I'd better check on Mrs. Jones."

Charles ventured down the dusty lane. He saw the astonishing sight of Addie Jones on her knees in the smithy yard, tearing at her bodice. Beddie darted around her in circles, too distressed to be still.

"Whatever has happened?" Charles called, moving into a loping run. He snatched up Beddie. The girl buried her head in his collar and went still.

"Mr. Jones is dead," Addie Jones cried, her face contorted with sorrow.

The child sniffled against Charles's neck.

"Your husband? Daniel? Something happened at Newgate?"

"No, Mr. Dickens. It's Mr. Edmund Jones, Daniel's father, who is dead."

Charles breathed in the sweet, dusty smell of the little girl. Her hair brushed against his cheek. "How? Where?" Had he been murdered, too?

"I found him bent over the anvil," Mrs. Jones cried. She took several deep breaths and spoke more calmly. "The heavy work was too much for him. His heart gave out, I think. Not a mark on him, poor man."

The hired boy appeared around the smithy. He must have washed his hands and face, since he looked cleaner than usual. "I'll get my mam," he said, coming toward them. "She'll help."

"That's a good idea," Charles said, grateful someone had a clear head.

"The body's still in the smithy. And it's very warm in there," the boy said.

Mrs. Jones moaned, her face going red.

Charles knew what he was trying to say, that the body would spoil quickly in the heat. "Where is the apprentice?"

"In there. He'll help you," the boy said, and then he trotted through the yard, toward the lane.

"Who will care for us now?" Mrs. Jones shrieked. "No men to protect us?"

Charles heard footsteps, then saw Hannah Jones, who was probably coming from her house. When she saw Mrs. Jones kneeling in the dust, she rushed toward them as fast as her bulky middle-aged body could handle.

"I'm so sorry," Charles said.

She shook her head repeatedly. "What has happened? What is wrong?"

Mrs. Jones lifted her hands to her aunt-in-law, as if offering herself for sacrifice. "It's Mr. Edmund, Hannah. He's gone to our good Lord." She broke into deep racking sobs as Hannah's lined face contorted.

"Where is he?" Hannah gasped.

"He's lying over the anvil." Mrs. Jones grabbed Hannah's arms. "Oh, don't go in there. It's awful."

"Please take Beddie inside," Charles said to Addie Jones.

The woman stared at him, wide eyed, then stood up, took Beddie from him, turned, and obediently trotted back into her house.

"Oh, Mr. Dickens," Hannah Jones whispered. "What will become of us now?"

"I don't know," Charles said honestly. "But first we need to see to your brother. Your hired boy has gone for his mother, and the apprentice can help us take the body into your house. Is your kitchen table cleared?"

"I was making a pie," she said hoarsely.

"Run back to your kitchen and clear it off," he said. "Scrub it clean, so the body can be laid out." He glanced around, knowing there must be a wheelbarrow somewhere. Edmund Jones was a big man, and he and the apprentice might not be able to manage him without the wheelbarrow.

Charles had no choice but to help in this situation. At least he could console himself with a glance at the body, to determine for himself if he thought the police should be called.

Charles entered his rooms wearily as the moon rose. He debated walking to the Hogarths to tell Kate about Edmund Jones's death, but he had to finish an article. He'd lost too many hours that day between Petticoat Lane and the latest death.

But he'd done what he had to do. He had helped lift Mr. Jones onto the kitchen table in his sister's house and had waited while he was partially undressed by his sister and the hired boy's mother. After that, he couldn't disagree with Addie Jones's conclusion. Indeed, there was no mark on the flesh or scent of poison or vomit. Just a heavy older man, worn out with work.

In his parlor, Charles lit the fire and put on the kettle. Fred came in from the bedroom. "I saved you half the pie. Well, at least I tried to. But Breese ate it and drank your half of the wine."

Charles shook his head. "Do we have anything to eat?"

"Just the bread we were going to toast for breakfast."

"I'll eat it now," Charles said. "And jam, if we have any."

Fred brought the bread and the jam jar, which had just a small smear left of strawberry at the bottom.

"This is poverty." Charles sighed, looking at the pitiful meal. "Don't we have any money?"

"Of course we do. I just meant this is how we would eat if we really had nothing. Anyway, I need to work. You can do sums at the other end of the table."

"I'll make tea first," Fred said, always eager to escape his mental labors.

A half hour went by. Charles lit a candle, devoured the bread, finished the jam, and drank two cups of scalding tea. Sweating, he opened the window and took off his coat, then finished writing a review and began to translate his shorthand notes about impropriety in a recent county election.

Nose deep in his notes, trying to discern what the vowel sounds might be in a confusing word, he didn't hear the knock. Fred rose, happily discarding his sums, and went to the door.

"Julie!" he cried happily after he flung open the door. "What brings you out so late?"

"I'd like to see your brother."

Charles set down his notes, almost glad to see her for once.

Julie didn't walk toward him with her usual bouncy step, though. She wore an apron over her striped silk dress from last winter, and her red hair had frizzed in a nimbus around her face. He hoped she didn't need to ask him to repay William's loan, but at least he had the clothing money now.

"Can I have a private word?" she asked uncertainly.

"Of course." Giving in to the rumbling in his belly, he turned to Fred. "Go over to the Royal Arms, would you? See if they have meat pies left, or anything really."

"Jellied eels? Pickled whelks?"

"Anything that hasn't gone off. Smell it first."

Fred saluted him, took the money Charles had pulled out of his pocket, and dashed out the door.

"Breese Gadfly ate my dinner," Charles explained. "And breakfast for dinner was not satisfactory."

"At least it's easy to get more," Julie said. "I'll cook you breakfast in the morning, if you like."

"William won't mind if you share his breakfast?"

"I'll cook your breakfast," she repeated. "Do you mind if I sleep on the sofa tonight?"

"Why? Do we have a ghost upstairs now?" he tried to joke, but his smile faded when she did nothing but shake her head violently. "What's wrong?"

"William is drunk."

"It happens. Is he sick?"

She shook her head again, her shoulders twitching.

"He hasn't a mean bone in his body," Charles said. "Surely he isn't . . ." He trailed off. He knew Julie had been hurt many times before, beaten by her mother as if she were a servant and not a daughter.

He didn't claim to understand, but after six months' knowledge of her, he could tell something was truly wrong, and better to keep her under this roof than send her to Lugoson House. "Very well. Fred would never forgive me if I turned you away."

Her gaze stayed down. "Thank you, Charles. I'm sorry to put you in this position, yet again."

"At least I know you aren't looking for work," he joked.

"Why do you look so tired?" she asked, looking up finally. "Haggard, almost."

He told her about the hard physical labor of moving Mr.

Jones's body. "I need to return to my work, but I'll keep the lamp close. Take a blanket from the bed and use the sofa as you will."

Charles woke the next morning to loud knocking on the door. Bleary eyed, he splashed water on his face and dressed quickly. The night before came back to him, the late dinner and drinking the ale Fred had brought. At least he'd finished his work. He merely needed to take it to Thomas Pillar at the *Chronicle* and move on to the next assignment. Resolutely, he pushed away all thoughts of Edmund Jones's staring eyes and the difficulty of moving the body. He ignored the pain in his biceps and back because of what remembrance they illuminated.

When he went into the parlor, he found the unholy trio of Kate, Mary, and Julie. Even Fred looked nervous, his gaze darting between them.

"Good morning, my dears," Charles said, heartiness projecting over his nerves. He kissed Kate on the cheek. "Very busy day ahead of me. If there is food to be had, I'll have a quick bite, but otherwise I am on my way into London."

"We arrived to make you breakfast," Kate said with an air of frost in her voice, "and found Julie already here. Doesn't she have a husband to cook for?"

Julie turned away, her mouth set. Fred drew her to Miss Haverstock's trunk, still against the wall, and she knelt with him and began to rummage through it.

"Don't trouble yourself," Charles said, a warning in his voice. He'd had about enough, between the money and the clothes and now Julie. Couldn't he do anything right? He needed to get back to work, where he was competent and well respected.

He caught motion out of the corner of his eye and managed to rescue his papers just before Mary slapped her basket down on the table. The look of alarm on her sweet face kept him from expressing his irritation.

"We brought bannocks and boiled eggs and things to make jam," she told him. "I know you were about out."

He smiled at her. *How thoughtful.* "I can eat quickly. And don't let Fred escape doing his sums again."

"Look," Julie said, holding up the silver dreidel. "I know how to play this game." She popped up, looking happier than she had since she arrived last night, and set the dreidel on the table. "Let's see. We need gelt."

She stuck her hand into Mary's basket and came up with a little stone container of currants. "Sit down," she told Mary and Fred, then poured out currants, counting out the tiny ruby globes for each of them.

Charles chuckled and reached into the basket for a bannock and an egg. He would eat while he walked and would find a cup of coffee at a stall somewhere along his way.

He tried to sidle out of his home, but Kate kept pace with him. "I was going to make fresh jam with those currants," she complained, standing by the door.

"Go easy on her. She's having some problems."

"Those should be managed behind her own doors, not yours, Charles. What if she asks you for money?"

Charles was uneasily reminded of his loan from William, quite the opposite situation. "She's the last person who would ever need to ask me." He walked into the hall outside his front door.

Kate followed him through the door. "What is she doing here? She's William's wife, not yours."

"Maybe he had to go out of town to a political meeting," Charles suggested. "Besides, we've hardly seen Julie in months. This tragedy with Little Ollie has her flustered."

Kate made a sour noise in the back of her throat. Charles was reminded that her father had once demanded he avoid Julie if he wanted Kate. But that was months ago, before Julie wed and he and Kate became engaged. "I don't like her being here. It's compromising," she said.

"Have you no charity in your heart, Kate?" he asked. "She's wayward—I'm the first to admit it—but Fred loves her, and she has a good heart under that lack of polish."

Kate's mouth screwed into a tight pink bud. "You won't have any fresh jam today, with the currants eaten."

"I understand," he said. "Tomorrow will do."

Chapter 14

Charles feigned shock when he saw William at his desk at the *Chronicle*'s offices. No scent of hair of the dog, no damp towel over his face.

"I thought you were still abed," he told William.

William set down his quill. "No. I was out all night."

"Drinking?"

William frowned at him. "No. I was out all night because Ned Blood has been captured."

"How wonderful," Charles exclaimed. "Any sign of Larsen?"

"Sadly, no. I understand you think he's the culprit, but hopefully, Ned Blood's story will lead the police to the other man."

"I hope we have news soon." Charles sat at his desk, then, turmoil clogging his thoughts, turned his chair around, ignoring the short stack of notes indicating his newest assignments. "Meanwhile, your wife spent the night on my sofa."

William picked up his teacup. "Was she frightened that I wasn't there? I'm sorry to hear that, but it's not the first time I've had to be out working."

Where was William's guilt at his misbehavior? "She said you were drunk and indicated that she was frightened."

William shook his head, looking confused. "Julie lied about my drinking. I wasn't even home."

Charles stared hard at his friend. He had to admit no sign of Julie's claims was evident on William's face. "She must have decided in the moment that it was the quickest way to persuade me to have her stay."

"She does tend to find the easiest ways," William agreed. "Julie has too much imagination."

"And not enough outlet for it, now that she's no longer an actress." Really, she manipulated more than anything, but he didn't want to disparage his friend's wife.

"I'm sorry you had to be involved in her little drama." William took a look at his own slips of paper. He pocketed a couple of them and handed a third to Charles. "Could you attend the Court of Common Council this afternoon for me if I'm not back in time?"

"Where are you going?"

William's usually charming expression set into a thin line. "Chelsea, to have a chat with my wife."

"I'm sorry I was the bearer of bad news," Charles said with sincerity. "I don't wish to cause problems."

William's face didn't change. "My wife cannot tell my friends lies about me. It could affect my friendships, my employment, my prospects."

Charles nodded. "You are correct, of course. Kate and I have misunderstandings at times."

"They are quite a bit younger than we are," William said.

"I know." Charles sighed. "We can rise out of chaos, and must, so that we can provide for our families."

Charles worked excessively late in order to do both his work and part of William's. He read through all the notes that came for William, but nothing about Ned Blood appeared. He stayed in Holborn to maximize his sleep hours and was back at the *Chronicle*'s offices shortly after dawn to continue. By the time his pay envelope was delivered in midafternoon, he'd put in a full day's work and then some.

"I'm going to go over to the prison and see if I can learn anything about Ned Blood, then head to Chelsea," he told William, who had come in at the usual hour. "And deal with Reggie Nickerson."

"Are you going to pay the new, inflated rent?"

"I don't have any choice, despite my bravado. I searched but found no sign of the rental agreement."

"You don't lose paperwork," William said stoutly. "Nickerson must have stolen and altered it. I am sorry, Charles. Do you have enough money?"

Charles nodded and reached into his pocket. "I forgot to give you this back." He placed the money he had borrowed next to William's hand. "I hate thieves."

William pocketed the coins. "Me too. But the murder is more important than Nickerson's petty thievery."

Charles sighed. "It could be connected."

He walked over to Coldbath Fields and tried to see the governor but could get only as close as the drunken servant.

"Is Ned Blood in your custody?" he asked after the servant said the governor couldn't see him. He wasn't even allowed into the office.

"Yes, but he has to go in front of the magistrate," the man said, breathing heavy gin fumes at Charles. His coat caught on a ragged brick in the wall.

"What will happen?"

He tugged at his sleeve, loosening a few strands of thread. "I don't know the law."

"What about the murder?" Charles demanded. "Did he admit to it? Did he claim Mr. Jones helped him?"

"'Ow would I know?" the servant groused. "Write a letter to the governor."

"I want to see him," Charles demanded. "I know you can get me in."

The man bared a mouthful of jagged yellow teeth and held out his hand. Charles gave him what spare coins he felt he could afford from his pay. They were very few, but it seemed sufficient. The man walked him to a turnkey, who took him to a block of cells that seemed to be used for more temporary prisoners. Though dank, they did not have the lived-in scent of human despair.

"You 'ave five minutes," the turnkey said. "What good it will do you, I cannot say. Second from the end."

Charles walked down to the cell and stared through the bars at the feral creature inside. Did he lay his gaze upon a killer or a common villain? Blood had lost the facial hair, as Kate had feared, though the fleshy lips remained. "I want to talk to you, Mr. Blood," Charles said, as if he were trying to catch the attention of a reluctant Member of Parliament.

The man glanced up. Charles recoiled. One side of Blood's forehead was a deep, oozing wound.

"God's teeth, man, what did it take to capture you?" Charles went to a water barrel and dipped his handkerchief in, then pushed it through the bars. "Clean off the blood, at least."

The man, dull eyed, did as he asked. Had he suffered a brain injury?

"I don't have much time," Charles said. "Did you kill a woman at Selwood Terrace?"

Blood spat into the dirt. Charles saw the reddish color and went back to the water barrel. Cursing the necessity of it, he dipped in his hat and managed to fill it with water. He carried the hat back, then lifted it above his head. The prisoner came up to the bars, and Charles tilted his hat so water flowed down Blood's face. He drank and coughed while crusted dirt and other things ran down his face.

"They offer no kindness here," Charles observed.

"We're animals to 'em," Blood rasped. "And I got no answers fer you."

"They'll hang you for a murderer," Charles warned. "I just want the truth. You were seen."

"My aunt lives o'er there. She took me in. I went to her 'ouse to 'ide and never left it until they found me."

"Not at Selwood Terrace?"

His voice stayed low and guttural, the intonation of a man who functioned in back alleys. "No. Near Arthur Street."

"Did you know Miss Haverstock?"

"Never 'eard of 'er." He shook his head. "More water?"

Charles went to dip his hat in the barrel again, then poured more water over the man's head. "Tell me about Osvald Larsen," he said when the hat was empty.

"Met 'im 'ere. 'E 'ad friends, money. It were 'is escape. Just needed me for certain, well . . ."

"You were part of the plan, but not the originator?"

Blood nodded, then winced and put his hand to his head.

"How did you get your manacles off?"

"Used a rock."

"In a smithy?"

Blood's left eye moved in its socket, while the right eye remained fixed on Charles. "Under a bridge."

The turnkey reappeared before Charles could truly process this bit of intelligence. Larsen had been the man at the Jones Smithy.

Charles looked at his soaked hat, sighed, and filled it again. Trying not to spill it, he pushed the sodden mess through the bars. "Maybe it has some value for you."

Charles followed the turnkey out, disgusted by the state of

the prisoner but not surprised by his answers. He had to find Osvald Larsen, but for now, he needed to deal with his rent.

An hour later, he walked into Mr. Ferazzi's office in a crumbling building on Paradise Walk that had once been a brewery. He could smell the stench coming off the Thames from here, just a couple of blocks south of the office.

"If it isn't Mr. Dickens!" exclaimed Reggie Nickerson, rising from his stool. He'd been scratching away at a ledger placed on his slanted desk. Another man faced away from them. Charles assumed the closed door in the far wall led to Mr. Ferazzi's personal chambers. "Aren't you in a sorry state of affairs."

"It's rent day," Charles said, ignoring the gibe about the state of his wardrobe.

"It is, it is," Mr. Nickerson said, rubbing his ink-stained fingers together. "But I do my rounds, sir, first in the morning, and then in the evening, as you know. I'd have reached your door eventually."

Charles grunted. "You and I both know that my rental agreement has been stolen."

"I don't know as how I can agree to that," the rent collector said, losing his smile.

"You know what my rent was, sir. I know what my neighbors pay, and it is impossible that my rent is higher than Mr. Gadfly's, whose rooms are much nicer than my own."

"What are you proposing?"

"I'll pay back rent to match his, and pay the same going forward, and that's an end to the extortion." Charles could afford that and still leave enough money for food for the week.

"That's not what you have due." Mr. Nickerson flipped through his book. He shook his head sorrowfully and turned back, his hand over the page.

Charles's natural grace aided him as he snatched the heavy book from under the rent collector's arm and looked at the page himself. "And here is the proof," he chortled. "My page, all crossed out and repenciled. Aha, sir, why does Mr. Ferazzi choose to torment me? Or is this your doing?"

Mr. Nickerson grabbed for the book, but Charles held it away. "I have no patience, sir. I will take this to the police."

"I can't change your rent without Mr. Ferazzi's approval." Mr. Nickerson reached for the book again.

"Who is pocketing the extra money? You or him?" Charles demanded.

The man's eyes narrowed. "It's not extra money."

Charles shook his head. "I have other rooms, ones that Mr. Ferazzi does not control. I can surrender Selwood Terrace in an hour's time."

"But what about your parents? Your siblings? Can they do the same?" Mr. Nickerson asked. "Do you know your father is behind in his rent again?"

"He is ill, and foolish with his funds," Charles cried. "Repair my agreement, and I will do my best to pay you what is due on his rent."

Mr. Nickerson's mouth twisted. "I will take your deal and rewrite the page."

Charles knew Mr. Nickerson understood exactly how far he could be pushed. He was, after all, a man of business.

Charles returned the ledger to Mr. Nickerson.

Mr. Nickerson scratched away furiously for a moment, then took out a fresh sheet of paper and wrote a new rental agreement and handed it to Charles.

Charles pulled out his money, one coin at a time, and slowly built a pile of currency. "A receipt, please, for all of it, with a notation that says, 'Paid in full through the eleventh of July.'"

Mr. Nickerson shook his head, then wrote out a new sheet, and Charles took it from him. Then the man wrote out yet another sheet and handed it to Charles with a nasty smirk.

What fresh hell was this? Charles read the paper and grimaced. "An eviction notice for my father?" Charles wanted to spit in the man's eye.

"What are you going to do about it?"

The other man turned from his desk. Charles recognized him as one of the thugs from Bloomsbury. He must box in his free time, for his neck was thick with muscle.

Charles stared at the amount that Mr. Nickerson had listed as still being owed. If his father was evicted, what would it do to his sisters' courtships? The families of their suitors might talk them out of wedding the daughters of such a man.

Throat so constricted with rage that he couldn't speak, he pulled the rest of his pay envelope from his pocket and handed it over.

"This isn't everything," Mr. Nickerson said calmly.

"But it helps," Charles said. "I want a receipt, and I want you to tear up this eviction notice."

"We will revisit this next week," the rent collector warned.

"I'm sure we will," Charles said wearily. "But I had better never hear about thefts in my neighborhood again. This is a far better racket for you than stealing."

Reggie Nickerson merely sneered and went back to his book.

When all the paperwork was transacted, Charles walked out of the building in a daze. How could all his money be gone again? When he found himself in front of his building, he went to Breese Gadfly's door instead of his own.

Breese opened it and exclaimed, "What's this? Are you ill?"

"An ache in my head," Charles said. "What do we have to do to finish that song? I could use the money you thought we could earn."

"Let's take a look," Breese said with a look of sympathy. "Come in. That was a fun evening, until the disaster with your young friend."

"Yes," Charles agreed as he went in. "At least Little Ollie's stump is healing well, but he lost his hand."

"Poor mite. Will he starve?"

"We will do what we can, but leaving the river is beyond these children's imagination."

Breese rustled through the music at his piano. "Pour yourself a drink and we'll get to work. Ah, here it is."

Charles sat next to him and recreated that night they had worked together on the song. When Breese found the paper with their melody, Charles sang the verse they had so far from memory. "In the sunlight, oh, my sweetheart, when your glove lays soft on my arm. I can think of your kisses when we know it's strawberry time."

"That's it," Breese agreed.

"It needed to be funny, if we can make it so," Charles said. "So next verse. It's a duet, right?"

"Sure," Breese agreed, pouring himself a tot of gin.

"In the moonlight, oh, my darling, I feel your hair brush my cheek. It reminds me of my puppy when he curls against me to sleep."

Breese laughed. "Oh, no. Here it comes."

Charles grinned at him, feeling better, and they developed the song from there over the next couple of hours, with the female singing about lovemaking and the man singing of things much more prosaic.

"We'll have the audience in hysterics," Breese pronounced. He rolled up the sheets. "I'll make a copy in the morning, when the light is good, and take this to my friend. I'm sure to receive payment right away."

"That would be good, or we won't eat this week," Charles said.

"The rent extortion stands?"

"More or less," Charles said, not wanting to explain about his father.

"I'll get you the money tomorrow," Breese promised. "I don't think it will be a problem."

Charles stood and stretched. "Thank you. I had better check on my brother, and I need to write a note to my parents."

"Will you be around tomorrow evening?"

"I can't afford to be anywhere else," Charles said frankly.

"Very well." They shook hands. "Until tomorrow."

Charles went across the hall and entered his rooms. Fred wasn't there. Maybe he'd gone to see their parents for dinner, since the larder was bare here.

All of a sudden, he remembered something important about Fred. *Botheration!*

How had he forgotten his brother's birthday? Of course Fred had gone to Bloomsbury. He hadn't wanted to be alone on his natal day.

Charles dashed for the door, wrenched it open and, despite his sore feet, went down to the street, hoping to hitch a ride with someone to Bloomsbury. He cursed himself all the way to the main street, then calmed himself enough to beg his way onto the back of a wagon heading to a dairy part of the way back into town.

The sun had almost vanished by the time the brothers returned to their rooms, the remaining light casting a pink glow across the horizon. Thankfully, his sisters had both made presents for Fred. They'd made a pet of him, with a fine new waistcoat from Fanny and a shirt from Letitia. His younger brothers had contributed a pint of early cherries, which Fred had exclaimed over, declaring they were his favorite. Charles had had only promises to offer, but at least his father had ordered a hackney for them, being concerned about having Fred on the streets after dark, as there were rumors of an extra-vicious cutpurse on the streets of Bloomsbury that week. He hadn't had the heart to admonish his father for the expense none of them could manage. At this rate he'd be borrowing from William again.

A knock came on his door shortly after he'd set himself down to do some writing. Fred had just gone to bed, sweaty and flushed with the heat and excitement of his birthday. With a sigh, Charles went to answer the door, frustrated that he hadn't even written a page yet or taken off his shoes.

Julie stood in the darkened passage, holding up a bowl. "A peace offering."

Charles's stomach growled, preventing him from shutting the door in his friend's wife's face. He turned away, thinking he would light a fire, but then decided against it. The illumination would be nice, but not the heat, and besides, coal cost money.

She followed him in, then set the bowl on the deal table in front of the fireplace. "I'm still not a very good cook, but I can make stew."

Charles sat down in front of it. He couldn't really identify any specific components of the dish, but it smelled fine, so he picked up the spoon she'd stuck in the middle of the steaming glop and took a bite.

She sat down at Fred's usual spot at the head of the table. "Do you want a glass of wine?"

"Don't have any."

"I'll make you a cup of tea."

"Don't want the fire lit."

She poured what was left in the water jug into a tin cup and set it at Charles's elbow. "I'll just go fill this for you."

"I'll get it, Julie. Where are you claiming William to be now?"

She licked her lips. "He's with the police. They are combing through the room where Ned Blood was staying. I had a letter from him."

He laughed. "So you've decided to tell the truth?"

"I didn't think you'd let me stay last night just because William was working," she said.

"So you lied to me about my friend?" Charles snatched up the cup and drank the scant inch of tepid liquid that had been left in the water jug. "You led me to believe he would scare you? Hurt you?"

"I'm sorry. I'm honestly surprised you ever believe anything I say."

"Don't worry. I won't make that mistake again." He finished the stew, which had been, after all, a rather small portion, and pushed away the bowl.

"Kate was very upset with me for using her currants for the dreidel," Julie ventured. "I'm no threat to her. You like a girl with a bit of polish," she said, some bitterness in her voice.

"You're my friend's wife."

"Yes, I am, and you must know that I'll never be a threat. Kate ought to know that, too, after all these months."

"Think before you act, before you tell lies." Charles stood up. "Now, if you don't mind, I've had a very trying day, and I need to spend a couple of hours on my work before I can sleep."

"You ate all the stew." She stood and picked up the bowl, looking at it with stupefied pleasure.

"William will let you know tomorrow evening if I survived eating it," Charles snapped.

Julie kept staring at the bowl.

Charles felt ashamed of himself. "Thank you, Julie. It was kind to bring me dinner. I'm sorry William is gone from home so frequently."

"It was a mistake to come to Chelsea for the summer," she said. "It's nice to be near my family, but I feel like I've lost my William. He has such a long walk to work."

"It hasn't been a great few weeks for me, either," Charles admitted. "Maybe we are Londoners at heart."

She nodded. "I think you are right. On a day like today, summer seems endless, but autumn will arrive soon enough, and we'll go back to our regular lives."

He forced a smile. "Good night, Julie."

"Happy writing." She reached for the empty jug and grinned slyly at him. "I will fill this for you. You'll need it to wash out your mouth if you become ill from my stew."

Chapter 15

⤭

The next morning he and Fred walked over to see Addie Jones and find out how she was getting on. It had been three days since old Edmund Jones had been found over his anvil.

When they knocked at the door, it took a couple of minutes for Mrs. Jones to answer.

"Mr. Dickens," she exclaimed, quickly wiping her water-beaded hands on her apron. Her eyes were rimmed with red, and Beddie clung to her skirt.

Fred showed the child a wooden ball he had carved. "Come and play with me," he invited.

Mrs. Jones stroked the top of the girl's head with work-roughened fingers. "Go along and play with young Fred in the yard."

The girl followed Fred past Charles, wide eyed. With a nervous glance inside, Mrs. Jones shut the door of her house and stepped into the yard, too.

Charles frowned. This wasn't like the usually hospitable Mrs. Jones. He and Kate had stopped in for tea more than once on their neighborhood walks. "I hope I don't make you nervous."

"No, no." She clutched his sleeve. "It's that terrible man, Mr. Bung."

"Mr. Bung?" Charles asked. He'd never heard the name before.

Dust flurried around Mrs. Jones's shoes as she swayed. "The broker's man. I could manage to stay calm when the coroner came to view Mr. Jones's body to make sure he died by natural means. I cried only a few tears when my husband was taken. I didn't want to make things worse for him. But this." She choked on her words. "Oh, Mr. Dickens."

He patted her arm. "Why is a broker's man here?"

"A distress has been levied. It must have been set in motion as soon as my husband was arrested."

"You have debts," Charles said, familiar with the process. The broker would value and take everything if the family couldn't pay what they owed.

"Yes, Mr. Dickens. Just the usual sort of things. But we've had my husband gone from the forge for two weeks. We've lost all that business, and then men won't pay their debt to us, since there's no one to intimidate them. You understand."

"I do," Charles said. "I take it you don't own this property?"

"No."

"Does Mr. Ferazzi own it?" Charles asked, thinking of his own misery.

"I don't know, but this isn't about the property. They are here to take everything. My pots, our clothes, our furniture. Hannah and me, we can't raise the money."

"I wish I could help, but I've run afoul of my evil landlord and don't even have money for food today," Charles admitted.

She, in turn, patted his hand. "I at least have that. Come in for some bread and cheese."

He shook his head. "Thank you, but I believe I will get a bit from cowriting a song later today. I am glad I spoke to you. This gives me an idea for one of my sketches."

"We always have loved reading them," Mrs. Jones confessed. "On Sundays my Daniel would read them out loud while I sewed and Beddie played with her dolly. Will I ever have him home again?"

He was pleased to have some news. "One of the escaped convicts, Ned Blood, has been captured."

She smiled tentatively. "If his confession doesn't save my Daniel, maybe it will at least lead to the other criminal being re-captured."

"I spoke to him. It must have been Larsen who came here, not Blood."

She sighed. "I keep praying. Why don't you leave Fred here? I'll feed him a meal, and he can play with Beddie while I keep an eye on that broker's man. I can't trust him to value our goods properly. Maybe I can save something."

Charles agreed. "I'll keep an ear out. Surely, when Osvald Larsen is caught, your husband will be released."

She pulled out a handkerchief and dotted streaming eyes. "Thank you, Mr. Dickens."

He turned away after she went back into her little house, and took Fred aside to explain the plan. Fred didn't argue, happy to hear he had a meal coming, so Charles went back to their rooms and picked up his pen.

He wrote across the top of the page, "The Broker's Man," then refilled his quill and bent to work, pouring out his sorrow but neatly switching the tale to be from Mr. Bung's point of view, instead of his victim's.

He didn't stop writing until someone knocked at his door. Breese looked at him strangely when he opened it.

"What?" Charles asked, stretching.

"You have ink all down your cheek," Breese said.

"I've been working hard," Charles explained. "Thanks for telling me. I'll clean it off."

Breese's lips curved. "Are you well?"

"I feel like I've let the Jones family down, but I'm not a Bow Street Runner."

"You work hard, Charles," Breese said. "But you're a slinger of words, not a coroner." He reached into his pocket, pulled out coins, and handed them to Charles.

"What's this?"

"Your half of the money. I told you I'd sell the song."

Charles counted out the coins, delighted by the sum. "Anytime you want a rhyming companion, please let me know. Thanks to this, we can eat well until next payday."

"Very good," Breese said. "I'm off for a long inspirational walk. Then I have an actor to visit." He winked lewdly.

"Have fun. You've earned it," Charles said. He closed the door after Breese and leaned against it, remembering uneasily Miss Jaggers's words about the songwriter. Surely Breese meant to say he was going to visit an actress?

All day long, he'd waited to hear if William returned home, but he'd never heard footsteps on the stairs.

Charles walked to the police station in hopes of speaking with Constable Blight. The sergeant sitting behind the front desk told him that Constable Blight wasn't there. The sergeant gave him a blank stare when he tried to ask questions.

"Will you tell me where to find the coroner Sir Silas Laurie?" he asked.

The sergeant directed him to Sloane Square, where Sir Silas had his London residence. He owned an imposing redbrick terrace house on the less fashionable end of the eighteenth-century square.

A footman opened the door when Charles arrived at Sir Silas's residence. Charles gave him his card, and the man directed him into a long, narrow sitting room with a loudly patterned carpet, ornate wallpapered walls, and a painted ceiling. The effect dizzied Charles, who clutched at the fireplace mantel for support after nearly stumbling over the painted stone legs of the fireplace. A mirror over the fireplace warred with the mirror across the room, sending images back and forth. Charles gave up on the fireplace and went to sit on a spindly settee in the corner.

A few minutes later a maid came in and lit lamps; then Sir Silas arrived, dressed for an evening society affair in a black tailcoat over fawn trousers. His man stood behind him, a cape over his arm.

"Mr. Dickens," Sir Silas said, brushing black hair off his brow. He'd started a narrow beard along his jawline since Charles had seen him last, but Charles's keen eyes saw an angry red scratch along his cheek, and he thought it too tender to shave. "I remember you from the Haverstock inquest. Is that what this is about?"

"Ned Blood has been arrested, and I saw him, but he does not seem to have been near the Joneses' smithy. I have a theory—"

"I'm aware that you are a newspaperman, Mr. Dickens, but kindly save your theories." The creases around Sir Silas's mouth deepened. "I deal in facts."

"Very well," Charles said, keeping his temper contained. "Has Osvald Larsen been captured, as well?"

"No, but that is a high priority. I'm about ready to pay a Bow Street Runner myself to add to the men looking for Larsen."

Charles crossed his arms as if that could contain the words that wanted to flow from his lips. This must mean that Sir Silas had the same theory that he did. "Can you tell me what has been determined about Ned Blood?"

Sir Silas chuckled grimly as he went to his fireplace and leaned against the cold stone. His man sighed and walked out of sight, back into the passage. "The police now admit that Blood isn't Miss Haverstock's killer, after all."

A muscle jumped in Charles's thigh. "What did they learn during questioning?"

"He'd spent the night in a 'cigar shop,' and a dozen people are willing to testify, even some who are known to be honest."

Charles pressed the spasming muscle. "'Cigar shop' being a euphemism, I take it. He told me he was hiding at his aunt's house near Arthur Street."

"She owns the building," Sir Silas said. "Apparently, he'd celebrated his escape with a cousin of his. They shared a quartet of ladies for the evening, but of course, there were other men about, too."

"I see." Charles, elated, forgot about his aching muscle. He'd been right. Larsen had been Miss Haverstock's killer.

"It's a neighborhood brothel, so easy enough for even the Chelsea police to discern who was there that night."

"Given that Daniel Jones is a devoted family man, and you must now realize that Larsen was the murderer, could you not release Mr. Jones? His father just died, and a broker's man has moved in with Daniel Jones's wife. They are in a sad way."

Sir Silas snorted. "Do you know that Osvald Larsen was a blacksmith? I suspect Mr. Jones was his friend."

"On what evidence?" Charles demanded.

"We know that one of the men's manacles was removed at the Joneses' smithy. I understand you found another set, which is all well and good, but it doesn't absolve Mr. Jones in any way."

"Why not pin the crime on Edmund Jones, then, Mr. Daniel Jones's father? He is closer in age to Larsen."

"I saw the man at the inquest. A cripple."

"He still had power. He did work at the forge sometimes. Please let Daniel Jones go free before his family is utterly ruined."

Sir Silas stroked his beard. "I am not the police, and they have him."

Charles had left his hat on Sir Silas's settee. His hands went into his unruly hair, even thicker and wavier than Sir Silas's mop. "I am quite desperate to help the Jones family before it is too late."

"A fine charitable impulse," Sir Silas exclaimed. "So help them, but not by trying to free Mr. Jones. It is quite out of the question. What will you do next?"

"What do you care?"

"Maybe you will save me the price of a Runner." Sir Silas picked up a miniature portrait from his mantelpiece and ran his finger over the tiny child's face. "Since you are doing the investigative work."

"I've spoken to Miss Evelina Jaggers," Charles said. "I have not yet spoken to the lad who accompanied her, Prince Moss. He's another one who knew Miss Haverstock. She seems to have been from the Limehouse area, and I can also place Osvald Larsen there as a child, but what can I accomplish? I'm certain now he killed her. Does it matter why?"

Sir Silas snorted. "Of course it matters. Assuming he's still alive at the end of this manhunt, he'll need to go to trial. There will be a case, and it's not just a matter of putting him at the scene of the murder. We want a reason for it, too."

"It's something to do with a wedding," Charles said. "She was murdered in an old wedding dress. But Larsen is documented well enough. He's not the Haverstock that the former Backy Adams married."

Sir Silas frowned. "So Miss Haverstock was really a married woman?"

"A widow," Charles said. "She was a converted Hebrew. Miss Jaggers had a family Bible, and I've been to the church where Miss Haverstock was baptized and married."

Sir Silas gave him an amused smile. "A childhood friendship gone wrong?"

"Very possibly."

Sir Silas tapped his fingers on the mantel. "Keep interviewing people who knew the victim. You may find a connection yet. It will help the court, if not Mr. Jones."

"That is my only reason for continuing with my research," Charles explained.

The coroner's brow creased. "Don't you want the murderer hanged? The victim was your friend."

"Miss Haverstock is dead. The Jones family is feeling the pain of their victimhood now. They could lose everything."

"You still must persist, in the hope that it can somehow help them," Sir Silas said. He clapped his hands together. "Now, I have an engagement, Mr. Dickens. I wish you the best of luck."

Charles followed him out of the room and back into the entryway. The valet settled the cloak over Sir Silas's shoulders.

"The carriage is outside, my lord," the footman intoned.

Charles realized that Sir Silas was actually a baronet, rather than just a knight. He must have a hereditary title. That explained the house, probably built by his grandfather.

Not that Charles cared. These rich people could not possibly understand how close to disaster a family like the Joneses could be. He followed the coroner to the street and refused the offer of a ride. The streets called to him on this fine night. He needed to think.

He left Sloane Square and walked through the heart of privilege in Belgravia, then along to the parks around Buckingham Palace. Feeling hungry, and grateful that he had some coin again, he paid for a dish of shellfish and some ginger beer. More than an hour later, as the sun began to descend in the sky, he found himself at the former site of the Eleanor Cross, which then became the hanging ground for the executioners of Charles I and now sported a decaying statue of that long dead king.

The bareheaded king sat on a fine Flemish horse. Some of his equipage was missing now, stolen a quarter century ago, but the king still looked on peaceably enough. No hint of the man's mortally foolish obstinacy showed in his calm features. His inability to bend had cost him his life.

Charles stared up at his namesake, wondering what his own faults had cost him. They would cost him Kate soon if he continued to allow Julie Aga and his father to run roughshod over his life. He had to stop defending her to his fiancée, and he had to have a large enough income to fend off his father's woes. Even if his impulse to spend was different from his father's, with him giving in to charitable needs rather than to endless bottles of wine, he still found himself with empty pockets rather than full ones.

He needed to be smarter, too, to guard his valuables from thieves like Reggie Nickerson. It had cost him dearly to lose his rental agreement. He must remember to be more careful, more diligent. Somehow, he needed to work harder and sleep less. The best daylight of the year had just passed, and he needed to rise with the sun each morning and go to his work, write more articles, more sketches, more songs. More letters, too, as he needed to build more useful friendships, seize more opportunities.

If Charles I had been friendly instead of quarrelsome, he might have lived. He'd had a difficult childhood, an unpopular marriage, and religious beliefs that did not mix well with the times. Success was built with mainstream beliefs, the support of others, a good wife.

"You are a lesson of what not to do," Charles called up to the statue, imagining his words bouncing off the brass.

He turned away and started the long walk home, making mental lists of whom to see, whom to write to, ideas for sketches. If world domination could be enacted on thought alone, he'd surely be king of England himself by the end of the night.

The next morning, he woke Fred, instead of the other way around. He found a note in the parlor that William had pushed under his door in response to his own note tucked under the Agas' door during the night. It contained Prince Moss's address. He and Fred went to Bloomsbury for church and a meal with the entire Dickens family. Charles saw his sisters, Fanny and Letitia, with their beaus, happy to see that his improvident father hadn't ruined the relationships, not yet at least.

As soon as their roast and summer vegetable meal had been eaten, Charles excused himself to follow up on the address he'd received.

Prince Moss lived near Miss Jaggers in a crumbling old house alongside a market garden. Charles banged on the front door. His knock seemed to shake the entire listing wooden structure. Instead of anyone opening the door, a window opened on the first story. Bits of debris rained down on Charles's head, part of the structure holding the window into the wall, no doubt. He blinked something out of his eye as an old woman shrieked at him.

"Is Mr. Moss home?" Charles shouted.

"Wot's that?" the woman asked, holding a gnarled hand to her ear.

"Prince Moss," Charles yelled. He heard a window open in the next old house, as his loud voice had disrupted the neighborhood.

Her face contorted as her mouth opened, displaying the remains of a couple of rotted teeth. " 'E's in the garden."

"Thank you."

"Wot's that?" she cried, putting her hand to her ear again.

Charles waved to her and turned away. The garden, a large plot that perhaps the inmates of the house farmed as tenants to a great lord, started behind an outhouse that smelled so badly that Charles had to pinch his nostrils shut with his fingers.

Grateful to reach the garden with its more agreeable odors, he walked down bare dirt paths between plantings. Beans were trellised on one side, blocking the view of the road. On his other side sprawled a vast bed of cucumbers.

A carrot suddenly sounded like the most delicious treat in the world to him. His fingers itched to pull one up by its curly top when he saw them over the cucumber vines. Then he spotted a youth bent over lettuces in the distance.

Prince Moss had not been well dressed at the inquest, but now he looked like a farmer. He wore thick boots, trousers and a waistcoat of cloth that could have been used to bag potatoes, and a dusty neckerchief. Had the dainty Evelina Jaggers of Eaton Mews ever seen her swain like this? Charles doubted it.

"Mr. Moss," he called, heading toward the lettuces.

The youth straightened, then stretched his back with his fists pressed against his kidneys. "Yes?"

"I'm Charles Dickens. I was Miss Haverstock's downstairs neighbor."

Prince Moss pushed his straw hat back out of his eyes, then reached down and picked up a stone jug half-filled with water. He spoke after wiping his mouth with his hand. "I remember seeing you at the inquest."

"I'm following up with everyone who seemed to be involved, because Daniel Jones is still in Newgate."

"That's the blacksmith who was arrested?"

"Yes, and a gentler soul you never met."

Prince Moss set down his jug. "If he helped the killer escape prison, it hardly matters."

Charles wiped sweat from his eyes. "I don't think there is any need to assume he did. Osvald Larsen was a blacksmith and could have removed the manacles himself after breaking into the smithy for tools. I don't know if you heard that there were two escaped convicts."

The youth shrugged. "It's no problem of mine."

"It's a great injustice to the Jones family," Charles insisted. "They are losing everything."

Prince Moss spit in the dirt. "Are they locals?"

"I believe so. Why?" Charles had the sense that most of his attention was outside of this conversation.

The lad squinted at the horizon. "She had a hatred of foreigners and always thought one would get her in the end."

Chapter 16

⁂

Charles tilted his hat to hide his eyes from the sun. Heat seemed to rise from the earth, and he wished he had his own stone jug. "Why?"

"I don't know, Mr. Dickens," Prince Moss said without looking at him. "Miss Jaggers took me to tea with her foster mother a few times, but I never really spoke to her myself. I might have been able to say if something was stolen from her sitting room, having been there a few times, but solving her murder is beyond me."

Charles could not help but think the lad hid something. Would praising him help to loosen his tongue? "You have the air of an educated young man, despite these humble surroundings. You must have some suggestion to make."

Prince Moss smiled for the first time, still staring at his boots. "I'm interested in improving crops. It's a passion of mine. I'd rather spend my time in a garden than in a counting-house, save up to buy land of my own."

Frustrated, Charles shifted the conversation in the right direction. "Does Miss Jaggers share your passion?"

"She's as ornamental as any rose." He picked up his jug again. "As long as the dirt is gone from under my fingernails when I go to see her, she doesn't mind."

Charles nodded. "Did Miss Haverstock speak specifically about any enemies?"

"Of course not. She was a retiring old woman."

Charles's gaze followed a trail of moisture as the lad drank. "Did she and Miss Jaggers have a good relationship?"

"The best." Prince Moss set down his jug again. "Only love between them."

Charles, finding that hard to believe when one was such a coldly beautiful young lady, pressed on. "And you? You were a suitable friend in Miss Haverstock's eyes?"

"She never expressed any concern. I can assure you that neither Miss Jaggers nor myself had any part of her death."

"I suppose Miss Jaggers has sufficient funds from her parents' estate?"

Prince Moss finally met his gaze. "She is in no need."

"Thank you." Charles turned away before the young man spoke again.

"Were either of the escaped convicts foreigners?"

Charles glanced back. "Yes. Larsen, the blacksmith."

Prince Moss picked up his hoe. "It will be him who did it, then. Will the police find him?"

"They found Ned Blood," Charles said. "So there's hope." He saluted the boy and waded back into the carrot patch, then the cucumber patch, thinking it wasn't a bad way to live, in the summer at least.

As the heat of the afternoon began to fade a bit, he drifted toward the Hogarth home. He hadn't seen Kate for a couple of days, and they needed to speak.

Mary opened the front door when he knocked. Her face looked flushed, like she'd been working hard.

"Are you well?" Charles asked.

"I was just chasing the twins," Mary explained. "They were trying to pull baby apples from the trees in the orchard."

"Ah," Charles said. "The little ones don't have labors to rest from on the Sabbath."

"Indeed not. Kate is in the kitchen. I'll get her." Mary started to shut the door, then opened it again with a grin. "Come in, Charles."

"I'll wait out here," he said. "It's pleasant."

She shut the door completely, and he went to sit in one of the chairs the family had placed in the front garden, a sweetly relaxing place. He tilted his hat over his eyes and closed them, wondering if he could wring another sketch about parish life out of an incident he'd witnessed at church this morning between a very old woman and her young grandson, an impoverished curate.

"Charles?"

He blinked, then sat up straight when he realized Kate stood in front of him, dreamy eyed, in a short-sleeved blue dress and a lacy shawl.

"I'm sorry, my darling. I must have nodded off there for a minute," he said.

She held a glass of lemonade out to him. "You should drink this. Your face is damp with sweat."

He wiped it with a handkerchief, then took the glass and downed the contents in one long gulp. "Thank you. That was perfect."

"Did you want something?" Her voice had a tenuous quality. "I've put up some more strawberry jam with the last of the harvest."

"I always love your jam. I thought we could take a walk," he suggested. "It is Sunday afternoon."

"Yes. Mother said I could, as long as I'm home for dinner. The little ones have been crazed today."

"It's the heat," Charles said, rising. He set his glass on the seat and offered her his arm, glad that she had not refused him.

She smiled and took it. They walked down the path toward her front gate, then headed down the dusty street.

"Look," Kate said. "The cemetery gate is open."

Charles glanced at the entrance to the Jewish burial ground. Kate was right. "It's very peaceful," he said.

"Can we walk there? I'd like to see inside."

He nodded. "Just be ready to leave if we're caught. The rabbi doesn't like interlopers."

She put a finger to her lips and smiled.

They walked through the gate and down the main lane. Kate's head swiveled back and forth as, wide eyed, she took in the exotic gravestones. Charles saw that the remaining leaves from last fall had returned to dust in the heat. Now the parts of the burial ground that weren't grassed over were gray with leafy remains.

Kate stopped under a tree's shadow and let out a long sigh. "It's lovely here."

Charles smiled at her, then leaned against the tree. After a moment, he took her hand between his. "Kate?"

"Yes, Charles?"

"I'm sorry if it ever seems like I am choosing Julie Aga over you. That is never, ever the case. I'm so grateful for your maturity and gentle good sense."

"She has a way of rattling your nerves," Kate said.

"She knows how to bend me to her will, for short periods, at any rate."

"How?"

"I believe she knows how to tug at my heartstrings. And she's not beyond lying or stealing."

"It's unfortunate that Mr. Aga married her. I think you will not be able to stay friendly with him forever."

He didn't expect to stay a newspaperman forever. "Perhaps not."

"Mrs. Aga has a very uncertain temperament, and she will create problems for him, probably in his professional life, as well."

Charles didn't want to speculate, so he changed the subject. "I am a very good reporter, one of the best."

She nodded enthusiastically, also happy to move away from an uncomfortable subject. "So Father says, and Mr. Black, as well, when he comes for dinner. They are full of praise for you as the most accurate taker of shorthand in the business."

Charles puffed up a bit. "That is good for us. But I won't be a reporter forever. I'm out of town too often. You won't want that when we are married."

"Do you have a plan?"

"I want to do two things. One is refocus on the law. The other is keep building relationships with like-minded men and see where that takes me. After all, I would not be at the *Chronicle* if not for my uncle."

She used the toe of her boot to scratch a *C* in the dirt, then a *K* next to it. "Do you have time to read the law?"

He added a heart between the two initials. "Not right now, certainly. But after we are married. I know your father went from the law to journalism, but that was in Edinburgh, not here. And I was a law clerk once upon a time."

She grinned at his heart. "You are a very good writer, Charles. Your sketches are so funny. You shouldn't give them up."

"Thank you. It turns out I can cowrite quite a good song, as well. That has saved my finances this week."

"Did you sort out your problem with the rent?"

"The agreement was stolen," Charles explained. "I would never have lost such a document, but it is no longer in my possession. I believe Mr. Nickerson searched my rooms when they were clearing out Miss Haverstock's space, and then took advantage of the situation."

"So now what?"

"I lost a fair amount of coin due to irregularities with my father's rent. But I proved to my satisfaction that I did not owe any money on my own rent."

"Oh, Charles." She blew out a breath, then picked up a stick and started to inscribe his last name under their initials. "I'm sorry."

He stared at a pair of stones with matching engravings. A married couple, perhaps? They were weathering together for eternity. "I have a responsibility for my siblings and mother. I'm sorry that this will put our wedding back a bit. It won't be Christmas, I'm afraid."

She focused on her stick writing. "Because you have to pay your father's debts?"

He touched her arm. "I'm sorry, darling, so sorry. I wanted to see more of you, so I took on the expense of these extra rooms for the summer, but it seems it's brought us little but grief."

She hid her face from him. "You work much too hard."

"I have to, as you have seen," Charles said. "It's all for our future. I'll be more careful now with my charitable impulses, and I'll make sure you come first. It won't be so much longer. Just a few months. I'll be able to save fast once I am back in Furnival's Inn."

"I know you will, Charles." She forced a smile, but her lips trembled. "But it is hard to wait to be your wife."

Her emotion pleased him. He didn't want to wait any longer than she did. "I know. Engagements aren't supposed to last so long."

She dropped her stick and buried her face in the crook of his shoulder. He put his arms around her, loosely, just in case the rabbi came upon them. But when she let her soft cheek drift up his jaw, he couldn't help but turn so that his mouth met hers.

Her lips parted, and he took her mouth in a kiss unlike any they had ever experienced together before. He tasted the gingersnaps on her breath and felt the hard pearls of her teeth against his tongue. *Heaven.*

An amused voice broke their reverie.

"Have you lost your mind?"

Kate broke away from him, her lips swollen and reddened. Charles could feel his heart pounding, and his arms ached to hold her again.

"Breese," he panted, catching sight of his neighbor, dressed like a summer dandy, complete with new straw hat and silver-tipped walking stick.

Breese lowered his voice. "I just saw the rabbi. He'll be here in a minute. You'd better leave, unless you plan to convert to Judaism."

Charles kicked leaves over their scribblings and grabbed Kate's arm. "Let's go."

She broke into a trot alongside him. The azure ribbons that were meant to tie her straw hat around her chin fluttered around her neck and shoulders. By the time they reached the gate and stepped back onto the road, they were both giggling madly.

Charles stopped and pulled her alongside the outer wall of the burying ground. "You're so lovely with your cheeks all flushed."

She stopped giggling and stared at him, then put her hands to her cheeks. "Oh, Charles, be careful with your money. I don't want to wait much longer to be yours."

He stared into her eyes, feeling like he was falling into the ocean. "Neither do I, Kate. Believe me, I am most sincere."

She swallowed. "What should we do now?"

"Will you come to see Miss Jaggers with me? I saw Mr. Moss this morning, and I want to follow up on what he said about Miss Haverstock's hatred of foreigners."

Her gaze lost a little of its romantic haze. "You think she hated Mr. Larsen?"

He tapped the elongated tip of her nose. "I do. If I can take some history between them to the police, it might help Mr. Jones. He wasn't a foreigner."

She nodded. "Where does Miss Jaggers live?"

"It's a walk. We'll stop at a cart and have some refreshment. Your parents know you are with me."

"Yes. Let's go. I need to settle my nerves."

He grinned at her. Oh, how he understood that feeling.

They strolled toward Eaton Square, stopping for lemonade at a cart where young children played in the street, next to their dusty parents. Not much of a day of rest for these people. Charles shared a glass with Kate so they wouldn't arrive at Eaten Mews with a parching thirst, but he didn't give pennies to the children like he might have if his finances were in better order.

When they arrived at the house, in honor of the day's warmth, the retired nanny's little maid took Charles and Kate to the back garden of the house where Miss Jaggers lodged.

Miss Jaggers sat in a chair in the center of the small lawn. The young lady wore white yet again and made such a picture she could have been posing for an artist. Gauzy fabric flowed around her limbs when she rose languidly to greet them.

"Mr. Dickens again," she sighed in obvious irritation. "And this is?"

"Miss Catherine Hogarth, my fiancée," Charles said, defensively putting his hand on Kate's arm. "You would have seen her at the inquest."

She held out her hand to Kate. "Yes. You also discovered Miss Haverstock."

"I am so very sorry for your loss, Miss Jaggers," Kate said with ardent simplicity.

"Please, have a seat." Miss Jaggers had been prepared for company. She gestured to a quartet of ironwork chairs on a stone flag terrace just behind the house. They surrounded a matching table. Glasses circled a sweating pitcher filled with something thick and purple. "Would you like to try my lassi?"

"What is it?" Charles asked, intrigued. He pulled out a seat for Kate, then for Miss Jaggers. Kate and Charles sat.

"An Indian drink from my childhood. Very refreshing. Made here with berries instead of mango."

"I'd love to try it," Kate said as Charles nodded.

Miss Jaggers lifted her elegant arm in a bird's swoop and poured the creamy stuff into two glasses, then filled her own. She perched on the edge of her chair.

Charles took a sip, then closed his eyes in ecstasy. "I am very tired of lemonade. This is an excellent alternative."

Miss Jaggers smiled with her mouth, her eyes narrowed as she watched Kate take a sip.

"How delicious," Kate exclaimed. "My, what an unusual beverage. Charles said you'd come from India."

"Yes, for my education." Miss Jaggers regarded Kate over her cup rim with suspicion. Charles had the sudden notion that she wasn't a girl who liked other girls.

"I spoke to Prince Moss," Charles said. "He seems an admirable young man."

"He has goals for himself," Miss Jaggers opined.

Unusual ones, for the swain of a lady like Miss Jaggers. Their conversation had boiled down to little but this. "He said that Miss Haverstock hated immigrants and expected to meet her death from one someday."

Miss Jaggers set down her glass. "She grew up in quite a rough neighborhood. I think she had trouble with the other children."

"Tormented for her religion?" Charles suggested.

"Tormented by her religion, more like," Miss Jaggers sniffed.

"What do you mean?" Kate asked as Charles's brows rose.

Miss Jagger's perfect chin went up. "I know rather a lot about my foster mother, things I haven't revealed, because they didn't seem relevant. But if you say this escaped convict may have been someone she knew long ago, maybe I was wrong to keep her history to myself."

"Please, do explain," Charles urged.

Miss Jaggers spread her fingers over the ends of her armrests. "Miss Haverstock married her husband in order to escape an arranged marriage with a fellow Hebrew."

"Surely you can't convert on a whim," Kate said.

"She studied with a curate during the period of her engagement to a foreign-born Jewish man. As you probably know, the Hebrew people have vast networks across nations, formed by blood. They all seem to be related much more closely than Christians. When she was able, she converted to Christianity out of disgust with her family."

"I wonder if Osvald Larsen is a Hebrew," Kate said. "Surely they must know at the prison."

Charles had read over the prison documents at Coldbath Fields. He closed his eyes, attempting to remember his review of the material. Seconds ticked by, punctuated by the clinking of glasses, birdcalls, rustling grass. Disappointment filled his thoughts when he remembered the relevant information. "No, he's not a Hebrew, on the paperwork at least." He opened his eyes again.

Kate frowned. "The wedding was obviously a pivotal issue in Miss Haverstock's life. Who would she have worn that dress for now?"

Charles suggested, "The man she jilted?"

"Not Larsen," Kate pointed out. "Not Blood?"

Charles said, "No, he isn't Hebrew, either, and too young besides."

Miss Jaggers rubbed her upper lip. "So neither of them killed her?"

Charles ran his tongue over his teeth. "Perhaps not. The convicts may be a dead end. We need to dig deeply into her past.

Miss Hogarth urged me to do this some time ago, and I was set on the convicts being responsible."

"I don't know any of the names," Miss Jaggers said, sounding plaintive for the first time. "I'm related to her husband, remember."

"It's time to find the Adams family," Kate said soberly.

Charles rose. "We should leave Miss Jaggers to her garden. Unless you know any Hebrews in Limehouse?"

Miss Jaggers's delicate eyebrows arched. "I don't know anyone in Limehouse at all."

"The Haverstocks were from Limehouse," Charles reminded her.

She waved an elegant hand as Kate rose. "Not in my generation."

Charles inclined his head. "Thank you for that taste of India."

"Yes. It was delightful," Kate said.

Charles steered Kate around the side of the house, where a freshly painted wooden gate let them back onto the street.

"We know one other Jewish person," Kate said. "Maybe he can help us figure out where to go next."

"Who?" His thoughts went to Breese, but Kate surprised him.

"Reuben Solomon, the old-clothes man. You seemed fascinated by him that day we sold the clothing." Kate took his arm. She seemed exhausted by the heat and clung to him.

He pulled her down the street. "We wouldn't be able to see him today."

"No, we'll have to go there in the morning, on your way in to work again."

"Do we have anything to sell him?" Charles said, not wanting to face the penetrating gaze of Mr. Solomon again. "Otherwise we are wasting his time."

"We could sell him the dreidel charm, perhaps."

"You don't want it?"

"I'm not sure I want anything of Miss Haverstock's, to be honest." She shuddered. "Murder. I find it a fascinating puzzle, and I can lean on my faith to get through someone dying, but the way she looked when we found her . . . Oh, Charles. She's someone we took tea with."

He squeezed her hand against his body, thinking how far off from death it seemed here, in this neat mews behind a great square, on a dusty, sleepy Sunday afternoon. "Forget, Kate. It's all we can do."

She nodded. "I'll bring you something to eat in the morning, and we'll go into London to sell the charm."

Charles calculated the expense of the hackney into London. Kate would never be willing to walk that distance. It would cut drastically into his food budget for the week. He and Fred would have to eat trotters and eels instead of meat pies. But it was all in the service of Mrs. Jones and her poor family. Still, how long would he have to wait to make Kate his own?

Chapter 17

❧

The next morning, he and Kate alighted from an unusually clean hackney on the corner of Middlesex Street.

Sunday's peace was broken by the cacophony of Monday. Wagons rattled in the street, the horses plodding along, raising clouds of dust, which caused people to cough and hack. Street sellers hawked their breakfast wares, rolls and fruit, ham sandwiches and coffee. People tore at the clothes hanging on the stalls, and doors slammed against brick, then closed again as people came in and out of the buildings behind the stalls.

They ducked under a procession of men's tailcoats hanging on a clothesline and found Reuben Solomon at his same bench, with the familiar women against the wall of the building, hiding in the shade.

Mr. Solomon wore a frock coat instead of his previous long black coat and was counting buttons into a wooden box. They waited until he had finished muttering Hebrew numbers and had set down his handful of buttons before they spoke.

"Back again?" he asked when they greeted him, his dark eyes raking over Charles.

Charles straightened, then gestured to Kate, who held out the dreidel on its chain. She had repaired the clasp.

Mr. Solomon's expression softened as he took it from her. "Very nice. A bat mitzvah gift, perhaps."

"It belonged to my friend who died. I purchased it," Charles explained.

Mr. Solomon let the dreidel dance in front of his eyes. "You don't want to keep it as a keepsake?"

Kate shuddered. "It was in the room where she died, for days with the body."

Mr. Solomon shook his head sadly. "She was not buried within a day of her death?"

Charles shook his head. "She was murdered, and besides, she had converted to Christianity. Jewish rituals might have been inappropriate."

Mr. Solomon raised his bushy eyebrows. "Then perhaps this token no longer meant anything to her."

Charles pulled the old wedding ring from his pocket. "We have this, as well."

"I am not the right person to sell these items to," Mr. Solomon said, handing the charm back to him. "I deal only in clothing."

"Ah, I apologize," Charles said, placing the ring back in his pocket.

"Can we ask you a question?" Kate asked. "Before we go?"

The corners of Mr. Solomon's eyes crinkled. "What is it, child?"

"How can we find any Hebrews called Adams?"

He rubbed his beard. "Do you have any idea where she came from? Check with the burial grounds there."

Charles waited but the old clothes man offered nothing more. "Thank you for your time, Mr. Solomon."

"I can recommend Mr. Levy, the pawnbroker, for your jewelry," Mr. Solomon added. "Near the docks in Limehouse."

"That's where Backy Adams came from, Limehouse. She

converted to marry someone other than the man her family had chosen." Kate nodded as Charles expounded.

The old man glanced through the hanging clothes at clouds moving across the blue sky. "My family has lived in London for a hundred years, but people who come from other places have sometimes endured the most terrible things. This girl who ran away from her family may have had a good reason to do so."

"She did end up a murder victim," Kate said soberly.

Mr. Solomon nodded. "Beware. You could find yourselves on a deadly path yourselves."

"We cannot quit," Charles said. "A good man's life is at stake. I must find out what happened so that we can free him from Newgate."

"An admirable quest," Mr. Solomon said. "But this lovely creature at your side will miss you if you become a desperate man's next victim."

Kate frowned at the old man. "He will be careful."

The old man spoke to one of the women against the wall. She walked back into the building. "This woman who died, what sort of person was she?"

"Very retiring," Charles said. "She saw her neighbors, the blacksmith's family down the lane, and her foster daughter. I had lived there only a few weeks before her death, but I saw no one else."

"Then the danger is very close, Mr. Dickens," the old man said. "You know the person who killed her. There are not many to choose from."

"But the wedding dress," Kate said. "It's important."

"Perhaps," said the man.

"It's not so simple," Charles explained. "There are escaped convicts, and manacles were found nearby."

The old man coughed. "You believe, therefore, that a man escaped prison and somehow got word to this retiring woman, and she dressed in her old wedding gown to greet him, and then he killed her?"

"Yes," Charles said after a pause. "Or at least, I did."

Kate nodded.

The old man's lips curved. "*Oy vey*, what a tangle."

"We should go," Charles said. "I need to be at work."

Mr. Solomon inclined his head. "Then I will pray your quest is successful."

They walked out from behind the clothesline. Everything was brighter and busier on the other side.

"I am frustrated by old men," Charles muttered.

"I agree that was frustrating," Kate said, trailing alongside Charles as he walked toward the *Chronicle*'s offices. "We have a perfectly good theory, and he thought it was silly."

"I feel like yelling at someone," Charles said.

"Who?"

"I have a good candidate. I want to give Mr. Ferazzi a piece of my mind. His Mr. Nickerson threatened my family's lodging in that other building. I'm not happy that we've all been targeted, and I want Mr. Ferazzi to know what is going on. I do not want to take on the additional expense of helping my family move."

"No, that would delay our wedding even more. Have they found a new tenant for the rooms above you?" Kate asked.

"No. Maybe that is at the heart of his thieving from me."

"Maybe Mr. Nickerson is acting on his own," Kate said with grisly relish. "After you tell Mr. Ferazzi what happened, a constable will discover the rent-taker's body in the Thames."

"I just want to ensure that my mother and siblings will not end up on the streets." Charles coughed as carriage wheels raised a cloud of dust just in front of him. "It is going to be a busy week."

Charles, still with a head of steam, planned to go to Mr. Ferazzi's office after he was done at the *Chronicle* for the day. Unfortunately, he had left no money with Fred and couldn't leave his brother hungry.

He sidetracked to the Apple Tree, a pub on Fulham Road, and downed a bowl of stew, then asked to borrow the bowl and have it refilled with stew to take to his brother. He was waiting for the refill when he saw Mr. Ferazzi himself enter, accompanied by two men similar to him in age and clothing. His gaze narrowed as he considered how to approach the landlord and his hands clenched. Time to release some frustration.

"Mr. Ferazzi," Charles said in a confident tone, walking up to him.

The landlord looked down his long razor of a nose at him. "Yes?"

"Charles Dickens, with the *Chronicle*," he said, each word measured. "I would like to speak to you about your employee Mr. Nickerson's extortion and threats."

"Go along, gentlemen, and I'll be with you momentarily," Mr. Ferazzi said to his companions. Their gazes drifted over Charles as they walked past him and went up the stairs to the second level. "Now, what is this about?"

"I'm your tenant at Selwood Terrace."

"Ah," he said dismissively. "You'd have to speak to Mr. Nickerson. I'm not that involved."

"You are involved enough to be involved in cleaning out rooms," Charles reminded him.

"I am a busy man," Mr. Ferazzi said impatiently. "If you think Mr. Nickerson has committed a crime, please speak to the authorities."

"He's your employee and follows you like a dog," Charles snapped. "Did you order Mr. Nickerson to steal my rental agreement or commit the robberies at Selwood Terrace before the murder? Did you order the murder?"

"You belong in Bedlam, sir." Mr. Ferazzi sniffed. "I shall call the authorities on you. After all, as you have told me, I know where you live."

"Did you know Miss Haverstock?" Charles demanded. The

two men at the table alongside him got up and left the pub. "Did you rob her, the way I was robbed? Did she try to stop you?"

"I don't know any of my tenants personally," he snapped. "I'm not a killer."

"Does murder happen often in your properties?" Charles asked, attempting a quieter tone, before one of the other customers called for a constable.

The landlord fingered his mustache. "I have owned property for twenty years, Mr. Dickens. Everything that can happen has happened."

"Can I quote you on that, sir?" Remembering the power of the press, Charles pulled a piece of paper from his pocket.

"I'll have your position, sir, and your rooms. I can terminate your rental."

"The same tactic as your employee uses," Charles growled. "You are a criminal, sir, and I will have justice."

Ferazzi looked over his head. "If I see one constable at my chambers, I will send my men to evict you, your family, and all your friends. If you'll excuse me." He moved toward the steps.

"Who killed Miss Haverstock?" Charles yelled at his back.

Mr. Ferazzi remained cool, no hint of a reaction in his body language as he went to the stairs.

Just then, the barmaid walked into the dining room with Charles's second bowl of stew, a clean cloth laid over it. She had not heard the fight, but the man behind the bar gave him a long hard stare.

"Thank you," Charles said, taking the bowl. He had to feed his family, rather than his ire. He'd had no satisfaction from the man, only threats. What would it take to prove Nickerson or Ferazzi or both were stealing from tenants? "I'll bring the bowl back."

He walked back to Selwood Terrace, careful not to spill his bowl of stew, his thoughts churning unproductively. Miss Haverstock didn't die in the commission of a robbery. Her home had been full of her personal belongings when he and Kate had entered. Why had he thrown her death into his attack on the landlord? He'd just made things worse.

Breese, arriving from the opposite direction, met him in front of their door.

"How kind," he exclaimed with a twinkle in his eye. "To bring me dinner."

"It's Fred's," Charles explained. "But I'll buy you a libation if you help me with something."

"Of course." Breese patted his stomach.

The front door opened. Fred stood in the doorway, his hands on his hips. "My belly is touching my backbone, Charles."

Charles handed him the bowl. "Here you go. Take the bowl back to the Apple Tree when you are done."

"This isn't going to be enough," Fred complained as he took it.

Charles fished in his pocket and gave him a few coins. His brother snatched them and went back inside their rooms.

"Tight on funds?" Breese asked.

"That song saved me," Charles admitted.

"Buy me a drink and we'll work on another song," Breese offered.

"Of course," Charles agreed. "I need to distract myself and coins are hard to come by."

"What is troubling you?"

"I had a confrontation with our landlord, but it got me nowhere."

"You are at their mercy if you don't protect yourself," Breese suggested.

Charles rubbed his temples. "You are right. I need to let it go until I have secured more funds."

The songwriter waited.

Charles forced his thoughts along another path. He still needed to solve the murder. Daniel Jones must be his top priority, not a crooked rent-taker. "I had a question for you. Do you know where the Hebrews who live in Limehouse might be buried?"

"I'm familiar with the cemetery at Brady Street," Breese said thoughtfully. "Would that do?"

"I don't know. I've learned that Miss Haverstock was originally Backy Adams. I want to find someone who knew her as a child and might have some insight into Osvald Larsen, who I believe knew her." Whether or not he was the murderer. How many fiancés might Miss Haverstock had had when she was young?

"Then why do you want to look at graves?"

"I thought I might find some likely names. I asked a Jewish old-clothes man in Petticoat Lane, but he didn't know anyone named Adams. I'm sure you're right. It is a silly idea."

"It's actually not terrible," Breese said. "Some of those stones have where people lived, the names of those that erected them, that sort of thing. It just seems that there must be a different way."

"She isolated herself from her former life, yet it seems that is what killed her," Charles said.

"It's a pleasant night," Breese said. "Why not walk over there? It's always quiet in a burial ground, and we had luck working in one before."

"I have paper and a pencil," Charles said.

"So do I." They set off together.

When they reached the main street leading into London, they had the luck to happen onto an omnibus and soon found themselves heading into Whitechapel. More walking, but eventually they arrived outside the leafy walled environment of the Brady Street burial ground.

The spiked iron gate wasn't locked, so they were able to step right in. Charles saw a vast cluster of gravestones of many different types, from short little stubs of stone to large monuments. "It looks rather full."

"I believe we want to avoid the south side. That has the oldest graves, and we want ones from when?"

"The last fifty years," Charles said. "If we could find her parents maybe or siblings?"

"Very well. Looking for Adams." Breese wandered through the uneven clusters of graves, muttering snatches of poetry as he went.

Charles stopped at a vault. A number of stones had been placed on top of the stone surface. "What's this?" he asked.

"The stones are a gesture of respect in the Jewish community," Breese said. He walked around the vault. "Ah, here's the inscription. This vault holds a rabbi."

"I left a stone for you, but you weren't buried there," Charles intoned.

"They staked you at the crossroad, but your heart is where?" Breese added with a chuckle. "Sounds like a very bad murder story that a street seller would have on hand. I prefer songs I can sell to the theaters." He walked down a row of graves on the opposite side of the rabbi's memorial.

"Fair enough," Charles said.

"Here we are," Breese called. "One Thomas Adams, of Limehouse. Died eighteen twelve."

Charles walked around the rabbi's vault and perambulated through the area Breese had found. "Here's another. Next to Hurwitz. This is Dr. Abram Adams, died eighteen twenty-two."

"Was her father a doctor?"

"I have no idea," Charles said. "She's a mystery. Let's keep looking."

Breese walked down the row. "Adams again, a Simon this time. Just died three years ago."

"I find it hard to believe that these wouldn't be her relatives. What other names are mixed in?"

"Levy, Hart." Breese's voice became harder to hear as he walked farther down the row. "Abraham, Moss—"

"Wait. What was that last one?"

"Moss. Susan Moss. Died five years ago." Breese looked up from the gravestone.

Charles lifted a finger emphatically. "We know a Moss—Prince Moss. Miss Jaggers's friend. She is a relative of Miss Haverstock's late husband. What do you want to bet that Prince Moss is a relative of hers?" Although the boy had claimed he didn't know Miss Haverstock well. He knew the youth had hid something.

"Have you asked him about Larsen?" Breese asked, crouching down to pick up a pebble.

"Yes. He assumed Larsen was the killer, because I told him that the man was a foreigner, but he didn't volunteer anything else."

"It's almost as if the young people in her life don't care that she was murdered," Breese suggested. "Which sends me down the path of another murder ballad. No more graveyards for a while. Take me to a public house, and let's enjoy some drunken men singing songs. That will put us in the right mood."

"I apologize, Breese, but I don't want to waste another minute of Daniel Jones's life. Can you go see young Moss with me first?"

"As long as you give over to me after that." Breese dropped the pebble on Susan Moss's grave and walked back to him.

"Of course, my friend." Charles followed him as he wound his way out of the cemetery.

When they reached the crumbling house, where Prince Moss lived Charles bypassed it, shielding his eyes with his hat from the slowly lowering sun. He suspected Prince Moss was in his beloved field still, since farmers didn't like to waste light.

"Is that him?" Breese asked. He looked unfavorably at the edge of the field. "My city shoes are going to be even dustier."

"Turn that into a song," Charles suggested. As Breese muttered rhyme schemes at his back, Charles stepped into the field.

Prince Moss indeed had decided to use what sun remained.

He had gloves on and was dropping weeds into a bucket as Charles approached him.

"You again, Mr. Dickens?" Prince Moss asked, shading his eyes with his hand as he glanced up.

"I felt like you had more to offer," Charles said. "Are you related to a Susan Moss who died five years ago?"

"My mother," the youth said. "Why?"

"I'm guessing you are related to the former Backy Adams?"

Prince Moss chuckled, his nostrils flaring with each hard laugh. "You figured it out. She was my mother's cousin. But I really did not know her well. And I had nothing to do with her death."

"What am I missing?" Charles asked, relieved to have solved one mystery. "I have her firmly placed in Limehouse, along with Larsen, who I assume was a Jew hater, given his treatment of the little girl Goldy in the article I read."

"She wasn't some poor girl," Moss said. "Her father was a doctor, a very old-fashioned sort of man."

They had found Dr. Abram Adams's grave. "Hence the arranged marriage."

"Yes. But Cousin Backy left her family to marry a man of business who had a very wealthy client. He speculated on banks and canals and had an uncanny way of getting his money out before things failed."

"Who was the arranged marriage with?"

"I don't know," he said with disinterest.

"Think," Charles insisted.

Really," Prince Moss exclaimed. "It was before I was born. I'm only nineteen."

Charles's jaw didn't want to form the words. "Then we will continue. Miss Haverstock was wealthy?"

Prince Moss sighed. "There is a warehouse full of property that Cousin Backy said was Miss Jaggers's dowry."

"Just portable property? Why did she live in two rented rooms? Why didn't she admit to having been married?"

"I told you she was afraid of foreigners."

"You think she was in hiding?"

Prince Moss shrugged. "She was eccentric. You knew her. She obviously had a reason to be afraid, given what happened. Not too many quiet widows are murdered."

"No," Charles agreed. "What else are you not telling me?"

"She deserves to have her privacy respected. What does any of this have to do with saving your Mr. Jones?" the youth demanded.

"I'm trying to understand her connection to Osvald Larsen," Charles explained. "Believe me, I'm confused myself, but someone put a magazine under my door, revealing a story about a long ago murder Larsen was involved in. Since Larsen is an immigrant, he isn't going to have much of a trail. Was he of the Jewish faith? Was he after her fortune? Did he know the Jones family?"

Prince Moss shrugged. "I need to finish my weeding before the sun goes down."

"Where is this warehouse?" Charles demanded. What if Ferrari or Nickerson had learned about her goods? They were greedy enough to rob the dead. Maybe the murder did revolve around an attempted robbery after all. They could have ignored the modest goods of her chambers for the richer pickings of the warehouse.

The youth stared at a tendril of weed sticking to his coarse trousers. "Down at the lower end of King's Road. There are warehouses between there and the wharfs."

"Can you be more specific?" Charles asked.

The lad gritted his teeth. "Milman's Street. The end of there, along the river."

"Did Miss Jaggers have the contents of this warehouse under her control before Miss Haverstock died?"

Prince Moss shook his head. "No. But she's just seventeen. She isn't ready to marry, yet. If anything goes missing, I'll hold you to blame."

"I'm hoping to protect Miss Jaggers's property from our greedy landlord," Charles snapped. "I'm not the criminal here. Come with me if you like."

The youth glanced between him and Breese. "Not tonight. I mean, it won't be safe. It's too close to the river. How about in the morning?"

"I have to work," Charles said. "Why don't you check on it in the morning? I will attempt to interest the police as soon as I am free tomorrow."

The boy nodded. "I'll do what I can."

Charles went to a political meeting the next morning and wrote up his notes in a jolting coach on the way back to Chelsea, trying to save time. He jumped off the coach at the inn nearest to the police station, then turned up his collar against an unexpected summer rainfall.

The sergeant on duty laughed when he asked for Constable Blight. "Blight's just brought in a drunk. Sick all over him. A dandy like yourself won't appreciate the smell."

Blight walked into the lobby just then, his clothing wet with stains. "Mr. Dickens, what is it now?"

Charles cataloged the dark circles under the man's eyes. Either he had a new baby or the police were working him to death. His hair hadn't fallen out from stress, though. The coarse dark locks twisted every which way as they sprawled out from his hat.

"Do you have time to go to a warehouse down by the river with me?" Charles asked.

The constable folded his arms across his chest. "Why?"

"It belonged to Miss Haverstock. I'm concerned about the safety of the contents."

"What's in it?"

"Goods meant for Miss Jaggers. Dowry items, supposedly."

The constable's eyes narrowed. "You're hoping robbery was a motive for her death?"

"It is a good motive. We know there were robberies in the neighborhood before the murder," Charles explained.

"Why don't you let Sir Silas handle this? You're just a reporter."

"The police have custody of Ned Blood and Daniel Jones. Sir Silas can't fully investigate the case as a result."

Constable Blight sighed and turned to the sergeant. "Do I need to get back to my beat, or will you allow this? He won't be able to get in without me."

"I'd be happy to never see the likes of him again." The sergeant stuck a tattered cigar into the side of his mouth. "Let this be the last time I see your face, Mr. Dickens."

Charles nodded, feigning sincerity.

The constable gestured toward the door. "After you."

Charles walked out, calling behind him. "Rough day?"

"The rain will help." The constable reached him and scratched his broad nose, as if rubbing his nostrils might make them smaller. "Or I can pour a bucket over myself from a trough. In this weather my clothes will dry, or they would if it stops raining."

"Messy business, your line of work."

The constable nodded. "It's a hard life, being with the police, but better than the army. My grandfather died fighting Napoleon, and my father spent years in India."

"I like London too much to go far," Charles said. "I have to travel for work, but never for more than a few days."

"I don't have your learning," Constable Blight admitted. "But I do enjoy reading the *Chronicle*. There's usually a copy or two lying about the station by the end of the day that I can take to the pub while I eat my dinner."

They discussed the newspaper, stopping just once at a hackney stand, and with the waterman's permission, the constable had poured a bucket of brackish water down his trousers, attempting to clean off the worst of the drunk's emissions. After that he'd become a more pleasant companion.

When they reached Milman's Street, they headed south toward the river. The houses became smaller cottages, then wrecks of cottages, then warehouses along the riverbank. The rank summer smell of the great river finally overpowered the man's odiferous clothing.

"Which warehouse?" the constable asked.

"I'm not sure. I guess it could be any of these four," Charles said.

The constable lifted his hand over his head and shook his rattle. "If any of my brothers are walking the beat here, this will bring them. Let's go down to the wharf and see if anyone knows the answer."

They walked across the foreshore to the rickety wharf that stretched into the Thames. Men were loading barrels onto rowboats, which then delivered the goods to larger boats anchored deeper in the water. Constable Blight seemed to grow taller as he took on an air of authority.

He pointed to a man who was standing at the end of the dock with papers in his hand. Though not dressed like a gentleman, he seemed to be in charge.

The constable waved and caught the man's attention. He came down the wharf toward them.

"Do you work among these warehouses?" the constable demanded.

"I do, Constable." The man's rabbity front teeth clicked nervously. "Is there a problem?"

"We're looking for the one rented by a Haverstock family. Any notion?"

The foreman pointed up the foreshore, his fingers black with grease and dirt. "It's not the second from the left. That belongs to my master. The one on the end on the right belongs to a brewery. That's all I know."

"Thank you," the constable said. "Any idea who might be able to identify the others?"

The foreman glanced around. "Eh." He turned in a circle, then suddenly called out, "Micky, me laddie." He pointed at a scrawny, barefoot boy talking to one of the laborers.

The boy glanced up and slowly finished his conversation, then came to them at a dawdling pace. "Wot?"

"You've worked for the people who own the warehouse on the left, haven't you? Who are they?"

The boy rubbed his nose with a ragged sleeve. "Wot's it to you?"

The foreman turned to the constable and shrugged.

With a roll of his eyes, the constable smacked the back of the boy's head. "You know what I am? I'm the police. Answer the question, or I'll clap you in Newgate."

The boy's eyes turned into little moons. "I don't know, sir. 'E's called No-nose, on account of the damage."

Constable Blight glanced at Charles. "It's got to be the other one, no?"

"I agree," Charles said. "Boy, have you ever seen anyone at the second warehouse from the right?"

The boy glanced up at the row of warehouses, then shook his head. "This morning a boy came by and looked around, but 'e left."

"That would be Prince Moss, Miss Jaggers's special friend. He said he'd check on them this morning, but I've had no opportunity to talk to him again."

Constable Blight nodded at the foreman, and he and Charles strode back up to the row of warehouses. They went to the one that must be Miss Haverstock's.

"Odd that she'd choose to store her goods so close to the river." The constable took a look at the hefty and rather fresh-looking lock holding the main door closed. "Easy to move from here. There's no sign of damage."

"Any windows?"

The constable raised his eyebrows, his dark under-eye circles deepening, and then they walked around the perimeter of the building. There were windows, though they were covered over from the inside. "We won't be able to get any of them open except in the back," he said. "Do you know anyone who has the keys?"

"Her solicitor? Miss Jaggers herself? Though it didn't sound promising," Charles mused.

Constable Blight smirked and pulled a long, thin tool from inside his reinforced coat and set to work on the window facing toward the road. "See if you can find stones or something so we can climb up there more easily."

Chapter 18

Charles wandered around the back of the warehouses, breathing shallowly through his mouth. The weeds smelled of spilled beer and urine, mixed with the stench of the river.

He found discarded crates in pieces but then saw a barrel that looked intact. When he pulled it over, he found the top was uncovered and it smelled worse than vomit, but the bottom seemed sturdy. He rolled it over to the Haverstock warehouse.

"I'll hold on to you when you climb up," Charles said to the constable. "Just in case it doesn't take your weight."

"It will be the other way around," Constable Blight said. "You're much lighter than I am."

"Very well." Charles took off his fine frock coat and set it over some clean-looking rocks. After taking the constable's hand, he climbed on the barrel and lifted the window.

"Are you going to be able to see?" the constable asked.

"Not without pulling the paper off the windows," Charles said. He knelt on the sill and looked down, hoping to see where it might be safe to put his feet. It didn't seem like there was anything just below the window, so he turned over and cautiously let himself down.

His shoes touched wood. He turned around, letting his eyes adjust to the dimness, then ripped off a strip of the paper covering the window. Once they did, he was unable to believe what he was seeing. "Well, if that isn't butter upon bacon."

"Hold." The constable spoke from outside.

Charles heard the man grunt as he climbed onto the barrel, then let himself inside. Charles stepped aside so that Blight didn't drop onto him.

"There's a bloody mansion's worth of furnishings in here," Constable Blight said after an awed pause to contemplate the glorious mess.

Charles edged along the wall, hoping to reach the next window and pull off the paper. When he achieved his goal, he found himself in front of a ghostly sheet-covered expanse. After dislodging spiderwebs as he cautiously lifted the sheet, he found an array of silver candelabras.

The constable had gone in the opposite direction. More rays of light appeared. The constable exclaimed as he lifted a sheet. "Old paintings."

They walked along the perimeter in opposite directions, gently lifting glued-on paper from the lower parts of the windows and exposing the glory of Miss Haverstock's possessions.

"You know what this means?" Charles said when they met again back at the opened window.

"What?"

"Miss Jaggers is an heiress."

Constable Blight coughed. "I expect you are right."

"You need to arrest her."

"Why?"

Charles lifted his eyebrows. "For the murder of Miss Haverstock."

"Why again?"

"Because she hid the existence of all this valuable property. Surely Miss Jaggers's culpability is more likely than a convict's, when there was no sign of forced entry to Miss Haverstock's rooms."

The constable stiffened at the mention of the lady's name. "You can't be serious."

"I can. Miss Jaggers is a very cold and superior sort of person, and I expect she wanted her inheritance sooner rather than later."

Constable Blight shifted from side to side as Charles continued. "Which means the manacles in the Jones smithy are meaningless to the murder." Charles said these words with satisfaction, feeling as though he'd solved the case.

The constable frowned. "I'll take the matter to my superiors, but we can't go about arresting women willy-nilly. You are sure that these items once belonged to Miss Haverstock and were not simply in her trust from Miss Jaggers's family? She is an orphan, correct?"

"My impression is that these items indeed belonged to the old lady." Charles pointed the constable toward the selection of candelabras. Once the man stood in front of them, Charles reached through a couple of tarnished three-pronged candleholders to the candelabra he'd spotted before. He tugged it forward, dislodging spiders' webs.

"It has nine lamps," Constable Blight said. "What a waste of candles."

"It's a menorah," Charles explained. "It's Jewish, just like Miss Haverstock. Miss Jaggers's family is not Jewish, so these must be Miss Haverstock's own possessions."

Constable Blight ran his fingers over the ornate branches of the candelabra. "This must be worth hundreds of pounds. I wonder where it came from."

Charles pulled out his handkerchief and rubbed at the base. "It's good silver."

The constable wrapped his fingers around the base of the candelabra to pick it up. "Bloody—" He drew back his hand.

One of the branch tendrils had cut into the base of his thumb. A thick drop of blood welled up, then dripped into his palm.

"More blood spilled for these treasures," Charles murmured. "Come. Let's clean that up before it gets infected."

Charles arrived at the Hogarths an hour later, so pleased with his solution to the murder that he couldn't wait until a more suitable hour to call on his fiancée. Kate would not be pleased if he waited to tell her about the warehouse. The fact that he'd seen no sign of the missing convict in the vicinity made it all the more implausible that he had anything to do with the murder.

The sun had almost vanished on the horizon, and the Hogarths had gone inside. However, he could see lights behind gauzy summer curtains in the windows, so he rapped on the door.

Mr. Hogarth answered, peering out. Pipe smoke rose behind him, presumably from his hidden hand. "Charles! What brings ye by at this time of night?"

"I think I know who killed Miss Haverstock," he exclaimed.

"Excellent news," Mr. Hogarth said. "Kate is reading in my study."

Charles stepped in and shut the door behind him, then followed Mr. Hogarth. Kate sat at a chair in front of her father's desk, reading a magazine by candlelight.

He took her hand. "Great news, darling girl. I've solved the murder!"

Mary tumbled into the room, pulling her dressing gown around her shoulders. "What's the news?"

Charles grinned at Mary. She perched herself on the edge of the desk and looked at him expectantly.

He drummed on the desk. "Ladies and gentleman, I present a killer to you!"

"Who is it, Charles?" Kate asked.

"Miss Evelina Jaggers, late of India. Age seventeen and already a cold-blooded killer," he said dramatically.

"Miss Evelina Jaggers," Mr. Hogarth said thoughtfully. "Ye don't say."

"I find that entirely shocking," Kate said.

"Thrilling," Mary insisted, clapping her hands with glee. "How clever you are, Charles. How did you figure it out? Is she in Newgate? Will she be hanged?"

"I went to see Prince Moss again after I discovered a Susan Moss had been buried near an assortment of Adamses in East London. It was a long shot," he said modestly, "but I had to do something."

Mary leaned forward. "What did you learn?"

"He is related to Miss Haverstock," Charles said. "Which he had lied about earlier. He admitted that his very eccentric relative had a warehouse of items intended as Miss Jaggers's dowry. I thought the murder might have occurred because Osvald Larsen or Reggie Nickerson knew she was wealthy and he wanted to steal her goods. So I collected Constable Blight, and we went to the warehouse, and . . ."

"And?" Kate prompted.

He grinned. "She was a wealthy woman. Miss Jaggers was an heiress, but with no access to the material goods until her foster mother passed."

"So ye think Miss Jaggers killed her foster mother to gain access to what?" Mr. Hogarth asked.

"Fine furnishings, silver objects, paintings." Charles ticked them off on his fingers. "Trunks rested along the walls. I don't know what is in them. The sun was going down."

Kate cleared her throat. "Surely slight Miss Jaggers didn't strangle her foster mother, then lift her onto a stool and drive a corkscrew into her neck."

Charles listened, then shook his head. "People can do amazing things under stress. Presumably, she wants to marry Prince Moss and wants her goods. Maybe Prince Moss killed her."

"He didn't look very strong to me, either," Kate said.

"He's a farmer," Charles protested.

"Maybe they hired someone," Mr. Hogarth said. "Like these escaped villains."

Charles waved his hands. "Don't even think it, sir. If we can connect the crime to Miss Jaggers or even Mr. Moss, or to them both, can't you see that it ought to lead to freeing Daniel Jones, which is why we were originally involved?"

"That doesn't mean you can think carelessly," Kate chided. "You have a rather implausible version of the murder."

"You see a pretty face and can't imagine the evil underneath," Charles snapped.

"I have no trouble seeing past a pretty face, Charles," Kate said calmly. "I appreciate that you can see past one, as well, believe me. But I don't think you've proven that Osvald Larsen is unconnected to the situation."

"Blast it," Charles muttered. "Why must it be so complicated to free Daniel Jones?"

"Because the strong arm of the law does not readily give back that which it has captured," Mr. Hogarth said. "No, Charles, I do not think ye are going to be successful with this quest. I am sorry for the Jones family, verra sorry."

"I will leave you, as the hour grows late." Charles sighed. "Thank you for hearing out my theory. We shall see what the police do with it."

"It's a very good find, Charles," Mary said. "You've done wonders, and I am sure you are right in the main, regardless of who actually killed her."

He saluted her, then bent and kissed Kate on the cheek. "You will be coming into the office late tomorrow afternoon, correct? We planned on attending the Colosseum Pleasure Dome opening?"

"I'm coming in with Father in the morning," Kate said. "I shall do some shopping for Mother and then meet you at the end of your workday."

"Very well. Good night, everyone." He walked out, stiff

backed. Mrs. Hogarth came into the passage, but he merely sketched a wave before he departed the house, in too much agony of feeling to do more. He knew Kate must develop her own theory of the murder, but he preferred his own.

Charles had forgiven Kate for her lack of support by the time he went to Mr. Hogarth's office to pick her up late Wednesday afternoon. She would come around in time, after the police proved their case. Someday Kate would shriek and turn away from the newspaper in which Charles's account of Miss Jaggers's grisly death from hanging appeared.

His breath left his chest when he saw Kate leaning against her father's shoulder as they both read something at his desk. She wore a walking dress, primarily of blue silk, with a white underskirt showing out of a triangular opening in the front. A pretty lace kerchief lay across the soft skin of her throat, and a cunning pink ribbon was tied in a bow over the lace. It matched the strings of her straw summer bonnet. She also had her hair tied up in ribbons, so that a bow lay across her hair, just under the place where the straw kissed her scalp.

"My goodness, you are a fetching portrait," Charles exclaimed.

Kate giggled as he kissed her hand. "La, sir, the things you say."

"She is ready for the fete," Mr. Hogarth said proudly. "I don't know that ye do her justice, Charles."

He knew Kate's father was joking, because he looked rather fine himself in cream trousers and a perfectly brushed black coat. William had helped him tidy up the sleeves, and he'd tied a fresh white neckerchief around his neck just now. His jaunty waistcoat had been cut from blue silk. "I think we match, sir."

Mr. Hogarth glanced at the waistcoat. "I see that ye do. Well, off ye go, the pair of ye, and don't forget to return and bring the article."

* * *

The Colosseum hulked at the east end of Regent's Park.

"Do you feel like you are in Rome?" Charles asked as they walked up the side of the long promenade, along with hundreds of others. Carriages filled the center of the drive as Londoners streamed toward the grand fete in the glorious sixteen-sided space of the large building.

"I certainly feel like I am somewhere special," Kate replied. "What a glorious night." She smiled at a little girl, her face covered with the sticky remains of an icy treat as she clutched at her fingers ahead of them.

Though as an attraction it had never been terribly successful, the cement-over-brick Colosseum looked astonishingly lovely with the summer rays hitting it, creating a golden hue on what was supposed to resemble white stone in the manner of the Roman Parthenon.

"I've always wanted to see the massive painting inside," Kate continued. "Have you seen it?"

"Oh yes," he assured her. "All three-hundred-sixty degrees."

"What is the perspective supposed to be?" she asked.

"It's the view of London from the top of the dome of St. Paul's Cathedral some dozen or so years ago," Charles explained. "One of those examples of artistry that, while a great achievement, was ruinous for so many involved in the financial sense."

"What do you think of it, then?" she asked as they came up along the side of the polyhedron-shaped building. "Should the project never have been attempted?"

"They should have reduced the scale to something manageable," he said. "Some of the backers had to flee to America to avoid being thrown into debtor's prison. They never were able to enjoy their achievement."

"I expect most people are happy to see what is in front of their noses, rather than a view from a bird's perspective. Maybe people aren't even meant to see things like this."

Charles considered her words. Was she offering him a warning about seeing what was only in front of his nose, like his quest to have Miss Jaggers arrested? He knew with sickening clarity that she'd been right that he hadn't done enough to free Mr. Jones with his theory. If only he had the bird's eye view of Miss Haverstock's murder. "You are wise, Kate. I will consider what you say."

She smiled gently, squeezing his arm, but her attention had shifted to a group of youths wandering through the crowd, tripping into each other as they sipped from flasks. Mostly, he enjoyed seeing the people milling around, but he could do without the rowdy boys, who were too callow to enjoy paintings, anyway.

"Flare-up!" one of them, a tender young dandy with flopping sandy hair who'd lost his hat, called in a high-pitched voice, lifting his flask. "Flare-up, you Englishmen!"

His friends chortled and tipped back their flasks for another libation. Charles could smell the fumes coming off them from earlier drinks and spills.

The tender youth's generously girthed companion tripped into another young man, perhaps one of a rival group of dandies. The rival youth, resplendent in a purple-checked waistcoat and a cream suit, snapped, "Not to cut it too fat, but just to throw in a bit of lean to make weight." He pushed against the round youth.

Kate jerked as the round dandy flung the contents of his flask at his rival. The rival threw a punch. Charles winced as the seam of the round dandy's coat ripped at the shoulder. He pulled Kate away from the combatants, then found himself face-to-face with Prince Moss.

Charles froze as he looked at the young farmer in front of Kate. His clothing was rougher than that of the other youths; his looks were more refined; his years, even more tender. And he was not alone.

"Miss Jaggers," Kate gasped.

For Miss Jaggers stood next to her young swain.

Charles blinked, disbelieving that he hadn't seen her right away, in her filmy white skirts and lacy bodice, an emerald-green ribbon tied around her neck in a manner similar to Kate's pink one. If it weren't for that ribbon, he'd think her a ghost, a figment of his imagination. Blast the police for not listening to him. Just because her arrest wouldn't clear Daniel Jones didn't mean she wasn't guilty.

"H-how pleasant to see you again," Kate stuttered.

The stunning Miss Jaggers said not a word. She merely inclined her head to Kate in regal fashion and floated past them. Prince Moss smiled faintly at Charles and moved in her wake.

Charles stared as they walked away in finery instead of chains. He took Kate's arm and pulled her up the walkway, under the huge Doric columns. "All this grandeur in London and no justice," he hissed.

"They can't simply arrest her on your say-so," Kate said. "She's a gentlewoman. It's a terribly awkward situation, and I'm still not sure she did it."

"They should have taken some action," Charles said, following the crowd. "I'd follow them if you weren't with me."

"Oh, Charles, if they did kill Miss Haverstock, you've ruined their goal, showing the police the goods like you did. They can't run off with them now."

"Perhaps. Perhaps they even hired Larsen and Blood."

"How would they have met two convicts?" Kate demanded.

"I have no idea." Charles frowned. "I've lost my sense of fun. Let's take a look around and then get back, so I can write my article."

Kate took his offered arm.

"Look up," Charles said as they entered the exhibition. "That, my dear, is the largest painting ever created. Forty thousand square feet, worked in oil."

Kate stared up at the dome, her lips rounding into an expression of delight. "If only so many men weren't smoking. The smoke quite obscures things, but it is amazing, nonetheless."

"This is what we can achieve when we dream," Charles said, staring not at the painting itself but at their fellow art viewers, from the elderly lady complaining that she couldn't see anything to the rapturous young artist exclaiming about the vision above him. "But I think my article will be more about the people here than the art. That is what fascinates me. Londoners. I am sure you can't find such a vast array of personalities anywhere else."

When Charles looked out his window toward the lane the next morning, he saw two wagons trundling by from the direction of the smithy. Their heads down, the horses seemed exhausted from working too hard. Perhaps they were too old for such heavy burdens.

Fred came into the bedroom with a fresh jug of water. He poured some into the bowl, then rubbed at his cheek. "I feel roughness on my upper lip, Charles. Do you think it is time for me to start shaving?"

Charles turned away from the window and wrapped his fingers around his brother's jaw, then pulled him gently toward the sunlight streaming in the window. Tilting his brother's face this way and that, he said, "A bit of fuzz, but I don't think it's noticeable yet."

"So a girl wouldn't notice it?"

"A mother might, but not a girl," Charles said. "Sorry, Fred. Maybe by autumn."

Fred grinned. "That isn't so very far away."

"No. Speaking of dates that aren't so very far away, I've felt bad for missing your birthday."

"It's fine. I know you've had a lot of expenses."

Charles smiled at his brother's downcast expression. "I managed to put a bit aside, and I did get you something."

Fred's dark brows lifted. "Oh?" He danced a little jig, his shoes making shuffling noises on the floor.

Charles opened the trunk they had brought there when they

first moved in, and pulled out a new piece of sheet music. "Here you go. Something new for your fiddle."

Fred reached for it and took it to the window. "Thank you," he exclaimed. He opened the sheet. "It looks like a fun piece."

"I'm glad you like it. It's Italian." Charles stared out the window as another wagon went by.

"What's going on?" Fred asked.

"I have a bad feeling about it," Charles said. "That's the third wagon." He turned away and quickly finished dressing, then washed his face.

"It has to be the Joneses, doesn't it?" Fred said when Charles was ready.

Charles nodded. "Let's see if they are still there. Maybe they are dismantling the smithy." He reached for the pages for Breese that he'd finished writing late the night before. They'd picked up the habit of sending lines back and forth, since they both kept unusual hours. Charles thought his latest phrases ought to complete another set of lyrics, and he knew Breese had a jaunty tune for the chorus.

In the hall, Charles slid the pages under Breese's door; then he and Fred left the building and walked down the lane. He saw Hannah and Addie Jones in the yard, their mourning dresses making them look like oversize crows, and poor little Beddie, an even thinner, droopier creature.

Charles raised his hand and headed toward them as two men came out of the smithy, hauling a heavy crate filled with tools between them. For a moment, he could believe that was the only part of the property being dismantled, but then he saw two more men walking out of Edmund and Hannah's small house, carrying a large mattress between them.

"Not your household goods," he gasped as he reached Mrs. Jones.

She nodded somberly. "With both men gone, we can't run the forge, much less pay the bills."

"But you had the apprentice and the hired boy," Charles protested. "Couldn't you manage them?"

"No. Both are too young," Hannah Jones said, dabbing at her red-rimmed eyes. "When my Daniel was arrested, two-thirds of our customers immediately switched to the Pirie Smithy down by the river, and the rest vanished when my brother passed. We didn't have the time to rent out the smithy to anyone else. The collectors came."

Charles shook his head. "I know. I saw the broker's man. What are you going to do?"

"At least the rent isn't in arrears," Mrs. Jones said, trying to smile. "The tools all have to go. They were on a payment plan, and, well, we've lost just about everything, but we still have family, and they have agreed to take us in."

"Where?" Fred asked, patting Beddie's shoulder.

"Limehouse," Hannah Jones said. "I had an aunt, and her children are a decade younger than me. One of my cousins has room in her house, since her children are grown now. She's an invalid, and we'll run the house for her."

"I'm glad you have both a place and a purpose," Charles said. Might their Limehouse relations have known Miss Haverstock? He couldn't trouble the Joneses with the question now, though.

"It's not far from St. Anne's," Mrs. Jones said, then suddenly, her face crumpled and tears ran down her cheeks. "Oh, Mr. Dickens."

"I'm sorry," Charles said. "I tried again. I found a suspect for the murder, a good one, but it still wasn't enough to free your husband. Those blasted manacles ruin all my attempts to out-reason the police."

Mrs. Jones's shoulders shook. "We've been told that my Daniel will be transported for 'being in the company of felons.'"

Charles put his hands to his temples. "I am so sorry. Can't it be blamed on Mr. Edmund Jones? I'm sorry to blacken his memory, but—"

"No, you are right," Hannah Jones said gently. "He'd have taken the blame, for Daniel's sake, but he's dead now, and a dead man can't speak. If only we'd thought of it before it was too late. They won't listen to us women."

"What happens now?"

"We wait for the next court session, and then he'll go to Australia," Mrs. Jones said glumly.

"Maybe we'll follow him," Hannah Jones said. "After my cousin is dead. If we inherit a bit, we will be able to go to Australia ourselves. Start over."

Charles was touched by the bravery of the women. "I'll keep fighting for you."

"It's no use." Mrs. Jones sniffed. "You've done everything you could."

"No," Charles insisted. "I'll find Osvald Larsen and make him testify that your husband had nothing to do with the manacles. Just you wait."

Mrs. Jones smiled, but in doing so, her lower lip cracked. A line of blood appeared on her pale skin. Fred turned away, sadness in his young eyes.

"How much longer will you be?" Charles asked.

"An hour or two."

"Can we take Beddie?" Fred asked. "You can collect her when you leave."

"That would be nice," Mrs. Jones said. She turned to the little girl and released her hand. "Go with nice Mr. Dickens, Beddie."

"I'll play you my new music," Fred said. "And give you some bread and butter."

The little girl's eyes widened, and she put her tiny hand in Fred's larger one. After a glance back at the Jones women, Charles took Beddie's other hand. How was he going to fulfill his promise?

They walked down the lane together. When they reached the front door of Selwood Terrace, Charles saw Mr. Ferazzi and Mr. Nickerson coming their way.

"Those are bad men," Fred told Beddie. "Stay away from them."

Beddie wrinkled her nose. "Uncle Edmund talked to the old man."

"What?" Charles said.

She shrugged. "They was friends."

Charles frowned at the little girl. "Are you certain?"

She nodded.

"It doesn't matter, Charles," Fred said. "Two old men who live in the same neighborhood."

"'E didn't have a wife," Beddie added. "Aunt Hannah cooked him dinner when 'e came."

Charles shrugged. "It's hard to imagine anyone wanting to spend time with Mr. Ferazzi who wasn't being paid for it."

Chapter 19

Despite the midmorning hour, Charles heard clattering on the steps as he exited his rooms after settling in Fred and Beddie. First, he saw William's legs appear, then the rest of him.

"You are leaving as late as I am?" Charles exclaimed.

"I'm afraid so." William made a face. "One of those days. I was up half the night writing a piece and then overslept. Julie hates to wake me after nights like this, but she needs to be cruel and simply pour water on my head."

Charles chuckled. "Fred loves to do that to me."

William opened the door to the front walk. "At least we can reacquaint ourselves while we walk. I feel like I haven't seen much of you lately."

"A new wife has that consequence," Charles said, tilting his hat to keep the sun's rays from his eyes. Of course, he'd bought food for his brother and not himself, and his stomach decided this was the time to remind him.

"And new relatives," William agreed. "Did I tell you my father came into London earlier this week?"

"Did he like Julie?" Charles waved at a dusty girl with a tray of rolls. She walked to the side of the road to meet him. He bought a couple and paid her, then bit into one before he'd even stepped away.

"Julie warmed up some ham for me before I left," William said. "Funny how a hot meal tastes good even on a summer morning."

"Yes, yes," groused Charles around his dry bite of roll. "But back to your father."

William's father was a widowed schoolmaster who lived in Harrow. He visited William only a couple days a year. "He met Julie at the wedding, but, of course, that day was overwhelming, to say the least. I have no recollection of him speaking to her."

"I suppose. I think we drank decidedly too much. That might have affected your memory."

"No doubt," William said. "Julie was on her best behavior for his recent visit. She brought in food from Lugoson House, so the eating was excellent, and she waited on my father like he was an earl."

"He's very quiet."

"Yes. I'm the loud one in the family." William grinned. "Anyway, he's gone now. What's been going on?"

Charles edged along a narrow strip between a dead horse and a building. Someone had pushed the horse to the side of the road, but no one had removed it yet. He averted his eyes, trying not to remember Miss Haverstock as he batted away flies. "I tried to talk the police into arresting Miss Jaggers on Tuesday night, but then Kate and I saw her on Wednesday night in Regent's Park, so I don't think my mission was successful."

William glanced away, too, his face shading toward green. "You think she killed Miss Haverstock?"

Charles's memory unhelpfully flashed to the scene as he'd first come upon it with Kate three weeks ago. "I did at first. Still, I think she was involved. Follow the money, right? It turns out that she has quite an inheritance."

They reached a crossroad, and both dashed across, satchels swinging, happy to get away from the horse carcass.

"Do you think Miss Jaggers hired the escaped convicts to kill Miss Haverstock?"

"I'd like to leave the convicts out of the equation entirely." Charles's throat had seized up between the dust and the smell and the flies. He pulled William into a coffeehouse and went to the bar.

"I don't think you can. I think they are in the picture somehow."

After Charles had ordered coffee for both of them, he said, "She should have been questioned as soon as we found the warehouse full of expensive goods. Who is protecting Miss Jaggers?"

William spotted an empty table and pulled Charles through the crowd of men to reach it. "Anyone who feels pity for the young and beautiful."

Charles pulled out a chair. "She's a cold fish. Young and beautiful doesn't mean honest or good."

"Is there a connection between Blood, Larsen, and Miss Jaggers?" William asked as they sat.

"She was in India for her earliest childhood, then went to boarding school." Charles rubbed road dust from his face as a waiter set down their pints of coffee. "Her family was from Limehouse originally, and Larsen lived there."

"Bread and butter, too," William said to the waiter. "This coffee is more than my stomach can take alone."

Charles stared at the oily brew. He didn't think he'd been in this coffeehouse before. Glancing around, he saw only the lowest kind of day laborers at the tables. Now he knew why. He took a sip of his coffee and grimaced before saying, "Tastes better than flies. At least a little."

"So, the convict has no connection to Miss Jaggers, in truth."

Charles set down his cup. "But perhaps to Miss Haverstock.

Backy Adams is from Limehouse. I do not know the years of Osvald Larsen's residence there."

"Anyone else?"

"The Jones women have relatives in Limehouse. I don't know if Daniel was raised there."

William snapped his fingers. "Mr. Pietro Ferazzi was raised there, as well."

"Pietro?" Charles said, almost knocking the bread and butter plate onto the floor. He hadn't noticed it being set down.

"Yes. I got to talking to that Reggie Nickerson one day, when he was collecting the rent."

Charles jumped to his feet. "Pietro and Osvald. That's it!"

"What's it?"

"What is the connection between the Jones siblings, Larsen, and Ferazzi?" Elated, Charles poked his index finger at the table. "I'll tell you. They were all the children who killed Goldy in that magazine article. I remember the names. Eddie, Han, Osvald, Pete."

"What about Miss Haverstock?"

Charles had been about to launch into a little jig, but William's words stopped him cold. "None of the children were named Backy."

"Goldy died," William said. "It was probably her sister."

Charles nodded thoughtfully as he sat back down. "This means that Osvald Larsen didn't know just Edmund and Hannah Jones. He knew Mr. Ferazzi, as well."

"Did he know Daniel Jones?"

"It was probably Edmund who helped Larsen or Blood with the manacles," Charles said. "But the police don't care. They've already scheduled poor Daniel for trial and have settled his charges. The Joneses who are left have lost their home. They are leaving today. I suppose my sympathy for Hannah is diminished, given that she must be the girl who was involved in Goldy's death."

"Since Edmund Jones is dead, do you think Mr. Ferazzi is

hiding Osvald Larsen?" William asked. "And they've turned Daniel Jones into a scapegoat?"

Charles folded his hands in front of his chin. Now there was a notion. "Perhaps."

"Why did they want Miss Haverstock killed?"

"To get at the warehouse?" Charles asked, shrugging. "But it was weeks after she died, and the goods were still there."

"Maybe Miss Haverstock threatened to expose them as Goldy's killers?"

"I doubt it would matter." Charles swallowed more coffee. "It was fifty years ago."

William poked a piece of bread into the butter. "Are you certain you can't free Daniel Jones, given the evidence of a connection between his father and Larsen?"

The rolls sat uneasily in Charles's stomach, so he shook his head when William offered him the bread and butter plate. "They'd just say Daniel had probably met him, too. After all, Larsen had been at Coldbath Fields for only eleven months. And he is a blacksmith."

"I think we should find him," William said around a mouthful. "I think we can find him. I'll bet Mr. Ferazzi has him. It's too much of a coincidence to find this group of men with a fifty-year-old connection."

William's enthusiasm infected Charles. "You're right. I have to attend some meetings this afternoon, but tonight let's go on the hunt."

"I agree. I'll find out where Mr. Ferazzi lives. I suppose he owns enough buildings that Larsen could be camped out anywhere, but we have to start somewhere."

Charles tapped his fingers on the table impatiently as William handed the waiter the coins for their food. Then they left.

William and Charles returned to Selwood Terrace together from London that evening. When Charles went into his rooms, he found Fred alone.

"No Beddie?"

"They came for her a couple of hours after you left," his brother reported. "Off to Limehouse they went. I used a bit of my pocket money to take her to a shop and buy her some boiled sweets. They kept her happy until Mrs. Jones arrived."

"That was sweet of you, Fred. She's had a rough time, that poor little girl."

Fred screwed up his lips into a tight pout for a moment. "I suppose we are lucky, really, to have our parents. They aren't perfect, but they are still alive, ready to pet and praise us at birthdays and at Christmas and such."

"Yes, parents are much better than the alternative," Charles agreed. Parents were all very well and good, but he'd prefer they cared for themselves. Fred was too young to have any real idea of what transpired when their father put himself and the rest of the family into difficulties.

"Did you bring any dinner?" Fred asked.

"Julie is going to cook for us. William and I bought sausages and summer greens on the walk home," Charles said.

"Oh, I forgot to tell you." Fred pointed up. "Someone is going to move in upstairs."

"Did you see them?"

"Another newlywed couple," Fred explained. "Young, pasty faced, blowing kisses at each other. They are waiting for their trunks to arrive from up north, and then they will move in."

"I can't imagine they know what happened up there."

"We won't be the ones to tell them," Fred said. "I plan to steer clear. I'm sure they will keep to themselves. The only possible irritation will be a squeaking bed overhead in the night."

Charles felt his cheeks go hot. "What would you know about that?"

Fred's face had gone very red, too. "I'm not a child."

Charles stared at him. Maybe he'd been right about a mustache starting. "I suppose so. You are fifteen now. After we go back to Furnival's Inn, it might be time to find you your first position."

Fred's mouth opened slightly, as if he were going to pant like an eager pup. "I'm ready to work, Charles, really I am. I can keep living with you and still learn things."

"Of course you can." Charles ruffled his hair. "You'll have a home with me as long as it makes sense. I'm going to wash my face and hands and put on my darkest clothing. Then we'll go up and see how Julie is faring."

"Greetings again," William said cheerfully as he opened his door twenty minutes later. "Ah, I see you are ready to skulk."

Charles patted his high-buttoned black waistcoat. "I've gone as dark as I can."

"You look like an undertaker." William grinned. "I shall dress accordingly, and Julie can wear mourning."

"Is she going out with us?" Charles asked as Fred added, "Can I come?"

"We are looking for a desperate escaped criminal," Charles said. "You are too young for this kind of hunt."

Fred protested, but Charles shook his head.

Julie stood at the fireplace, an apron covering her summer dress of sheer white muslin printed with pink flowers. Her red hair had fluffed into a nimbus despite her neat bun as she turned the sausages in an iron pan.

William pointed to the table set away from the fire under an open window. A salad of summer greens and a wooden platter with a loaf of sliced bread took the center, and the table had been neatly set with plates, utensils, and glasses of ale.

Charles leaned on the windowsill and surveyed the peaceful scene beyond their building. Yet a villain had crept inside and murdered an old woman. He jiggled his legs, anxious to get on to the hunt for Osvald Larsen.

"How is Ollie progressing?" William asked.

"I visited Dr. Manette's home and surgery today," Julie said, carrying her smoking pan over to the table.

"So Ollie is still there?"

She used her fork to spear each sausage in turn and set one on each of the four plates, then placed the pan in a wooden bucket to cool. "Yes, but the doctor said he's past the possible infection stage now, and the wound is healing. He's insisted that Ollie needs somewhere clean to heal completely, as the stump will have to go through various stages of change for months." She gestured everyone to sit and they followed suit.

William winced as he tucked a napkin over his waistcoat. "Such a sad situation. I know you haven't a penny to spare, Charles, but Julie and I have talked, and we can afford a bit. I don't want him to go into the workhouse."

"It's unlikely he'd survive there," Charles agreed, passing the plates of greens and bread around. "Could you afford to send him to school? If he learned the skills of a clerk, he could do well in life."

"I agree," William said, cutting into his sausage. Juice spurted but was caught on the napkin. "He won't do well as a laborer. Let us hope he has the intelligence to learn to read and figure. I spoke to my father when he was here. He's offered to take Ollie as a charity pupil, if I'll pay some of the fees."

Charles lifted his glass to his friend. "I feel so remiss. Good work, William."

William nodded. "The other mudlarks will hate me for it. I will have to break the news, since Ollie is ready to leave Dr. Manette very soon."

Julie patted his hand. "They'll forgive you, William. And Ollie is so young, he'll probably forget his former life in time."

William smiled at his wife. "We cannot all have good starts to life, but in the end, Ollie may come to find this disaster a blessing in disguise if it gains him an education and a better life."

"Or any life at all," Julie said quietly. "I don't like his prospects if he remains on the streets."

"Are we done?" Charles asked, after ten minutes of hearty eating by all. Shall we depart?"

Julie rose. "I'll change into mourning."

William rose, as well. "I'll find something like Charles is wearing." The couple went into their bedchamber.

When they were out of earshot, Fred said, "I hope I land on my feet like she has, with her aristocratic relatives, more money than we have, a good husband. I mean, for a woman, she is doing exceedingly well for herself, and she's only a couple of years older than me."

"You want aristocratic relatives, more money, and a good wife in two years?" Charles asked.

"I'll settle for more money," Fred said, "but I don't suppose we're going to get any better relatives."

"No," Charles said. "We'll have to make do ourselves. You have a brain, and if you apply yourself, you can rise quickly. Look at me. Five years younger than William, who you think is such a fine husband, and I'm already being paid more than he is."

"Are you?" Fred asked.

"Yes, because of the sketches. What I don't have is Julie's dowry. So think about that when you choose to marry."

"Why are you marrying Kate, then?"

"Connections," Charles said. "And she'll make a fine wife. I'd rather have comfort in my home than dramatics. Besides, I love her, and even if she didn't have those connections, she would still be a worthy choice."

"I like Kate, too," Fred said, rising. "She's a very different choice from Julie. I don't know what I want yet."

"You have plenty of time to figure it out." Charles stared at the littered table and turned away, flustered and uncomfortable. He went back to the window and watched the setting sun, while Fred piled up the dirty dishes and put them in the bucket on top of the cooled pan.

When the Agas returned, "ready for skulking," as William announced, they all went down the stairs. Charles directed Fred into their rooms, where he went after one final grunt of irritation, and then the trio left the building and walked south toward the river less than a mile away.

"I always appreciate that moment the river air hits me," William said.

Julie's nostrils flared. "Not at this time of year. Fresh sewage instead of that cold watery smell."

"You couldn't pay me to live down here," Charles said, "no matter how nice some of the houses are."

"Mr. Ferazzi lives in the most southern row of terraced houses," William said.

They crept behind the stables of the Royal Hospital to the row of late seventeenth-century terraces. A horse neighed, perhaps sighting a rat in its stall. Visible in the dim light were the elderly two-story houses built of brick. Attics with variously shaped windows looked functionally large under tiled roofs.

"No lights at all." William pointed to the last house. "That's Mr. Ferazzi's house. Though you can see lamps through the windows in the next two houses."

"Let's investigate the other two walls," Charles said over a sudden burst of piano music from one of the houses, reminding him that if they could hear what was happening inside a house, those people could hear them speaking in the street. He lowered his voice. "Maybe the lights will be on in the back. It appears to have a large interior."

They crept across the street and down the lane to see the side of the house, but darkness folded over the windows there, too, despite the sun being too low to provide illumination indoors. Then they went into the stinking alley behind the house, the smell of garbage only somewhat distinguished from the smell of raw sewage coming from the river, but they saw no lights there, either.

"If they are inside, they are using lights only on the side of the house that is shared with the next house," William said.

"I don't know," Charles fretted. "It has an air of disuse. Maybe Mr. Ferazzi sleeps at his office."

"I could inquire into a maid position with him," Julie said with a low laugh. "See if I can be hired in some capacity and find Larsen that way."

"Don't even say that," Charles gasped, the memory of finding her crumpled at the base of a staircase last winter, during her brief employment as a maid, still fresh in his mind.

William took his wife's arm and whispered emphatically, "You will never, ever serve as anyone's maid again. I pay on a survivorship policy just for that purpose." He shuddered.

"I'd like to do something to help, William," she insisted. "I am going to be as mad as Lady Macbeth if I don't do a proper job soon."

"I know, darling," he said in a low, intimate tone. "But you'll soon be recovered from losing the baby and will be able to work again in the fall."

Charles went still. *Losing a baby?* Had Julie? "Oh," he murmured, so much coming into understanding. Why he'd hardly seen her for months. Why she seemed to be so thin now. He counted in his head. She couldn't have been far enough along to even know she was expecting for sure. Unless she and William had both lied to him about that night she'd spent in his rooms last winter. No wonder William had been so eager to marry her. It hadn't been about the money at all, but about his child.

Charles glanced away from the pair, pretending he hadn't heard anything, but he felt sorry for them. What a baby the pair of them would make, their combined personalities and personal charms together. What a loss. "A villain or a king," he whispered.

"What?" William asked.

"Nothing," Charles said. "We've been standing here for five

minutes, and the house has been still as stone. I don't think anyone is inside."

"Five minutes is nothing," Julie said. "We should investigate more than this."

"You want to go through the garbage middens?" Charles asked. "See how fresh they are?"

"Not especially," Julie said. "But light a match."

"I can do better." William pulled a stump of candle from his pocket and lit it. He prowled around the alley. The trio crowded together in the dim light, checking out what the household had thrown out.

A gray tabby howled and dashed off when Charles disturbed it, and he heard rustling noises behind a pile of kitchen scraps.

"I don't think any of this is fresh," Julie said. "This is last week's rubbish, or even older."

"I can't think of anything else to do," Charles said. "Let us return home. I will put my head together with William tomorrow, and we will see if we can find a complete list of Mr. Ferazzi's holdings. I think our theory is good, and he owns more properties elsewhere."

"Do we know Larsen isn't in Bloomsbury?" William asked.

"Yes, I'm sure of it. My parents know all the tenants in their building, and as far as they are aware, Ferazzi doesn't own other buildings nearby."

William squinted into the alley as his candle flickered in the breeze that was rising. "He might own the rest of the terrace."

"We'll look into it tomorrow, have records pulled."

"What will you tell the *Chronicle* staff?"

"You covered the inquest for the newspaper," Charles said. "I'm sure they'll send a clerk for the property records. It's more effective than trying to get the information out of Reggie Nickerson. He'd tell us about all but the one where Larsen is living, right?"

"If he's a part of this," William said, reversing out of the alley. "But I think the ties between these two men, Larsen and Ferazzi, are very old and very personal."

"I wish I knew how Goldy fit in," Charles said. "I haven't found any personal papers of Miss Haverstock's. Nothing was in what was sold to me, no diaries, no old family documents, nothing. I didn't see a grave for Goldy Adams at the burial ground, either."

"Mr. Ferazzi was in Miss Haverstock's rooms after she died," William said. "He'd have been smart enough to destroy whatever was there to be found."

"What about the warehouse?" Julie asked. "We should look through it."

"I know how to get in," Charles said. "I saw trunks."

William nodded. "Let's do it."

They walked along the twisting streets above the river until they reached Milman's Street. Charles was about to step on the wharf when Julie grabbed his arm.

"Don't," she whispered. "Guards."

Instead of progressing carelessly, Charles let his senses open to the night. Soon he picked out what Julie had spotted. Two dark shapes at each end of one of the warehouses.

"They aren't guarding Miss Haverstock's," Charles said.

"I doubt they'd ignore us while we broke in, though. We should go." Julie urged.

"What if that's Osvald Larsen?" Charles argued. "If we capture him, this might all be over, at least for Daniel Jones."

One of the men lit a cigar. By the light of it, Charles could see his face. He glanced at William, who shook his head. Too young to be Larsen.

Julie rolled her eyes at Charles and stepped forward before either of the men could stop her. The cigar-holding man let out a low whistle as she sauntered up to the warehouse.

Charles grabbed for William's shoulder before he could go after his wife. "We're close enough," he whispered. "Let her work her magic."

Julie was speaking to the men. "Oh, dear, neither of you can afford me. Big Aga would have your heads if you touched me," she bragged.

"Never 'eard o' 'im," said the second man, stepping away from the wall.

"Sounds like a local," William said. "Doubt he's our man."

Charles nodded. "How do we get her away?"

"Wondering about the action hereabouts," Julie said to the men. "My man wants to prig the swag out o' one o' these warehouses. You the only guards?"

"Lookee, you saucebox, we're 'onest men," said the first man. "Paid to guard."

"I could pay you more," Julie said in a wheedling tone. "Just look away. We can be in and out in the blink of an eye."

"Be away wi' ye," growled the other man.

Julie put her hands on her hips and jiggled a little. "I'll cut you in. You gotta screw?"

The first man dropped his cigar and grabbed her arm. William roared and raced down the wharf. Charles swore and went after him.

The guard dropped Julie's arm, and she turned and fled up the wharf. William grabbed her, and the trio ran for home, not stopping until they reached the front door of Selwood Terrace.

"Don't ever do that to me again," William wheezed.

Julie giggled uncontrollably. Charles threw up his hands and went to his bed. He'd meant to solve a crime, not have an adventure fit for a bedlamite.

Chapter 20

∿

Charles had forgotten he needed to travel to Sudbury early on Friday morning. He slept on the coach since he'd been up half the night. On his return, he had to bribe the hostlers at the inn to put their best horses on the stage so he could turn in his story on time. At the *Chronicle*, he worked with Thomas Pillar to clean up the version of the article that he'd written in the coach on the way back to the Strand.

William's desk had an air of neglect. Dust marred his inkwell, and a pile of mail had slid across the left side. He didn't appear to be in today. Had he learned more about Mr. Ferazzi's rental holdings?

Charles decided to go home and see if he could find William. Maybe he'd beg dinner from Mrs. Hogarth and spend some time with Kate. But when he reached Selwood Terrace, needing to change his waistcoat before he paid his call, he found Breese in the front yard with a flute, playing trills.

Breese took his mouth away from the instrument. "I'm almost done, Charles. I have a buyer, too. Do you want to sit with me for a minute and try to finish the last verse? It needs a suitably happy ending."

"Certainly." They were halfway through when the front door opened and Fred came down. He sat in the grass, in front of Charles, listening to them sing.

"That was nice," the lad said when they were done, "but what about my dinner?"

Charles handed his brother a pie wrapped in a handkerchief and helped Breese finish the song. When they were done, Charles went inside and wrote out a good copy of the lyrics in ink.

"Thank you, good sir," Breese said grandly when Charles brought the copy back out. "I'll write up the sheet music and take it tonight. I should be able to turn this into money right away."

Fred cheered and shook out Charles's handkerchief. "Is there any more food?"

"No. Have you checked with Julie? Does she have anything to feed you today?"

"She isn't home, neither she nor William. Did they go somewhere?"

"Maybe they were promised to her aunt." Charles stared at the sky. Hours of daylight remained. "I don't want to waste the evening. I think I'll go to the Blackfriars Bridge to check in with the mudlarks. I don't know if William has told them that Ollie is going to go to school in Harrow, and I'm wondering if they can help me find Larsen."

"Did they figure out where those manacles came from?" Fred asked.

"They were Ned Blood's. Walk with me a ways. We can stop in somewhere for more food."

Fred jumped to his feet. Charles had already put his satchel in his rooms and had hidden away his weekly paycheck in its box. He might as well splurge on a nice meal. The pubs would be busy tonight, but the food would be better.

They walked deeper into Chelsea and chose a new pub, the Sheep's Head. Charles ordered mugs of ale and a plate of cold meat and pickle.

"Am I going with you to the river?" Fred asked.

"No. They can be a mercurial lot," Charles said. "And it's dangerous. Look what happened to Little Ollie."

"He's lucky," Fred said, a serious expression on his face. "You always say education is important, and he wouldn't have one if not for this. He'll probably live much longer."

"If he recovers completely," Charles agreed. "Some people, though, they don't want to leave what they know. All our mudlarks could have been moved on by now, thanks to our charity, and all of them chose to stay."

"They don't have anyone to guide them," Fred said.

"At least ours are a nicer bunch than Pietro, Osvald, Edmund, and Hannah," Charles mused.

Fred had read the magazine article, too. "They were savages. But Edmund and Hannah turned out well enough, didn't they?"

"I don't really know. Maybe Edmund did help with the manacles."

"I expect it was Edmund who helped Osvald Larsen," Fred agreed. "And then he died for his sins."

"If that's true, then why does everyone else have to suffer, too?"

"That I don't know," Fred said before draining his mug. "I'm not much for theology."

Charles chuckled. "I'm more interested in people, anyway."

"Maybe you'll find something by the bridge," Fred said. "You've got a good eye."

"I never keep what little I find down there. I give it to the mudlarks or bargain with them. So there's no point in me searching."

"It's too bad we stopped finding coins," Fred said.

"I suspect we found the contents of someone's dropped purse, rather than an actual buried stash," Charles said. "Still, we had fun searching for them last winter. But I think my income is very sufficient to our needs, once we return to one set of rooms. I'll save up quickly and be able to wed, and you'll start contributing to the household, too."

"I'll never go hungry again," Fred said.

Charles ruffled his hair. "You never go hungry now, except when I forget to feed you."

Fred pushed back his chair. "I suppose I'll go to Bloomsbury tonight. Father will have all the papers, and I can start to see what sorts of positions are available. I'll see you on Sunday?"

"If you like," Charles said. "I will be writing most of the weekend. I have a lot of catching up to do."

They left the pub and walked into London. Charles was footsore by the time he left his brother on Bloomsbury Street and headed toward the river.

When he made his way down to the foreshore, he saw the little cluster of mudlarks bent over, staring at what the river had tossed up for them that evening.

Poor John had outstripped Lucy Fair in height over the past couple of months, though Brother Second still lagged behind, and the new child, Cousin Arthur, was only half Poor John's size. He had acquired a bucket, however, maybe Ollie's, to help him in his search for goods.

He heard the child chortle as he lifted a nice bit of coal from the rocky surface.

Lucy Fair stood, stretched her back, and saw Charles. He waved and walked down toward them.

"Did Ollie go to Harrow?" she asked.

"It's possible," Charles said. "I haven't seen William today. I was out of town myself."

She sighed, then retucked her hem into her leather belt, to keep the fabric dry. "Will he thrive there?"

Charles kept his gaze on her face. She was coming to the age where she couldn't risk continuing to expose her ankles like this. "Mr. Aga will take good care of him. It's not like Ollie is going to live with complete strangers."

She shook her head. "I'm glad I learned how to read, but I can't understand the point of the rest of it."

Charles picked up a piece of metal that glinted on the beach and showed it to her. "This is why. To you, this is just a hunk of metal. But I know it's a military badge."

"How?"

"See? It sort of looks like part of a coin, but do you see the letters? W-a-t-e-r-l?"

"Yes, I see them."

"I bet this was something very precious once. The word was *Waterloo* once, but it was cut up somehow, and this part of the bottom was lost."

She shrugged. "It's not precious now, unless the metal is worth something."

He handed it to her, and she dropped it into her bucket. "Why are you here tonight?"

"I'm desperate to find Osvald Larsen. He grew up playing on the river. He has no connection to shipping that I know of."

"In Limehouse, right?" she asked, bending down again.

Charles nodded. "He was a blacksmith and a thief. The other escaped convict has been found, so I think that means Larsen has better contacts. Of course, he's also older and had a proper trade."

"I wonder why he became a criminal," Lucy Fair mused.

"I don't know, except he helped accidentally kill a girl when he was around your age. Poor John knows the story."

"I've heard it, too. They stuck her in a barrel that went out into the river. That would mark a person who cared about others," she said slowly. "But other sorts of people would shrug it off as an accident, and it wouldn't trouble them a bit."

"Something about that past clung to these people, because they seem to have still been connected some fifty years later."

Her poking dislodged something. She picked it up and showed

him a small pipe, then gently set it in her bucket. "Maybe they were all related? Cousins?"

"No, that isn't the case," Charles said. "Good idea, though."

"Maybe that wasn't the only death," she said. "Maybe Osvald Larsen knows the others' secrets. It has to be like that, doesn't it? Why would anyone help an escaped prisoner? It's very dangerous."

"An excellent question." They heard shouts behind a large rock, and Brother Second held something up in the air. "Edmund Jones might have been forced to help him, because he had a son who is a good man, and he didn't want his son to know. But if Pietro Ferazzi helped him, a man who doesn't have any family, what was the reason for that?"

When Charles and Lucy Fair reached the other children, they saw the prize was a gold ring.

"I saw it on a dead cat!" Brother Second crowed triumphantly. "It was caught in its fur."

Charles stepped away from the sad corpse.

Poor John clapped the younger boy on the shoulder. "You'll get a pretty penny for that, eh, Lucy Fair?"

"Absolutely." She took the ring and added it to the strip of leather she had tied around her neck. "Anyone find anything else?"

Cousin Arthur held up a pipe. "It's old, but it's perfect. And five lumps of coal."

Charles held out his hand for the pipe. "I'll buy it as a gift for my fiancée's father," he said. He haggled with the children, then passed over coins in good humor. But what had really been helpful this evening was talking over his problems with Lucy Fair.

"It's been days and days," Kate said to Charles as they walked down the front path from her house to her garden gate. She straightened her gloves and fixed her straw bonnet.

"I'm here now," Charles said in an apologetic tone. "Ready to discuss the situation with the missing Osvald Larsen."

"Do you have news?" Kate asked, shading her eyes as she checked out the sky.

Though there were a few clouds, the sky was as bright blue as it ever blazed above London. Kate adjusted her bonnet again, and Charles tipped his hat lower over his brow.

"I spoke to the mudlarks last night, and Lucy Fair had an interesting question."

"What was that?" Kate asked, a touch of sourness in her voice.

"She asked why anyone would help an escaped prisoner," Charles explained, craning his neck to see the gate of the Jewish burial ground as the passed by. This time, the gate was not open in welcome.

"It's a good question, given the danger," Kate mused.

"Exactly. Why would Edmund Jones help Larsen with his manacles? Why would Pietro Ferazzi hide him?"

"Why are you so sure he is?" Kate countered.

"Because Larsen hasn't been found, and Ned Blood has."

"He could be anywhere."

"No," Charles said, gesturing grandly around the street. "He's been a Londoner since childhood. Anyone he knows in the entire country is right here. He's not leaving the streets he knows, and who better than his old friends Edmund, Hannah, and Pietro to help him?"

"Pietro?"

"Pietro Ferazzi," he said.

"Oh. You have learned some things since I saw you last," Kate admitted. "Are those the names from that old magazine?"

"Yes, or close enough. The article had child's nicknames, but they all match to the people we know. In order to figure it out, we went to Ferazzi's house," Charles said.

"You and Lucy Fair?"

"No, I went with the Agas."

"Ah." She kicked at a pebble, raising a cloud of dust, then sneezed.

Charles sighed. "My dear, I do think there is something you should know about Julie Aga."

Kate pinched her nostrils. "What?"

"Everything has been a bit strange with her for months, but I finally found out why."

"Did her mother persuade all the theater managers in London not to hire her?" Kate lifted her brows.

"No," Charles said. "She lost a baby. I didn't know. I'm sure she doesn't want to discuss it."

Kate stopped dead on the street. "A baby? How is that possible?"

"Shhh," Charles said, noticing that an elderly couple, moving very slowly, had managed to listen to their every word. He tipped his hat to them and watched as they passed at a snail's pace.

To their left, a nanny came out the front door of a terrace house, holding the hands of two small children. The little girl might have been dressed in a miniature of Kate's clothes, with gloves, ribbon-trimmed straw bonnet, and floaty cream dress all the same.

Kate's expression softened as she looked at the children. "Soon," she murmured, squeezing Charles's arm.

"Soon," he agreed.

"How did Julie Aga manage to lose a baby when she's been married only three months and a couple of weeks?" Kate demanded, going flinty around the eyes.

Charles glanced away. "I don't like to tell you this, but she did disappear at one point when she was my maid of all work, and we discovered she had stayed with William."

"Charles," Kate shrieked. "And you continued to see her?"

"They swore their innocence. You remember what last winter was like. Don't forget she almost died."

"Good gracious," Kate said, her gloves going to her lips.

"She must have been expecting when she was pushed down those stairs."

"No wonder she lost the baby," Charles said. "I am sorry that happened to her. Some women can move on, but for others, it is very hard. One has to lean on one's faith, and I don't know that Mrs. Aga has had a proper religious education."

"I now have the sense that William kept her from the stage deliberately, so that she could recover her health." Kate made a frustrated noise. "I hope she can return soon, so she doesn't create more mischief."

Charles agreed, remembering Julie's claims that William was off drinking when he was merely away for business. "I think it would be good for her to have work in the evenings. The life of a reporter sends William away all too often."

Kate took the opportunity to have a poke at him. "Must you work so hard?"

He nodded adamantly. "It is the job. We are paid well for it."

"Yes," Kate murmured, "but—"

"Charles!"

The houses were behind them, and they were now in an area with shops. They had just passed a pub, and a cobbler's shop had come up on their left, with an assortment of repaired shoes that had never been collected exhibited in the window.

Charles turned around, back toward the voice. It had come from the pub. Breese stood in the doorway, waving his hand. Charles turned Kate around, and they retraced their steps.

"Good evening, Breese. Having a jolly time?" Charles asked.

Breese grinned. "This is where a couple of composer friends of mine spend time." He fished in his pocket and pulled out a handful of coins, then counted some into Charles's hand. "I told you I had the song sold. Here is your take."

Kate's eyes widened.

"See, darling, I told you I'd catch up quickly," Charles said, pocketing the coins. "Thank you, Breese. Enjoy your fun."

"Oh, yes," Breese said. "I deserve a break. What about you?"

"I wrote all day. One of my sketches. I had an article to fin-ish for another little magazine, as well. Every little bit helps to refill the coffers."

"Then we m-must work together again soon," Breese said, slurring a bit.

"Of course. Kate and I were just going for a walk. We thought we might visit with my sisters."

"I saw William in here a couple of hours ago. Have you been home? He said there was big news about our landlord." Breese threw his arms up in the air.

"What is it?" Charles asked.

"Did you know that the Jones family didn't own their houses or the smithy?"

"Mrs. Jones said as much," Charles said. "Why?"

"Mr. Ferazzi owns the smithy, not the Jones family."

Kate gasped. "Do you think Larsen is hiding on that prop-erty?"

"I wonder," Charles mused. "It's empty now, and he is a blacksmith."

Breese blinked, then straightened his body. "We should inves-investigate," he suggested.

"We should," Charles agreed. "Kate, darling, do you mind if I take you home instead of going to Bloomsbury?"

"I can go with you," she suggested.

"To find a murderer? Your father would insist we break off our engagement immediately if he found out."

"But—"

"But nothing. Larsen's a dangerous man, darling. Think about what he did to poor Miss Haverstock." He slid his finger under her chin. "You know I can't live without you, my sweet. Let's take you home."

She shuddered. "Very well, but if there wasn't anyone else, I would go with you, Charles. I'd even hold a weapon."

"I know you would." He kissed her cheek. "Darling Kate."

"We are inves-investigating?" Breese demanded as Kate smiled into Charles's eyes.

"Get back to your rooms," Charles said. "Drink coffee. I'll take Kate home and then be along. We'll gather up William, if he's home."

"But not Julie," Kate said tartly.

"Of course not. I know the Joneses took some of the fittings from the smithy, but I'm sure there are quite a few dangerous metal objects about. There is no place for a woman in this search."

"And not Fred, either," Kate added.

"No, not Fred," Charles agreed.

Breese seemed to have dozed off against the pub door. His eyes were half closed, showing a disquieting sliver of white between the lids and the under-eye area.

"Breese!" Charles called.

He jerked up like a marionette, all bending legs and flailing arms. "Yes, yes, I'm here."

"Coffee." Charles pushed him into the pub and waved toward the bar. "Coffee, then home."

"Aye, aye, sir." Breese gave him a mock salute, then staggered toward the bar.

"He's not going to be good for anything for a while," Kate observed.

"It might be best if we do our search later in the day, anyhow."

"Shouldn't you bring in the police?"

"I'll have time to look for a constable," Charles said, promising nothing.

By the time Breese was sober enough to walk in a straight line, the clock at St. Luke's had chimed seven times and was about ready to resound across the parish again. Charles stood from Breese's piano bench in the songwriter's rooms when the man pulled the damp towel from his head and yawned.

"Maybe we should forgo the pleasure of your company," William said, setting down the deck of cards he'd been toying with, a pint of ale at his elbow.

"No, I'm fine. Forty winks did me good," Breese said. He stretched his arms over his head and yawned again. "Do either of you have weapons? It doesn't escape me that we intend to search for a man who may have killed an elderly lady."

Charles and William glanced at each other. "I hadn't really thought about that," Charles admitted. He remembered what Kate had wanted him to promise. "I suppose we should find a constable first."

"Gather up a few sharp sticks and we'll be as well armed as a constable," William said. "I actually have a truncheon upstairs, but if I go up there, Julie will start begging to join us."

"No women," Charles insisted. "I told Kate she couldn't come. I jokingly told her she could join us for a consultation after our investigation."

"Right, because sweet, well-bred Miss Hogarth will climb down a trellis and come to visit you in the dead of night," William said sourly.

"She's no Julie," Charles admitted. "But we weren't looking for the same thing in a wife."

"No," William said.

"Why didn't you tell me that you had to marry?" Charles asked.

William's normally open countenance shuttered. "I can't say that I did."

"But—"

"But nothing," William interrupted. "Not everything is your business, Charles."

Charles did math in his head again. He was certain that he was right about when Julie must have conceived, and that it wasn't after the wedding, but these things did happen all the time. It was simply that he didn't like to be misled.

Breese scratched the top of his head. "I shall venture to the necessary, gentlemen, and then be ready to go."

Charles nodded and retied his neckerchief, which he had loosened after it chafed his neck.

William glared at him and tossed the rest of his pint of ale down his throat. "I'll follow Breese and meet you in front of the building in a couple of minutes."

After a couple of minutes, Charles walked out of Breese's rooms. He didn't lock the door, since he didn't know if Breese had a key. When he went outside, he found his fellow investigators testing green sticks they had torn from an ornamental tree in the front.

"I hope Mr. Ferazzi isn't lurking around to catch you damaging his property," he joked.

Breese tossed him a stick. "It isn't exactly a cudgel, but I wouldn't want one of these coming at my eye."

Charles caught the stick and pulled off a few leaves. "I could pretend a sword battle with it when I was ten, but beyond that, I'm not sure of its use."

"At least we look armed," Breese said cheerfully. "All for one and one for all!"

Chapter 21

William shook his head at Breese's Musketeerish battle cry. He gestured down the lane with his stick. "I'd like to point out that the smithy is not that far from here, less than a city block, and we may consider silence as our best policy from here on out."

"Maybe we could tie knives on the end of our sticks," Charles suggested, ignoring him.

"Why don't any of us have theater swords?" Breese mused. "We all spend a good deal of time at the theater."

"None of us are in the habit of putting on amateur theatricals," Charles said. "I do look forward to moving into that time of my life."

"When does that come?" Breese asked.

"When you have more than three rooms," Charles explained, swishing his stick around and enjoying the whooshing sound it made. "One needs room to rehearse and have a stage."

"Room for guests," William suggested. "Honestly, Charles, other than the fact that Selwood Terrace brought you closer to your Kate, and me closer to Lady Lugoson's money, moving here has been a terrible decision."

"Financially ruinous," Charles agreed.

"You met me," Breese protested. "Aren't you the lucky ones?" He struck a pose, reminiscent of certain actors that Charles had met at parties.

"Have you ever considered marrying?" Charles asked the songwriter. "You need a wife to be friends with our ladies."

Breese put his hand to his head, scratched his cheek with his stick, then dropped it. "Good heavens, I've forgotten my hat. You didn't lock me out, did you? I must still be rum dum." He tottered back into the building, holding his cheek, after Charles assured him that he had not been locked out.

"It's better not to push the issue," William said softly. "It's his private life, and you know the severe problems his predilections can cause."

Charles bit his inner cheek. "He should hide it better, for his own sake. Someone made a comment to me, and he could risk arrest."

"Not your business," William cautioned. "Don't mix yourself into it."

"I just want to help him," Charles snapped.

William dropped his stick and held up his hands. "You can't, Charles, except by merely being his friend. Here is poor Gadfly, a Hebrew, among other things. He must hide his true self in order to have any hope of success."

Charles snorted. "He has no trouble writing one love song after another."

William picked up his stick. "But who are they written to? Are they all about a love that can never be returned, never shown openly?"

Charles opened his mouth, then closed it.

William looked down his nose at Charles, his expression uncharacteristically severe. "Exactly."

Breese reappeared after a couple of minutes, holding a walking stick. He brandished it at Charles. "Sword cane. Thought it might come in handy."

William bent over it. "Looks like an antique."

Breese pounded the grass with it. "Belonged to my great-grandfather. Family lived in Germany then."

Charles picked up the stoutest of the remaining sticks from the tree. "Let's get going."

"What about a lantern?" William asked. "Let me run in and get one, just in case."

He vanished back inside the building.

"I start to wonder if we will ever make it down the lane," Charles remarked.

"Just because you are both men of adventure doesn't mean any of us are exactly men of action," Breese pointed out. "You like to travel around reporting, but you aren't involved in what goes on."

"No," Charles admitted. "But the three of us should be able to take on one fifty-eight-year-old man."

"A blacksmith? Powerful bodies," Breese mused.

Charles felt a frisson of discomfort at Breese's tone. Too dangerous.

William reappeared. "I have it."

"Sticks, a sword, a lantern," Charles said. "Now can we go? The mere thought that his friends might have been hiding Larsen so close to us all this time makes my blood boil."

They walked down the lane. The sun hung low in the sky. Smoke from cooking fires obscured some of the pinkening horizon, but the moon had already appeared. In only a few minutes, the smithy appeared. Behind it were the two small houses.

"Do we separate?" Breese whispered.

"Let's stay together," Charles said. "Our quarry will be desperate."

"What first?" William asked.

"The smithy." Charles's fingers felt slick along his stick. "We don't want him escaping into it if he hears us."

Charles crept alongside the woodshed and peered into the dark. He recalled that the logs were stacked across the rear wall, so no one should be able to hide in there. After he motioned the other two men to the opposite side of the door to the smithy, he pulled up the latch and opened it.

Holding his stick in front of his face, he stepped into the doorway. He breathed lightly through his nose as he listened intently for other sounds of breathing or movement. When he moved inside, William opened the lantern shutters and lifted the lantern high.

Charles saw the shadowy shape of the anvil, and the forge, less intimidating with its fire gone out. The room was laid out in a long rectangle. "No real hiding places in here," he said in a low voice.

"They cleaned it out well," Breese said.

"That explains why the door was unlocked," Charles agreed. "I did wonder."

They spent a couple minutes poking around, but the dirt floor didn't appear to be hiding a storage space in a dug-out basement.

"If someone has been hiding on the property, they'd probably want a bed," Breese said after they all met at the door again.

"Makes sense," William agreed.

"Very well." Charles pointed his stick at Daniel Jones's house. "Let's search there next."

They formed a triangle as they moved through the yard, watching for any sign of light or movement. Charles heard rustling in the woodpile as they walked by, but suspected rats. A flock of birds flew overhead. He accidentally kicked an anthill that had already started forming a few feet in front of the abandoned house. The ants streamed out, and the men danced around them, trying to get away from the nest before ants crawled up their legs.

William reached the front window and shined the lantern inside. No curtains blocked the space now. They must have belonged to the Jones family. "Just an empty room," he reported. "How large is the house?"

"I'm not sure," Charles admitted. "Maybe four rooms."

Breese tried the front door. "Locked, Charles."

"I recall the houses share a kitchen in the back, so there must be another door." He led the way. That door was locked, too, but the window showed another room was vacant.

"That's at least half the place empty," William said. "And I bet there are only three rooms."

They walked together to the small kitchen building. The unlocked door allowed them instant access. William shined his lantern around. The light illuminated a long, bare wooden table and a squat stove. On the other side were cupboards, but none large enough to hide a man. The ghosts of old meals clung to the air, potatoes and fish stew.

"No one here," William noted.

"Let's try the other house," Charles said. "But I admit I'm discouraged."

"This is a perfect hiding place," William argued. "Since we can't risk breaking into the houses, Larsen could be hiding inside."

"Let's check the last house and then go to the police," Charles suggested.

"Bravo," Breese said, breathing harder than was warranted by their exertions. "Brilliant plan."

They left the kitchen building and went to the window in the back of the Edmund Jones house. Through the glass, Charles saw a dilapidated armchair next to the fireplace. Hannah Jones must have decided not to move it. The floor didn't have the scrubbed-clean look of the one in the other house. She must not have been as house proud as Mrs. Jones.

Breese tried the back door. "Well, well. It turned."

William blew out a breath and lifted the lantern high as Breese stepped aside. Charles stayed close behind his friend as light swept over the fireplace and the armchair. When the light reached the opposite wall, Charles saw a clean square where an embroidered hanging with a religious verse had hung.

William walked on. "Just three rooms," he reported. They swept through a dining room in the back and a bedroom with an old bedstead that looked like it had been built into the house.

"No bedding or curtains," Breese said. "She took those."

"I think this was Mr. Jones's room," Charles said. "I can smell the tobacco."

They returned to the dining room. Charles pointed to a bright rectangle on the floor to the right of the fireplace. "Looks like a second bed was under the window."

"This means there's a bedroom with no windows in the other house," William said. "Assuming the floor plan is the same. We can tell the police that and call it good."

Charles circled the rooms once more, but this wasn't a house that held secrets. Nothing remained.

They returned to the yard. Trees rustled at the far end.

"A person?" Breese asked, stepping closer to William and the lantern.

Charles heard an owl hoot. "I think it is the owl's prey escaping."

"Let's go," William said. "My candle is down to a stub, and I don't want to be attacked from behind."

Charles led the way to their building. "Let's go to the main road. If we don't see a constable, we'll walk to the station, though I think that sergeant is tired of me."

William blew out his candle and shuttered the lantern as a curricle went by, the young man working hard to keep his horses in step. The lady next to him held on to her bonnet with one hand and the seat with the other.

"That's an accident waiting to happen," Breese said. "He didn't seem skilled enough to manage his cattle."

"Let's hope we don't see them in the road," William said.

They walked past a coffee cart, which was not doing brisk business at this time of night.

"Good evening," called a soft voice from the shadows between a pub and a row of terraced houses.

They kept walking. Even a soft voice could be a harbinger of danger where no light existed.

"Constable across the street," Breese said when they were only a couple of streets from the station.

They crossed, and Charles waved to the constable. "Blight!" he called, recognizing the man.

"Now what is it, Dickens?" the man said laconically. He spit tobacco into the street.

"We think the Joneses' smithy should be searched for Osvald Larsen," Charles explained. "We just had a look around ourselves, but one of the houses is locked, and there's a bedroom without any windows."

"Why do you think he's there?"

"We think he murdered the woman who lived above me. She might have been a childhood friend of Edmund Jones and Ferazzi, the property owner," Charles said. "It's a good hiding spot. He's gone to ground somewhere. I still believe Daniel Jones is innocent, but I'm not convinced his father was."

The constable nodded and lifted his rattle to signal other men close by. "We'll have a look around, gentlemen."

"Thank you. Would you like us to help the search?" Charles asked him.

"No, my sergeant would not approve. We'll be in touch if we need any more information."

Charles turned away, suddenly realizing how stiff he felt

across his shoulders. "A rum and water sounds like a capital notion right now, my friends."

William clapped him on the shoulder. "More than one, I hope, and I'm buying."

"Why?" Charles asked.

William grinned at him. "Nothing like a candlelit search, holding nothing but a stick, to feel like a man!"

Breese laughed. "I prefer a sword cane."

"We can't all be dandies," Charles said. "But I think I might like to have one of those myself. Oh, to be done with Selwood Terrace and to be back in London again, with money in my pocket."

The trio was worse for wear by the time they returned home, singing one of Breese's comic songs that had been in a theatrical show the year before. Charles stumbled as he entered his parlor after saying good night to his friends. Unaccountably, he still had his stick. He, William, and Breese had used it as a prop while entertaining the other pub denizens with their antics.

He set it next to the fireplace and unbuttoned his frock coat, dancing a jig as he did so and singing softly. Fred snored in the bedroom, syncopating his song.

"That's it!" he exclaimed, sure he had the idea for another collaboration with Breese. He lit a candle and took it over to his desk, then dipped a fresh quill into his inkpot. Black tendrils of ink splattered on paper as he rushed to write down his brilliant rhymes before he forgot them.

After six or eight couplets, his mind lost focus. He yawned. The candlelight seemed to grow before his eyes. Catching himself, he jerked back before his nose hit the hot brightness. He blinked, then heard a scratch at the door.

As he stumbled toward it, he yawned hugely. Was Breese pursuing a similar burst of inspiration? Or was Julie or William escaping a spat?

Instead, when he opened the door, he found a little figure covered in a dark cape. A pair of rosebud lips poked out from the encompassing hood.

"Kate?" he asked.

"See, I came," she whispered.

"What do you mean?"

"If this is the only hour to reach you, I'll sneak out and walk over here." She pushed back the hood so he could see the outline of her oval face and pointed chin.

"I didn't suggest you wander about in the dead of night," he said around another yawn. "Between escaped convicts and other villains, your father would have my head."

More roughly than he meant to, given that he wasn't so steady on his feet, he pulled at the cape to bring her inside. The tie tightened around her neck, making her cough.

"Sorry, sorry." He reached for the ribbons and untied them, then let the heavy fabric drop to the floor. He could see trails of perspiration on her neck, for the cloak had been too heavy for the warm July night. "Why are you here? You are more sensible than this, Kate."

"You certainly aren't acting happy to see me." She pouted. "You can't be irritated with me, because I'm working so hard to secure our future."

"I never see you," Kate said. "Surely tonight you haven't been working. You're drunk, Charles, I can tell."

He giggled. "We celebrated after our convict hunt."

"Did you find Larsen?"

"No, but the police are looking into it." Charles shook his head, overbalanced, and caught the back of his sofa for support.

"Oh, Charles. I'll make you some tea."

She moved toward the fireplace, but he caught her arm. "Don't. I don't want any more smoke in the room. I'm dizzy enough."

She looked around his arm and saw the quill on the scrap of paper. "You've been working?"

"On a song. More ready money."

"If you say so," she said doubtfully. "Shouldn't you be working on your prose pieces?"

"Whatever makes money. Here, give me a glass of water. That will sober me up." He went into the bedroom while she put water jug to cup.

When he came back out, she handed the cup of water to him. He ignored the brackish taste and drank it down. "Thank you, my dear."

"Of course, Charles. Will you walk me home now?"

"You don't want to stay?"

They stared at each other. Charles wished Fred had gone to Bloomsbury for the night, but how could he have known his Kate would be so daring? Besides, he couldn't afford to marry her yet. No, a chaperone was best, even a sleeping one.

"Kate, I'll walk with you, but I'll have to let you go at the burial ground. I can't risk your parents seeing me with you at this hour."

"You do look rather drawn," she said, putting her hand on his cheek. "But I hate that I see you so little. You are solving our murder with your friends rather than with me."

"Looking for a poisoner as we did in the winter, among the drawing rooms of the Brompton elite, is far different from looking for a desperate blacksmith who may have brutally murdered an old woman," Charles explained. "This is not a genteel situation. The police won't even consider Miss Jaggers, as best as I can tell, so all we can do is find Larsen."

"Murder is never genteel," Kate said. "Oh, Charles, do just walk me home. I'll deal with the consequences."

"Very well. I'll, err—" He realized he'd taken his shoes off at some point. Glancing around the dark room, he couldn't see them anywhere.

"What?"

"Shoes," Charles said. "Do you see them?"

"No. I'll help you search."

She went toward the door, while Charles stood in the center of the room, trying to retrace his steps. After a couple of minutes, he sat back down at his desk. His toes immediately touched something hard.

He reached beneath his desk. "Found them." After pulling the shoes up by the laces, he turned his chair so he could see.

Kate returned to him. Above her head, something thumped softly, a meaningless sound unless one knew the chambers above were unoccupied.

Charles stood, only one foot in an unlaced shoe. "What was that?"

Chapter 22

Something slid across the floor above. This was no time of night for people to be moving about in their parlor. Charles bent and laced his shoe. "I know that new tenants have been chosen, but there's been no sign of them yet."

"Might they have moved in?" Kate whispered.

Charles reached for his other shoe. "In the middle of the night? No, this is a time for thieves, not newlyweds."

"We didn't hear anyone on the stairs, and you were gone earlier," Kate said.

Footsteps walked over their heads, a heavy, slow tread.

"Moving toward the fireplace," Charles mused as he shoved his foot into his other shoe. "Doesn't sound like the walk of a young man or woman."

"There's a drag to it, like one leg is wounded," Kate agreed.

"I'd better investigate." Charles finished with his laces. "If it is only the newlyweds, then I can apologize and be bashful."

"I don't want you to risk injury," she protested.

"I'll take my stick and bang on the Agas' door first," Charles said. "I owe Julie an uneasy moment."

"Be kind, Charles. She lost a baby."

He chuckled. "How the tables have turned." He kissed her cheek. "Stay down here and don't unlock the door until you know it's me."

"I'm going up those stairs behind you," she insisted, handing him his stick. "I'll stay out of the way, but I can't let you go alone."

"Fred's here."

"Lock the door. If he can sleep through all that noise upstairs, he'll sleep through everything else."

"Fair enough, but keep your hood over your head, so you aren't seen. If it is the villain and he somehow escapes, I don't want him to see you."

She touched his cheek. "Thank you. I appreciate your concern."

He stared at her. "Are you always going to be this brave?"

She lifted her chin. "I hope so."

He couldn't help tucking two fingers under that stubborn chin and tilting her toward him. When he had her mouth positioned under his, he pressed a soft kiss to her lips. "You are a darling."

"Yes, I am." She grinned at him, then winced as another thump resounded. "What is he doing?"

"I have to wonder. I thought nothing remained up there." He took her hand and pulled her to the door. When they were in the hall, he locked the door and handed her the key. "Put it in your pocket."

She complied as he lifted his stout stick and put his foot on the first step of the staircase. He went up slowly, trying to remember where the squeaky treads were.

When he reached the top, he whispered, "I'm going to try to open that door. As soon as I do, start banging on the Agas' door."

"Create confusion," she whispered back.

"And gain backup. On the count of three." He counted slowly, raising his arm. Behind him, he heard the whisper of cloth as she moved toward the other door; then he slapped the pinkie side of his fist against the door.

Bang! Bang! Bang!

Charles reached for the doorknob. It turned, unlocked. He pushed the door in, hoping his banging had startled whoever was inside. Across the hall, Kate had done the same with her smaller hand but was still making a good amount of noise as she attempted to rouse the Agas from their bed.

Creeping into the dark room, Charles kept his stick in front of his face, his other arm crossed over his chest for protection. He blinked, realizing light glowed in the fireplace. Had they lit a fire on this hot July night?

Then he realized it wasn't a fire, but a lantern on the grate. Bricks were scattered across the floor. A man turned to him. He must have been dismantling the fireplace. Charles saw a gaunt, late middle-aged face, the lower half covered with whitish whiskers.

The old man threw a brick at him.

Charles leapt out of the way. "Osvald Larsen?"

The man grunted and pulled another brick from the fireplace, then threw it. Charles rushed forward. He swung his stick and caught the man on the shoulder.

The man grunted again and went down, then came up with the lantern. When he threw that at Charles, aiming for the center of his body, Charles jumped to the side. He dropped his stick and stumbled as he reached for it.

Glass tinkled when the lantern broke. Charles sniffed instinctively, afraid of gas, but the light had gone out. A candle, probably. Now the room was pitch black. Glass on the floor. Had the man left the apartment?

"Dear God," he said aloud. Kate was in the hall. He straightened and ran for the door.

A heavy mass blocked his path. The man. Charles grabbed him around the waist. The man turned, fighting back. Charles attempted to land a punch and had his ear pulled. He heard shouting in the hallway; then a light flared outside the door.

"Give over," Charles puffed. "We've got you, Larsen."

The next thing Charles knew, he'd been slammed against a wall. His head went back, and he struck the plaster hard with the back of his skull. He saw stars and began to slump down but then recovered himself. Kicking out, he caught the man's shin.

The man grunted, the only sound he seemed to make. Charles pushed off the wall and head-butted him. The man stumbled back and fell over, Charles on top of him. Charles's head swam as he struggled into a sitting position on the man's chest.

A light appeared in the doorway. "Take this," William said to somebody; then he came into the room.

"I think I'm sitting on Osvald Larsen," Charles said through his haze.

"Go for a constable," William called. The light went away as footsteps made their way down the stairs.

Charles heard hands moving against fabric; then William knelt down next to him on the wood floor.

"Get up," he instructed. "Turn over slowly, Larsen."

Charles came up on his knees, then went into a crouch, as the man turned over, groaning. In the dark, Charles felt rather than saw William confining the man's hands with a neckerchief.

"Do you have any weapons?" William demanded.

The man didn't answer.

"I'll search him," Charles said, poking around the man's torso, trying to feel for hard objects.

"What was he doing here?"

Charles gingerly patted the man's trousers. "He was pulling bricks out of the fireplace."

William rose.

"Watch out. There's glass," Charles said.

"Can I leave you while I get my shoes?"

"No," Charles said. "My ears are still ringing. From my head being slammed against the wall."

"Right," William said. "At least I was still dressed. Why are you up?"

"I was writing lyrics, then . . ." Charles trailed off. While his friend knew Kate had been with him, he didn't want Larsen to hear about it.

Long moments passed. The man on the floor breathed hard but said nothing. Charles's ears started to lose the annoying noise. He blinked hard, trying to quell the dizziness.

"What were you looking for in the fireplace?" he asked. "Is there a secret hiding spot?"

Larsen didn't answer.

"We'd better turn him over so he can breathe," Charles suggested.

William swore under his breath. "You didn't kill him, did you?"

Together, they forced the man over.

"No, he's breathing," Charles reported. "Just not talking."

The man sniffed. The sound was so liquid that Charles guessed he'd possibly damaged the man's nose. He didn't feel the least bit sorry.

"What do you think is in the fireplace?" William asked.

"We know Miss Haverstock was wealthy," Charles said. "They must have been looking for something valuable. Maybe she had jewelry to go with her goods."

"Makes sense." William chuckled. "I'm sorry we didn't look."

"It would belong to Miss Jaggers, anyway, and I'm not particularly fond of her," Charles groused. He heard a rattle in the street. "That will be a constable."

The darkness in the hallway diminished as a small group

came up the stairs. First, a constable appeared, holding a lantern high; then the two young women came in behind him.

"Watch for glass on the floor," Charles called, not sure if Julie was wearing shoes or not.

"Wot's all this?" demanded the constable.

"The new tenants haven't moved in yet, so we knew what we heard overhead had to be a thief," Charles explained. "I believe you'll find that this is one Osvald Larsen, escaped from Cold-bath Fields Prison and the murderer of Miss Haverstock, formerly of these premises."

The young constable lifted his lantern high over the prisoner's head. "Oh? What do you have to say for yourself?"

Charles could see blood had spilled from the man's nose and had clotted around the whiskers on his upper lip. The prisoner spat and turned his head away from the light.

"Not a good sign if he won't talk," the constable said.

Charles stared at the man on the floor, trying to picture him versus the sketch he'd seen at the prison. "I do think we're right. I've seen a sketch, and this man is the right age and has the same square face. Besides, anyone who lives nearby would know these apartments are empty and wouldn't bother trying to rob them."

"Could be a vagrant simply looking for a warm place to sleep."

"Not needed in July," William said. "Look, we're reporters. Professional observers."

More footsteps sounded on the steps. Two more uniformed men came into the room. Charles stood, happy to recognize Constable Blight.

"I believe we've found your escapee," Charles told him.

Blight stepped forward and glanced down at the man. "Very good. What's he doing here?"

"He was ripping apart the fireplace," Charles reported.

Blight turned to look at it. Bricks littered the floor. "You don't say. I look forward to sorting all this out. Haul him to his feet, men, and let's get him back to the station."

Charles watched impassively as the two other constables lifted Larsen. He kicked out with his feet, a last act of defiance that earned him a thump on the head.

"Watch it, you, or we'll throw you down the steps," the first constable said in a menacing voice.

Larsen stopped fighting. His dark gaze met Charles's, and Charles felt sure he'd just locked eyes with a killer. As much as he wanted to understand, he needed to free Daniel Jones even more.

"How did you remove the manacles?" he asked. "If you have any love left for the Jones family, please tell me."

Larsen stamped his foot.

"They've lost everything, Mr. Larsen," Charles pleaded. "Your old friend Hannah has no home. Edmund died. Daniel is rotting away in jail."

A bead of sweat trickled down the old criminal's temple.

"You know what it's like in jail. But he's in Newgate. Sweet, kindly Daniel Jones will never see his family again if you don't tell the police the truth."

"It were Edmund," Larsen admitted. "Edmund, me old cove. Never even met his lad."

"Thank you," Charles said. "Thank you. You heard that, didn't you, constables?"

Soon the remaining inhabitants of the room listened as three pairs of feet sounded on the steps.

"Shall we have a look?" Constable Blight said, gesturing at the fireplace.

"Isn't it more important to send to Newgate and have Daniel Jones released?" Charles asked.

"It's not that simple. But we all heard the confession. It will have to be sorted out with the magistrates. I think he will go free now."

"Thank God," Charles breathed.

"What do you think that man was looking for?" Constable Blight said.

"Impossible to know," Charles said, coming to stand next to him by the fireplace.

The constable grunted. "I need to get back to the station if you want Daniel Jones added to the docket. If you find anything here, make sure the heir's lawyers are notified."

"Aren't you going to help us?" William asked.

Constable Blight gestured at the mess. "It's too dark to search, and I'm not about to be further involved in the demolition of property."

"Fair enough," Charles said. "But I'm afraid Mr. Ferazzi will have whatever ought to be Miss Jaggers's property stolen if his men find something here."

"Demolition of property, eh wot?" came a voice from behind them.

Charles turned to see Mr. Nickerson in the doorway. "What are you doing here?"

"I was walking by, and I saw lights and police," the rent-taker said. "Why are you destroying Mr. Ferazzi's property? I 'ope you're arresting this man, Constable."

"'E didn't do it," Constable Blight said. "Osvald Larsen did."

"Did Mr. Ferazzi tell him to do it?" Charles demanded. "I know they were old friends."

Mr. Nickerson screwed up his lips into a tight O. "I don't 'ave any idea wot yer talking about."

"Maybe you came here to help Mr. Larsen," Charles said. "I wonder what you are hunting for in these empty rooms. I'd understood new tenants were moving in any day now."

Constable Blight sighed. "I need to return to the station. Mr. Nickerson, I know you work for the owner. What do you want to do here?"

"Board up the door," Mr. Nickerson said with a narrow-eyed glance at Charles. "I'll have a bricklayer in to repair the damage."

"Do you have the wood?" the constable said. "I don't."

"I'll take care of it." Mr. Nickerson stared at Charles, then pointed at the door. "You need to leave, Mr. Dickens. I remember 'ow we were once friendly-like, and I won't put in a complaint against you. I want to get 'ome to the missus."

"He's a thief," Charles told the constable. "They are looking for something that must belong to Miss Jaggers."

"Who you thought was a killer," the constable pointed out. "So why do you care?"

Charles went across the hall to his friends. Kate clung to his arm when he walked in.

"We heard everything," she said softly as footsteps went down the stairs.

"Why don't Julie and I walk Kate home?" William suggested. "Leave you out of it?"

"Are you certain?" Charles said.

"A walk will do Julie good."

"Very well. Thank you. But then what?" Charles asked.

"We can unboard a door, as long as no one is around to hear us."

Charles gritted his teeth. "That Nickerson character tends to appear out of nowhere. We'd better not try it tonight. Tomorrow?"

"We can have someone stand guard," William said. "Fred, maybe."

"We can't," Julie said. "Remember? Lord Lugoson is taking us to Tatersalls with him to look at a horse tomorrow."

"As if either of us would have any advice for him. Can't we put him off?"

"It is his birthday," Julie explained. "I promised."

William worked his jaw. "I really wanted to be on hand for the discovery of buried treasure. What do you think is hidden in the fireplace?"

"Jewelry," Charles said.

"Proof of Miss Haverstock's original identity," Kate suggested. "Something that ties her to Osvald Larsen, that would give him a reason to kill her."

Charles leaned over Kate and stole a sip of tea from her cup. "I'll have to find some proper tools. I'm not about to tear apart a fireplace with my bare hands."

"There will be a hidden compartment." Kate leaned forward. "It's not as if Miss Haverstock built that fireplace herself."

"Just needs a clever eye," Julie said. "We'll be home by dark tomorrow. No one will be in the street, and we can have a very quiet little treasure hunt."

"Come along, Kate Hogarth. We need to take you home. Let's leave Charles out of it this time," William said.

"Yes. I'll see Charles at St. Luke's in a few hours." She glanced shyly at Julie. "My parents are having a garden party on Monday evening. I hope you and your husband will come."

Julie smiled and chose her words with care. "What a kind offer. We would be delighted to join you."

Charles watched the trio leave before going back down the steps to unlock his own door. Inside, Fred still snored away. Charles stretched out on his sofa and closed his eyes and tried not to worry that Mr. Ferazzi would demand another search of the fireplace before he and his friends could sneak in.

Twilight came the next night, and Charles was alone. Fred was in Bloomsbury, and the Agas had not yet come home. Charles grew impatient as the light diminished. He crept upstairs with his coin-digging trowel and pried the nails holding one board over the door. With minimal noise, he made it inside and figured he was safe enough until the Agas returned. He had a view of the lane from the window.

The air still reeked of Osvald Larsen's musky sweat. Charles opened the parlor window, hoping for a breeze, and removed his frock coat. He set it on the floor by the door, trying not to remember the final sight of Miss Haverstock's body screwed into the far wall.

In his shirtsleeves, he shifted the five bricks the blacksmith had pried out of the mortar, and stacked them against the wall, under the window. Larsen had attacked only one part of the fireplace, but Charles didn't know if he'd had any intelligence about an actual secret compartment. Still, he must have been tearing it apart for some reason.

Why hadn't Larsen conducted his search the night he'd killed Miss Haverstock? Had something startled him, or had he learned something later? If Mr. Ferazzi had known the fireplace's secret, he'd have investigated the day they tossed the possessions out of the rooms.

Charles forced his memories back to the morning he'd discovered Miss Haverstock. Nothing had seemed out of place around the fireplace. Had Osvald Larsen assumed some particular item would be found among her possessions that had not?

After removing the grate, Charles stepped into the fireplace in a crouch. Chunks of mortar crunched under his feet. Within seconds his fingers were dark with soot as he poked and prodded. A disgusting taste coated the back of his throat. "A future as a chimney sweep, I have not," he muttered.

He spent twenty minutes searching the bricks on the damaged side, poking his trowel into the mortar, but did not find any signs of secret compartments. Then he quickly swept eyes and fingers over the back of the fireplace, though it was an odd place for a hidden compartment. Finally, he tackled the right side.

In exactly the same spot where, on the opposite side, Larsen had pulled away bricks, he found a brick that wiggled. He pushed hard. It didn't move back. After wrapping his hands around it, he attempted to shift the rough surface. The brick moved about an inch. He tightened his grip and put his entire body into it.

Behind him, he heard a door open but didn't cease in his attempt to shift the brick. "I may have discovered the right spot," he called. "Did Lord Lugoson find a good horse?"

"The dead never stay dead," said the voice of an older man, with a whisper of an accent. "They keep haunting you."

Chapter 23

❧

As Charles jerked his head around, the brick came away with him. He toppled against the other side of the fireplace, shoes skittering on the broken bits of mortar. His palms went damp with sweat. Why hadn't he waited for the Agas? Mr. Ferazzi would toss him and Fred out on their ears.

But instead of ordering him out, Mr. Ferazzi spoke as if Charles was one of his employees.

"Did you find the papers?" the old man asked. "Every last remnant of her must be erased."

"Why?" Charles asked, not knowing if Mr. Ferazzi recognized him. The old man looked drugged, his eyes hazy. "Is Mr. Nickerson with you?"

"She destroys my dreams." The landlord clutched at the knot at the front of his cheap black neckerchief as if it was choking him.

Charles tried to right himself, but he went down on one knee before he regained control. The knee of his trousers tore. Was the man superstitious? Was he afraid Miss Haverstock would haunt these chambers if anything of her remained?

"I'm sorry I came in here. I know Mr. Nickerson didn't want me upstairs. Can I take you home?" Maybe he could remove the old man and then go back in later.

The landlord didn't look at him, just continued worrying at the knot at his neck. "Goldy tortured me. I had to end it."

"Goldy?" Charles asked, rising to his feet. He brushed at his knees. "Who was Goldy?"

Mr. Ferazzi blinked at his question as if he hadn't noticed before that an actual person was in the room with him.

"Miss Haverstock died here, not Goldy." Charles climbed out of the fireplace, holding the brick still. He added it to the neat pile.

The landlord ripped away his neckcloth. "Don't confuse me."

Charles could see long red streaks on the man's neck. Scratches. His pupils were tiny in the limited light. He looked like an opium eater. Was he having hallucinations? "Who was Goldy?"

"A survivor," whispered the old man. He swayed.

"The only Goldy I know of died as a child. But she died in the river. I read the article about it. Were you the person who put it under my door?" Maybe he would finally get to the bottom of that mystery.

"No."

Charles frowned, not liking the sound of that. Unease prickled at him. Maybe he should have kept the brick in his hand. He touched his pocket where his trowel rested. "I wonder who wanted me to know about Goldy's death. You had a part in that, didn't you? You were the leader of her mudlark gang all those years ago?"

"She survived," Mr. Ferazzi said in a hollow voice. "Then she lived."

A connection formed in Charles's brain. "Are you saying Goldy became Miss Haverstock?"

The old man nodded. "We called her Goldy because her father was rich."

So Rebecca Adams had been Goldy all along. Charles kept a light note in his voice. "Then she can't be haunting you now. She's buried. Er, somewhere." He hadn't thought to ask where, much less visit her grave.

Mr. Ferazzi clutched at his head. "She still has a hold on me."

Charles's reporter's instincts snapped into place. He had in front of him a man who wanted to tell a story. "Start at the beginning, please."

The man's lips curved under his mustache, but no hint of warmth reached his eyes. "None of our parents ever knew what had happened on the river." The man winced. He pulled a little black vial from his pocket and drank down the contents. Laudanum.

"Did you help free her?"

"No, we all left her to her fate. Goldy reappeared the next day."

Charles opened his mouth when Mr. Ferazzi paused, but then his fingers opened and dropped the vial on the floor, and the noise seemed to rouse him again. He continued. "Years later, our parents promised Goldy to me. An arranged marriage. She was a beauty then, black hair, fiery eyes. Her personality softened some as she grew into womanhood. I thought she had forgotten."

Charles's brain snapped onto one piece of that narrative. "You're Jewish?"

"Yes. Italy has rarely been a good place for my people. My father moved us here from the ghetto in Ferrara when I was a child."

Charles glanced out the window, wishing he'd see his friends in the lane, but he seemed to be on his own. Without knowing what Mr. Ferazzi wanted, and given that he was blocking the door, Charles continued the conversation. "I take it that Goldy didn't want to marry you."

A growl emerged from Mr. Ferazzi's throat. "She would have, but Elijah Haverstock stole her away with his wealth."

"I'm sorry."

Mr. Ferazzi bared his teeth. "He paid for it, for taking her away from all of us, stealing her from her family and heritage."

"She married Mr. Haverstock. Was she afraid of you?"

"She had no reason to fear me, unlike her husband. I admit she had suffered that day, would have drowned if she hadn't been picked up by a ferry, but—" He shrugged as if he hadn't been responsible.

"You went on as if nothing had happened," Charles pointed out.

Mr. Ferazzi's lips peeled away from his teeth, an involuntary grimace. "I made it my life's work to ruin the Haverstocks. Anyone connected to that family."

"You never married? You let revenge blacken your soul."

His eyes glowed hollowly when he lifted his head. "The Haverstocks took in my bride, treated her like a daughter as she made arrangements to join the Church of England. I never spoke to her after she left her parents' home, but I was the specter in the corners of her life."

"You hired your old friend Osvald to kill her all these years later?"

The landlord spoke as if to himself. "I am not such a hard man. I found her again after she was widowed and offered her a home in one of my buildings."

Charles frowned. Mr. Ferazzi had been watching her all those years, waiting for the opportunity to offer his twisted love again. "Why did she need that? She seems to have had a great deal of money."

"Property, not money, by then. She wanted to keep all the Haverstock possessions for Miss Jaggers's benefit. She adored that pretty, spoiled girl. She had no children of her own. None that lived."

"You told me at the inquest that you didn't know the girl."

"I knew of her. She was a Haverstock connection."

"You wanted to court Goldy? After all this time?"

"She continued to haunt me. I wanted her forgiveness. My lust to destroy the Haverstocks wavered once most of them were gone."

"What happened that night?" Charles asked softly, trying to be the voice of conscience in the man's mind, rather than another person talking.

"I suggested we wed. She excused herself for a time. When she came back, she was wearing that old dress, the one she'd married Haverstock in. She insisted I look at her, told me we were both decayed, like that dress, and I had no business talking about wedlock." Mr. Ferazzi rubbed his eyes with the back of his sleeve.

"What did you say to that?"

"That she was still beautiful, still mine." He paused. "I was holding her arm. She wrenched it away. She turned. Her spittle hit my eye when she said she was never mine. We'd been about to open a bottle of wine. The corkscrew was in my hand."

Charles pressed his lips together tightly as bile rose from his belly. He knew she'd been strangled first, but now he knew Mr. Ferazzi was Miss Haverstock's killer, not Osvald Larsen.

The landlord passed his hand over his eyes. "It was in my hand, then—" His fingers shook hard as he gestured. He folded his arms across his chest. "I slammed it into the wall. I hurt her."

Charles took stealthy steps, trying to get between the door and the evil old man.

But Mr. Ferazzi's gaze tracked him, and a little smile edged around the corners of his mouth. Charles stopped moving. He noticed how long the man's fingers were, and wondered what it had taken for him to choke the life from Miss Haverstock.

His voice trembled as he spoke. "Why don't we go for a

walk? It's stuffy in here. You'll be able to think more clearly."
Could he lead the man to the Chelsea Police Station, or at least
to a constable on the beat?

"I hate this building," Mr. Ferazzi said, his hand dropping to
his side. "I should sell it, but the rents are excellent."

Charles took another step, his back brushing along the wall,
hoping to herd him out the door. "Don't you still smell her
here?" he asked. "I do."

The man shuddered and took a step backward.

Charles moved again, an agonizing step closer to the door. He
had to get this murderer to the police. "It must torment you,
being in the room where you made such a desperate move."

Mr. Ferazzi's fingers went to his temples. "It happened so
fast."

"Your mind will be clearer somewhere else," Charles said
soothingly. "The brick dust is heavy here. Let's go downstairs."

"I might feel better," the man said tentatively. He coughed.

Charles's heart pounded in his chest, but he took the steps,
anyway, ignoring his fear that the man might attack. He was
young, after all, and a match for this madman, unlike poor,
dotty old Miss Haverstock. He set his fingertips on the man's
sleeve and gently pulled him through the door and to the stairs.
The old man went with him down to the main door of the
building.

Charles felt faint with relief when they reached the walkway
outside. The cool air felt blissful on his cheeks after he'd
breathed in old mortar and brick dust. He led Mr. Ferazzi
south, planning to turn off onto the network of roads leading
to the police station, but after a block or two, the man's agita-
tion returned. He pulled away from Charles's gentle hand on
his sleeve and began to touch his face, his mustache. His nails
scratched his cheeks.

"I need to go home," he muttered.

"Home?" Charles said. "But you haven't been staying there."

The landlord's head snapped in Charles's direction. "What do you mean? Have you been following me? Who are you?"

"I'm your tenant," Charles said patiently, patting his arm. "I passed by your house one night while looking for a friend."

Mr. Ferazzi wrenched away from him with far more force than was needed. Then with one leg lifted high and his knee bent, the man took off at a run, to Charles's shock, belying his age and his drugged state as he bolted in a southward direction, rather than toward the police station.

Charles raced after him, thinking he was heading toward his house, but instead of veering off eastward toward the Royal Hospital, he kept heading toward the river.

Chapter 24

❧

"Mr. Ferazzi!" Charles shouted, chasing his quarry past a pub. He couldn't let the man out of his sight. Murderer or not, in his deranged state, he might harm himself. Closing in, Charles reached his hand out but just missed the man's shoulder. Focused on grabbing, he didn't mind his feet. His arms windmilled as he lost his balance, his feet slipping, but he stayed on his feet.

Charles stalled to scrape old potato peelings from his shoe, using a sharp chunk of rock. His knee gave a twinge of pain when he moved it. But the Italian kept running, and no constable appeared.

Frustrated, Charles retraced his steps, opened the pub door, and waved until he caught the eye of the man behind the bar. "Summon a constable!" he called, then reversed and continued to follow in Mr. Ferazzi's footsteps.

Down the street, the landlord's feet flew past an array of artisans' cottages. Charles followed him down the quiet, darkening street, wincing each time he put his weight on his knee. Seagulls circled overhead as the sluggish brown river came into view beyond the tangle of trees and vegetation. The scent of raw sewage assaulted his nostrils.

Charles shouted again. The Italian didn't look back. "What are you doing?" he yelled.

Mr. Ferazzi didn't pause at the end of the street, merely leapt over a bush and disappeared.

Charles reached the bush and paused, massaging his knee, then slowly made his way across the uneven surface of the vegetation-covered dirt beyond the bush. A few feet later, he could see the rocky foreshore below a rickety staircase next to an abandoned building that had probably been an unsuccessful pub.

His mouth dropped open as Mr. Ferazzi waded into the sunset-dappled but filthy water, the tide so high that little of the foreshore was evident. The mudlarks and other riverside dwellers had not yet come out.

He kicked at the dirt with his good leg. "I'll stop chasing you," he shouted at Mr. Ferazzi. "You'll make yourself ill. Come out of there!"

The Italian didn't look back. At first, Charles could see his knees pumping as he lifted them, wading, then walking. Soon the water was waist high on him.

"Stop," Charles cried, holding what was left of the bannister as he stumbled down the stairs. A splinter bit into his palm, and he yelped but kept moving. He hurtled over a missing riser at the bottom of the stairs and came down hard on his bad knee. Gasping past the pain and limping, he made his way over the foreshore and stopped at the water's edge.

The smell of the river was indescribable, even to a newspaper-man. At his feet, the water lapped at his shoes, which were already stained with water. A dead bird floating in the water touched the leather at his toes. He jumped back, hoping he wouldn't see a human corpse next.

Behind him, he heard a yell as he waved his arms in the direction of Mr. Ferazzi. What was the landlord trying to accomplish? Was he trying to mimic Goldy's experience?

Giving up on the man hearing him, as he was already out in midstream, the water up past his abdomen, Charles ran down the foreshore, ignoring the voices behind him. He tripped over a derelict boat but then found a rowboat at the water's edge, probably left there while the owners went up the waterside stairs to dinner.

He pushed the boat toward the water, thinking to rescue Mr. Ferazzi himself. The man had gone mad, utterly mad. No one responsible for their actions would run into the filthy river. But behind him, shouts rang out again, and he heard the telltale rattle of a constable. Not wanting to be arrested as a thief, he stopped short of climbing into the rowboat.

He focused back on the river, squinting his eyes. When he found Mr. Ferazzi again, he was only a head. His mustache had gone flat with dampness. Mr. Ferazzi sank into the water. Charles held his breath, waiting for the man to bob up. But he didn't. He didn't come up again.

When Charles put his hand to his cheek, the splinter in his palm speared his tender flesh. He yelped and worried at the splinter with his teeth and waited for the uniformed constable to make his awkward way down the stairs.

Long after dark, Charles sat in a room in the Chelsea Police Station. Sir Silas and Constable Blight had questioned him, conferred outside, then come in again to continue with him. Constables had gone door-to-door down the street and had found a couple of artists who had been drinking on their roof and insisted that Charles had never touched the man, merely chased him.

"At least we finally know who killed Miss Haverstock," Sir Silas said.

The door to the room opened. "We've found Reggie Nickerson," the sergeant said.

"Bring him in," said the coroner, rising to his feet.

Charles stayed where he was. His knee had swelled, and he was bone tired, as if he'd escaped from the river himself.

Reggie Nickerson swaggered in. He'd tied up his oversize neckerchief until it thrust his chin high above his neck. The coat he'd donned was oversize, too, almost as if it wasn't his. "Wot's all this?" he asked. "Me missus might think as if I've done somefink wrong, being dragged out at all hours."

"Have a seat," Sir Silas said calmly.

Charles pushed out the chair next to him.

"Well, I'll be blowed," Mr. Nickerson exclaimed. "If it isn't that reporter fellow."

Charles looked up at Sir Silas, not sure why he hadn't yet been dismissed.

"Your employer has died," Sir Silas said calmly.

The factotum cupped his hand around his ear. "I can't be 'earing you proper, sir. Wot's all this?"

"Mr. Ferazzi killed himself in front of witnesses," chimed in Constable Blight.

Mr. Nickerson's lower face slowly elongated, his mouth falling open as the truth sank in.

"There will be an inquest," the coroner said. "But for right now, I want to know who is to take over the businesses."

"I'm 'is right-'and man," said Mr. Nickerson, uncharacteristically slowly. "I know it all best."

"Do you know who his heir is?" Sir Silas lifted his fingers above the desk as if to rap out a beat, but then settled them back down again.

"Why, it's that Miss Jaggers," Mr. Nickerson explained. "Miss Haverstock's ward."

Charles's eyes widened. Mr. Ferazzi would never have made a Haverstock his heir.

Sir Silas's fingers went to his chin. "Are you the appropriate person to notify her? Can the business run without her intervention?"

"She hasn't reached her majority," Charles said. "She's only seventeen."

"Was Mr. Ferazzi her guardian?" Sir Silas asked.

"Miss Haverstock was her guardian," Charles explained. "Did she have a will? Did she leave the guardianship to Mr. Ferazzi? It seems unlikely, though not out of what is possible."

Sir Silas nodded. "I'll call on the lawyers. I'll want them at the inquest." He turned to Reggie Nickerson. "Give the constable the lawyers' names on your way out. We'll have to send word to Miss Jaggers in the morning."

"When will the inquest be?" Charles asked.

"Tomorrow afternoon," Sir Silas said. "Clear enough situation. Three witnesses to most of it."

Mr. Nickerson glanced at Charles. "What happened?"

"He was drinking laudanum. I think he hallucinated," Charles said.

"You think he killed Miss Haverstock?" the factotum gasped.

"He confessed," Charles said wearily. "He confessed and then ran down the street and drowned himself. Clearly, he'd been consumed by guilt about what had happened when they were children."

"I'll be blowed," Mr. Nickerson whispered. "I'll be blowed."

Charles was suddenly fed up with the entire situation. "Sir Silas, I know this might be outside of your responsibilities, but we had robberies in the neighborhood before Miss Haverstock was murdered, and I can't help but think Mr. Nickerson was involved somehow. In my dealings, he has proven himself to be quite dishonest, and I would hate to have him allowed to continue in his present sphere of responsibility."

"You've nothing on me, sir. Why, I did what Mr. Ferazzi told me!" Mr. Nickerson shouted.

Sir Silas nodded. "But you don't deny the accusations, Mr. Nickerson. I'm sure all this will be taken into consideration as the heiress's guardianship is resolved by the courts."

"Not only that, but I don't know why Miss Jaggers would be Mr. Ferazzi's heir. They were not related," Charles explained, "and Mr. Ferazzi told me he'd spent his lifetime intent on destroying the entire Haverstock family."

Sir Silas's gaze went shrewd. "Miss Jaggers is part of that family?"

"Exactly, sir. If there is a will naming her as Mr. Ferazzi's heir, and Mr. Nickerson has such a document, I would investigate the relationship between the two of them." Charles thought of that shining girl, Evelina Jaggers, a newly minted heiress. First, Miss Haverstock had died, and now Mr. Ferazzi, and the deaths had freed her to be rich. How could she be entirely innocent?

"You must be mad," Mr. Nickerson exclaimed.

Sir Silas turned to him. "Are you any relation to the Haverstocks?"

Mr. Nickerson stiffened. "What does that matter?"

"Just answer the question," Sir Silas ordered.

Charles glanced at each man in turn, holding his breath.

Mr. Nickerson passed his fingers over his mouth and wiped away a sheen of moisture at one corner. "Wot we have is a situation of extreme delicacy, wot wi' a lady who wasn't very proper, but 'oo my father loved."

"Was that father a Haverstock?"

Mr. Nickerson laced his fingers over his midsection. "Yes, but I never did Mr. Ferazzi any 'arm."

"Except forging his will," Charles snapped.

"You can't prove it, Mr. Dickens." Mr. Nickerson's upper lip twisted. "Miss Jaggers is the only heir he's got."

Charles wondered why he felt sorrier for the suicidal murderer than he did for the victim's ward, but Miss Jaggers was not one to elicit sympathy. Had he sensed evil in her from the start?

＊　＊　＊

The next morning, Charles rose from his bed early, though it had been nearly dawn when he retired. He went down the lane at a trot, his sore knee reminding him of the previous night when he had run after a remorseful killer.

Instead of heading toward town, he went in the opposite direction, toward the Hogarths' house. One of Kate's brothers opened the door and escorted him to the dining room, where Mr. Hogarth sat with an early newspaper and a pot of tea. A rack of toast waited nearby.

"If it isn't Charles," his editor exclaimed, setting down a butter knife. "What brings you here so early?"

"I needed to tell you that I won't be able to come into the office today. I have to testify at another inquest. I'm sorry for it."

"Who died?"

"Mr. Ferazzi. I was a witness to his suicide. He admitted to killing Miss Haverstock." Charles heard an exclamation and saw Kate coming through the kitchen door with a basket of hard-boiled eggs.

"Truly?" Kate asked. "The mystery is solved?"

"Part of it," Charles confirmed. "But in order to get any sleep, I was unable to finish searching Miss Haverstock's fireplace."

"We'll look tonight," Kate promised.

"You will not," her father interjected as he tapped on a brittle eggshell with a knife. "You will be helping your mother with her party this evening. You are attending, are you not, Charles?"

"Of course," Charles agreed, though he had completely forgotten about it.

Kate looked stricken. "What if the treasure disappears?"

"There might not be a treasure," Charles said. "And it's possible the Agas uncovered it while I was at the police station. For now, I need to get such writing done as I can at home this morning, and then go to the inquest."

"I'll see you tonight, though," Kate said.

Charles smiled warmly at her. "Yes, and again, Mr. Hogarth, I am very sorry."

"Canna be helped," said the editor. "Sit down and eat, Charles. There is plenty for ye." He fluttered his copy of *The Observer*.

"Anything exciting?" Charles asked.

"I thought ye might like to take Kate to *Cupid in London*," Mr. Hogarth said. "At the Queen? Mrs. Nisbett is claiming to have fixed the theater's ventilation problem."

"I'd be happy to write an article," Charles promised. "Tomorrow?"

Kate smiled and wiped her hands on her apron, then vanished back into the kitchen.

"What do you think about this election of David Salomons to be a sheriff of London?" Mr. Hogarth asked.

Charles perused the article as Mr. Hogarth poured tea for him. "This alleged screaming of agony by the lord mayor of having the election of a Jewish man after a Catholic is troubling. It seems that the men in power fight what the citizens don't mind."

Mr. Hogarth nodded and passed him the cream jug. "We need different sorts of men in power, otherwise thinking will never liberalize. I am glad Mr. Salomons was elected. I hope the lord mayor does not succeed in preventing him from taking office. Salomons is considered a man of great ability."

"Better to openly be Jewish than to hide it," Charles said.

"Did the religious issue have anything to do with Miss Haverstock's death?"

Charles took a piece of toast from the rack and stared at it, considering. "Perhaps not, but her mistreatment at an early age by her friends might have stemmed from her religion as much as from her personality, and her later behavior seems to suggest a constant pattern of secrecy. I was surprised to learn that Mr. Ferazzi was also of that faith and background."

"As ye can see, it hardly matters," Mr. Hogarth said. "Religion and race are no marker of ability."

"Nor background, as long as you can find an education," Charles said. "I want to persuade all the mudlarks to leave the river. Maybe the examples of Mr. Ferazzi and Miss Haverstock, no matter how tragic in the end, will help persuade Lucy Fair and her little band. Their starts in Limehouse did not preclude them from being financially successful and living to old age."

Mr. Hogarth chuckled. "A murder victim and a suicide, role models for a group of wild children?"

Charles sighed. "I know, but what else have I to work with?" He coated his thin round of buttered toast with strawberry preserves and stuffed it into his mouth. "I'd better return to my desk."

"Not going to keep hunting for that treasure?" Mr. Hogarth lifted a bushy gray brow.

"No, sir. I have the discipline to finish my work." Charles picked up three of the eggs, forced a smile while juggling them, and left.

He was glad to learn he was still in good graces with Kate's father, despite not having spent much time at the *Chronicle* over the past few weeks, but his time had been entirely too broken into bits. What could he do in order to be entirely his own master? The discipline of reporting on meetings had begun to chafe him.

Charles yawned through the inquest, which didn't reveal anything new or exciting. Miss Jaggers and her swain did not appear. After his hand was shaken by everyone who'd seen his mad chase through Chelsea, he returned home, ready to spend the evening in more lighthearted pursuits.

"I've been neglecting Kate terribly," he confessed to Fred as he looked through his meager wardrobe an hour before the party. "I should do something to amuse her."

"You should perform for her," Fred said. "You refused to join in at our parents' rooms that night, and I remember she pouted and said she wanted to see you dance."

Charles narrowed his eyes at Fred. "I don't want to make a fool of myself."

"Go in disguise," Fred suggested.

Charles rubbed his chin. "I could be in character. That would disguise any imperfection."

"You can do a hornpipe," Fred said. "What will you wear?"

"I'll borrow your cap," Charles decided, "and wear simple workman's clothes. That will do for a sailor well enough." He grinned and clapped his brother's shoulder. "Will you play the fiddle for me? Stay outside in the garden and start the song when I burst in through those French doors they have?"

"Of course," Fred promised. "We'll flare up and have the best time!"

The party began after the dinner hour. Charles and Fred sneaked in through the apple orchard and around the vegetable garden. A gate led into the back of the property, which had a lawn edged by flower beds.

"There is your stage." Fred pointed at the French doors, which were open to the early evening air.

Mrs. Hogarth's roses were still in full bloom. Charles took a deep breath of the delightful fragrance as Fred opened his violin case and took out his instrument and bow.

"Stand by that bush over there." Charles indicated a spot in front of a massive purple-flowered rhododendron. "The sound should carry."

Fred bounced into place and set the cheap instrument against his shoulder, then placed his bow. Charles stood next to him, peering into the room at the very edge of the opened doors.

Quite a crowd had gathered in the drawing room. He recognized John Black and Thomas Pillar from the *Chronicle*, along with the Agas. Lady Lugoson, ethereally beautiful as ever, sat in the corner, speaking to Mrs. Decker, another neighbor they had met last winter. Charles saw Breese Gadfly sit down at the Hogarths' cottage piano. He waved his hands wildly, and somehow Breese saw him. His friend raised his eyebrows, and Charles shook his head.

Charles shook out his arms and tilted his hips from side to side, warming up his joints. He hoped his knee, which seemed recovered, could take the strain of the dance, but he planned to do it only for a couple of minutes, before grabbing Kate's arms and swinging her into the dance for a moment before he ran out again.

He nodded to Fred, who put his fingers to the strings and commenced the first notes of the famously rollicking tune of the "College Hornpipe."

Charles dashed into the space between the open doors and paused until all eyes were upon him. Robert Hogarth called something out, but Charles's ears were deaf to anything but the music. He began his dance, imitating the work of a sailor upon a ship. His hands pulled a rope, swabbed a deck, and did some sort of cleaning before he grabbed his laughing Kate and swung her around in a circle. As soon as she was breathless, he sped out the doors again while Fred still played, to the general laughter and huzzahs of the crowd.

Charles tossed Fred's sailor's cap from his head and ran around the side of the house. Once he was at the vegetable garden, he took his neckerchief and coat from the edge of a bean trellis where he'd left them in preparation, and shrugged into his coat, then tied his neckerchief while he walked through the other side of the yard and to the front.

He went in through the front door and stepped into the drawing room. Little Georgina pointed at him, goggle eyed, and he winked at her.

"If it isn't Charles Dickens," John Black, one of his biggest supporters, cried and came to shake his hand.

Then all was a blur as he shook hands all around, everyone

keeping up the fiction that he was just entering for the first time, despite their winks. Mrs. Hogarth put a dish of trifle into his hand, and Mr. Hogarth, a glass of wine.

When he had caught his breath and drunk his wine, Kate came with a bottle and refilled his glass, then set the bottle on the table and clutched his sleeve, her cheeks pink and her entire face a little sweaty from exertion, but happy indeed.

"Did I please you?" he whispered in her ear.

"Very much," she said with a blush. "My old Charles is back."

"Now that the murder is solved, I feel much better," he said. "I hope we can sneak away later and see what is in the fireplace."

"Tell us about the inquest, Mr. Dickens," said a voice behind him.

Charles recognized the voice but thought he might be imagining it. He turned around and saw Daniel Jones, the blacksmith, with a much thinner face wreathed in smiles, his wife, Addie, clutching his arm. Kate laughed and cried as Charles whooped in delight.

Charles stepped forward and clasped the man's shoulders. He could feel the bones underneath, where there had been muscle before. "You're here! You're free! What blessed news!"

Daniel Jones's eyes welled up with tears. "I have you to thank, Mr. Dickens. We cannot stay, as there is nothing at the house to feed Beddie or Aunt Hannah, but I was told you were here, and we wanted to thank you."

"With all our hearts," Mrs. Jones said, beaming.

Charles wiped at his eyes, quite as overcome as Mr. Jones. "Oh, I have never done anything better than this. I am so happy you won't be transported. And back at the forge, too? Despite everything?"

"Mr. Nickerson gave us permission to resume our business," Mr. Jones explained. "I cannot wait to be back at that happy old place."

Charles kept his thoughts to himself with difficulty, just beamed his praises and walked the Joneses to the door. "I will stop by tomorrow. We'll bring you some of Kate's jam." After another round of praise and thanks, he returned to the party.

"Tell us the whole story," young Lord Lugoson exclaimed. "It must be a corker."

Robert Hogarth brought a chair into the center of the room, and Charles sat down.

"Come now, ladies and gentlemen," Charles said, arranging his features. "I shall tell you a tale of wealthy young Goldy Adams and her poor but hardworking swain, Pietro Ferazzi."

"Start at the beginning," Lord Lugoson said. "The day you found the body."

Kate waved her hands. "No. It was too gruesome, my lord."

"Begin with the magazine," Mr. Hogarth said. "Who delivered the magazine to ye in the first place?"

Charles explained the events of that June morning to the assembled crowd. "To conclude, I believe Mr. Ferazzi himself did put it under my door. The man was tortured by the past."

"If he wanted ye to discover the truth, why did he try to extort money from you?" Mr. Hogarth countered.

Charles rubbed his chin and crossed his eyes. "Another glass of wine!" he called, for the general merriment.

The roomful of people laughed as Kate filled his glass. Before he could speak again, the crowd thinned at the end of the room, and in between two senior reporters stood Miss Jaggers and Prince Moss.

Chapter 25

❦

Prince Moss was dressed like a young gentleman, in new clothes of a fine summer-weight wool. Miss Jaggers wore deepest black, but the fabric was so superior and so well fitted to her sylphlike form that it complemented her loveliness rather than detracted. She walked up to Charles. The entire room seemed to stop breathing. Even Fred, who had come into the room carrying his violin case, sat down next to Breese on the piano bench and said nothing.

"I slipped the magazine under your door," Miss Jaggers said in her beautifully modulated voice.

"Why?" Charles asked, genuinely confused.

"I discovered my foster mother's body first." Miss Jaggers's finely curved mouth tensed. "I wanted someone to know the truth."

Charles glanced around the room. If all the world was a stage, Miss Jaggers had found herself a prime one. "What is the truth?"

"Pietro Ferazzi stole my inheritance." Her mouth twisted. "My foster mother had not the strength to stop him."

"What happened?" Charles asked. Mr. Hogarth stepped toward him, but Charles put out a hand to stop him. He wanted to see this conversation through to the end.

"My parents trusted her to keep my property safe. They had no idea there was a Mr. Ferazzi lurking around the edges of her life, causing mayhem, hoping to bring her to dependence on him. He forged documents of sale and took all my properties while I was at school, leading me to a life of dependence on others."

"I am sorry," Kate said.

Miss Jaggers gritted her teeth. She lost some of her shining beauty. "I wanted him to pay. Him and men like him, who prey on the defenseless."

"He didn't steal everything. She had that warehouse full of goods," Charles said.

"What about her investments?" Miss Jaggers cried. "Why was she living in his rooms, his two small rooms, if he had not stolen everything her husband had built over a lifetime? What good were plate and furnishings in that tiny space?"

Charles winced. She had a point.

"He is dead now. How do you make him pay?" Kate asked.

Miss Jaggers smiled coldly. "I am his heiress."

"So Mr. Nickerson said." Charles lifted his brows. "How did that happen?"

"He wrote a will," she said, then smiled. On her lovely face, the smile should have been angelic, but even so, it had a hint of the devil in it.

"Did he repent?" Charles asked sarcastically. "Or did you or Mr. Nickerson forge his signature?"

She sneered. Prince Moss took her arm, sending the message that she had his support. "I won't discuss the details."

"How do we know you didn't kill your foster mother?" Charles said. "We have only the word of a desperate man."

She pursed her lips. It didn't create wrinkles around her

youthful mouth. "I have not the strength to do what he did to her."

"You are not without friends," Charles said. "Mr. Moss. Your cousin, Mr. Nickerson."

"He was a sick old man," Miss Jaggers said in the tone of a governess encouraging a slow student. "Mr. Nickerson had to purchase medicine frequently." Her lips curved.

"He bought the laudanum," Charles whispered. "What was in it that night?"

Miss Jaggers's smile widened.

Charles remembered that Prince Moss farmed. He suspected the boy had known what to add to laudanum to make a man go mad.

"You have done a terrible thing," Kate gasped.

Miss Jaggers clicked her tongue. "The will is sound. The courts move slowly, too slowly to trouble me any. Mr. Moss and I will liquidate all the properties and emigrate. You will never see us again, Mr. Dickens. Surely we have been through enough. Let us continue our lives in peace." Her nose went up as she glanced around the room, which was full of newspapermen.

Charles knew Miss Jaggers hadn't killed Mr. Ferazzi outright, nor had Prince Moss, but nonetheless, this was a girl who was capable of forgery, possibly even of poisoning. Why had she not lawfully fought in the courts what she claimed Mr. Ferazzi had done to her inheritance, instead of mimicking his own bad actions?

Miss Jaggers, her head high, turned away, pulling Prince Moss with her.

"Don't go with her," Charles said to the lad. "Stay in England and continue with your farming. You may still be able to put yourself on a sound path."

"I love her," the lad said simply.

"Please don't sell the smithy out from under the Jones family. Show them some compassion," Charles said.

Miss Jaggers did not look back.

"I think you should ask these people to leave," Charles, frustrated, said to Mr. Hogarth. "For myself, I will be having a conversation with the coroner and the police."

Prince Moss said nothing, merely walked away, his love next to him. No one stopped them, and the room remained silent.

When they were gone, Kate asked Charles, "Was justice served?"

"She became a criminal to save her fortune. She knew Miss Haverstock was vulnerable, and she did nothing to protect her foster mother, only cared for her own interests. I hope she goes away and stays away." Charles sighed and took Kate's hand, then squeezed it.

The room of people crowded around them, discussing the appearance of Miss Jaggers. Charles found himself next to Lady Lugoson. "What did you think?" he asked Julie Aga's beautiful aunt.

"Beauty does not preclude evil," she said. "I suspect her difficulties twisted her mind. But she is the rightful heir if Mr. Ferazzi did as claimed."

Charles nodded. Kate walked up to them. He kissed her cheek. "In order to spend time with a better sort of person, I suggest we avoid crime in the future," he said.

Kate laughed. "The world is complex enough to amuse both of us unavoidably, Mr. Dickens. And you know how I love a mystery."

"Is the mystery solved?" Lady Lugoson asked. "I understand there is a half-dismantled fireplace. My niece Julie mentioned it."

"Didn't she and William finish the excavation?" Charles asked. "I was gone most of the night, what with Mr. Ferazzi's death."

"No," Lady Lugoson said. "They stayed overnight at my house."

Kate clapped her hands. "Oh, Mr. Dickens! We must take a look."

"But your parents' party," he protested.

"We'll take the Agas with us to chaperone. Come, we have only an hour or so of light left."

Lady Lugoson shook her head in maternal tenderness. "You must please your lady, Mr. Dickens."

He inclined his head and thanked her; then he and Kate went to round up the Agas. Fifteen minutes later they were walking down the Hogarths' front path, and ten minutes after that, the foursome climbed the stairs up to Miss Haverstock's former rooms.

"What do you think it will be?" Julie asked. "Gold coins? Jewelry?"

"Religious artifacts," William suggested. "A gold menorah."

"The lost Ark of the Covenant," Kate said.

"How about we hope for the Holy Grail?" Charles said sarcastically. "Come now. It will just be some deeds or shares or something like that."

"So unromantic," Kate chided him.

"We'll know soon enough," William said, pushing open the door.

The foursome went to the fireplace and took turns glancing into the space.

"This must be an older building than I realized," William said. "The fireplace is really rather enormous."

"Which one of us is going to reach our hand in?" Charles asked. "I do think I found the hidey-hole when I pulled out that last brick."

"I'll do it!" Julie squeezed past the other three and ducked into the fireplace. She dropped her shawl into her husband's hands and pushed her arm, bare in her summer evening gown, into the hole. Her first reaction was unladylike in the extreme. She swore like a sailor as the rough bricks scraped her flesh.

Charles began to laugh as she rooted around in the hole he'd made, a comical expression on her freckled face. Then her eyebrows lifted and her arm pulled back, her hand clutching a narrow, long box.

"Metal," Charles said.

"Too small to be much of anything," William said, his forehead scrunched as he concentrated on the item in his wife's palm.

"Shall I open it?" Julie asked. Her fingers played with an edge of the box before anyone could respond. "No keyhole. Oh look. There's a latch."

The trio crowded around her as she stepped out of the fireplace and walked toward the window. Her fine, gauzy green skirt caught on the stacked bricks, but she paid it no mind, simply lifted the box to the available light and pulled the latch over the knob holding it in place.

"Five shillings on gold," William called.

"Tuppence on silver." Kate laughed.

Charles kept his counsel as he trained his gaze on the box.

Julie gave a little cry when she peeked at the contents. She reached into the box and lifted something toward the light, then sniffed.

"What is it?" Kate asked.

"A lock of baby hair," Julie said softly. "Tied with a faded ribbon."

Charles stared at the wisp of fine black hair. The strands were held together by a scrap of what had probably been a red ribbon.

"Miss Jaggers's hair?" William guessed.

"No," Charles said. "Hers would not have been black."

"I think Miss Haverstock and her husband lost a child," Julie said softly. "Poor woman. That must have made her relationship with Miss Jaggers all the more precious."

"Mr. Ferazzi indicated as much," Charles said. "Is there anything else?"

Julie handed him the memento and reached back into the box. "I feel cloth." She scrunched up her face and lifted a round of waxed cloth.

While she held it, Charles unwrapped the cloth. Inside were papers. A little brittle but still able to be spread out.

William leaned over them. "Deeds," he said. "I'll bet this is evidence of the property Mr. Ferazzi stole from the Haverstock family. If Miss Jaggers had been patient, all would have come to light in the end."

"The original tale of Goldy was a sad one," Charles said. "And the ending isn't much better."

"No," William agreed. "But I don't imagine the courts will rule in favor of anyone but Miss Jaggers in the end."

"A generation from now," Charles said sarcastically. "When they manage to process the case. I hope Miss Jaggers does emigrate and we never hear of her again."

Kate patted his cheek.

"I wonder if all of this will allow us to get out of our rental agreements early," Charles mused. "And get me back on track with my wedding savings."

Kate squeezed his arm. "I'm glad our wedding is foremost in your thoughts again, Charles. For that reason alone, I'm willing to forgo crime for the rest of the year."

He smiled at her, then stared out the window, toward the lane that led to the smithy. The Joneses had paid a heavy price for the sorry lives of Miss Haverstock and Mr. Ferazzi. Miss Jaggers and Prince Moss were out there, trouble on the loose. Charles wondered how long they'd be able to avoid more crime, now that they had had a taste of it. He had a bad feeling that he hadn't heard the last of either of them.

Acknowledgments

I want to thank you, dear reader, for picking up this second book in the A Dickens of a Crime series. If you haven't read the first book, *A Tale of Two Murders*, yet, I hope you take the opportunity to enjoy another Dickensian adventure through pre-Victorian London. An audio version of *A Tale of Two Murders* has been released, and I have to give a special shout-out to Tantor Media and their wonderful production, with voice acting by Tim Campbell. Give it a listen!

I am so grateful for the book reviews you have written, and please keep them coming. I had a wonderful time doing live and online events to celebrate the first book's release, and I am grateful to everyone who came out and spent time with me. I especially want to thank the bookstores, book clubs, Facebook groups, and libraries who hosted my presentations. VIP status goes to my parents, who attended three events!

Thank you to my beta readers Judy DiCanio, Walter McKnight, Mary Keliikoa, and Red Jameson on this project. I also wish to thank my writing group for their support: Delle Jacobs, the late Peggy Bird, who helped me with some of the Jewish material, Marilyn Hull, and Melania Tolan. Also, a special thank-you goes to my agent, Laurie McLean, at Fuse Literary, and to my Kensington editor, Elizabeth May, for their work on the series, as well as to many unsung heroes at Kensington.

I have continued to respect the life of Charles Dickens and kept him doing the work and walking the streets that he did during the timeline of my book, to the best of my knowledge. Not that I think he was ever an amateur sleuth. My plot is entirely fictitious, as is most everyone in the book. Attitudes between the sexes and toward minorities, certain sexual orientations, and so on in the pre-Victorian era were not what they are today, and I beg your indulgence when these unpleasant facts creep into the narrative.

I learned just as I began to plot this book that my maternal Jewish family lived in London for a couple of generations. My ancestors were there from the 1880s until the 1920s, not the timeline of this book, as they were refugees from Poland and Russia, but their recovered history inspired me to learn more about East London life in the nineteenth century, and I dedicate this story to them.

BOOK CLUB READING GUIDE for

Grave Expectations

1. Charles Dickens's novel *Great Expectations* inspired aspects of this novel. What themes did you recognize from the classic novel? Does reading this book make you want to read or reread Dickens's work?

2. What did you know about Charles Dickens before reading this novel? How do you think his career as a journalist informed his fiction writing?

3. Charles Dickens and Kate Hogarth are engaged by this point in my series. What do you think about the limits that are put on them during this period of their romance?

4. Charles and his parents have a difficult relationship, stemming from when his father was imprisoned due to unpaid debt and Charles had to work in a factory. How would you feel if your parents did so much damage to your education and your prospects?

5. The Dickenses are considered of a lower class than the Hogarths. What evidence did you see of this in the book?

6. Did you feel that any of the characters are stereotypical?

7. It was illegal to be homosexual during this era in England. Can you put yourself in Breese Gadfly's shoes and imagine what his life is like?

8. What do you think of the Miss Jaggers character? Do you think she'll return to plague Charles down the road?

9. Would you have bet on Charles Dickens as a romantic partner? Some reviewers have been disturbed upon learning the real-life story of the Charles and Kate relationship. Does that color how you read this series?

10. Some of the characters in this novel are real, like the Dickenses and the Hogarths. Are you content to leave them on the page, or do certain aspects of them fascinate you?

11. Readers may be horrified to learn that at least sometimes, according to records, bodies were left in place before inquests were completed, and were even temporary tourist attractions during this era. How does this contrast with the way murder and human bodies are treated nowadays?

12. Policing was very different in 1835. The Metropolitan Police Service didn't have detectives yet, and there were conflicts between the coroners and the police. How would you have protected yourself and your family in the pre-Victorian era?